Desire for Chocolate

CARE SANTOS

TRANSLATED BY JULIE WARK

ALMA BOOKS

ALMA BOOKS LTD
3 Castle Yard
Richmond
Surrey TW10 6TF
United Kingdom
www.almabooks.com

First published in Catalan by Editorial Planeta, S.A. in 2014
First published by Alma Books Limited in 2015
This mass-market edition first published by Alma Books Limited in 2016
© Care Santos, 2014
Translation rights arranged by Sandra Bruna Agencia Literaria, SL
All rights reserved
Translation © Julie Wark, 2015

The translation of this work was supported by a grant from the Institut
Ramon Llull

Care Santos and Julie Wark assert their moral right to be identified as the
author and translator respectively of this work in accordance with the
Copyright, Designs and Patents Act 1988

Printed and bound by CPI Group (UK) Ltd, Croydon, CR0 4YY

ISBN: 978-1-84688-394-1
eBook ISBN : 978-1-84688-369-9

Contents

DESIRE FOR CHOCOLATE   5

Prelude: *Resurrection*   7

Act I: *Chilli, Ginger and Lavender*   13

First Interlude: *The Lid*   135

Act II: *Cocoa, Sugar and Cinnamon*   147

Second Interlude: *The Chip*   287

Act III: *Pepper, Cloves and Achiote*   297

Finale: *Madame Adélaïde*   429

NOTES   437

LIST OF CHARACTERS   440

AUTHOR'S NOTE AND ACKNOWLEDGEMENTS   447

Desire for Chocolate

For Deni Olmedo,
for everything *che dirsi
mal può dalla parola.**

Prelude

RESURRECTION

Sixteen white porcelain fragments of different shapes and sizes and a tube of superglue. Max sets about the tedious task of putting this puzzle together. It's half-past three in the morning and he should be in bed because he has to get up in three hours' time, but he promised Sara he'd do it and doesn't want to go back on his word.

He picks up the shards one by one and looks for a possible match. The more pieces he finds, the fewer possibilities for error are left on the table. He applies the glue, joins the broken edges and lightly presses the pieces together until they're firmly stuck. He checks the result and feels satisfied. In some parts the join is barely visible. In others, it's not so easy because it's not such a clean break and the porcelain is slightly chipped. Yet Max is gradually reconstructing something that was apparently lost for ever. It's worth the effort, though he's dead tired after tonight's long dinner. It will be a nice surprise for Sara when she comes into the kitchen later on this morning and sees that he's taken the trouble to do this.

It's been a great night. First, the feelings of sharing and trust in a conversation between two old friends who meet up again when they're both at the peak of their careers. Then, there's Sara, so enchanting, so gorgeous and so together. What happens to women after they turn forty? Their qualities become more concentrated, making them more intense, more intelligent, more serene and more attractive than they were twenty years earlier. This is how he perceived his wife tonight and he's proud of her.

Proud that she's his. This is such a primitive, wrongheaded feeling, Max thinks. It's also out of character, yet he has to admit that this is what has made it such a good night.

After Oriol left, he and Sara spent some time clearing up and chatting about the evening. He washed the dishes and she put things away, a division of labour they've perfected after years of practice. It's good that their friend has at last decided to settle down, but they both think he might have found a wife a little closer to home. "If you want to marry and marry well, marry within the sound of your own church bell," Sara murmured, imitating her mother's sing-song cadence as she scraped the remains of the salad into a clear plastic container. "What sort of father do you think he'll be?" Max asked, and she replied, "Hopeless, like he is in everything." Ever the faithful friend, Max leapt to his friend's defence. "Oh, come on! Not in everything! That's a bit excessive. He's done very well for himself." But Sara didn't answer. She looked tired and seemed flat. She was upset about the broken chocolate pot. She'd looked at the bits, desolate but resigned. "Don't worry, I'll stick it together," he said, trying to comfort her. All he got in response was a glum: "Even if you can, I'll always know it's broken." Then, methodical as always, she neatly piled the plastic containers of leftovers in the fridge and said, "Do you mind if I wait for you in bed?"

Max didn't mind. On the contrary, he knows that Sara needs time to herself so she can take it all in. Tonight's just the start of a long haul. Perhaps the scars will never heal – like those on the surface of the object that's starting to take shape in his hands – yet it will be necessary to learn to admire them for what they mean.

There's an undeniable, different beauty in what we're able to salvage.

The inscription in blue letters on the base of the pot has been broken in the middle. Max is holding "*Je suis à madame Ad…*" in his right hand, while the other bit saying "*… élaïde de France*" rests in his left hand. Fortunately, there's no chipping here and the two parts make a perfect fit. Madame Adélaïde de France, whoever she was, can breathe easy.

"There are stories inside objects and voices that tell them," Sara had said some years ago. "Sometimes, when I'm touching the white porcelain chocolate pot, I have the sensation that I can hear them." When he'd asked, "Are there many?" she'd said, "A few. Can't you see that it's a very old piece that's had a lot of owners?" He, always the scientist, probed a little deeper: "But that's the same as accepting that everything's full of ghosts, like mansions in horror films." She shook her head. "That's precisely the point, Max. People believe in haunted houses when, actually, these presences usually prefer to inhabit small, almost insignificant objects." Max was amused by his wife's little foibles. "So they don't have to dust, no doubt," he'd added.

Once he's put together the three pieces of the broken spout, which he then sticks onto the pear-shaped body, he can see the rest clearly. Only two fragments of the handle remain on the table. Once they're in place, elegant and bow-like, the puzzle will be completed. *Here you have your chocolate pot, Madame. I hope it keeps you good company for many a year. In a few hours you will be able to fill it with chocolate*. He smiles at what the voice in his head has just said. He has no idea where that came from. He keeps sticking the bits together with the skilful hands of a surgeon finishing a delicate operation. Then he pours some alcohol onto a cotton ball and wipes away the remains of the glue from around the cracks.

The chocolate pot reminds him of a battered war veteran who's somehow survived and managed to limp home. When Sara bought it in the antique shop, well after closing time one night, the spout was already chipped and the lid and swizzle stick were missing, but even so, it was beautiful. She's never told him what she'd learnt about its origins from the man who sold it to her. He only knows that he was an elderly, strange and garrulous antique dealer who'd reduced the price when he saw how young she was and how she'd been so drawn to it. Then the chip had been noticeable and spoilt the harmonious appearance of the pot as a whole, but now it isn't at all out of place. Max caresses the old wound with a fingertip. It has the roughness of ceramic fresh from the kiln. The roughness that all beautiful things must have when seen from inside. Roughness of the passage of time. Although the whole pot is now a patchwork, it can still be used. It holds exactly three small cups of hot chocolate, no more, no less. He can't help thinking that, now Oriol has left the country, this is one cup too many. It will always hold one cup too many.

Then he tidies up. Resuscitated after its near-mortal accident, the chocolate pot takes pride of place in the centre of the table. Max tears a page from the pad they use for shopping lists, writes "*Voilà!*" and slips the note under his handiwork. Then he turns out the light.

He fears he might find Sara awake, brooding over what has happened. But no, she's sleeping like a baby. When he gets into bed he sees that she's naked. This is an invitation he can't turn down, yet the time isn't right. After weighing up all the pros and cons, he sets the alarm clock half an hour later than planned and closes his eyes. His heart is beating very fast.

Act I

CHILLI, GINGER
AND LAVENDER

Emotional hurt is the price a person
has to pay in order to be independent.
HARUKI MURAKAMI

Behaviour of Polymorphs

People – and such is human nature – get bored with everything: objects, distractions, family and even themselves. It doesn't matter whether you have everything you want, or are happy with your life, or share your days with the best person in the world. Sooner or later you get bored.

That's how things are. Any evening, any month, you can tear your eyes away from the television screen and glance across to the other side of the living room where your husband is sitting in his usual place, just as he does every night between dinner and bedtime. Nothing you see surprises you. The coffee table in the corner has its pile of about twelve de-rigueur books, some already read, some still to be read, and some both things at once, and Max is there in the place he's occupied every night ever since they had the duplex renovated, sprawled in his reading chair (the only piece of furniture he chose), feet up on the footrest, glasses balancing on the tip of his slightly beaky nose, light pouring down, straight onto the pages like a spotlight on a cabaret star, while the book in his hands has him so absorbed that he's completely oblivious to anything that might be happening around him.

Max is one of those people who don't need silence in order to read. He only needs the usual props – the chair, the footrest, the light, his glasses and, of course, the book. His unvarying presence in his corner of the living room is like that of a good-natured pet. He makes no noise and bothers no one. It's only once in a while when he lets out a sigh, discreetly changes his position in the chair or turns a page that Sara knows he's still alive and still present. Yet, in these few moments of looking away from the television and seeing her husband in his usual place, doing what he always does, she thinks that if he wasn't there she'd miss him, because she's used to his silent company in the way you get used to seeing your furniture in the right place. He's her surety, her security, her stability, everything she has in this world. But none of that spares her from the question that immediately follows: *Why am I married to this man?*

This is one of those doubts that pop up when your conscience is momentarily off guard and, of course, you immediately feel ashamed. It's one of those questions that Sara would never ask aloud, would never voice in front of anyone else because they somehow attack what she believes is most sacrosanct in her life. Indeed, her conscience is already preparing a whole battery of responses, artillery fire in the form of other questions: *Wherever did that come from? Haven't you got everything you could possibly have (and not just material things but others that are more difficult to obtain)? When you had the chance, wasn't it you who chose in total freedom who you wanted to be with? Have you ever lacked for anything? Haven't you prided yourself, time and time again, on having made the right decision? And aren't you absolutely sure, without the slightest shadow of doubt, that Max wasn't just a good choice, but your choice, the one that was right for you, the one that was somehow your due? Don't you have two beautiful, tall, intelligent, fantastic children, with the best qualities of both parents and who absolutely adore you? Aren't you secretly proud that your and Max's ways of being in the world have come together in the almost perfect – of course! – characters of your children?*

Just then Max looks up from his book, takes off his glasses and says, "Hey, Mama, I nearly forgot! Guess who phoned me today. You won't believe this. Pairot! He's in Barcelona and says he's free the evening of the day after tomorrow, so I asked him to come over for dinner. Won't it be great to see him? It's so long since we last got together!"

Max only takes off his glasses when he has something important to say. And this is important, so he waits a moment for Sara's reaction. She doesn't react.

He puts on his glasses again and goes back to his book, *Frequent Risks in Polymorphic Transformations of Cocoa Butter*, as if he hasn't just said something important.

"Did he tell you why we haven't heard a word from him all this time?" she asks.

"He's a very busy man. We could have phoned him too. Anyway, it doesn't matter. When did we see him last? Do you remember? Was it that night in the Hotel Arts, perhaps, when they gave him the prize?"

"Yes, that's right."

"How long ago was that? Six or seven years at least."

"Nine," she corrects.

"Nine? Wow! Are you sure? Time certainly does fly. That's truer than ever. I can't believe you aren't keen to see him. You've always liked hanging out with Pairot." Max starts reading again.

Sara wonders how this man can read a treatise on the physical properties of cocoa butter with the same interest as if it were a Sherlock Holmes novel, but then, on second thoughts, realizes that, after all this time, she shouldn't be surprised. She's much more surprised by what she's just heard, and for more than one reason: that Oriol's in Barcelona (and not in Canberra, or Qatar, or Shanghai, or Lithuania, or whatever remote place where people can open shops) and, moreover, that he's remembered that in this small city on the western shores of the Mediterranean there are two people who once – many years ago when he was a long way from being this Oriol Pairot now endowing luxury establishments with his own name and making his former fellow citizens so proud that he's on telly, day after day – shared a few things (well, a few important things) with him. She's also very surprised that her husband should have arranged to see Oriol before she has, because the priority of the phone calls used to be different. But what has really astonished her, completely dumbfounded her, is that Max seems unaware of the importance of the announcement he's just made, and that he should have just let it out like that, between one page of polymorphic transformations and the next, only to revert immediately afterwards to his absent-minded presence of every night, when they sit down in the same old places to digest their dinner – or digest their life, maybe – letting the last hours of the day sneak away.

Sara wonders what she should say now. She could respond like one of those characters in the soaps she no longer watches because she got too hooked on them: *My God, Max, I knew he'd be back sooner or later!* Or she might wind herself up and throw a ridiculous tantrum: *So when were you planning to tell me, Max?* But she decides against that, because he's no good at arguments. He always agrees with her before she can even begin to get angry, so it's no fun fighting with him. Anyway, she's too tired to get worked up so she decides to take the easy way out.

The least complicated solution is the most conservative one, the most selfish one and also the most cowardly one: cop out.

"Aren't we going to the Liceu the day after tomorrow?"

"No, I checked. That's Tuesday next week and that's sacred: *Aida*."

"Yes, it certainly is. Anyway, I can't do it that night. I've got a work dinner the day after tomorrow," she says, pursing her lips and looking peeved. "Can't he come another night?"

Max removes his glasses again. The polymorphs wait, stoical as usual.

"I didn't ask him, but you know he never stops. He's probably totally booked up."

"Like everyone else. We've all got a thousand things to do."

"I don't disagree. I'm just saying he's different. He's always running around all over the place, from airport to airport and to some weird and wonderful countries as well. It looks like he's in Japan this year. He says he's very happy and he's going to tell us all about it. What a guy! He's a nomad warrior. Meanwhile, we're the ones who stay somewhere safe, with the table set. Someone has to prefer a peaceful, orderly life. Basically, we've always been like that, wouldn't you say?"

Peaceful, *orderly*, *basically*, *we*. These words weigh on Sara like four tombstones.

"I'm sorry, but I can't back out of my dinner. It's been scheduled for weeks."

Scheduled. Now there's an expression that shows how things are. Sara, too, is a busy, important, modern woman who uses horrible expressions invented for people like her who can't afford to waste time paraphrasing.

"Can't you reschedule it?" Max asks.

Why should I be the one who has to reschedule? Can't the great Oriol Pairot be asked to make a small change in his plans?

"No way. It's with the editor of the magazine."

"Oh well, that's bad luck." Max's usually amiable lips contract in a grimace of sincere disappointment. "What if I phone Oriol and ask how long he'll be here?"

Sara shrugs to show she doesn't care. It looks very natural (which is just what she wants).

"Don't worry, my love. I'll have coffee with you when I get back. I'm sure you'll still be going in the wee hours."

My love is a calculated strategy for undermining one's opponent. In this case, *my love* means lots of implicit things. It means *Everything's fine*. It means *Don't worry*. It means *I'm OK with this and am doing what I want*.

"All right then, let's leave it at that," Max says. It's now twenty years since they first met, and they've been married for seventeen, so his Catalan accent is almost perfect, polished as a river stone. He's particularly proud of it. Before replacing his glasses and putting an end to the matter, he has one last practical question. "Shall we set the table on the terrace, or inside? Will you organize something for our dinner?"

"Of course I will, Papa. As always."

Max puts on his glasses and returns imperturbably to his polymorphs and their very odd way of being part of the world, adopting different shapes but never ceasing to be, in essence, themselves. Seeing that he's once again absorbed in his book, Sara makes the most of it to start thinking about her plans for tomorrow. She has a couple of appointments jotted down in her diary. Her manager wants to talk about this year's range of *torrons** and, in the afternoon, she has to meet a journalist who's writing a piece on Barcelona's best chocolate shops. Of course, Casa Rovira will be the star turn. However, before dealing with all that, she makes a mental note of a new, hitherto unforeseen task, which suddenly turns out to be more pressing than anything else: she's going to pay a visit to her next-door neighbour's presently unoccupied flat. She should have gone there ages ago but has been too lazy. Now, she has a very good reason for going to check it out. She wants to be sure it's what she needs and will go early in the morning. She has to engage in some rearguard action and prepare a good observation post.

Sara doesn't remember the first time Max addressed her as "Mama" instead of using her name or one of those early-days sweet nothings like sweetheart, honey or darling, but it's clear that the nickname was yet another consequence of the birth of their children and also – especially – carelessness on her part. Sara has always blamed herself for this. She should never have allowed the woman that she was to lose ground to the mother that she became. Effect gradually replaced cause and, as the years went by, Max forgot to call her sweetheart, honey or darling in his clearly American accent, and only called her "Mama". Not even in public was she Sara, or if she was, it was only very rarely, when they were with people they didn't really know. Always, and in front of just about everyone, she was "Mama". She didn't like it at first, but now she's stopped grumbling about it like she used to when they were still very young: "Don't call me Mama! I'm not your mother, I'm her mother," she complained, pointing at Aina, who only laughed, happy to learn that language, apart from being fun, was also problematical. Max stood his ground. "But you're Mama in this house! You're the most important person here! And this should be said loud and clear." That was when Sara discovered, to her horror, that Max found her more attractive after she'd given birth. When she was sitting in his reading chair with their daughter in her arms, feeding her with saintly patience she didn't have, she sometimes caught an awestruck Max gazing at her as if he were witnessing some kind of miracle. Now and then that look seemed tender, although there were other moments when it was ominous, because she felt as if a strange woman had usurped her place.

Sara recognizes that her maternal instinct in these suckling matters left quite a lot to be desired, that she never found in the act of breastfeeding the self-affirmation or delightful intimacy proclaimed by the mother's-milk militants and, even though she deeply admires these women who can breastfeed for years, she left this phase behind her as soon as she could, no matter how horrified Max was, which was no help at all in making her feel any less guilty than she already felt. She bought six baby bottles and six cans of the best-quality powdered milk and closed the chapter called "Mother's Milk" only four months after Aina made her appearance. The books in the reading corner were now covered with bottles and teats, while a bemused Max contemplated the scene and the battle for her name was lost for ever.

Now, fifteen years on, she thinks it would be ridiculous to tell him that she doesn't like being called "Mama". Like Oriol's silence, this territory is out of bounds. If there's one thing she's learnt in her forty-four years, it's that there's no point wasting your energy on hopelessly lost causes.

Next morning, just as she does every other day, Sara watches the television news while she's having breakfast in the kitchen. She's especially interested in the weather forecast, but only the short-term one. Tomorrow night: cloudless sky, pleasant temperature, slightly higher than usual in mid-May, low humidity. Although the day hasn't begun well, the forecast is perfect, exactly what she needs. Max left for the university a while ago, after his first cup of coffee – which she always makes for him – kissing her on the forehead and saying, "Have a nice day, Mama."

The moment she hears the door close, Sara runs to get her phone. For hours she's been suppressing the urge to check her messages, very carefully, in case she's missed one. She reads them all, one by one: the usual text messages, ads, emails, Facebook, Twitter and finally voicemail. The last three days. It takes a while but yields no result. This is very strange. He hasn't even tried to contact her. She writes him a message. The first thing that comes into her head.

When did you arrive? Where are you staying?

No, no, no. That's too direct. She deletes it. Tries again.

Are you OK?

That's too ingenuous. She deletes this one too, puts the phone down, gets a slice of bread from the bag in the freezer, puts it in the toaster, picks up her phone and makes a third attempt.

Can't wait to see you.

She's about to send it when something stops her. It's forced, not very natural. She deletes this one too. After so many attempts, she's not sure of anything. Would it be better not to send any message at all? Maybe he has a reason for not saying anything.

The toast pops up, the toaster turns itself off and everything's left in abeyance. She doesn't sit down until she has everything nicely set out on the table: a plate, a tray, a butter knife, the phone, a linen napkin with her name on it and the remote control for the TV. She turns up the volume, but only a little, and watches the news as she spreads butter and lime marmalade on her toast, just like she does every day.

A black man with blood dripping from the palm of one hand and brandishing two enormous knives in the other is raging at the cameras. She can understand him without reading the subtitles, although her English is terrible. "You people will never be safe. Remove your governments, they don't care about you." The newsreader explains that the man and a companion have attacked a soldier on a street in south-east London, and stabbed and hacked him to death in broad daylight. *Now we've seen it all.* Sara turns off the TV.

After she's had her breakfast she's twitchy again. She needs three more tries before she decides on the right message.

Hello.

She hits "send" and, with no sense of relief whatsoever, gets moving with today's agenda. However, there's an unavoidable change of plan when someone rings the doorbell at half-past eight, an absent-minded delivery man who's turned up before the shop opens. The manager hasn't arrived yet, but Sara doesn't want him to drive off again as she believes he's bringing the chocolate they needed in order to cover all the orders. They'd told her about this yesterday. Sara answers the intercom and a hoarse voice tells her, "I've got thirty boxes from Callebaut."

"Just a moment, please."

Sara quickly grabs the keys – hers and the neighbour's – and goes out onto the landing. While waiting for the lift, she looks to see if there's any message. She checks her reflection in the metal door and fiddles with her hair. When she's tense she keeps touching her hair. But she doesn't want to get strung up now. Everything's fine. Everything's under control. The chocolate they needed has just been delivered, her visit to her neighbour's flat is nothing more than reconnaissance – nothing's decided yet – and Oriol will answer her sooner or later. Perhaps he's still sleeping off his jet lag. The lift door closes. She presses the button for the ground floor and starts her descent. Not only the descent inside this metal box but another, more intimate one. She reminds herself that things are a long way from being under control, however much she tries to convince herself they are. As always, when Oriol appears, everything flies out of control. And, by the way, she'd like to know why she's feeling so pissed off when no one's done anything to her.

Sara quickly deals with the delivery man. She opens the door and asks him to leave the boxes in the corridor. Before he's finished the job, the shop manager arrives and takes over everything. Sara says she has to go to the bank and disappears. In the last couple of minutes she's checked her phone five times. Still no answer.

Her neighbour's flat is in the house next door. If it wasn't older and narrower, and if it had undergone the same thorough and extremely expensive renovation as the one where Sara lives, this building could be its twin. It has no lift, so she has to take the stairs up to the fourth floor. No problem. As a member of an exclusive women's gym in the top part of town, Sara has been keeping fit for quite a while now. She goes there from time to time, swims a little, plays paddle tennis with the manager of a luxury hotel in Avinguda Diagonal – with whom the relationship is confined on every side by the four walls of the court – and then treats herself to a sauna.

She gets to Raquel's flat without puffing. She finds the general state of the stairway distressing. It needs rather more than a coat of paint. She turns the key in the lock and goes inside. As soon as she crosses the threshold, she notes her neighbour's smell, as if she's about to come and greet her any moment. Sara's only been here once before, the day when Raquel came into the patisserie to ask if she'd do her a "very big" favour, which she could only tell her about in private. Sara went to have a cup of coffee with her that afternoon. Until then, she only knew this woman because she sold her croissants, Kaiser rolls, the occasional *ensaïmada** and a lot of drinking chocolate. Raquel is a small woman, closer to sixty than to fifty, a widow with one daughter who lives abroad. She says her daughter needs her and she's decided to go and stay with her for a while, though she doesn't know how long. "I thought I might be able to leave my keys with you. In case anything happens so you can get in. I also wanted to ask, if it's no bother and if you know anyone who's looking for a flat to rent, whether you could mention it. Someone trustworthy and reliable of course, and who won't wreck the place. I'd be very grateful. Since you know everyone, I was wondering if you'd do me this favour, but I don't want to give you any more work than you've already got. Only if you can. To be honest, I could really use the money right now."

This conversation took place more than a month ago, and Sara has at last eased her conscience about not having come to check the place, not even once, although not a day has gone by without her telling herself that she really must do it. She's surprised to see everything so shipshape. Raquel has left the windows closed and there's hardly any dust on the furniture. No disagreeable smells. After a quick once-over, she goes directly to what interests her most of all, climbing up the spiral staircase to Raquel's bedroom, groping her way through the darkness – the skylight blind blocks out practically all the light – and going out onto the terrace.

She's happy to see at once that this is the perfect spot for her plan. The heather hedge has crept up higher than the dividing wall, so it's enough to conceal someone of her height. There are a few gaps, but that's no problem. In fact, they'll make useful peepholes and she'll still remain hidden. The terrace slopes slightly, so she'll have to be careful not to trip. Anyhow, the measures she'll need to take in order for this to work are minimal. Black clothes – camouflage – a comfortable chair that doesn't squeak or wobble, a jacket and maybe a scarf at her neck. With this humidity it's quite chilly at night. Ah yes, and switch her phone to silent mode. She mustn't forget that.

There's still no message, but she keeps glancing at her phone. She lingers a little longer in her lookout. She stares at the terrace of her flat, which, seen from here, has a slightly aristocratic air with its wooden flooring, the teak table, the area of artificial grass – smaller than Max wanted and bigger than she would have preferred – the three-seater garden swing, the designer deckchairs with six different reclining positions which they'd bought in Vinçon, the plants lovingly tended by the number-three programme of an automatic watering system, the awning with an automatic wind detector so it knows all by itself when it has to be retracted... They'd been lucky to get in before the prices shot up, as they were able to buy two flats – on the third and fourth floors – in the building in which her parents had lived all their lives. They had also been fortunate in finding a good architect who did the renovations at an acceptable price (all of that thanks to Max and his sangfroid in negotiating, something which makes her feel quite hysterical). And the final piece of good fortune was being able to take it slowly without having to worry about delays in the work or unexpected extra costs. That very year, her parents had decided to retire and went off to live for a while in Menorca. Sara, Max and Aina, who hadn't yet turned one, had gone to stay in the flat where she'd grown up while their paradise was being created. They were hardly aware of the workmen's presence.

It had always been a magnificent listed building, right in the middle of Carrer de l'Argenteria, renovated and with a lift – which was most unusual in her neighbourhood – but it was even better after the residential association decided at the end of the Eighties to agree to the city council's improvement plan and restore the façade. The value of the flats shot up immediately, of course, but then went down again – though not much – shortly after the Olympic Games. Max and Sara had first visited what was to become the top part of their duplex in 1995. As soon as he saw the views of the basilica of Santa Maria del Mar, Max said, "I want to have dinner up here every summer night for the rest of my life." The original terrace was small, but they both believed that an architect could sort out this and other problems. As for the other flat, the downstairs one, they'd had to wait three years for it, until the death of the old lady who'd lived there all alone since the year dot. They would have bought it sight unseen, but they played their parts. Max haggled, Sara nearly had a nervous breakdown and the real-estate agent acted offended, but the very next day, first thing in the morning, he phoned to say that their offer had been accepted. While the flat was being renovated, everyone involved was extraordinarily keen to knock down walls. Consequently they all got along very well.

The duplex was so beautiful and spacious that when Sara's mother came up to see it for the first time her eyes filled with tears and she gushed, "This is exactly the flat you two deserve, my darling!" Three years later they ended up buying the second-floor flat, the only part of the building they didn't already own. For the time being, they'd use it for storage but, one day in the future, Sara wanted Aina to have the first-floor flat and Pol the one on the second floor. Sorting out such an important part of their children's future before either of them finished primary school was an unambiguous sign of their prosperity.

Sara has one last look at her phone, sighs and selects "New Message".

Hello?

Send. Sending. Sent.

She puts the phone in her pocket and goes back into Raquel's bedroom, leaving everything exactly as it was. She goes down the spiral staircase, steps out onto the landing, locks the door, thinks that a coat of paint would make a huge difference, and also that what's happening to her, this wanting to see Oriol and yet not wanting to see him, is very weird. She doesn't want to know anything about him and yet she's desperate because he's not answering her messages. She's lucky to be able to use Raquel's flat. It's perfect for her needs, precisely because of one of those things she does – or doesn't do – without knowing why. The point is, she still hasn't told Max that Raquel is away, perhaps for quite a while and, meanwhile, she's left her keys with Sara.

If anyone asked Sara why she likes her husband she'd come up with a lengthy reply full of heartfelt reasons. Max, and everyone would agree, is a delightful man, starting with his looks: the eternally rebellious adolescent with light, ageless eyes and an unruly fringe that used to drive his mother mad. His appearance only caused him serious problems when, shortly after he got his PhD and started teaching, he discovered that most of his students were taller, stronger and looked older than him. He didn't exactly resort to a strategy to earn their respect, but just slightly played up his way of being in the world. Distance and extreme rigour, academic strictness and seriousness. In the beginning at least, these were the aces up his sleeve for getting them to take him seriously. To his great surprise, he soon found they were winners, with both male and female students, although the latter had the embarrassing habit of falling in love with him and assailing him with very uncomfortable declarations in office hours or around exam time. He, however, never felt attracted by undergrad nymphets, not even physically. He thought they were superficial, silly and, in particular, ignorant. He couldn't imagine any serious relationship with a girl who didn't even know who Mendeleev was.

Max has everything that any mother-in-law could possibly wish for. He's the perfect son-in-law. He is so respectful when he speaks that he sometimes gets lost in labyrinths of compliments, he never gets up later than seven, is as punctual as a bell-ringer, never loses his temper or raises his voice, whatever the situation – and still less with his wife – has no big, medium-sized or small vices (not even one that might look quite admirable like being a collector or a bibliophile), and doesn't find household chores beneath him. When the children were small he said he'd broken the world nappy-changing record; he understands the washing machine much better than Sara does; and he re-sews anything that comes unstitched. If that weren't enough, he never sets foot in the kitchen, because Sara can't stand anyone else stirring pots on *her* fire.

Obviously, if Sara's conscience asked her why Max sometimes isn't the kind of man she wants to share her old age with, she'd also have a heap of ready-made answers. The only difference this time is that she'd reply to herself alone, and even that would require a special dispensation from her sense of guilt, which isn't too generous when it comes to making exceptions. She'd say, for example, that Max is prematurely old. It's not that he's become old at the age of forty-two, but that he's been old for about twenty years, and that's more serious. Living with him, it's impossible to make plans to go out at night because his morning timetable is sacred and, if he doesn't get eight hours' sleep, he can't function. On a couple of occasions, when the message hadn't quite sunk in, she'd dragged him off to the theatre and a concert and then had to deal with the consequences. Max went to sleep during the play and at the concert and, moreover, when they'd hardly begun, both times. He also suffers from a syndrome which tends to be confused with the nature of a genius. While socially appealing, it's a pain in the neck to live with. He's absent-minded and gets distracted with irritating ease. In fact, he spends so much time up in the clouds that it's often difficult to bring him back to the real world where normal people's lives run their course. Max takes a break to come down for dinner in the real world, but immediately afterwards returns to his parallel existence from where, of course, he teaches, lectures and reads in his chair. Finally, there's sex. Naturally, sex always has its place. Whether this is first place or fourteenth place depends on the person concerned. Anyway, Sara can't say that Max is lacking. He's pretty good and she has no complaints in general. For a while now, however, the problem's been in small details. For example, he's taken to fucking without taking his socks off. At weekends, he neglects his obligation to shave and, *even so*, comes on to her, wanting sex on Sunday afternoons. When she informs him that it's shave or nothing, he opts for nothing, giving her to understand that he prefers getting around looking like a hobo to having sex with her.

Sara realizes, every time she runs through her list – she's still too young to work out the final tally of the pros and cons – that, actually, she has no real reason to be bored with Max. Maybe it's a kind of snobbishness, like this latest fashion of making chocolates with strange things like onion or *botifarra*,* which is really over the top. Not that she can talk. She has a whole display case in her shop devoted to Oriol Pairot products (complete with the man's photo) and, surprise, surprise, the best-selling item by far is the famous box of chocolates in three flavours, "Three Very Different Friends". Ginger, chilli and lavender, for Heaven's sake. That mixture could only occur to Oriol Pairot, who is a genius.

What Sara is very well aware of is that there is only one person at fault as far as Max is concerned, and that is her and her alone. Ever since they first met she's known that he's an innocent, incapable of doing anything that might upset or offend her, and unable even to begin to suspect the confused or hateful thoughts that sometimes occur to his wife. If he knew, it would drive him mad, poor man.

As for gaping at her like an idiot, that's nothing new. Max has been devouring her with his eyes ever since that first night in April, or the beginning of what one might call their shared story. Actually, it started before then. His staring had flustered Sara throughout the whole Techniques for Chocolatiers course, where they first met.

"I wish to welcome all of you," Ortega began ceremoniously, the first day. "My name is Jesús, I'm a chocolatier and shall spend the next three weeks doing my best to turn you into chocolatiers too. I'd like to begin by drawing attention to what that actually means in a city with such a long chocolate-making tradition as Barcelona's. Many of you are perhaps unaware that you live in one of the first places where chocolate became a delicacy for aristocrats; home of the first chocolatier – Fernandes by name – who dared to produce a device that would make the production process easier; the port from which all the great nineteenth-century chocolatiers, with names like Sampons, Amatller, Juncosa and Coll, sent off their products, creating a tradition and making fortunes in the process; it is also the place where chocolate figures were first invented for Easter, and where Joan Giner, maestro of maestros, turned this invention into an art, which he exhibited in the display window of the well-known patisserie Mora. And, of course, if we're talking about shop windows, we can't fail to mention his great friend, Antoni Escribà, who was known as the Mozart of chocolatiers because of his incredible imagination. Finally, Barcelona, thanks to her own merits, now occupies a prominent place on the world chocolate map, and you must be aware of this if you want to add your names to the illustrious list I've just mentioned. Now, let's get to work as it's getting late. Let's start with the introductions, so we can get to know each other."

It was all very inspiring, but every time Sara looked up she noticed Max's light-blue eyes watching her. Then he took fright, like a startled bird, his eyes trying to light on any other object he might feasibly be looking at while the ripe-fruit blush on his cheeks betrayed him anyway. He was so sweet, such a bungler, such a good man. Anyone could see he'd fallen in love with Sara the moment he set eyes on her. Sometimes he got so distracted that Ortega had to bring him back to earth again. "I'd like you to keep your mind on the job, Senyor Frey. This looks more like gruel than truffle filling." Max looked down at the truffle mix that refused to bind, sighed heavily enough to ruffle the incorrigible fringe that kept escaping from his chef's hat and, for some minutes, didn't dare to raise his eyes.

Sara felt flattered when Max was around. Every time he looked at her like that he puffed up her insufferable immature girl's pride. She was still too young then to understand that if others make you feel good, it is more a plus for them than for you. She also basked in her classmates' professional admiration, because her technique was by far the best and she was constantly leaving them gaping over what she could do with her hands. She shrugged it off, saying it was a family thing, because she'd grown up with chocolate, in her father's kitchen, where she'd witnessed the whole process of making *torrons*, cakes, Easter eggs and every imaginable chocolate product since well before she was tall enough to look over the counter. She seemed convinced that the art of patisserie ran in her veins, that her talent was a kind of heirloom. Her classmates didn't dispute it.

During the three weeks the course lasted Max kept staring at her and she was soon fed up with his lovesick mooning. If anything saved Max from Sara's total indifference, if she still spoke to him or looked at him sometimes, it was for reasons that might be called strategic.

Sara had learnt a lot in the course: how to make a white-chocolate picnic cake, what temperatures are really risky during the tempering phase, why she preferred traditional recipes to new trends and innovations, and that, more than anything else, even before the end of the course, she was desperate to fuck Oriol Pairot, Max's best friend and the most eccentric student in the class.

This last, non-academic question was the one that gave her the most headaches. She could produce a list of ten points (or more) explaining why she was more interested in classical pastry-making than using the new exotic ingredients that were forcing their way in everywhere. Yet she was completely unable to put together any logical sequence of thought that might explain why, when the charming Max Frey was head over heels in love with her, she only and desperately wanted his arrogant friend. Maybe it was only that: unfathomable irresistible attraction. Peering over her horizon of half-worked chocolate while Ortega did the rounds of the workbench to supervise the exercise, she slyly observed Oriol Pairot and his different way of being in the world, an ugly duckling in a clutch of fluffy chicks.

The original Oriol Pairot, who may have been more genuine than the present one, had the haughty, indifferent air of people who don't give a damn about what's happening around them. He'd left home and earned his keep working as a waiter or delivery boy. Somehow he'd managed to pay for the chocolatiers' course, but it was clear that his next steps in the profession would be learning by trial and error because of lack of funds. He lived near the Sants railway station, perhaps with some relative or friend who was never mentioned in their conversations, and in the morning, having slept four or five hours at the most, his eyes were impressively black-ringed. Sara has never forgotten how Oriol had introduced himself in the first class: "Hello, my name's Pairot. I'm from Reus, but I've been living in Barcelona for two months. I want to make chocolates, but something different."

Everyone was waiting for the next revelation, watching Oriol, who was staring at the floor.

"Could you explain what you mean by 'different'?" Ortega asked.

"Just that. I don't want to be like the rest of them."

"In what sense?"

"In every sense."

"And where might your taste for chocolate come from?"

"My family."

"Ah." At last Ortega had something to go on, or at least he thought he did. "So, do your parents have a patisserie? Maybe you could tell us a little about it."

Oriol wriggled uneasily on his stool. "Um… I thought I only had to talk about myself."

Ortega was a very good man. He moved on to the next one. Max.

"My name is Max Frey and I'm nineteen. I'm from Illinois in the United States, but when I was very young my parents moved to New York, which is where I think I'm really from. I've been living in Barcelona for two years and am in my third year in Chemical Sciences. I also work with the Molecular Alloys Group in the Department of Crystallography, Mineralogy and Mineral Deposits, and with another university in Japan that has a very long name, which I won't bore you with. If you're wondering why I'm doing a course in chocolate-making, you should know that I'm also wondering the same thing (especially because I'm hopeless with my hands and don't believe I'm going to learn much). Well, actually it's because my thesis is about how some lipids (and especially cocoa butter) behave in different conditions, and how we can get them to behave in an exemplary way, so to speak, which in this case would be equivalent to producing the perfect chocolate. I guess I'm trying to say I'm a mad scientist who's infiltrated the group, seeking an authentic chocolate-making experience. If all goes well, I'll present my thesis in eighteen months' time. You're all invited if you want to come along. Sorry about all the rigmarole, but my Catalan's not good enough to improvise. I wrote the speech yesterday and learnt it by heart. I hope I haven't bored you. Thanks for listening to me."

Max's speech was greeted with a spontaneous ovation, which made him go bright red.

"Did you say you're nineteen?" Ortega asked.

"Yes."

"Do you know you're the youngest in the class?"

"Yes. I'm used to it." Max looked down. "I'm two years ahead of my age group."

Max sounded embarrassed and, to tell the truth, he was. He was very embarrassed. This happened every time he was required to talk about his academic history, because sooner or later he had to confess his great intellectual gifts and the assessment that had been made by an eminent psychologist specializing in people with high IQs and exceptional talents, which was precisely why his parents had decided to move to New York, the beginning of a new life for the whole family and also the worst possible academic nightmare for a boy of nine who is suddenly thrust into a class of highly gifted eleven-year-olds. For him, it was a horrible experience.

Max wasn't asked to give any further explanations to the chocolate-making class that day. Ortega, with his sixth sense, had already guessed it all.

Now it was Sara's turn.

"My name is Sara Rovira. I'm twenty-one and am finishing a History degree. I decided to do this because I like understanding things. I think that we can never know anything about ourselves if we don't understand the past. I mean, I think we're just a heap of piled-up past... well, that's one way of putting it. Sorry, I'm rabbiting on too much. The thing is, I'm studying History, but I've always known that my future lies in the kitchen of my father's patisserie. My parents started the business in the Sixties and it's still doing well, with a lot of regular customers. My father wants to retire two years from now and I'm an only child. So I have to take over. This is fine by me: I'm really excited to think that I can be in charge, that I'm the second generation and will be continuing something that's really worthwhile. That's why I'm here, to learn techniques that will help me now and in future. And also" – aiming a mischievous smile at Oriol – "I'll need to know what the competition's up to, just in case."

"That's the spirit!" Ortega hasn't got the real drift of the last few words. "Very nice, Sara, what you said about the present and future. Very nice indeed!"

The friendship between Max and Oriol was difficult to understand, because they were so different. Or perhaps the most wonderful thing about friendship is that, unlike other relationships, it's not based on things you have in common or the need to create them. It's about knowing how to enjoy differences. You only had to see them together to realize they were chalk and cheese. Pairot got around looking half hippy, half rocker, always dressed in rigorous black and with a certain touch of elegance which made him stand out from any tribe or trend. Pairot was simply himself and it would be hard to find another like him. He was much taller than the rest of them, a little over six foot two with broad but slightly stooped shoulders, like a lot of other people who spend their whole lives talking to people shorter than themselves, an athlete's waist and powerful thighs evoking a classical statue. He had bony hands, as if his skeleton was trying to escape through his skin, and a prominent Adam's apple, which Sara couldn't stop looking at. For some strange reason, she found this the sexiest bit of the male anatomy, and every time she saw Pairot swallowing saliva she wanted to lick his neck like an ice cream, and nip the busy jack-in-a-box that so enchanted her, even though it was only a bit of thyroid cartilage protecting his larynx.

In fact, Sara had always envied men for their camaraderie. Those male get-togethers had always seemed deliciously vulgar, vaguely alcoholic, complicit in a slightly tribal way, trite because they never pause to analyse themselves or philosophize about life – which is something women do when they get together

– exultant because they get excited in each other's company and, most important, exclusive. When the males of the tribe are busy with men's talk, women aren't invited. And that's that.

When the first week's classes finished on the Friday afternoon and after all the other students had rushed out of the classroom as if a fire alarm had just gone off, Ortega saw that the odd threesome were still hanging around.

"Don't you lot want to go home?"

None of the three showed the slightest enthusiasm about going home, which only encouraged the maestro – who was about to retire, who loved his job and who was in no hurry to go home either – to suggest something he would never have done with anyone else.

"Would you like to learn a few decorating tricks?"

They all jumped at the chance and, feeling very privileged, went off to fetch their aprons, gloves and all the paraphernalia they needed. Ortega locked the classroom door from inside, thus creating a feeling of intimacy, which only heightened the wonder of his incredible master class. What came next was the most sumptuous treat. A treat of an hour and three quarters in which the incredibly experienced and, in particular, generous Ortega shared his knowledge and a few trade secrets.

"Teaching people who want to learn is a wonderful thing," he said at the end of the class, his eyes shining with the emotion of having spent this time with new blood, these youngsters who, he believed, had a great future ahead.

They too were excited when it was over.

"What now, mate?" Pairot asked, looking at Max. "Shall we go for a beer?"

"Of course," Max said and disappeared behind the toilet door.

Sara and Pairot were left alone. She was disconcerted at not being included in the invitation. "I like beer too," she said.

"Oh, sorry, I didn't imagine you'd want to come."

"Can I?"

"I don't know. Max is a mess and he wants to talk."

"Ah, so you have to give him advice…"

"Yes, he needs another guy."

"You mean he's got problems that we women can't understand?"

"I mean he's got problems *with* women."

"Well, well, well. So that has to be discussed man to man."

"Yeah, that's right."

It sounded falser than anything Sara had ever heard in her life and, since Pairot had started this dangerous game of lies, she decided she could lie just as well as he could.

"You don't have to worry. In that regard I'm like a guy."

Oriol's eyes were as wide as saucers. It wasn't often that the tough guy of the class was impressed, and Sara savoured the moment like a scrumptious *petit four* fresh out of her kitchen.

"What do you mean exactly?"

"I like girls."

She blurted it out without any thought for the consequences, which were immediate. Pairot had never met a lesbian, and curiosity took precedence over the man-to-man chat with Max.

"Bloody hell, I've never talked about boobs with a woman." He was incredulous.

"Well, don't miss your chance."

By the time Max came out of the toilet, the beer had three heads and a most titillating touch of sapphism.

That was the night when their triangular friendship officially began, though it would be hard to say whether it was an equilateral triangle or some other form. What is for sure is that the base consisted of not one but two lies.

On the day of his dinner with Pairot, Max goes about his morning routine. Sara doesn't. Sara's not in the mood for routine. She lazes in bed until half-past eight and, as soon as she gets up, takes two blue headache pills. She phones the shop and tells the manager to see to everything, because she has to write an article and won't be coming down this morning. This is her most genuine excuse (though if she wasn't in such a state, it wouldn't be an excuse). The magazine people are very patient with her and never pressure her for articles even if she delivers weeks late. They publish her immediately and pay punctually, which is a lot more than one can ask for in these times when the traditional press is facing such difficulties.

Sara doesn't like being away from the shop all day because she has the impression, somewhere between responsibility and hubris, that nothing works the same if she's not around. She's had the same kitchen staff for years now. They know her style and aversions and can manage all the techniques, but for some reason their work lacks spark, that little bit extra, which is what Sara has, a special, unique touch, and, moreover, it's impossible to teach. In the nineteen years she's been running the patisserie she's been absent very few days, and always because of some major reason, like going to hospital to give birth to her two children.

Today she has a major reason.

That morning Sara spends a couple of hours frittering away her time on a thousand trifles. She paints her toenails dark purple, "Dominatrix" according to the bottle which she bought on her last trip to Andorra but hasn't wanted to use until today. She tidies the cutlery drawer. She has three cups of coffee, the last of which washes down another blue pill for the nagging headache. She wonders if she's turning into a codeine addict. That done, she decides it's time to do something useful and begins to think about the dinner menu. Pairot's allergic to shellfish. That complicates things somewhat, but not too much. Fortunately it's Wednesday and a relatively quiet day in the kitchen, so she can ask them to make something a bit special without affecting the orders. Tabbouleh would be a good idea, and maybe fish as a main. Truffled sole would be excellent, but monkfish with strawberries is more exotic and her cooks make it beautifully. Or maybe Max would prefer a cold dinner of salads followed by a mouth-watering dessert. Innovations are not the best way to impress the man who's invented – and sold for a fortune – a chocolate cake that one has to sniff instead of eating it but, if it's about tradition, then Sara's clearly on home ground and the odds are stacked against Oriol. She ponders serving her special *catànies** – which are certainly exquisite – but that seems rather meagre, so she decides on bitter truffles, made with very dark chocolate and served with *crème anglaise* and raspberry coulis. They can make the *crème anglaise* and the coulis in the kitchen, but she'll take care of the truffles. She'll rise to the occasion, astound Pairot and give her husband a good reason to be proud of her.

Just when she's wondering whether Max will approve of her menu, the phone rings. It's Max asking if she's thought about tonight's dinner and wanting instructions. He's also wondering about other details, like their chances of eating outside and if she's checked the weather forecast. She's bothered by having her thoughts so attuned to her husband's, as if their brains are connected by Bluetooth. It would seem that conjugal coexistence synchronizes spouses' neuronal synapses so that they end up like identical twins, which may be inevitable, but it's also very depressing.

"I'll set the table outside," she says. "You'll find everything ready. You just have to take away the cloths covering the dishes and serve. Ah yes, and take the dessert out of the fridge fifteen minutes before you eat it. The weather forecast's good. I think that's about all."

"Wonderful!" says Max on the other end of the line. "You think of everything. Thanks, babe. We'll miss you a lot."

They hang up simultaneously.

She's in no doubt about the sincerity of Max's last words, but she's also well aware that, without her, the dinner will be a perfect reunion of a couple of old friends. Her presence would only complicate things. Then, though she's promised herself not to succumb, she looks at her phone again to see if there's any message from Oriol, knowing – the worst part is that she knows – that there is no message and there will be no message.

Sara uses the remains of a bag of ninety-nine-per-cent chocolate to make her truffles. It's strong and bitter, with a lot of personality, so good that it would be a shame to serve it to any old guest. She phones the shop manager and tells her there's a slight change of plans and she needs to have the kitchen and all her utensils ready by three, as she's decided to make some truffles out of the leftover bitter chocolate.

She spends half the afternoon working hard, concentrating on the truffles. They're divine, exactly as she knew they would be. She then takes everything up to the flat, sets the table and greets the kitchen hand, who brings her the truffled sole and a bulgur-wheat salad, a last-minute decision. She decorates the table with a couple of aromatic candles, but then thinks this is a bad idea and removes them. In their place she puts a bread basket full of all kinds of bread – even *sobrassada** bread– which she covers with an immaculate white linen napkin. She has a quick last look and is happy with everything: table setting, cushions on the chairs and the awning sheltering the diners from inquisitive eyes and endowing the scene with a more intimate atmosphere. She then decides to make a small change in the decoration of her dining room.

She opens a china cabinet and takes out the fine porcelain chocolate pot. It's pear-shaped and about twenty centimetres high, its missing pieces a testament to the passage of time. It doesn't have a lid and the swizzle stick is gone. On the base, an inscription in slightly sloping blue letters evokes the distant, unknown hand that once wrote, "*Je suis à madame Adélaïde de France.*" Reading it again, Sara thinks that she should continue her enquiries, research or whatever, about this woman. Right now, she hasn't got a clue where the pile of papers is, but decides she'll dig them out as soon as she can and do something about it. After all, she and Madame Adélaïde are part of the same story, joined in this lovely, delicate object which by some lucky chance came into her hands. She strokes it as if it were a small animal, seeks the roughness of the chipped spout. She's sad about that. It's strange the way objects become part of our lives, as if they were living beings.

The chocolate pot has been used only once since she became its owner. She was with Oriol and Max at the time. That's how they discovered that it contained just enough for three small cups. It's a strange number – three – but this made her believe from the very beginning that she was fated to have it. In those days, Sara still thought that everything happened for a reason. How naive! Incredible.

As she suspected, the chocolate pot needs a wash. She takes it to the kitchen sink and cleans it with soap and water very slowly and carefully, as if it were a baby, dabs it dry with kitchen paper and then takes it back to the dining room where she leaves it on the table, to one side but positioned in such a way that anyone walking past will see it. She wants the chocolate pot, this small item with the shred of shared history it bears like a frieze stamped on its skin, to emanate its influence tonight. She's sure Oriol will remember as soon as he sees it. And with his memory duly prodded, he will end up where she wants him to be, in a place which, if Sara had had her way, he would never have left.

Once the stage is set, she dresses as if she's going out for dinner, puts on her make-up and does her hair very carefully. She gets her handbag and leaves only ten minutes after Max arrives with the wine – one red and one white, as usual – kisses her on the forehead and wishes her a nice evening.

Sara stealthily takes out her neighbour's keys before stepping out into the street. She doesn't believe Max will be checking on her – he's never done it before – but she wants to be sure, just in case. The coast is clear. She enters the next-door building, slipping inside like a shadow. She doesn't turn on the light. She's a thief. She goes upstairs, fumbles, trying to find the keyhole like a cuckolded husband who wants to know the whole truth. Only when she's inside the flat does she relax, but she still doesn't turn on the lights. She goes up the spiral staircase, opens the terrace door and wedges it so it can't blow shut. Then she turns her attention to the chair. She's already spotted one in a corner of Raquel's bedroom. She takes it outside, placing it next to one of the holes in the hedge, and peers through. She's delighted to confirm that it's perfect.

She can see Max checking the dishes under the linen napkins. She catches him nicking an anchovy from the top of the salad. She watches him gazing happily at the dinner table and checking his watch. Two minutes go by. When the doorbell rings – although it seems out of character, Pairot has always been punctual – Sara's heart flips. Max goes offstage to open the door. Sara readies herself.

What is it like to see someone you've thought about every hour for the last nine years?

For better or worse, she's about to find out.

Here's to Madame Adélaïde de France

That night of beers and abstract lesbian frissons was the one that officially launched the three-way friendship. It must also be said that, whatever came afterwards, the friendship endured. It was indestructible.

They had the first beer in a Basque tapas bar in Carrer Montcada. Since it wasn't yet dinner time, not even for tourists, the place was empty and they claimed some stools and a stretch of bar. They made a vague toast, confronted by a trio of slices of bread spread with salmon paste – or something of the pink and greasy ilk – and took the first sip looking at each other over the foamy horizons of their glasses. The second beer, in another bar, made Max feel more at ease, less shy, but it was still painfully obvious he was a virgin. He stared at Sara, even more smitten than he was in the classroom, while she challenged Oriol with her gaze as if to say, "Look how besotted your friend is."

During this second stop they hadn't yet progressed from the clichés about being in the same class and were still chatting about the course and their classmates whom they were unanimous in badmouthing with all the superiority of their twenty years. It was also time for a few biographical details to emerge. Max told them about his parents, enlightened farmers from Illinois, who owned vast expanses of land where they grew soya beans, plus soya-bean-processing plants and a shop specializing in soya-bean products in the centre of Chicago. They were so enamoured of the Old Continent that, although they missed him, they compensated for his being so far away by bragging to all their friends that their son was living in Europe. They phoned him every Saturday and punctually sent him a more than generous allowance, which Max saved because he didn't share his family's heartfelt conviction that in order to be happy you have to be a big spender. He spoke of his parents with a mixture of respect and admiration and was determined to achieve something that would make them proud of him, which is why it would never have occurred to him to do anything irresponsible, and why he continued to be the perfect son. While telling them all this, he was gazing at Sara, perhaps trying to convince her that nice guys have their advantages, or maybe he was trying to convince himself.

The main problem for Max was that he was dying to be bad, a rebel, but he was too scared to attempt any of the transgressions that occurred to him and that might be necessary to achieve that status. He had to settle for the inconsistency that governed all his actions, starting with not being able to stop staring at Sara's breasts, but being unable to make any move towards achieving any kind of intimacy with her. Or that little speech of his, all that hot air trying to prove he was a nice guy, when all he could think about was fondling those breasts.

She told them about her preordained destiny as an only child, hastening to add that it wasn't a problem for her. She'd always liked the patisserie and believed that when she took over she'd do a good job. She had a great deal of respect for her father and felt a kind of tender wariness in her mother's case. She was studying history because she didn't want to be "just a chocolatier", and because she'd always wanted to know about where we come from, but she was also resigned to the fact that history would have to be an unrealized vocation.

When it was Oriol's turn to talk about himself, he said, "Let's go somewhere else."

The third stop that night was in Carrer Vidrieria. The idea of moving on to something stronger than beer hadn't occurred to them yet. It was a warm, balmy night, one of those March evenings that presaged the coming of spring. They'd only just started talking and were showing no sign of flagging. Oriol scrutinized everything Sara did, as if analysing a very strange species. The alcohol had loosened Max up, made him more resolute, and by the fourth beer he was spurring on the conversation with a loquacity that was a quite a feat for him.

"Why does this patisserie thing run in families? Oriol's parents are pastry chefs too," Max said.

"I guess it's because you get hooked on chocolate!" Sara laughed. "Why won't you tell us about it, Oriol? So your parents are in the trade too? What's your shop called?"

"It's not 'our' shop. It's their shop." The genius doesn't mince words.

Max shook his head. "That subject's taboo," he warned, opening his eyes very wide.

Before realizing there was a problem, Sara would have asked at least a dozen more questions about Oriol's parents. (Where's the shop? What's its specialty? Do you make a good butter croissant? Have you got any brothers or sisters? Will you take over the business?) Problem notwithstanding, she still had at least six questions. (Did you fight with them? Have you left home? What do you want to do? How come you want to be a pastry chef if you can't stand your parents? Are you sure you've chosen the right job? Are you prepared to go into competition with them? What do you think about butter croissants?)

Butter croissants: now they really separate the sheep from the goats, as she'd learnt from her father, who was proud of the fact that he was "one of the few remaining pastry chefs in Barcelona who know how to make a genuine butter croissant like they do in France, crescent-shaped and all". Of course he always went on to add, "But you need to be aware that people here won't tolerate the quantity of butter that goes into the original recipe, so you only use about half, or no one will want to eat your croissant."

"Do you know how to make butter croissants?" This was a question from her personal exam. She wanted to know if Oriol would pass.

"No," he replied, utterly indifferent.

Sara pulled a face expressing all the contempt, all the haughtiness she could muster, as if to convey "I might have guessed", or, worse: "Yes, well, you certainly don't look as if you'd know".

"I don't give a damn about croissants. Butter or no butter."

Max, who was quite tipsy by now, wagged a finger. "It would be a waste if Oriol made croissants."

"A waste of what?" enquired Sara, who was about to declare the War of the Croissants.

"Of creativity. Energy. Oriol's an innovator. He's brilliant. He has ideas that no one else has ever had. He'll be famous one day. Mark my words."

"Bollocks!" Sara thought all this drunken praise for his friend was hilarious. She burst out laughing. Max took advantage of this to order another round and waffle on.

"This guy you see right here is the as yet unrecognized inventor of revolutionary recipes, with ingredients that have never been used before. He presents the things he makes like perfect gems of design. As soon as he can, he'll found a business on this, and it will be a huge success because people won't have seen anything like it. It won't be long before everyone will know who he is. We're lucky. This guy, our friend Pairot, is amazing." Max was so drunk and so worked up that his eyes filled with tears. Oriol, meanwhile, had gone bright red.

Yet the genius said nothing. He neither defended himself nor went on the attack. He settled into a sort of meditative smiling complacency which let the other two take the floor, even if only to talk about him.

"Ingredients that have never been used before?" Sara was still laughing. "So what are they then?"

She aimed her question at Oriol, but Max answered:

"I can't tell you. You're the competition."

"But you know what they are."

"Because I'm a fake chocolatier. A lost cause. I can't even make a cupcake."

The weirdest phenomenon of the night was Max's accent. The drunker he got the more American he became. Now, after they'd put away more than half a dozen beers and his resistance was plummeting, he sounded like a very weird kind of Texan. It was quite difficult to understand him.

Any notion that this might have been a three-sided conversation was mere embellishment, a cover. The true discussions of the evening were one to one, for example when Sara went to the toilet. Max and Oriol, left alone gazing at three empty glasses as they waited for her to emerge so they could move on to another bar in the Passeig de Picasso, argued about the scope of people's sexual preferences.

Oriol urged, "Try, at least! You might redeem her."

"Redeem? What do you mean? I want to be a lesbian too."

"Maybe if you bed her she'll like it."

"But I'm a virgin!"

"One of these days you'll have to leave that behind you, won't you? Or are you planning to be a monk?"

"Do you think monks are virgins?"

"I doubt it, but I couldn't give a shit."

"Do you know if she's got a girlfriend?"

"No, she didn't tell me."

"But did you ask her?"

"No."

"Because what I'd really like is to see her and her girlfriend together."

"Man, you're off your head. So don't you want to lay her?"

"No. I mean, yes. When the time is right."

"And do you know more or less when that will be?"

"When God permits."

"You need more *pebrots*, Max."

"*Pebrots*?"

"Peppers, capsicums. It's our word for balls!"

"Aha!"

"Go for it."

"She's coming back now."

In the bar on the Passeig de Picasso, which was actually the terrace of a Greek restaurant, they asked for a plate of hummus and three nips of some liquor that would have resuscitated the dead. When Oriol went to the loo, Max was at last alone with Sara. He made the most of it by trying to sort out some of the big unknowns of the night's equation in his typically clumsy style, and with what he considered was a good dose of bravado. In other words, Max was himself but with a few drinks on board.

"I agree with you that butter croissants are very important. Someone has to keep up the traditions," he began.

"Right."

"Are you going out with anyone?"

"Not at the moment."

"But have you been with someone before now?"

"Of course. Like everyone."

"With different people?"

"Yes, but not all at once." A giggle.

"Do you remember their names?"

"Some."

"Will you tell me please?"

"You ask the weirdest questions, Max. Are you OK?"

"Ah, sorry. I'm drunk."

"So I see."

"Do you often have sex when you're drunk?"

"Not always. Why? Do you want to fuck?"

"Nothing would make me happier, Sara."

"But you can't fuck me."

"Right. Because you like women."

"I see that your soulmate doesn't hide anything from you."

"Nothing! He tells me everything."

"Really? And has he told you if he fucks when he's drunk?"

"Oriol fucks whenever he likes."

"Does he now? How come?"

"I don't know. He's got some kind of weird set-up with the woman he lives with."

"He lives with a woman?"

"He sublets from her. She's an older woman."

"How old?"

"I don't know. He hasn't told me. OK, he doesn't tell me everything."

"Have you been to his place?"

"No. That's strange, isn't it? He never wants to go there. Anyway… Er, just one thing, Sara. Are carnal relations an integral part of love for you, or do they have their own inherent sense?"

"Max, can you please ask questions I can understand?"

"OK. Would you fuck a man? Yes or no?"

"Not you."

"Oh dear. Do you think you might change your mind later?"

"No. You're too much of a good boy for me, Max. Don't get upset."

"But I'm changing." He drains the glass of liquor that's still left on the table to prove it.

"You know what I think? People don't change."

"You might be right. Thanks for your sincerity."

"No need to thank me. I want you to know that I like you a lot, Max. As a friend. We can be friends for ever, if you like."

"That would be very nice, yes."

"Ah, Oriol! You took your time! Where to now?"

It was half-past twelve. The last stop of the night was a tavern in Carrer de Sant Pau, where they landed after following Oriol's siren call: "Have you two ever tried absinthe? I'll take you to the only place in Barcelona where you can drink it, with the whole ritual and all!"

Even before the ritual Max was legless. Oriol and Sara were on their feet but definitely woozy. The much vaunted absinthe temple was a run-down place with small, round, cracked marble-topped tables. Sara tried to sit next to Oriol, but Max was too quick. They huddled round a small table next to the door, Max in the middle, and asked for three absinthes. The chlorophyll-green liquor came in conical glasses with a bulb at the base for the absinthe. Resting on the top of the glasses was a spoon unlike any Sara or Max had ever seen. It was silver, somewhere between a fish knife and a cake server, bearing a sugar lump on its perforated surface. The set-up was completed by three small jugs of cold water. As soon as the waitress had left everything on their table, Oriol became the officiator of the ceremony.

"You two, my friends, are about to lose a very significant kind of virginity." Oriol was the consummate showman, complete with guttural voice. "Pay your respects to *madame Artemisia absinthium* who, mixed with hyssop, orange blossom, angelica and other plants of the wild, all sweetly marinated before distillation, produces the most inspiring green nectar that was ever invented by our species. In order to drink this, you have to pour water on the sugar cube, very slowly and lovingly until it is completely dissolved. Remember that absinthe is like life. It's too bitter and needs sugar in order to be palatable. Next, you mix it all together at the bottom of the glass. Then you savour it in small sips, very slowly as if it were excruciating. But first, let's make a toast. May what we have begun tonight last for ever." They clinked glasses and drank, Max and Sara still dazzled by Oriol's lesson. "And now, if you have any questions…" Oriol added.

Sara had a lot of questions, but none of them about absinthe. They sipped their drinks in silence until Max stood up and said very politely, "Excuse me, please. I need to go and vomit a little."

This was Sara's big chance. The only one she'd had all night. She slid into Max's chair, very close to Oriol, thigh to thigh, faces almost touching. But he didn't respond, either positively or negatively. As if that was how things had to be.

"Your friend has a very high opinion of you," Sara offered.

"Yes, he's very generous, a really good guy."

It was difficult to start a conversation that seemed natural. The words got tangled in long, disturbing silences, at least for Sara, who could feel her heart beating all over her body, except where it was supposed to be beating. Oriol was as cool as ever, which made her even more flustered.

"I think he doesn't feel very well," she said.

"He's not used to drinking. He's always locked away, like some kind of lab rat."

"Shall we take him home to sleep it off?"

"We'll have to, like it or not."

"And after that?"

"We'll go off to sleep too."

"Together?"

Oriol's Adam's apple did an enchanting little dance. Up, down, up again… Watching it, Sara was getting more and more turned on as she sipped the former green distillate, which had now turned into a milky concoction, and felt the warmth of his body seeping into hers.

"I don't know if you realize, Sara, but Max really fancies you. He's my best friend. I mean, there are certain rules that have to be observed."

"What rules?"

"The obvious ones. You and I are a no-go. That's rule number one."

"As easy as that, eh?"

"Things tend to be easy before we complicate them."

"Max is my friend too, I'll have you know. I don't want to hurt him."

"I'm glad we see things the same way."

"If we don't tell him it won't hurt him."

"If we don't tell him what?"

"Look, do you want to fuck me? If you say no, I won't believe you. Or do you think I can't see the way you look at me?"

"Of course I want to. But I won't do it."

"You don't have to be so…"

Something so steely that it was scary shone in Oriol's eyes. "I won't and that's all there is to it, girl. Not now. Not ever. There are some things that can never happen. It's not the end of the world."

Sara desperately wanted to run away. She'd never felt so humiliated. This was rejection. He might as well have put it in writing. She wanted to cry but couldn't. She never cried over things that made other people cry. Instead of escaping, crying or punching Oriol Pairot in the stomach – which is what she really wanted to do – she stayed put and said, "Another round?"

Oriol said yes. They repeated the whole ritual with the sugar cube and little jug of water. This time there was nothing to toast. No desire to either. Now chastened, they drank without speaking. Max still hadn't reappeared.

After some brooding Oriol finally said, "You're lucky I'm not angry with you. You deliberately deceived me. You aren't into women at all."

"Look, I think you should just shut up. You don't know the first thing about me."

Oriol agreed. He'd been talking for talking's sake. He was almost certain that she wasn't into women, that she'd invented the story so she could go drinking with them, but wasn't totally sure. Anyway, he was too worried about Max's long sojourn in the Gents to bother with such intricate anthropological disquisitions.

"I'm going to check on Max," he said and went off to the men's room, aware of Sara's eyes clinging to his bum like a couple of ticks.

When he could at last raise his head from the toilet bowl, Max felt terrible. He thought he was going to pass out. He was whiter than a snowflake, with hot or cold sweats (he wasn't sure which), a spinning head and a total lack of coordination. His tongue, too, was out of control, although that had its appealing side. He immediately threw himself at Sara: "I feel really bad. I've ruined your night. Will you look after me a little bit?"

"Oh, you poor thing, what are you saying? You haven't ruined anything. What's wrong?"

"I'm hot. It hurts here," pointing at his right temple, "and I really fancy you. I need to go and sleep."

"I'm sure I have some tissue wipes in here," Sara said, rummaging in her bag, observed by Max's half-closed eyes and ignored by Oriol. She found a small sachet, tore it open, took out a tiny napkin that smelt like babies and wiped Max's forehead and the back of his neck with all the tenderness of a veteran mother.

Max happily submitted while his body swayed, dangerously close to keeling over.

"Let's go outside and get some fresh air," Sara suggested while Oriol paid.

Max had a tiny rented flat in Carrer de la Ciutat. Now in the street, they walked arm in arm, Max in the middle in case he stumbled, clinging to Sara like a small child who won't let go of his teddy bear. This was his big chance to be close to her, and he was making the most of the apparent unawareness of his drunken state which, although not totally convincing, gave him carte blanche.

They had to make several stops along the way. Sometimes it was to let poor Max rest and gather strength. Other times it was to let him vomit again in a litter bin, the gutter or on the odd street plant. A couple of times Sara tenderly placed her hand on his forehead, holding up his head, just as she was to do years later with their children on those wretched, exhausting nights when they were sick. Anyone wishing to follow their trail through the Ciutat Vella only had to sniff out the stink of Max's stomach juices liberally splattered along the way.

One of their last stops was on a corner of Carrer de la Canuda. This time Sara remained sitting on a step while a solicitous Oriol led their patient to a spot behind some large street planters. They took quite a while. So long that Sara had time to look around and take in a few other details of this place where they'd stopped by chance. The step she was sitting on was part of a shop window; it was an antiques shop; the light was on; the door was ajar. Since boredom is a powerful force and she could never be still for more than two minutes at a time, she dusted down her dress and hesitantly pushed the door open, asking, "May I come in?"

Although she didn't expect it, a frail voice answered from the depths of the shop, "Come in, girl. Come in... of course you can. Come on, come on. Can't you see the 'Open' sign?"

When her friends reappeared, Max was as pale and floppy as a rag doll. Oriol was also starting to look ill. Sara, however, was euphoric. She was holding a white porcelain pot in her hands.

"I prefer throwing up with you," said Max, sitting down next to Sara and resting his head on her shoulder, which wasn't soft enough.

"Look what I just bought. It's very old, made somewhere near Paris. It might have belonged to a high-society lady, but that's not certain. It's incredible, isn't it?"

Max was in no state to find anything incredible, except for the fact he hadn't died that night. His only response to Sara's announcement was to change his position, sliding down her bony frame to sink his face in her much more comfortable skirt, his nose only a couple of centimetres away from her vagina, separated only by the flimsy material of her dress and cotton knickers.

Max breathed in deeply and then made a noise that sounded like a whimper of pleasure.

"I think we should look for a taxi," Oriol suggested. "Poor thing, he's getting worse by the moment."

"No, no, no!" Max's hand flapped in the air. "Let me stay here a little longer."

He let his head drop like a dead weight, as if he'd gone to sleep. In fact, he did nap for five minutes in which he dreamt that he'd stuck his nose in a pubic zone as sweet as an *ensaïmada*, unhindered by the lady who tousled his hair as if he were a little boy.

"Don't you think that everything happens for a reason? I do," Sara whispered to Oriol. "Look, it's a bit battered and it hasn't got a lid, but there's a strange inscription."

She showed him the base of her acquisition and he, squinting, read, "'*Je suis à madame Adélaïde de France.*' Yes, that's quite odd. What is it? A coffee pot?"

"It's a chocolate pot, you idiot. You can see by the spout. Look. It's high up and quite wide so the chocolate pours well and makes foam in the cup. It would be more obvious if it still had the lid because it would have a hole in the middle for the swizzle stick. This is very fine porcelain. You can see because it's translucent if you hold it up to the light. At the time it was fired it would have been a luxury item. Now it's mine and all because of a series of coincidences that might not have happened. Like the three of us going out together for the first time. Or the antique dealer who couldn't sleep and who sold it to me because he happened to be in the shop doing some paperwork. I think everything happens because it has to happen. The chocolate pot and the start of our friendship on the same night. That can't be coincidence."

Oriol didn't know what to say. He believed in chance. Full stop. He thought the world was a place of utter chaos where, from time to time, something fell into place, for better or worse, but there was no point trying to try to work out why.

"It's chipped here," Sara observed, running the tip of her finger over the rough edge of the spout. With a melancholy sigh she added, "I think it's full of stories that someone wants to whisper to me."

"Maybe we could christen it tonight." Oriol dragged her back from faraway realms. "Some hot chocolate would be good for our friend here, and I know the perfect recipe for him."

Max raised his head. "Shall we have a second-to-last one?"

"No, sweetheart, no. You're going to bed," Sara informed him.

"Whatever you say."

"You can't even stand up, Max. Right now you're going to have some hot chocolate and tomorrow will be another day."

"OK."

He seemed slightly more alert. Helping him to stay upright, Oriol and Sara managed to steer him back to his flat, get him upstairs – luckily it was on the first floor – sit him down on the couch in his tiny living room, which was also kitchen, laundry, library, guest bedroom and lookout onto the neighbouring flat, where an elderly man in a tracksuit spent the whole day talking on the phone. Oriol opened a cupboard and took out a glass jar full of dark powder sparkling with coloured shavings. He rinsed Madame Adélaïde's chocolate pot, put some chocolate powder inside it, mixed it with tap water and put the whole thing in the microwave oven.

"It would have been better with mineral water heated in a kettle, but we'll have to make do with what we've got, right?"

"If I died right now would you be sad?" asked Max, who was clasping Sara's waist.

"Of course, you idiot, but you're not going to die just yet."

"You're right. I feel better."

"You're only pissed."

"I really like the way you say 'pissed'. Can you say it again?"

"Pissed."

"That sounds so lovely."

Sara wanted to know about Oriol's recipe, but he, as usual, wasn't giving anything away. He only said, "It's my secret recipe for reviving Americans who can't hold their booze!"

"Sara-a-a-a! I can't untie my shoelaces. They're wriggling around all by themselves," Max bellowed, and Sara went to kneel down in front of him and undo them. This foreigner's cunning, Oriol thought. With these skills he'd soon stop being a virgin. He hadn't stopped groping Sara, not for a single second since he'd come out of the toilet in the absinthe bar. Trying not to watch, Oriol concentrated on his recipe.

"This is very uncomfortable," Max said, pulling at his clothes.

"'This' means your trousers. Do you want me to help you take them off?"

"Yeah. And my underpants. With you, sweetheart, I don't need clothes."

"If I'm in the way, I'll leave. You only have to say the word." Oriol pretended to be joking, but this situation was starting to bug him.

"Yes, Oriol, off you go!" Max wanted him out of there.

"No, of course you mustn't go, Oriol. You're a perv, Max. If you weren't so drunk I'd be very angry with you. Don't take anything off. Don't throw Oriol out. Aren't you ashamed of yourself? He's your friend and he's making you some hot chocolate."

Now contrite after being ticked off, Max gazed at Sara. "You're right. I won't do it again."

"That's better."

"Will you come and sleep with me?"

"No, Max. As I already told you, that's not going to happen."

"Only as friends. Like boy scouts, I won't do anything. I'm a virgin. Don't you feel sorry for me? I'll do anything you tell me."

"That's enough, Max. This is getting boring."

Oriol served the resuscitating potion in three small plastic glasses he'd found in a drawer. It was chocolate-coloured, not very thick, but the aroma was something else.

Max sniffed it and announced, "I'm going to bed. If I stay here any longer I'm going to die. Sara, do you mind if I have erotic dreams about you?"

Since she didn't reply, Max zigzagged off down the passage, leaving his hot chocolate.

"You make a nice couple," Oriol remarked as soon as they heard Max's door close.

"Why do you say that?"

"He's a nice guy."

"Yes, but not for me."

"Try it." Oriol pointed at the steaming hot chocolate.

Sara brought the glass to her lips, but stopped. She had something to say.

"I think you and I would make a better couple."

"If you say so."

"What shall we drink to?"

"Whatever you like."

"We'll drink to your taking back what you said to me tonight."

"OK."

Plastic against plastic, their glasses made an imaginary clink. The taste of the chocolate brought a strange grimace to Sara's lips. It wasn't very sweet, or very thick, or very dark. There was a blend of some very spicy flavours, like vanilla, cardamom or maybe... She took her time. Maybe black pepper? The oddest thing was the aftertaste this mixture left in the mouth. Sara realized that the reddish shavings she'd seen in the bag were dried chilli. They added a delicious touch and the whole effect was very well balanced, but more than anything else, it was infuriatingly original. Or so she thought before Oriol unveiled the mystery.

"This recipe's based on the original Aztec one. It was something like this – more or less – that Montezuma offered that cretin Hernán Cortés when he turned up. The same thing, but mixed with blood, was used as an offering for the gods. Maybe I should try it – I mean with blood."

"If you want a volunteer..." Sara murmured provocatively.

Oriol pretended he hadn't heard.

"Today it's a bit spicier than it should be because Max loves spicy food. So, what do you think?"

"I think I'm going to get what I want."

"Listen here, Sara Rovira," and Oriol drained his chocolate in one gulp, threw the glass in the rubbish bin and picked up his jacket which was languishing on a chair. "If I'm sure of anything, it's that you'll always get what you want. Pity the person who stands in your way."

Sara frowned. It would have sounded like praise without the clearly recriminatory tone.

Before leaving he asked, "Now, are you going to tell me whether you liked the chocolate or not?"

Basically, the only thing Oriol Pairot really wanted was to impress her with a new recipe. But Sara wasn't going to give him the pleasure. He didn't deserve it. She just shrugged and said, "Could be better."

"I'm off now. See you."

"Sure," she said before going out onto the balcony to watch him walking away (and get another eyeful of that bum, which was really gorgeous). She picked up her things, especially the chocolate pot, and left, carefully closing the door so as not to wake Max.

In fact, the most absurd thought of the evening came to her in the street. At this time of night, no one was out in the deserted city. She stopped at every corner, as if they were intersections on a maze, peering around, trying to find Oriol, but her eyes could only make out the familiar grotty paving of empty streets. Oriol had vanished. That was that. *You're an idiot. Men are slippery by nature and easily distracted. Always distracted. You can never totally trust them.*

A woman spurned, clutching a chocolate pot, wandering around a deserted city at five in the morning: what a ridiculous sight.

A new day was dawning.

Twenty-three years have gone by and a whole lot has happened since then, but tonight, sitting on a borrowed chair, on a borrowed terrace with views of her life, Sara has the impression that, as far as Oriol's concerned, she always has been and always will be a rejected woman. So many things have changed: them, the world, life. Even the past looks different now. Sara is the boss of a famous patisserie in Barcelona where a lot of people come every day for their breakfast croissants, for the pleasure of eating a proper one, made with butter, tailor-made for local tastes and beautifully served. At Christmas she sells two thousand slabs of her chocolate praline *torró* (speciality of the house), not to mention the Easter eggs, the *sares*, her *crema de Sant Josep*, the *coques de Sant Joan* or her *tortell de reis*,* all of which have contributed to the happiness of so many inhabitants of Barcelona, children or grandchildren of the ones who ate the same delights made by her father. This sense of continuity is what makes her happiest, as if life had presented her with a very difficult exam and she's passed with flying colours. Well, she hasn't invented anything, she knows, but she's given her very best to perpetuating the legacy that has come down to her from her forefathers, who go back more than one generation: those Barcelona chocolatiers who turned breakfast or any other snack into an art the whole world could fall in love with. Perhaps it was the first art to shine in this city where everything shines. It hurts that Oriol has never recognized the merits of her work in cherishing this continuity. And that Max has always been such a fervent admirer of his daring, innovating, globetrotting friend, inventor of the little box of chocolates called "Three Very Different Friends", one of the Pairot brand's best-selling products. They had inspired it and their friend had added one of his own essential ingredients: a big dash of boldness. In the first year alone, the famous Three Very Different Friends brought him half a dozen of the most prestigious awards and opened the doors of the whole of Europe, as well as those of some very interesting foreign importers. Today people all around the world, from Norway to Japan, from the United States to New Zealand, are all fans of his little box of chocolates, and for the last few years, production has been doubling every season.

The "Three Very Different Friends" are three egg-shaped chocolate bonbons made from white creole cocoa, grown on just one property in the south of Mexico (to which Oriol has exclusive rights because he owns it). White creole is one of the best cocoas ever – aromatic, delicately flavoured, slightly bitter and very different (in price too) – and Oriol had the audacity to add Mexican jalapeño chillies, ginger from India and lavender syrup. The chillies, he said, were in honour of Max and his love for spicy food. The ginger was for himself and his fondness for the raw materials of oriental cooking. And the lavender was for Sara and her sainted tradition, and also because it was her favourite colour. That summed it up. On the black lid of all the boxes – with three, six, twelve and twenty-four bonbons – one could read in nineteen different languages (depending on the country) the gold letters that spelt out the inscription, "For Max and Sara, in present, past and future." How beautiful.

Very profitable and very untrue. But very beautiful.

They also squabbled and this had consequences.

The first Monday after Absinthe Friday, Ortega informed them, "This week, you'll be working in teams of three people to make desserts that will define you. Not as individuals but as a team, and I want that to be very clear. You'll never be alone in the kitchen and one of the most valuable lessons you'll take away from any school you might go to is the spirit of teamwork that will be so necessary in your professional life. We'll spend some time organizing the teams and defining the projects. I'll also need one representative for each group."

Max, Oriol and Sara were already a group. Everyone took it for granted that they'd work together. Their teacher more than anyone else. Max saw the exercise as a wonderful opportunity.

"I'll do something great if it's with you two," he said happily.

Sara saw the practical side.

"This is our chance to combine tradition and modernity. We'll cook up a bombshell of a recipe. Any ideas, Oriol?"

Like Sara, Max was certain they'd make a good team, but Oriol wasn't convinced. He'd never been good at teamwork. Throughout his childhood and adolescence he'd heard the same words, over and over again: "You're too individualistic. You have to learn to share." In the kitchen, his idea of a team consisted of several people unquestioningly obeying his every order, army style. He was fairly sure that Sara wouldn't go along with this. The mere thought of it was utterly exhausting.

Nonetheless, there was no choice but to work as a team. In the first hour, the only thing they came up with was that their dessert would be a *torró*. It was perfect, a classic with a wide range of possibilities, yet urgently calling for innovation by creative spirits. It was the base to which they could add anything, and Oriol was very excited by this. For him "anything" had a complex, unpredictable meaning.

"But a bit of common sense, please. You can't ask us to make *torró* with *escalivada*,* right!" Sara guessed what was going to happen.

In the first few days they progressed from the original idea. They'd work with Grand Cru chocolate, the purest in the market. They'd think up a new and different filling that would slightly disconcerting but not alarming – hence they'd have to keep a watchful eye on Oriol – and they'd also work on the form, which they wanted to be as attractive as a special gift. What about a *torró* dedicated to an artist? Antoni Tàpies, Picasso, Miró, Gaudí? Or one in honour of Barcelona, the would-be Olympic venue. The design used by the city to promote itself in those pre-Olympic years was something all three of them thought they should exploit. They met up a couple of times outside the classroom to talk about it, in the afternoon and without absinthe. Things went well in the beginning and they all seemed very clear about their respective roles. Max was the technical advisor and a kind of executive producer. They knew that things would go well if they kept Max out of the kitchen. Their discussions were heated.

"So you're saying it has to be cooled fast but never below nineteen degrees unless we use another kind of butter—"

"But what are you saying, man! We're not going to use any crap in this. It has to be as healthy as possible."

What concerned Sara most was the praline. She was certain that Oriol wasn't planning to make it with hazelnuts, sugar and honey, the way it was always made. She was right. Oriol was thinking only about flavours no one had ever tried, and crunchy textures. Sara, who didn't know that yet, was already feeling the fury build up inside her. This had to flare up sooner or later. She'd worked out the division of labour from the very start.

"Right, lads, we've got to get organized. Max can deal with the technical part, Oriol the topping, and I'll do the filling."

Since nobody squawked, she understood they were letting her be boss. It wasn't until that afternoon, when they were sitting around a table and three coffees in the Plaça de les Olles, that Oriol informed them how he planned to go about things.

"I'm doing the filling. I'm working on it and, I can assure you, you'll be gobsmacked. Sara, you go and find the best chocolate for the coating and give it whatever shape you like. I won't interfere too much with that. Since we are fortunate enough to have a historian in our team, maybe you can go and find some special date in the history of the city. Perhaps we can pay homage to one of the great pastry chefs of the olden days, or the first chocolatier, or Joan Giner and his Easter figures, I don't know, but something that's worthwhile. Max could help you, so you two will be finished first. I tell you, Ortega will be astounded and we'll win."

"Since when has this been a competition?" Sara enquired.

"Everything in life is a competition," Oriol replied.

"So when did you take over? Didn't we agree that I'd represent the group?"

"Team representative isn't necessarily the same as the person in charge."

"Ah, so you've unilaterally decided that you're in charge?" Sara was gasping with rage and her voice was getting louder. She couldn't believe her ears.

"I only said I'm working on the filling. And I've left the showiest part for you, which is the coating."

"No, that's not on. You have to let me do the praline, Oriol. Don't you understand that I have a lot more experience than you? We've been making *torrons* for years and years in Casa Rovira, and the sales keep going up."

"Since when did sales success mean 'best'?"

"I was talking about praline. You don't have to be nasty."

"There can be many kinds of praline."

"Not in Casa Rovira."

"That's why I want to make it!"

"Sara's right." Max intervened, trying to arbitrate. "She knows a lot about praline."

"You know what, if everyone thought like you two, we'd still be eating berries!" Oriol was incensed, gesticulating wildly, banging the table, turning his eyes skywards as if demanding justice from a God who'd forsaken his children. "Anyway, what have we got to lose? Forget about the bloody boring praline that's been around for ever. Anyone can make that. Let's do something really original, something that bears our own brand!"

"Our own brand can be quality too. You don't have to go inventing things every second of the day."

"I agree, yes, yes, I totally agree. But don't you like being a little, even if only a tiny bit different?"

"Different? Like what? Let's see, Oriol, how about telling us what you'd put inside our poor *torró*. Have you thought about it, at least?"

"Of course I have! There are a thousand possibilities." He leant forward, speaking with contagious fervour. "For example, a tropical-style crunchy filling made of freeze-dried fruits, like mango or mandarin. Or papaya, maybe. Yes! Papaya would go fantastically well with seventy-per-cent chocolate. Or a sour-apple filling with a touch, but just a whisper of cinnamon. Or, even more daring, a *torró* which, with one bite, brings you all the flavours of the end of Christmas lunch: Baileys, cappuccino, *neules**... and slightly crunchy of course! Crunchiness would be great but, technically, it might be more complicated. We'll have to think about it."

A pensive silence fell on the group after Pairot's ardent monologue. Sara acted offended, or was offended, and Max felt uncomfortable because, for all his wishes to the contrary, he'd been unable to prevent them from getting into an argument. This histrionic bickering made him feel quite ill. It was not his thing at all, especially when they were quarrelling over praline.

"Hey, come on, you two, let's go back to square one. We're not making any progress." Max was doing his job. "We'll take a vote on it. Who votes for praline?"

Sara raised her hand.

"And who votes for the other filling?"

Pairot raised his hand.

"You have to give the casting vote," Sara said.

"Don't make me do that," protested the arbitrator. "I can appreciate both points of view. Are you sure we can't find a compromise between the two things?"

"But can't you see there can be no meeting between traditional praline and a *neula* shoved inside a *torró*?" Sara was aggrieved. Her tone was sharp.

Then it was totally clear that the praline issue was blocking all progress. Max felt terrible.

The hours and days went by and they could all see that there was no way they were going to sort out the praline question. Sara and Oriol were carrying on as if this was a duel between two rivals who wanted to be right at any price, and poor Max was the trusty friend who, once the wounds were inflicted, would have to take stock of the damage. The same old argument went on day after day. Sara turned up with a perfectly classical praline and, putting it on the table, made her challenge.

"Go on, taste it. Let's see what you think of that!"

Oriol tasted it, affecting an air of indifference. He then took out a bundle containing his strange concoction, as if to say, "Now here you have a proper filling." Sara reluctantly put some in her mouth, ready to say it was horrible.

Max thought they were both wonderful. Sara's praline was "unbeatable" and Pairot's filling was "fabulous". Even if he sometimes he ran out of adjectives, he always spoke with the same sincerity.

"We can't go on like this. You have to choose one or the other or we'll never finish this," Oriol demanded.

"It's difficult…" said Max.

Sara smiled triumphantly and Oriol couldn't bear it.

This also had its consequences on the friendship between the two men after Oriol accused Max of favouring Sara because he was in love with her. Max, who until that point had been

– because he'd wanted to be – a paragon of impartiality, was terribly hurt by this. He felt obliged to remind Oriol that, like it or not, Sara was "just as good" as he was. Oriol was so incredulous he asked him to repeat what he'd just said. Max had no problem with that and threw in a few even more wounding comments.

"Whether you like it or not, she's good and she'll go a very long way. She might go further than you because she knows how to treat people properly and not leave them feeling like a piece of shit. She's also a hard worker and very organized. It's about time you learnt that being a genius is all very fine but it isn't enough."

Oriol took these words as a terrible betrayal and spent hours muttering to himself and sulking. Max, who couldn't stand glum faces, and hated anyone being upset with him, tried to say it again in different words, but nothing could compensate for what he'd blurted out and there was no way he could erase it. Words often make more formidable barriers than a wall, and wound more than the sharpest blade of any knife. In this case, the worst consequence wasn't the distancing between the two friends but a little light that started flashing in Oriol's brain, signalling something very urgent that needed attending to.

Now they were no longer friends, certain things could be reconsidered, perhaps.

When Pairot phoned Sara that very afternoon, inviting her to go and have "a bite to eat" with him, she couldn't believe it. He didn't say "dinner", because he was broke and couldn't afford that. She meekly accepted, as if the praline question was no longer a bitter conflict. They arranged to meet in the bar in Carrer de Sant Pau, but it was closed, as it was still too early for the absinthe drinkers. They went to the London Bar, where, with two glasses of tonic water on the table, he launched himself at her, as if he wanted to glue his lips to hers.

Sara let him, but when they separated she asked him, "What about the rules?"

"Abolished. Max and I had a fight."

"About the filling thing or for some serious reason?"

But there were no further explanations, because Oriol didn't feel like giving them. Moreover there were problems to be sorted out. For example: the location. At this age when you're still dependent, the first step in having sexual relations is dealing with the question of the venue. Oriol never showed anyone where he lived and didn't even mention the possibility of going to his place. Luckily Sara's parents, who had season tickets to the Liceu, were at the matinee performance and would be out for a while. She wasn't at all keen about letting Oriol into her room, but this was an emergency and their range of possibilities wasn't exactly vast.

There was nothing for it but to go to Sara's place. "Casa Rovira, Chocolatiers and Pastry Chefs since 1960" was downstairs and connected with the family flat by a stairway that opened into Carrer de l'Argenteria. The kitchen backed onto Carrer del Brosolí, where the service entrance was only used to unload raw materials. This was years before Sara embarked on her real-estate-expansion strategy to become owner of the whole building – including the magnificent duplex with views of Carrer de l'Argenteria and the slender bell towers of Santa Maria del Mar – and the two business premises adjoining hers into which Casa Rovira spread like an oil slick to become the distinguished establishment she had already begun dreaming about. Back then, that afternoon, Oriol stared at everything with admiration disguised as curiosity.

He was amazed at Sara's naturalness when she invited him in, asked him to wait a moment while she closed the street door and gestured vaguely saying, "Look, this is the kitchen."

He glanced inside, just enough to see the stainless-steel worktops, sniff the good smell of tempering chocolate and ask if the posters on the walls were originals.

"I think so," Sara said, stopping for a moment to look at the two modernist-style gems of advertising which had always been there, claiming, "The best desire of all is desire for Sampons chocolate."

"They must be worth a fortune." Pairot, climbing the stairs behind Sara, was giddy with the enthralling swing of her hips.

He was amazed yet again when, once they were upstairs, she very serenely asked him if he needed the toilet or if he wanted anything, and he, well on the way to being the seducer he was to become, answered, "Yes. You."

The response was a smug, mischievous smile as if she'd won the battle in which she'd fired the first shots the night they'd gone drinking. Then she said, "Keep going. It's down the passage, the last door on the right." And he kept going to whatever place he had to go to at a time like this.

Oriol walked along the passageway as if he was about to be interviewed for a job and entered a room that would be engraved on his memory for ever afterwards. There was a bed with a pink crocheted bedspread, a white wardrobe with a mirror and built-in cupboards above, a shelf from which six formally dressed dolls smiled enigmatically, a shutdown computer, a bedside table with a telephone and a chest of drawers on top of which Sara had placed the white porcelain chocolate pot she'd bought from the night-owl antique dealer. Light poured in from outside, filtered by the curtains and joined by muffled humming from some faraway part of the world. Oriol imagined that Sara's life was an oasis of bliss in a world of lunatics and was, of course, envious.

"I thought you would have got your gear off by now." Her voice came from the doorway.

Sara was completely naked. Her body was as pale and delicate as the pink crocheted bedspread. Small breasts, tiny waist, flat belly, an impeccably manicured rectangle of dark fuzz over the vulva, dainty feet with toenails painted apple-green and lips with a condescending smirk that was enough to make anyone want to murder her.

Oriol knelt down in front of her and buried his face between her legs. She separated them slightly, cupped his head in her hand and gently pushed it farther in. This elementary choreography brought on the erection which, still confined in Oriol's jeans, was painfully cramped. He tried to stand up, but Sara put her hand on his shoulder and said, "Just a bit more," in such honeyed tones that he couldn't refuse. Oriol slyly observed her shifting expressions on the far side of the dark fuzzy trench. In terms of sexual pleasure, observation was as important as action. He liked watching girls losing control. He liked seeing them with their eyes closed and covered in sweat. He liked this abandon and surrender to sex as much as sex itself. But Sara didn't let herself go. She was watching him. She was doing the same as he was, examining him the whole time with unwavering interest, even when he was sucking her nipples in an upwards course which he wanted to finish in an upright position himself and a change of scene more in keeping with his own interests. She kept looking at him while she undressed him with an urgency he'd never seen in any other girl (not to mention surprising dexterity and, unlike other girls, without a moment's fumbling with his double-tongue belt buckle or fly buttons). She kept looking at him when they changed roles and she knelt in front of him. The oral stage, too brief for Sara's liking, came to an end when Oriol put his hands under her arms and pulled her to her feet saying, "Come here." Before he could get her onto the bed, she'd swept off the crochet bedspread so it wouldn't get soiled (nothing ever escaped her, even in such irrational moments), and before he'd decided which was the best angle from which to go about things, she was already putting the condom on him and asking him to lie down so they'd be more comfortable. As he went to do so, she said, "No, it'll be better with your head the other end."

He didn't protest, partly because he didn't care where he put his head and partly because he was so excited that his decision-making skills were seriously impaired.

It didn't take long for him to work out what Sara had in mind, though. She straddled him and did all the work, first avidly sucking his Adam's apple – at last, after so long gazing at it from afar, that naughty little bulge was all hers – and then rhythmically moving her hips as she clutched the end of the bed with both hands and watched the scene in the wardrobe mirror with the eyes of a woman possessed. Scary even. Oriol had never seen such a transformation and could never have imagined that Sara was so good at what she was doing. She was so terribly good that he'd never experienced anything like this. He abandoned himself to pleasure with a strange feeling of serenity, as if this was something normal, savouring the agreeable sensation of being stripped of all authority and not having to make any decision. It was only at the last minute that he wanted to do things his way. Since his hands were free he covered Sara's mouth and eyes; her mouth because her moans were getting louder and louder at an alarming rate, and her eyes because he didn't want to see that expression in them, which was so eerie it was interfering with his breathing. This move, something completely new for Sara, made her go berserk. Her body convulsed violently and she let out a terrifying howl even though her mouth was covered. Witnessing this majestic spectacle, Oriol also came. It was an orgasm unlike any other he'd ever had.

Afterwards, they lay side by side on the bed, their heads where their feet should have been, and briefly discussed their achievement.

"That was great," he said.

"Really great."

"You're very good."

"Ah."

"I see you're experienced."

"Not really. I just wanted to grab you."

"And you're gorgeous."

"You're a flatterer!"

"I hope your chocolate pot won't spill the beans."

They laughed. Four eyes gazed at the porcelain object on top of the chest of drawers.

"Can you still hear those voices you told me about?" Oriol asked.

"Yes."

"What are they saying now?"

"We're a pair of bastards. They're very jealous."

"Why? Don't they fuck?"

"No. They're spirit beings."

"Tough luck."

"Yes. I'm thinking about writing something about them."

"So the historian in you is coming out."

"Maybe. Yes."

"Will you let me read it?"

"Of course not."

They lay there, waffling on about nothing in particular. At half-past nine Oriol, now standing in the kitchen, downed a glass of water, kissed Sara on the lips and bounded down the stairs. In Carrer de l'Argenteria he walked past Senyor and Senyora Rovira, who were coming home after seeing *La Bohème* in the Liceu, arm in arm and humming Musetta's beautiful aria from Act 2. They didn't know him and he had no idea who they were. They only saw a gangly young man rushing past them.

Now she can see him. Oriol is on the terrace, sitting opposite Max. Sara squints, trying to see him better. He doesn't look much like the idealized image she's nurtured in her memory. Or maybe he does. Slightly unsure of himself, perhaps. Must be the circumstances. Coming back can't have been easy for him either. Max looks very stiff. After nine years, naturalness needs time.

Predictably, Oriol has brought an extra-large box of his "Three Friends…" He's smiling as he looks around the terrace and at the beautiful illuminated bell towers of Santa Maria del Mar.

"What about Sara?" he asks.

She has butterflies in her stomach, from the satisfaction of being the first person the prodigal son asks about on his return home.

"She's at a work dinner, but she'll be back in time to have coffee with us."

"Ah, wonderful."

Now she can see Oriol facing her, holding his glass as he waits for Max to open the bottle of wine. He's still lean. He's still dressed totally in black. He's got the snooty laid-back air of someone who thinks the world revolves around him, although it would now seem that the world concurs with him. He looks much the same as he did years ago, but it's also very clear that he's improved with money, even if only because of the expensive brand of his shoes, the fountain pen sticking out of his shirt pocket and the very pricey watch adorning his wrist. His Adam's apple is in the right place and Sara hasn't got over her craving to lick it.

"Did you cook this spread?"

"No."

"Phew!" He giggles. Max echoes him.

When Max has poured a little wine into the glass, he asks Oriol to taste it.

"You don't have to stand on ceremony with me," Oriol protests.

It seems that he's forgotten that, for Max, this kind of gesture has nothing ceremonious about it. He likes things to be done *properly*. In this regard, he and Sara have come to resemble one another over the years. Sara would have invited a guest to taste the wine. It's good manners, an elegant formality. But Oriol has never been a lover of formality.

"I'm sure it's excellent. Come on, top up my glass," he adds. Max fills the glass. "Let's drink to all this time we haven't seen each other." He raises his glass and clinks it against that of his friend. The tinkle is the happy sound of things that never change. "I was afraid you wouldn't want to see me," he now confesses, venturing into the terrain of sincerity.

"What! That's crazy. Why wouldn't we want to—"

"I don't know. Sooner or later you two will have to stop loving me, won't you?"

"I don't think so." Max shakes his head. "People who come back are loved."

"I thought the ones that don't leave are more loved."

Aina appears. She's barefoot, wearing jeans, and has her hair loosely coiled at the nape of her neck. She instantly breaks the intensity of the scene. Her hair's the colour of cherry wood. She's as slim and dainty as a young doe, and perhaps a little bit too serious and responsible for her age (fifteen), just like her mother was as an adolescent. Max, of course, thinks she's absolutely perfect. He gave her the title of Apple of Papa's Eye ages ago. Although Sara is blessed with the advantages of having a fifteen-year-old daughter who converses and behaves as if she were thirty, she sometimes wishes that Aina was a little more normal, with scatterbrained but amusing friends to go partying with, making her parents suffer and fret: *whatever could they be up to at this hour of night, running around wherever they are?* But Aina doesn't go partying and doesn't want frivolous friends. Her best and only friend – who may have been conceded some or other sexual privilege, but that's by no means certain – a boy a year older than her and as freaky as they come, dreams of being an astrophysicist and collects minerals. Sometimes Aina goes to his place "to help him classify geodes", and she's been known to spend hours on the Internet waiting for the seller of a piece of amethyst druse to respond to her counter-offer. However, when Sara saw the stone with its incrustation of lilac-coloured crystals, she had to admit that it really was beautiful – as beautiful as her daughter's habit of giving rocks to her friend was strange.

"Good evening," says Aina making her entrance on the terrace. "Enjoy your meal."

Her appearance totally changes the tone of the reunion. Oriol leaps to his feet as if set off by some mechanism. "Little Aina, but you're so grown up!"

Aina smiles faintly, her automatic response to the same old comment, which she's been stoically putting up with for the past five or six years, as if adults can't think of anything better to say as soon as they lay eyes on you.

"Do you remember me?" he asks.

"Of course I do. We've seen you on telly lots of times. And my parents often talk about you."

Her use of the formal form of you, *vosté*, is hitting below the belt. A lovely girl comes out onto the terrace and addresses you as *vosté*. Something serious has happened to you, Oriol. You have to deal with this immediately, sort it out, if only for your own self-esteem.

"Hey, none of this *vosté*, please. I'm not that old."

"Of course. Sorry. It's just a habit."

Aina is perfect, a marvellous combination of her parents' best qualities, and they are only too aware of it. They can hardly believe their luck.

"Is that what I think it is?" Oriol asks, referring to an item Aina's carrying in her hands. Then Max sees that his daughter is holding the porcelain chocolate pot, which is usually kept in the living-room china cabinet.

"I wanted to ask you, Papa, if you know why it was out on the table? It could have easily got broken, because it was just where everyone walks past. Mama would have a fit if she saw it there."

Sara smile gets even wider (if that's possible). How could her daughter know her so well that she divines what Sara wants and does exactly what Sara would have done? What she's just done with the chocolate pot is incredible. She's brought this memento to precisely the place where it can inflict most damage. If she'd wanted to enlist her daughter as an accomplice in this project (unthinkable, of course), Aina couldn't have done a better job.

"I haven't got a clue what it was doing there," Max says. "Maybe the cleaner took it out? You're right, sweetheart. Leave it here and I'll put it away."

Aina puts the chocolate pot on the table, checking out the food as she does so.

"I'm going to study for a while," she says.

"What about your brother?" Max asks.

"He's coming. He's cleaning his teeth." She now moves into slightly scandalized mode. "I'm sure it's the first time since this morning."

Aina's tone, when referring to her younger brother's substandard hygiene, makes Oriol smirk. He disguises it by picking up an anchovy nestling in the *coca de pa** and putting it in his mouth.

Aina takes her leave, once again wishing them goodnight and a nice meal before disappearing inside. Oriol, still eating the anchovy and with a look on his face somewhere between shock and admiration, says, "She's the spitting image of Sara, this girl! Amazing! It's like seeing Sara when she was that age."

You didn't know me when I was that age, you cretin.

"Everyone says the same." Max picks up a plate and starts serving the bulgur-wheat salad. "Tell me when to stop."

"God, I thought I was seeing her. She even has Sara's serious, perfectionist air. Amazing!"

"Yes, that especially," Max adds.

"But you're in there too. Good grief!"

"Yes, I'm in there too."

Oriol now focuses his attention on the food, smiling as he looks at the dishes and their contents. Sara doesn't miss a single detail of his reaction. She wants his approval of her choice.

"Ah, hang on, I brought you something." Oriol stands up and dashes inside. Max stops serving and stands there motionless, as if he's acting in a play and the lights have suddenly gone out. Oriol is back in a second.

"I fear your son took me for a thief when he saw me squatting down and retrieving this from a corner. Tell him I'm not, please."

Pol eyes him cautiously from the terrace doorway, as if trying to work out why this man who's come to dinner is an adult and he isn't.

"Good night, Pol. Are you off to bed now?" his father asks.

"In fifteen minutes or so."

"This is my friend Oriol."

Pol is a gangly, cheerful boy. Despite the thousand and one complications life constantly lumbers him with (especially when he has to enter the orbit of adults and, much more, when he has to move through the strange, hostile universe of his older sister), he's a kind of happiness pro. Or he's got a cheek, as his mother sometimes says. Come what may, he's not going to let anything in the world spoil his upbeat nature, his nonchalance and scatterbrained way of being in the world. Everyone wonders whom he takes after, where this baffling character comes from.

"We've already met," Oriol says, "but the last time I saw you, you were still in nappies. And if I remember correctly you were sleeping like a log."

Pol guffaws, half surprised and half embarrassed. Then he can't stop laughing. He looks as if his theory has just been confirmed: *that guy can't possibly be an adult!* When he stops laughing, he asks, "Where's Mama?"

Another shiver of satisfaction runs through Sara, cloak-and-dagger Sara hidden behind the neighbour's hedge. She's immensely happy to see how her children won't let her be totally absent, how they bring her into the gathering whenever they can. Her heart puffs up like a balloon. A moment later she finds it sad and deplorable. The Sara of twenty-three years ago would have been fuming at the mere suggestion of justifying her existence through her children.

"Your mother's at a work dinner," Max explains. "She'll be here later. Are you hungry? Do you want something to eat?"

"Mama left us some crepes. I just had them. They were great."

"Right, well get inside now. And clean your teeth. Your sister's outraged."

"I did clean them." He pulls a gruesome face. "Aina's a pain in the neck. She's worse than Mama."

Sara's trying not to laugh. Pol goes inside, looking scruffy in his pyjamas. They're navy blue, a grown-up colour. At twelve, however, Pol's in some ill-defined space between boy and man.

"Here." Oriol hands his friend the item he'd gone to get from inside. "I'm also making my particular tribute to the good old days. You probably suspect what—"

"No! Impossible!" Max exclaims as he opens the gift. "I don't believe it!"

While Max confirms his suspicions on freeing the bottle of emerald-green absinthe from its tissue-paper wrapping, Oriol picks up the chocolate pot from the table and studies it carefully: the generous handle, the high spout, the missing lid and swizzle stick and, on the bottom, the inscription that declares that it's the property of Madame Adélaïde, whoever she was. He rubs his finger across the chipped part of the spout. It reminds him of a war wound. It is as scratchy as memories, as things that end, never to return. He puts it back on the table and stares at it, recognizing its elegance, quality and arrogance of having emerged from clay to climb to the summit of a waning society. A society that could indulge in possessing the very best of everything. The whole lot vanished, but the chocolate pot is still here, sitting on the table between Oriol and his friend.

"Does Sara know who she was, this Madame Adélaïde?"

"She says – but I'm not sure why – she was one of Louis XV's daughters."

"Louis XV? King of France?" Oriol frowns. "Are you sure?"

"I think it's pushing things a bit too, though I recognize that, if she's right, the whole story's very interesting. The fate of the last two daughters of Louis XV was very tragic. They were fleeing across Europe, farther and farther away from France after the revolutionaries chopped off the heads of all the other members of the family, including their nephew, King Louis XVI. Sara's documented all that very well."

"Knowing Sara, I'm sure she has."

"She wrote something about it years ago, but she's making very slow progress. She gets very worked up when she's being a historian. If she discovers that the documents aren't yet catalogued, or she can't find information about something – as if it never happened – she gets very frustrated. I tell her that most of us are invisible to history, but she finds that hard to accept."

"Of course, that was before the Internet came along. I mean, not leaving a trace of our journey through history. Now our descendants inherit a whole pile of shit they'll never get through. Blogs, websites, emails, idiotic comments on Facebook, tweets that are supposed to be witty but are downright pathetic... the generations to come will take us for imbeciles, and they'll be totally right."

When Oriol returns the chocolate pot to the table he puts it near the corner, close to his elbow and, from the distance, Sara thinks, *No, not there, put it somewhere else*, the way she used to when her children were small and left a glass near the edge of a table, and she knew it would be knocked off in no time at all and smashed to smithereens. Sometimes she can even calculate when the accident is going to happen. She's always been able to foresee accidents, with the same sixth sense that sends dogs into hiding at the approach of a storm, or makes swallows set off on their flight to Africa every September.

"I'd like to read what she's written."

"To be honest, I doubt we'll have that privilege."

Sara has always told Max that she had undertaken this work of historical documentation because she needed to earn his respect. Without Max's respect she wouldn't have written a word or made any progress at all. The truth, however, is considerably more complex. When she started, more than two decades ago, she did so hoping to get a clearer idea of the stories tucked away inside her chocolate pot. She said it was like listening to whispering voices. When she started looking for solid data to support her theories she found much less material than she expected. Then again, there is the fact of never having enough time, which is the worst stumbling block. Or sometimes lack of faith in the project is, perhaps, even worse than that. After all her efforts, she now thinks that her notes could be the basis of a fairly interesting novel, if at some point she wanted to write it, or tried, or knew how to.

This lack of confidence that Max has just expressed loud and clear has, of course, taken her by surprise and immediately put a damper on her project. It makes her think that he knows how insecure she is but has never dared to be totally honest with her about it. Right now, she feels as if he's sorry for her because she's so tough on herself, on everyone around her, and even on history. It's not a nice feeling and she'd prefer not to have it.

"We won't open the absinthe till Sara arrives," says Max.

"Of course we won't. It has no meaning without her."

"I hope I can hold it better now than last time."

"If not, we'll put you to bed like we did then. I've always thought that was the beginning of your relationship."

"No, Sara and I took a good year and a half to—"

"I know, but one way or another, everything followed from that."

"Maybe."

No. That long-ago night didn't lead to anything related with Max. That night, twenty-three years ago, Max was a virgin and it was painfully obvious. Sara wasn't remotely interested in virginal boys. She can't believe that Oriol has said what she's just heard. How's that for a white lie?

The dining-room curtain flies up in the breeze, giving the conversation an unnecessarily theatrical setting. Max stands up to tie it back and makes the most of the trip to bring another bottle of sparkling water. He pours the drinks, offers more food. He's the perfect host, doing everything at the right time and not letting a single detail escape his eye.

"Why has it taken so long for us to get together?" Max looks at his friend in the way that only someone over forty can do. "I thought you'd forgotten all about us."

"I've been very busy." Oriol lowers his eyes when he says this. Sara can't see very well, but she interprets it as a sign of embarrassment. So he's still capable of that, it seems. Like Sara. More or less. "How long has it been exactly?"

"I haven't counted. Not since the night of the prize, unless I'm mistaken."

"Ah yes, the prize. Now that was a strange night."

"Very."

"You were babysitting."

"I had no choice. Sara was doing public relations."

"We hardly talked. Not even ten minutes. I don't remember what it was about."

"You had your head elsewhere. You were the star that night."

"I would have preferred to have more time for you two."

"I understood that you couldn't." A silence augurs what has to come next. This trying to make sure that nobody takes his words the wrong way is typical of Max. "What hurt was the fact that you disappeared afterwards. Not as much as a phone call or message in all this time. Sara was really upset by that."

Sara bites her bottom lip. Now the universe is starting its drum roll for the high point of the night. Oriol Pairot is about to offer his friend an explanation for something that can't be explained and which Max had just summed up as follows: after the night at the Hotel Arts when they gave him the prize, Oriol decided to disappear from their lives. He slipped away like one of those nineteenth-century escape artists who vanish from a tank full of water.

"I'm really sorry. It was a difficult decision."

The word wounds everyone. *Decision*. It wasn't carelessness but something he'd done deliberately. Oriol adds, "I had to escape, man."

"From what?"

"From you two."

Oriol puts down his glass, picks it up again, crosses his legs and rolls the bottom of his glass around his knee. He mumbles. "The jealousy was killing me, Max. That's the truth. It was totally unbearable."

Jealousy. That's a good one. It took him a while, but he's finally settled for the cliché.

"Jealous? Of me?"

A disconcerted Max raises his eyebrows. He doesn't have to wait long for the explanation.

"You had everything you always wanted. Your university chair, the business, the flat, the children, you were about to publish a book…"

"Sara…"

"I won't deny it."

Is that all? *I won't deny it*. Is this the only balsam she'll have to soothe the burning that has lasted all these years? To be precise, it started the night Oriol got the prize, that night at the Hotel Arts when he got up from the super-king-size bed in the Junior Suite with views of the sea and asked her if she wanted to have a shower with him. She said no, because, right then, what she needed most was to stop thinking about what she was doing and go home. And meditate. More than anything else, she had to meditate about what her life was like and what she wanted it to be like.

When Oriol asked, "Are you going to tell Max you've been with me?" she answered, "I have to think about it." And he said "OK" in the same way as he might have said "So let's leave it there" or "Bye-bye, that was nice" or whatever other senseless remark he might have thought up. Sara could still taste his kisses as she got dressed, glanced in the mirror to see what an adulterous woman looked like and left the room, trying not to slam the door.

The next few days she waited for a phone call, a text message or one of the absurd postcards he occasionally sent from surprising cities, but the phone only rang for the usual reasons, and Oriol, as usual, had vanished into the paving stones of the streets of life. Not long afterwards, as they sat in their chairs in that damn interlude of after-dinner togetherness, she saw him on television. She started to cry so wildly that Max dropped his book and rushed to console her, for the first time ever, without even knowing what it was about. Or maybe he did know.

But the worst was yet to come: resignation. Resigning herself to the fact that there was no future in it, that Oriol hadn't been born to share his life with any woman, and Sara in particular. Understanding that she wanted Max and, despite everything, that she loved him with a serenity she liked to feel, and didn't want to be apart from him. Burying the stupid fantasies of a different life she'd dreamt up after that night in the Hotel Arts, after what Oriol had said in the super-king-size bed, and seeing the good side of her everyday routine once again. *Tortell de reis, crema de Sant Josep, bunyols de Quaresma,* Easter cakes, *coques de Sant Joan, panellets, torrons de Xixona,** cream-filled *torrons* and the house specialty, the praline-filled dark-chocolate *torró.* Life rolled on, year after year; Max's unconditional love, without passion, or encumbrances or accounts to settle; the thousand obligations that came with being a mother, a role which she loved and hated at the same time; the comfortable routine of the Casa Rovira kitchen; the steady success of the business.

Deep inside, Sara knows she would have done a good job at Oriol Pairot's side. She would have been a perfect partner, steady admirer and selfless helper. And the aura of the adulterous woman who's left her family to run away with her husband's best friend would have given her a gloss of depravity she'd always lacked. She would have needed two lives to be everything she might have been.

"You've got guts, telling me this…" Max says.

"Nine years later? I'm not so sure."

"Can I ask why now?"

"Things are different now. I have some news for you."

"Something important?"

"Metaphysical."

"Shoot."

"I'm married. We're having a baby."

Max can't contain his joy. He waves his arms in the air and shouts, "Bloody hell, Oriol! You're settling down at last!"

Then it happens. Exactly what Sara feared. The sweep of Max's arm in this moment of sincere euphoria couldn't have been clumsier. A moment ago it might have been avoided, but now the die is cast. His elbow hits the chocolate pot perching too close to the abyss, a hand – Oriol's – shoots out, but isn't quick enough to avert the catastrophe, and echoes of shattering porcelain clink painfully through the street.

Madame Adélaïde's chocolate pot is a mess of very fine, translucent shards scattered over the terrace's red tiles. The remains of a long and eventful life.

The Multiple Talents
of Oriol Pairot

"What if we mix Sara's praline with your crunchy apple and cinnamon? That would be good, wouldn't it? That way neither of you has to give up your idea and we can finish the job on time. We're really behind schedule."

"Shit, Max, in the real world you always have to give up something! Every choice you make means fifty sacrifices. That's what life's all about: choices and renunciation. I'm asking you to say which of the two you think is better. Please."

"But the thing is, I'll always feel that the other one was—"

"Look, Max," Oriol interrupts, very sure of what he's saying, "until you learn not to keep fretting about what you've left by the wayside, you'll never discover what life's about."

The twenty-year-old Oriol Pairot was already an expert in renunciation. Some sacrifices had been imposed on him, for example the death of his mother at the age of fifty-five from a sudden fatal stroke, which in cutting short her life also drew a clear dividing line in his. In time, Oriol would come to realize that his mother's death had also been the death of his youth, that he'd never get it back and that everything that came later would have to be, for better or worse, part of the complex, free and often preposterous world of adults. Only a week after his mother was buried another woman was sleeping in the double bed beside his father, who was now a total stranger. He could hear their frenzied sex at night. It revolted him. During the day they made no effort to conceal things either: they walked around the street, ran errands and had lunch together, hand in hand or stealing kisses like two enamoured teenagers who have to go sneaking into doorways because they can't wait a moment longer. A few days after her first appearance she bought herself a ridiculous frilly apron and settled in behind the cash register in the patisserie, the same place his mother had occupied for more than twenty years. Unsurprisingly, the customers couldn't believe their eyes. Some tried, not very successfully, to hide their dismay. One indignant woman did an about-turn and walked out muttering something about the unseemly haste of widowers. Oriol's father was silent, saying nothing, making no comment, barely uttering a word, as had been his way since the day he was born. Neither did he speak to his son, who more than once wondered whether they should have a man-to-man chat but ended up doing nothing about it. There was no point and, anyway, he wasn't used to talking to his father.

Oriol drew his own conclusion. The woman who'd replaced his mother in just seven days had probably been waiting in the wings for a long time for the chance to occupy the place she'd so easily waltzed into. Putting up with his father, though, was no easy task, and to tell the truth Oriol was grateful to her for relieving him of all responsibility. He decided, then, to look on the bright side and went off to Barcelona without offering any explanation to anyone.

The first night he slept on a bench in Sants railway station, but the second day he got himself a job in the station's main cafeteria, where he'd gone to ask if they needed a waiter. The boss said they did and asked if he was interested. These were the years of pre-Olympic euphoria in Barcelona and it was easy to find work, especially for young people who were willing to do whatever needed doing, years when everyone was convinced that nothing would ever go wrong again, as if the Olympic spirit, the omnipresent construction projects, the closed-off streets, the Cultural Olympiad, Mayor Maragall inaugurating things every fifteen minutes and traffic jams entering and leaving the city were things that had to last for ever.

Oriol's most pressing problem on arriving in the city was finding somewhere to live. Getting a roof over your head when your pockets were empty wasn't easy. He'd spent his meagre savings on trousers, a shirt, new shoes and two nights in a pension in Carrer de Numància, but the month had just begun and he only had enough cash to get to the end of the week. He asked the boss for an advance on his pay, but the man glared at him – "An advance, you say! You don't mess around, do you!" – and answered with a resounding no. Then he had the good luck to spot a note stuck to a doorway. *Room to let. Clean, responsible young man. Economical. 3rd floor, Flat 2. Ask for Senyora Fàtima.* Oriol thought he met at least two of the three requirements and had nothing to lose by trying. He entered the grotty doorway of the rundown building, climbed the ill-lit stairs to the third floor and rang the bell of Flat 2. Just when he was getting tired of waiting, he heard the sound of iron screeching on iron, and the door opened, revealing a woman wearing only an oriental-style dressing gown. She was well on the wrong side of fifty and looked much older than that.

"Did you see the sign?" she asked as soon as she saw him.

"Yes, but I can't pay till the end of the month."

"Come in. I can't see your face."

Oriol stepped into a flat, which was as dilapidated and shabby as the street entrance. The once decorative tiles of the flooring had lost all their splendour. The passageway seemed interminable. He could see a light at the end and worked out that it had to come from the dining room.

"How old are you?"

"Twenty."

"Got a job?"

"Kitchen hand at the bar in Sants railway station."

"If I go there will I see you?"

"Of course."

"Will you invite me to breakfast?"

"No."

"What did you say your name was?"

"I didn't say. Oriol."

"All right, Oriol. You look like a good person. Your room is the first on the right, the one closest to the front door. You'll have a bit of privacy there. You have a bathroom for yourself. It has a shower. I don't want you using the other one, which is mine. You can use the kitchen as long as we can agree on a schedule. You can't have pets, or make a noise late at night, or bring girls here. I want ten thousand pesetas a month, in advance. But I'll make an exception for you. But if you don't pay me before the first of the month you'll have to go."

"All right."

"My name's Fàtima." She held out a hand with bitten nails.

As soon as he was paid, Oriol divided his wages into three parts: one for his rent, one for living expenses and the third for his savings account. He wanted to save up for something worthwhile, but wasn't sure what. When he went to pay his rent,

Fàtima said, "You can pay me eight thousand if you spend the difference by taking me out to dinner."

That seemed fair enough. After twenty-six days of living with Fàtima he had no doubt that, one way or another, he could make the most of the way she was looking at him. The second month she said he only had to pay four thousand. The third month she wouldn't accept his money. "You need it more than I do," she said, pressing it into Oriol's hand and closing his fingers around it. Fàtima was thrilled with her personable young tenant. His kitchen rights had expanded slightly and sometimes he slept in his landlady's bed. The ban on using her bathroom was also lifted. In those months, Oriol saved a lot more than he expected.

The bank also had a surprise for him when he went to make the first deposit. Two hundred thousand pesetas had suddenly appeared in his bank book. When he asked the teller about it, the man informed him, "Senyor Oriol Pairot Bardagí made the deposit," adding that he had done so three weeks earlier. Oriol called his father from the first public phone box he could find.

"I don't need you to send me money," he lied.

"Hello, son. Are you all right?"

"Why did you make that deposit of two hundred thousand pesetas? I never asked you for anything."

"Hang on, boy. Don't get worked up. That money's from your mother. The will's been read and it's legally yours, your inheritance, so go and spend it on something that will be useful to you, which is what she would have wanted."

After giving it a lot of thought and wavering till the last minute, Oriol decided to spend a good part of the money on the Techniques for Chocolatiers course at the Pastry Chefs' Guild, and buying the utensils he needed. He was never in any doubt that he liked the trade, but didn't want to do what his father did. He wasn't going to waste time making products that only last twenty-four hours. No croissants, or brioches, or *ensaïmades*, or sponge fingers for him. He wasn't interested in celebrations either and couldn't see himself making *coques de Sant Joan* or Easter cakes. All that stuff about "the long tradition of this patisserie" didn't interest him in the least. He had plenty of innovative ideas, but realized they were worth nothing if he didn't learn something about the trade. He renounced other ideas for spending his little fortune – a motorbike, for example, which would have been very good for getting round all the road works in the city; a trip around some of Europe's most famous patisseries, having a look (and stealing ideas) – but in the end he settled for the course. He knew the rule: *we pay for every choice we make in life with fifty sacrifices, and I'll have time to do other things. Until you learn to stop fretting about what you've left by the wayside, you can't say that you really know how to live.*

Hence, sacrifice stole into the conversation and took root when a stricken Max looked at Sara and gave his verdict: "I choose sour apple." The expression on his face was tragic enough to break anyone's heart. He blinked in Sara's direction and then added, "I'm really sorry."

Oriol clenched his fists, raised his eyebrows and opened his mouth to utter a mute cry of victory.

"I had a formidable rival," he said. The words sounded like a consolation prize.

"What you had is a biased judge, so the rival doesn't count." Sara was on the attack. She'd never been good at accepting defeat.

Max was still feeling terrible after being forced to choose. He took Sara's hand, trying to console himself.

"I'm really sorry, Sara. Your praline is fantastic."

"Forget it," she snapped, removing her hand from his.

Losing is a difficult art. At the age of forty-four she still hasn't learnt it. Right now she'd cry her eyes out if she knew how to, but crying with rage or impotence is not one of her skills. She only cries about stupid things: when Aina puts on a new dress and Sara can't believe she's so grown up, or if the dinner burns when she's in the shower. Yet, when her life falls apart and she knows that it's for ever, when one of the two men she loves has chosen but hasn't chosen her, she can't shed a single tear. She can only grit her teeth and stay silently contemplating his existence from the safe distance of Raquel's terrace.

Max and Oriol have just picked up the fragments of Madame Adélaïde's chocolate pot and set them aside on the table, heaped on a linen napkin.

"Sara's going to be upset," Max says.

Oriol presses his lips together and nods meditatively.

"We'll get her another one. I'm sure it's not difficult to find these things on the Internet."

"Not like this one," Max murmurs as he refills their glasses.

It's almost time for her classical dessert to make its appearance. Sara longs for this moment with every fibre of her being.

"So, who's the lucky lady then? How did you meet? You must have been together for a while, eh? Why didn't you bring her with you so we could meet her?"

"I didn't bring her because she's in Tokyo and eight months pregnant."

"You've married a Japanese girl?" Max is full of admiration. Oriol nods. "Bloody hell!"

"I met her through that guy you told me about… Do you remember? Sato Whatever, or Whatever Sato, the one from the university in Hiroshima…"

"The Laboratory of Food Biophysics at the Faculty of Applied Biological Science at Hiroshima University," Max specifies. He'd worked with the lab for more than five years.

"That's the one! In fact, there was a whole string of coincidences. I was looking for someone to design my shops in China and Japan. I wanted something that looked very Japanese but European too. I interviewed several candidates and looked at their projects. I thought hers was excellent. It was exactly what I was looking for. Her ideas are scarily clear, she's very intelligent and she immediately understood what I wanted. We've been working together to conquer Japan and, make no mistake about it, a lot of the success of this venture is due to her and the line she designed. I wanted to open a shop in Tokyo, but with Hina my plans have become somewhat more ambitious. You can't begin to imagine what the market's like! They're addicts, they're mad about chocolate, they've got good taste and they're happy to spend plenty of yens. Maybe they've realized that chocolate consumption is one of the indicators of a country's standard of living. In fact, they're opening up impressive shops and whole supermarkets just for chocolate and pastries. I'm about to open my fifth *confiserie* in Osaka. I say it in French because that's what they prefer. I guess they think it's more sophisticated. I'm gobbling up the market."

"Did you say Hina?"

"Yes, Hina, with an H. I'm telling you, it's impossible not to fall in love with her. What I can't believe is that she loves me. She's so young and beautiful she could have aspired to an emperor's son at least."

"How young?"

Oriol looks slightly embarrassed, as if he's apologizing for something. But he's having fun at Max's expense. He knows that his forty-one-year-old friend will automatically envy him.

"Twenty-five."

"Twenty-what? You've got a nerve, pal!"

"Well, she's twenty-six now. She's getting old on me. Look, let me show you a photo."

Oriol fiddles with his phone, Max puts on his glasses – which he's been wearing round his neck on a fine gold chain for the past three or four years – and there's an awed silence as the two men gaze at the vertical photo, showing in the middle distance a very pale-skinned girl with jet-black hair and almond-shaped eyes. She's wearing pink shorts.

"Wow, she's gorgeous, Oriol. You're a lucky guy."

"She even more gorgeous *au naturel*. This is our wedding day." He shows Max another photo.

"Shit, is that you? You're very dashing in that kimono."

"That's the traditional clothing for businessmen, which, by protocol, was what I had to wear (you've got no idea how complicated everything is in Japan). She's wearing the mandatory kimono for honouring her family. They're descendants of samurais."

"Samurais! Shit a brick!"

"Yeah, man, that's right. Look, here she's taken off the *shiromuku*, which is totally white and only used for the ceremony. You see? Now she's wearing a *hanayome*, which is a festive kimono for newly married women. As I say, it's complicated."

"And this couple here?"

"My father and his present wife."

"Ah, and these are your in-laws, of course."

"Yes, look, you can see them better here."

"Fuck! Is he the samurai?

Oriol laughs. "No that was the great-grandfather, I think. This one only manages a string of service stations."

"Well, I'd be bloody scared if this gentleman filled up my petrol tank."

"No problems, man. He's been eating out of my hand ever since he discovered he's going to be a granddad."

"Girl or boy?"

"We don't know. Hina prefers the surprise."

"The baby will be born in Japan, of course."

"Of course. It's a great country to be born in. It's a great country for everything, in fact. You two will have to come and visit me there as soon as you can."

"Bloody hell, Oriol! It's not like coming to see you in Paris."

"Come on, talk to Sara about it. It'd be great if you could meet Hina. I'm sure you'll like her."

"We have to celebrate this." Max stands up, goes inside, leaving Oriol with a slightly idiotic smile on his lips which is just starting to fade when his host reappears with a bottle of Moët et Chandon in his hands. "I was keeping this for a special occasion, and I think this one's more than special. I want to drink a toast to your marriage and your future son or daughter."

The cork pops and flies into the air, bubbly liquid overflows from Bohemian crystal champagne glasses which ring with a pure note, almost like a violin, when they meet.

"I'm going to send a message to Sara to see if she'll be back soon," Max says, getting up from his chair after gulping down his champagne and refilling the glass. After the alcohol he's been mixing he seems a little tipsy, but he can't keep still. "And, yeah, the dessert, man. I mustn't forget that! If only you knew how much love Sara put into those truffles, and all because of you. Hang on a moment, I'll be right back."

Left alone, Oriol heaves a sigh of weariness, or resignation, or all the pressure of *noblesse oblige*.

Sara's phone vibrates with the message she's just received.

Max reappears on the terrace with a tray of truffles and another of *catànies*. He offers them to Oriol, who takes a *catània*, puts it in his mouth and savours it slowly.

"Sara's chocolate has always been unbeatable," he pronounces, almost snarling.

At last. Sara, on her side of the barricade, thinks at last the great Oriol Pairot, one of the two men she's loved the most – and she'll never been able to stop loving him, although she'll have to love him differently from now on – at last Oriol Pairot has recognized that she's the best. If he'd done that fifteen years ago, she might have cried with emotion.

"And what about you? With all this talk about Hina, I haven't asked you about anything. How are your parents?"

"The same as always. They're living the life of a typical retired American couple. They get off one cruise ship in order to board another. I think they spend more time floating round the Caribbean than they do at home."

Max is the oldest of their offspring. His parents, who are almost seventy, are unaccountably youthful and Sara sometimes thinks they have more energy than she does.

"Do you still all go to visit them in New York every year?"

"Yes. They're coming here to celebrate Thanksgiving with us and we'll go to see them in spring, though actually we prefer New York in autumn."

"In November it's the best city in the world."

"I couldn't agree more."

"What about your mother-in-law? What's she doing?"

"She's been in a retirement home for the last year." Oriol raises his eyebrows in surprise, as if he can't quite take it in. "Strange, isn't it? But she decided this all by herself. One day she announced that she had nothing to do here and that she wanted to go and live in a very expensive retirement home where her best friend is. This friend is also her bridge partner."

"Bridge?"

"The bad influence of my mother, who wouldn't let up till she'd taught Sara's mother to play."

"I can't imagine Sara's mother playing bridge."

"She's really good. She's got a poker face and she never loses her cool. Not like my parents. If they ever get divorced, it will be because of bridge."

"What about Sara's parents' flat?"

"It's exactly the same as it always was, right down to the last detail. Even Sara's old bedroom, with the bed still made and clothes in the wardrobe. It's a bit spooky, actually. It's like going into a museum."

"And haven't you thought about what you could do with it?"

"Not for the moment, at least not while my mother-in-law's still alive. Then, we'll see. I'd like to persuade Sara to expand the business. We could connect the shop with the flat and have a restaurant upstairs."

"Great idea, Max! That's perfect. Have you thought about what kind of restaurant?"

"Not really. Sometimes I think about it a bit, but it's not the right time yet."

"Of course. Well, I can see that you're busy too, at least above your eyebrows."

"I have no choice in the matter. I've got to do something to ward off depression, especially now that the university's such a shambles. Now we have to be marketable and profitable. Our success is measured by the number of students who enrol in our courses. If you want to be a tough guy and pressure them a bit so they work better and more rigorously, they badmouth you and you pay the price. Now we're submitted to the laws of the market. And you know what marketing is, don't you? It's not about selling what you've got but producing what you can sell." Max pauses and sighs. "It's hopeless, man. We've copied the academic model of the United States, but only the bad things. I've decided not to let it get under my skin. I'm counting the years till I retire and hope they'll go fast. I don't complain. Since I haven't joined the resistance I'm on the enemy's side."

"But… what about the job as head of department they offered you?"

"No, no, hell no!" Max flaps his hands as if shooing away a swarm of mosquitoes. "I turned it down. I don't want problems. The university is a fiasco, as I said. If I was a physicist there might be some hope, but the problem's intellectual. We're done for. Right now, it's better to think about opening a restaurant."

Sara didn't know that Max was thinking about expanding the business. She likes the idea, though she would have preferred to find out about it in other circumstances. Her man, with his cautious ways, was always trying to get the timing right for whatever had to be done or said. Maybe this is one of the underlying problems of their scant sex life. Timing. Max won't throw himself into anything unless the circumstances, absolutely all the circumstances (including atmospheric, biological, timetable, health and emotional factors) are in his favour. Naturally, at his age and with his lifestyle, that rarely happens.

Oriol is as glib, self-centred and aloof as ever. They'd both benefit if each borrowed a bit from the other, Sara thinks. Now she's worried because Oriol's just made a huge, colossal blunder, but without consequences so far. Luckily, Max is absent-minded and isn't good at paying attention to small details. He hasn't stopped to wonder how Oriol knows about the job as head of department. He obviously hasn't done the sums. The sums would more or less involve certain question-and-answer steps. When did they offer him the job? January 2004. How long did it take him to say no, after brooding and more brooding about it? More than six months, and his definitive rejection was in September 2004. When was the prize-giving ceremony in the Hotel Arts, the last time Max and Oriol saw each other? On 8th April 2004, when there was still a chance Max would say yes, or at least Sara thought there was. But it was a secret then and Max didn't want to talk about it. Not even with Oriol. At least in the brief ten minutes of their conversation he didn't bring up the subject. And Oriol wasn't listening anyway. He'd just won the most prestigious prize a chocolatier could aspire to and was exultant and extremely busy.

So?

So, the bits don't fit but Max hasn't realized.

"Hey! Sara's answered me!" Max is happy. He puts on his glasses and reads out her message. "'With you in half an hour. Leave me something to drink.' She asks if everything's all right. I'll say yes. It'd be better to tell her about the chocolate pot when she gets here."

"We'll tell her it's my fault," Oriol offers.

"No, no, no. That wouldn't be right. Hang on." Max frowns as he taps out his message.

OK. Hurry up. xxx.

"Done! Pour me a bit more of that Moët et Chandon, mate."

"Sara's going to find us well and truly sloshed."

"All the better. Pour. Right up to the top."

The glasses are filled and emptied. The two men fall silent for a moment, lost in their own thoughts.

Just then, the lights in the towers of Santa Maria del Mar go out.

Oriol's phone lights up with a message. Sara now realizes that the number's the same, but his phone's in silent mode. That means, although he hasn't answered them, he's received all her messages. She wishes she knew what all this is about, but can't come up with an explanation. Oriol looks at the screen.

Blabbermouth

Oriol glances at the dining room and, more discreetly, at his general surroundings, looking for Sara. He then nonchalantly puts the phone down. Sara's hurt by this. It's clear that he's not planning to answer this time either.

Max has stretched out his legs with one foot balancing on the other, hands resting on his belly. He's talking with his gaze lost in some unidentifiable patch of the night sky. He looks very serene. Also very drunk.

"Do you remember that time in Paris? Man, did we do some drinking then! Now we can hardly hold a drop. We're getting old."

"That Paris thing was fantastic. You're dead right." Oriol laughs as he lets the memories flood over him. "You were crazy about the Louvre. Wild horses couldn't have dragged you away from there."

"You can't imagine how bowled over Sara and I were when we saw you at Fauchon, in that chic black uniform and bossing all those people round in your perfect French." Oriol raises his hand in protest, modestly suggesting there was nothing perfect about it. "I reckon it was then that we understood what kind of beast you are. What a genius! But you were only a kid… And we weren't even married then!"

"Of course you weren't married. That's when you told me there that you were going to get married. Don't you remember? 'Oriol, we have to tell you something. Sara and I would like you to be best man at our wedding.'"

"Bloody hell, that's right! I'd forgotten."

"I took the flowers to the bride and I read her a poem."

"Horrendous! We wanted to frame it, but it was too bad."

"That was the summer of '92. Remember we watched the opening ceremony of the games in my flat on Allée de la Surprise?"

"Yeah, yeah, of course! Holy shit, holy, holy shit! All three of us sunk into that sagging couch, watching your mini-TV, sweating like pigs…"

"And eating chocolates."

"Yeah, that's right! Those terrible chocolates made with the weird things you were testing. You couldn't even chew some of them. Then Sara said to me, 'Max, don't you have something to tell your friend?' I told you and you were totally dumbstruck."

"I wasn't expecting that."

"Then you started getting out more and more bottles, as if you'd gone crazy, and the three of us ended up pissing ourselves laughing and drinking toasts to everything, especially us."

"That night was the beginning of the 'Three Friends' box, even though it took me a while to be able to do it…" Recalling this, Oriol can't help thinking that it was a very profitable night, despite their drunkenness and the bad news.

"Then you were very happy to take on my wedding cake, man! My parents still remember that it was very strange and tasted like cologne."

"Your parents are American! The best-selling chocolate in the United States is Hershey's, Max. Enough said."

"My aunt Margaret got stomach cramps and, when I was escorting her to the toilet, she kept asking, 'Isn't it much too spicy, honey?'"

The two men roar with laughter, just like that night on the sagging couch in one of Paris's outlying neighbourhoods. The echoes of their laughter bounce from the corners of Carrer de l'Argenteria, from one house to another, gathering speed, rushing up to the top of Santa Maria del Mar's towers, swirling in and out as the bells strike midnight, disappearing into Carrer de l'Espaseria and eventually reaching Pla de Palau in their quest to join the murmuring of the sea and the warmth of the night.

Oriol gets another message, but he keeps laughing.

709

He understands – he definitely understands! But it no longer means anything to him.

The night Oriol Pairot was awarded the most prestigious prize of his career, Sara and Max were the first to arrive. *To get front-row seats*. But Max didn't know that Oriol had reserved four seats with the organizers in the Gran Saló Gaudí, where the ceremony was to take place. Four seats. But they'd only need three: they'd brought the pushchair for Pol, since they expected that, at best, he'd get tired and grizzly and they'd need somewhere to put him. Aina was very good. She stayed put in her seat, quiet and serious, through the whole ceremony, and only once did she succumb to a rather indiscreet yawn, which brought a smile to the lips of the Catalan Minister for Culture, who was sitting just in front of her. Then, when the canapés were passed round, she ate so much and so quickly she made herself sick.

Sara did much more networking that night than she would do for the rest of her life. She met up with Ortega again, after all those years. He was older, still lovable, as generous as ever and very proud to say that he'd been the teacher of the star of the night. He might have been a wee bit inebriated as well, but she wasn't sure. He was alone and wearing an old-fashioned, slightly shabby navy-blue suit.

"I hate these shows. If it hadn't been for Oriol, I wouldn't have come," he told her.

She also saw some of her colleagues and got into a heated discussion about the new European regulations allowing chocolate makers to use up to five per cent of vegetable fats, apart from cocoa butter. Some saw this as an opportunity and others as a disaster of cosmic proportions. Sara tended more towards the second opinion, but was in no mood to get embroiled in Byzantine arguments. She ended up – how she didn't know – in a huddle with some other people including the editor of *Cuines* magazine. As soon as he saw her he asked if she'd like to write for them: pieces on the history of chocolate and pastry-making. "A little bird told me you have a degree in History," he added. Flattered by this, Sara took the man's card and put it in her handbag, promising to give his proposal some very serious thought.

Meanwhile, Max was looking after the children. The three of them made a strange little island in the middle of the restless sea of people. In the distance he could see Oriol's head standing out above the crowds of people who were hanging round waiting to speak to him. He could see him smiling, shaking hands, having his photo taken with ladies who glowed as brightly as the light fixtures, chatting with personalities he'd just been introduced to, receiving the embrace of the President of the Pastry Chefs' Guild, being congratulated by the Mayor and hanging out with famous chefs who were talking to him as if they'd known him all their lives. Slowly, at a rate of about a millimetre per minute, Oriol was advancing towards the spot where Max, attentive father of two children who were too small to know what they were doing there, was waiting.

Oriol was making progress, but would never get there. Aina had a major emergency.

"Papa, I have to do poo." No beating around the bush there.

Max asked the invariably futile question that parents come out with at such times.

"Can't you hold on?"

But Aina was in no doubt. "No. I need to do poo, *now*."

Max set out on a very complicated expedition through the hotel's plushly carpeted corridors, complete with pushchair, Pol's nappy bag and a little girl who was about to burst. It was a miracle they made it in time, but when Aina was perched on the toilet in the Ladies' with the door open and offering a detailed account of the state of her evacuation – "It's coming out, Papa. It's coming out!" – Pol started to cry, because with all the excitement he'd woken up and couldn't get back to sleep. He was thirsty too, and his water bottle was empty. Max lifted him out of the pushchair and took him into the Gents' to fill it up. After he'd had a drink, Pol made himself comfortable in Max's arms and snuggled his head into his right shoulder, closed his eyes and let himself be rocked for ten minutes until he was out like a light.

Aina was very thrilled and continued with her chronicle. "Papa, I've done lots and lots of poo. It's green!"

Max issued instructions from outside, getting some very peeved looks from several ladies who, dressed up to the nines as one would expect from clients of a luxury hotel, had come to use the toilets. Perhaps they were the type of person who'd never had any contact with the bowel movements of others.

"Wipe yourself clean. Drop the paper in the toilet and flush it, darling."

"Yes, Papa."

"And wash your hands."

"Yes, Papa."

The green poo was a little disturbing, especially because, now that Aina had (literally) emptied herself out, she wanted to go back to the Saló Gaudí to start stuffing herself all over again with canapés, petits fours and orange juice until it was time to go home. Max was at the end of his tether.

Once he'd returned to the party, with Pol asleep at last and Aina wolfing down everything she could get her hands on, Max finally managed to have a ten-minute chat with Oriol. He congratulated him with a tight hug, telling him that he and Sara were very proud of all his achievements. He then introduced his children, although they weren't at their best (Aina now heavy-eyed, and Pol as red as a lobster, sweating profusely and fast asleep). Oriol asked him about his work and Max gave him the short version of his last fifteen years in the Department of Food Biochemistry at the Faculty of Chemical Sciences at the University of Barcelona.

"Nothing new."

Then Oriol said it was a shame they had so little time together. There was so much to talk about. He asked if Max and Sara had any time the following night because he had a couple of hours free and maybe...

"Tomorrow? Impossible. We're going to the Liceu tomorrow and, as you know, that's sacred," Max said and, fearing he'd been too brusque, asked, "Why don't you come along?"

"No, no, let's leave it!" Oriol made a great show of his distress at the very idea. "I don't understand opera."

"There's nothing to understand, Oriol. Music is a universal language."

"No, I'm telling you, no."

"They're doing Donizetti tomorrow. Easy-peasy. Even for an ignoramus like you."

"Next time then, OK?" Oriol ended the conversation. He couldn't stand feeling left out. Then he walked away because a young lady in a smart jacket murmured in his ear that the media were waiting for him. In total good faith he said to Max, "Wait here, I'll be back in a moment." But Max didn't wait. He knew how these things worked even though he was one of the world's docile creatures, the ones that always wait while other people finish all the important things they have to do. Then Aina announced that she had a very bad tummy ache and Max decided that enough was enough. He went to find Sara, who, looking very beautiful and with a glass of cava in her hand, was chatting animatedly with some of Barcelona's most famous pastry chefs. Max told her not to worry about anything, but he was going home.

"I'll come with you," she offered.

"No, sweetheart, you stay here. This nightmare is a professional commitment for you. I'm going because the kids are getting out of hand and they're the perfect excuse."

"Are you sure?"

"Of course I'm sure. No need to go on about it. If you finish very late, get a taxi, OK? They'll find you one at the entrance."

"OK…" Once again Sara thought how lucky she was with this man. With anyone else, things would have been very different.

"Have fun," Max said, pushing Pol's buggy with one hand and holding Aina's hand with the other. Aina was waving at everyone like a princess.

Sara felt queasy as she watched them leave, but it was short-lived, because the president of the guild told her that her praline was the best in Barcelona and that he bought *torrons* at Casa Rovira every year to send them to the Catalan President as a personal gift. The politicians who'd graced the ceremony with their little speeches had disappeared a while ago, as had the official guests, and now there were only a few of Sara's colleagues plus a couple of old friends she hadn't seen for ages. Oriol was circulating among journalists and admirers, but it was hard to catch him. She was just starting to think about going home when she received an SMS. From Oriol.

709

Saying goodbye to everyone was a fairly slow process, although she only took leave of the people she could see, asking them to say goodbye to the others she'd lost sight of, especially the president of the guild who'd been so nice to her. She was very excited when she left the Gran Saló Gaudí, which is what always happened when she was about to have time alone with Oriol. She got lost in a very long corridor, trying to find a lift, retraced her steps and asked a waiter who, treating her like a little girl, showed her the way and even pressed the button for the seventh floor.

The whole operation, from the moment she received the message until the lift let her out on the seventh floor, lasted about twelve minutes, an eternity for Oriol, so she ran along the last section of the corridor from 730 to 709. The door of 709 opened before she could knock. Oriol was waiting for her on the other side, still dressed in his dinner jacket, with the usual sly smile on his lips. He closed the door and pushed her against it, kissing her urgently, painfully. He was much taller than Sara and, even when she was wearing high heels, had to stoop to kiss her, like an insect feasting on its victim. Sara slipped off her shoes, dropped her bag on the floor and let out a long sigh. As always happened when she had Oriol to herself, she had the sensation of having missed him terribly when he was away and hence an urgent need to do things that would make up for so much nostalgia. Without moving her lips from his, she stepped out of her dress. Now there was only the thong she'd bought with Oriol in mind a few days ago, and a strapless bra which left her still-tempting shoulders bare. Oriol threw himself on her with frenzy of a predator, a vampire. The shoulders, the neck, the chin and, once again, the lips of Sara. The lips, a thousand times yearned for, of Sara Rovira. She wrapped her hands round his neck, as if wanting to strangle him, her thumbs resting on that little bulge, the temptation that never changed, surrounded by whitish skin, rough and smooth at the same time, reminding her of the soft underbelly of a reptile. Now that she was barefoot, Oriol's Adam's apple was at eye level, the perfect target for her attack.

"Just a moment, I'm not totally free yet. Some French journalists are waiting to speak to me," he complained, still panting. "Why don't you pour yourself a glass of something and wait for me? I won't be long."

"All right, but if you take too long I'll go to sleep."

"If you're asleep I'll find a way to wake you."

Oriol took more than two hours and Sara had time for everything. She explored his room, a two-storey luxury suite with fabulous views of the Olympic port and the sea. What a shame it was night-time and she wouldn't be able to wake up looking out of those big windows. Then she spent a long time looking at herself in the mirror, admiring the still-young, agile body that showed no sign of her two pregnancies. She checked out the toiletries, had a shower and put on one of the dressing gowns bearing the hotel's logo. As Oriol had suggested, she poured herself a glass from the bottle in the champagne bucket at the foot of the bed, but then left it untouched and slid between the sheets, where she lay very still, monitoring her own breathing and the impatient beating of her heart, getting aroused every time muffled footsteps came along the corridor.

Then she suddenly remembered Max and called him to see how everything was going. As always, his voice soothed her. Everything's fine, he said. The kids were asleep and he was reading in the living room for a while before going to bed. There'd only been one problem. Aina had a stomach upset, had gone to the toilet Heaven knows how many times and had a spoonful of that wonder medicine, so now there was no need to worry about anything at all. "And you? Are you still there?" Max asked. "Yes," she replied, "and it's not going to end soon. The party's still going strong." Max didn't ask for further details – and if he had, Sara would have got flustered and not known what to say – but merely repeated his earlier wish of "Have fun", except that this time he added one word. "Have fun, *Mama*."

After speaking with Max, Sara felt drowsy. Oriol had been gone for an hour. Surely he wouldn't take much longer. The journalists must have him in their clutches. They're such a pain in the neck. Normally, Oriol wouldn't want to be hanging around with them, but tonight he was obliged to wait until everything was finished. That was the price he paid for being a famous man, and that she paid for being the famous man's secret lover. That was fine by her.

She covered herself with the feather duvet, which smelt deliciously clean, and then, all of a sudden, that other Room 709, the one in Paris, popped up in her head. Was it really 709? Why was she so sure of that? She hadn't remembered it until just then, but had to recognize that the coincidence would be amazing.

709. What's the total if you add 7 and 9? Sixteen. Sixteen, 1 + 6. In other words, 7. Seven's her lucky number, or at least that's what she's always believed since she was a little girl. It may seem silly, but Aina was born on the 7th, Sara was born in the seventh month, the years ending in 7 had always been the good ones in her life and, right now, she was on the seventh floor of the best hotel in town waiting for the man she desired more than any other in the whole world.

Sara was thinking about the things the sea washes up on beaches and no one knows where they come from or what they are. She thought that the number 709 was like one of those enigmatic jetsam treasures. In the other 709, the one in the Hôtel Madeleine in Paris – yes, of course, it was definitely 709 – they had been wildly happy. It was Barcelona's Olympic year, Oriol was head chocolatier in Fauchon, and Max and Sara were two fairly typical tourists in a city that had a lot to show them.

Max was mad about the museums in Paris. He wanted to go to the Louvre three days running and still hadn't tired of mummies, sculptures and painting. He had to spend a quarter of an hour contemplating every work because he wanted to know everything about it, had to read everything, had to see everything close up, then from a distance, and then close up again. The second day, Sara told him to go without her while she slept in at Oriol's flat. When she woke up at half-past eleven, there was a thermos flask of coffee and a little basket cradling some excessively buttery croissants on the table, together with a note from Oriol reading, "If anyone's free at lunchtime, phone me on…" and giving his work number. She lazed around until half-past twelve, snooping in his drawers for signs of the presence of some other woman in his flat, but finding nothing. It seemed that Oriol didn't fancy Frenchwomen. Then she got dressed and took the Metro to Place de la Madeleine. As soon as she surfaced she realized that there was a hotel right next to the sophisticated, very expensive establishment where her friend worked. As if it had all been prearranged, she went to Reception to enquire whether they had a room free, "with a double bed" please, and how much it would cost. The concierge was most charming. He smiled very graciously, said "*Oui, Madame,*" and asked for her passport. Once she was in the room, she phoned the number Oriol had jotted down and told him she was waiting, naked, in 709, and that he should ask for the rest of the day off. Oriol, dissembling, replied, "*Oui, Madame, naturellement.*"

It took him only half an hour to appear, bearing a little box with four delicacies of the house and an erection that augured a splendid afternoon. As soon as he saw her, he said, "You're crazy."

She agreed.

It was the best afternoon they ever spent together. It was only their second sexual encounter, but the waiting, the memory and desire did the rest. An eternity of two years had gone by since that first time in Sara's room.

Lying across the bed, her head hanging over the edge, hair brushing the carpet, ankles on Oriol's shoulders and blood beating in her temples, Sara envied the vigour of his thrusts, the powerful, active role nature has reserved for men in sexual matters. She would have liked to have a man's attributes for a while, just to know what penetration or the male orgasm felt like. *La petite mort*, the French call it. A little death that must be very different from her own, and that she'd never experience for herself. Mysterious impotence!

When they'd finished and were lying together, now respecting the layout of the bed, they ate the little cakes Oriol had brought – two lemon and two chocolate, exquisitely presented in their box – washed down with a miniature bottle of white wine, which was lukewarm because they'd forgotten to put it in the minibar. Then they got to work again. They thought they'd take it slower this time, but the plan was short-lived because, playfully sliding around, as if inadvertently, Oriol's index finger snuck between her buttocks and began to check out what was on offer.

"Will you let me in there one day?"

"One day?" she laughed. "Do we have to ask permission?"

"What if you don't like it?"

"If you do it, I'll like it."

"What if it hurts?"

"I'll yell."

"Aren't you scared?"

"Yes, but that's why I want you to do it."

"Now?"

"Up to you, Oriol Pairot."

Everything Sara said or did turned Oriol on. He didn't know anyone who came near her in bed. No one. The man of forty-three he would become in the not-too-distant future would have died of envy at his present capacity for rising again and again to the occasion, but Sara did her bit too. She was fantastic. She inflamed him. He was mad about her.

"Do you say these things to Max too?"

"Shut up, idiot. There are some things you don't ask."

The second part of the afternoon was even better. You only have one chance to do things for the first time in your life and they really made the most of it. After such an active session, multi-orgasmic, as one might imagine with two bodies as young as theirs were then, they both needed to freshen up. "Will you have a shower with me?" Oriol stuck his head around the bathroom door and issued his invitation with a beguiling smile. A compliant Sara joined him. "Will you soap my back?" Oriol asked. She soaped it. "And now the front?" She soaped that too. "Close your eyes." In the darkness she could feel his hands soaping her so slowly that it might go on for ever, and if only it would, because Oriol was getting lost in her body again, and starting to breathe heavily once more. Sara smiled, feeling very pleased with herself, and asked, "Haven't you had enough yet?" – to which he answered, "I can never have enough of you." She was exhausted, but they kept going. "If you want me to stop, I'll stop," he offered. "Don't stop. Don't ever stop," she said.

He wanted to keep going, and Sara had decided that she could never say no to Oriol. They got back under the shower, Sara clutching a very strategically placed towel rail and Oriol doing a balancing act, trying not to fall flat on his back. Before they were done, now with Sara's arms and legs wrapped round his palpitating body and Oriol's nose brushing against her ear, he departed from old scripts and whispered, "I've missed you so much." And she replied, "Why? I'm here for ever."

It was the only moment of weakness, and only the second of their thirteen assignations. Sara always kept count. She was a specialist at that. Thirteen trysts, not counting that of the night of the prize, which was yet to come, the one she was now waiting for, cradled in her memories. But, back to Paris: as she was attending to her hair, still holding the dryer in her hand, Oriol asked, "What are you going to tell Max about where you've been this afternoon?"

"I've been with you, of course," she replied with such logical ease that, then and there, they set out the rules that would thereafter govern what was to be their life, the life of all three of them.

And she got it absolutely right.

It was very late when Oriol finally returned Room 709 of the Hotel Arts, fed up with conversing with people who thought they knew him when they didn't have a clue. Yet he'd played his part, that of the man who appears to be as others want him to be. So draining. When he came into the room, Sara was sleeping like a baby. He shed his elegant suit and shoes, and drank from the glass she'd left untouched, gazing out of the picture windows and wondering whether to let her sleep or wake her up. He decided to wake her. He didn't want Max to be worried if she didn't get home before daylight. He took off his underpants, slid under the sheets and caressed Sara's waist with his large, warm hand. She turned to him, still half-asleep, but smiling and opening her legs. Oriol clasped her small body, and then turned her over. He knew every nook and cranny of it, knew exactly what he was doing. He pressed her belly slightly, felt her buttocks against him, found her vagina and entered from behind with the ease of someone who knows the way very well.

Sara let out a long moan but without opening her eyes, as if she was dreaming, as if she was suffering (but not much), and didn't move a muscle. Her floppy rag-doll body was there, as always, to satisfy Oriol's every desire, which was her desire. Panting faster and faster, he nuzzled her hair and said, "I couldn't stop looking at you tonight. You were so gorgeous." Sara smiled more, still with her eyes closed. She was happy with this. They were still good at it, in spite of everything. They were no longer twenty-year-old kids, and maybe they knew a lot more now than they did that afternoon in Paris. They both seemed as willing as ever to offer everything and accept everything. "But I would have preferred it if you'd been at my side," Oriol added.

Once, a long time ago, she'd said, "You, on top of me, thrusting as hard as you can, in those three or four seconds before coming: for me, it's an image that has all the best things in the world. Being young, being happy, being so alive. I promise you, I'll summon it up when I'm dying so I can take it with me as the best thing life has given me." She still thought the same, all those years later.

In Room 709 in the Hotel Arts, the sex was as splendid as always. Maybe they were a little wiser with the years. Now they didn't make as much noise as they used to and Oriol needed a few hours to be ready for another round. Yes, that much had changed. The double sessions were unthinkable now. The triple ones long gone.

As Oriol poured some drinks, Sara put on the hotel dressing gown and they sat down together, looking out over the sea.

"You know what? I have a spare ticket," he said. "It's first class! When they gave me the prize they thought I'd be coming with a partner and got me two tickets. Will you come with me?"

She looked at him, narrowing her eyes, trying to work out if he was joking. He wasn't.

"Where are you going this time?"

"Tokyo."

"Tokyo's a little too far away, Oriol."

"Have you ever wanted to leave Max?"

"Never."

"Not even in the early days?"

"No."

"Not even when you sleep with me again?"

"Especially then."

"Not even when, after sleeping with me, you have to get into bed with him? Are you going to tell me, Sara, that it's as good with Max as it is with me?"

"I don't want you to talk like that about Max. He doesn't deserve it."

A silence for things to settle down once more where they belong, so that what should never have been said aloud can vanish in oblivion.

"You'll have to leave soon, I guess," Oriol says.

"Soon? It's nearly five in the morning."

One last sip before Oriol's final offer. "Will you have a shower with me?"

He went into the bathroom and turned on the shower. Outside, Sara, thinking about the consequences of things, was petrified. Room 709 in the Hôtel Madeleine, the shower, the whispered words which had not totally faded away, two first-class tickets to Tokyo, the years going by, the empty chair at Oriol's side tonight, her two children and Max waiting for her, dozing in his reading chair.

It was even later when she decided that, this time, Oriol would have to shower alone. She didn't have it in her to say goodbye. That would have been too sad, utterly ridiculous. She wouldn't be able to find the right words. She got dressed in silence, picked up her things and left.

She walked home, taking a detour along Moll de la Marina so she could sit, just a little while, to look at the sea and calm down. Her head was full of unresolved problems, but she didn't have the slightest doubt about what to do, because she'd always known what she wanted: to go home to her husband. But, whether she wanted to do that just then, at quarter to six this April morning in 2004, was another matter.

The new day had dawned when Sara got home with a bag of still-warm *ensaïmades* which her shop manager was about to put in the display case. She found Max fast asleep in his reading chair with the light still on. She had a quick shower, made two cups of hot chocolate and woke him up as amorously as she could, telling him that breakfast was on the table.

"Did you have a nice night?" he wanted to know.

"It was great."

"So you had fun."

"Yes, I really did."

"That's good, Mama."

The next few weeks were unbearable. Sara found that the best way to cope with her contradictions was to retreat into herself. Max constantly annoyed her. She couldn't stand him. Everything he said was wrong, but she was mature enough to understand that his worst defect was that he wasn't Oriol Pairot. She spoke rarely, not wanting to hurt him, trying not to make any inappropriate remark, waiting to get over this thing that was happening inside her and not letting her breathe. She'd turned into a monster. Max was infinitely patient with her.

It took more than two months for her to stop looking at her phone a thousand times a day. She was waiting for some message from Oriol, some plea, some news of his despair which, perforce, had to be the same as hers. But not a word. Only silence. Maybe he was upset about the way she'd walked out of Room 709. Maybe he wasn't suffering much. The silence dragged on for nine years, suggesting that he was very angry or had forgotten all about her. Either answer was intolerable. No matter how many years went by, the pain of his absence was always too easily revived. It was a kind of desire, always alive, always with her. On and on it went until that evening, when she was watching telly after dinner and Max was reading his book on the risks of polymorphic transformations, that evening when he looked up and said, as if it was the most natural thing in the world, "Hey Mama, I nearly forgot! Guess who phoned me today. You won't believe this. Pairot! He's in Barcelona and says he's free the evening of the day after tomorrow, so I asked him to come over for dinner. Won't it be great to see him? It's so long since we last got together!"

Sara is about to leave her secret lookout. But she immediately sits down again when she hears Max say, "By the way, Oriol, there's something I want to tell you, now that I can see you're so much in love with Hina and that you're finally doing something good with your life."

A preamble like this guarantees the attention of the audience. No one would dare to leave before hearing what the speaker has to say. Oriol waits impatiently for Max to speak. Sara, behind the hedge, is all ears.

"I don't want to be melodramatic. You know I'm not into listening to or making bombastic speeches. And I don't want to play Mr Mysterious either. The thing is I know that over the years you and Sara have had several sexual encounters, the last one, if I'm not mistaken, at the Hotel Arts, the night you got the prize. Hang on, don't speak. I haven't finished yet. Please, pour yourself some more wine. I don't want you to think that

I expect any kind of apology, or that I'm going to pull out a gun, or do one of those things that husbands do in books. I'm a real, flesh-and-blood man, Oriol, and I've been lucky because there have been times when you've given Sara something I didn't even know she needed. Things are complicated and the passing of time doesn't make them simpler. I don't know if the same thing happens to you, but as I get older I can see that I'm getting weirder too, as if something's adulterating my make-up, so to speak. You're a charismatic, rich, famous, good-looking guy. You're also somewhat insufferable, but I think your virtues make up for your defects, at least in the eyes of women. So what's this all about then? In the last nine years, during which we haven't seen hide nor hair of you, I've become too accustomed to having Sara, this marvellous woman, all to myself. It's not a question of being stupid enough to think that you can possess another person. Of course you can't. Sara's not mine or yours or anyone else's. But it's just that, recently, I've had a feeling I've never had before. I think she really wants to be here, with me, because you get to a certain age in life when what you've done starts to be more important than what you can still do. That's why I wanted to tell you all this, Oriol, and, in passing, to ask you a question, if you don't mind. I'd like to know, to the extent you can predict it, of course, whether your marriage might represent for me a reasonable expectation that I can have my wife all to myself."

Oriol says nothing. He's at a loss for words and his hands are shaking.

"You've got nothing to say, Oriol? Can't you think of something?"

"Shit, man."

"I can see you're gobsmacked by what I've just said, but maybe you could be a little more forthcoming, pal."

"I think that, right now, I can't be anything. Fuck, Max! What you just told me! So… so, you've always known everything?"

"Come on, man, everything… everything… well, to tell you the truth, I never really wanted to know everything. There are things it's better not to know, don't you think? It's bad to have too much information sometimes. Anyway, perhaps *know* isn't the right word. At times I had an a-priori suspicion when she invented excuses so she could meet you and, though I never asked for explanations, she offered them, which made me smell a rat. Sometimes my hunches were a posteriori, when she came home with a sort of sinner's look about her, making her even more beautiful, and then she'd be evasive for days afterwards, pretending she was very busy. Sometimes they were only little things, but I noticed, because I've always been very observant, and of all the things I can observe, I like watching her most of all. For example, if she did something new in bed, I knew she hadn't invented it for me. Or if she bought some new lingerie just before you were about to turn up, it wasn't for me either. I can't give you all the examples. There are lots and they're not important. I've forgotten most of them anyway. But I think I've made clear enough what I wanted to talk to you about, haven't I? Come on, man, cheer up. It's not the end of the world."

"I'm dumbfounded, Max. I feel so ashamed. I don't know what to say."

"You don't have to say anything. And I don't see why you need to feel ashamed, not now. As far as I'm concerned, nothing's changed. I don't expect anything extraordinary. I just want to be able to talk about it like two men who care about and respect each other. We've been friends for twenty-three years, mate. If I'm sure of one thing, it's that you have some respect for me. It's a lot more than one might expect in this situation. If I look at the whole thing objectively, I can see that I'd never have stood a chance if I'd had to compete with you for her. Don't you remember that first day when I was so besotted and she only had eyes for you? I didn't have a hope. I was such a loser. I blushed every time she spoke to me and there was nothing I could do to stop it. I was so green. If it hadn't been for you, Sara would never have even looked at me."

"Me? What are you saying, man? You two started going out when I was in France."

"Because I was the only way she had of staying in touch with you. Of course I smartened up bit. I had no choice. I dared to suggest things (she always said no), to steal the odd kiss (she got so angry that sometimes I thought she was going to hit me), and I think that, in bed, I even managed to surprise her the first time. Believe me, I made a huge effort to keep it up! But I didn't make any real headway until I invited her to my PhD viva. Much to my amazement, the polymorphs won the day. She liked my intellectual attributes more than any other. Women are crazy about good-looking, swashbuckling men like you, but then they settle for the boring, normal ones like me. Do you know why? Because, sooner or later, they discover that you spend a lot more of your life out of bed than in it. Of course, Sara did better than most. She chose both of us, each for his own speciality. She's always been very intelligent, as you well know. A lot of women should do what she did."

"Don't say that, Max. She chose you, with everything that meant. When I found out, I cursed you to hell and back."

"Did you now? Well, I think she'd like to know that, because I'm pretty sure she believes she never meant anything to you. I mean, nothing more than an easy lay waiting for you every time you get to pass Go. Don't get me wrong if I choose the words she'd use herself. For me, Sara is anything but easy."

"Well, she's mistaken if she thinks that."

"That's what I thought, Oriol, but I couldn't tell her, of course. I mean, I suspected that you were in love with her too at some point. In fact, I don't understand why everyone doesn't fall in love with her. I've never met anyone like her. In your own way, naturally, and perhaps obliged by the circumstances to put on an act, you were in love with her, and I knew it. Sometimes I wanted to tell her, to make her happier, but I couldn't. I couldn't suddenly look up from my book and say, 'Hey, come on, you don't have to suffer so much. Oriol loves you too and, right now, he must be as wretched as you are, missing you every millisecond of the day, remembering every detail of your last sex session and counting the days till he sees you again.' Maybe, if she'd known... Oh, Oriol, man, if she'd known... I think things would have been different. Look, you know what, let me correct myself. I would never have said anything to her, because if Sara had left me for you I don't know what I would have done. Basically, I've put up with it because I was always sure she'd never leave me. Or almost always."

"I don't think she would ever have—"

"Listen, when all's said and done, it doesn't matter. It wasn't that often, eh? How many times was it exactly? Did you keep count?"

"No, I didn't, actually."

"You didn't? Well, I'd say Sara did. It's a pity I can't ask her. I kept a tally too. My estimate is fourteen times, counting the last one. I might have missed some occasion, but I doubt it. Fourteen. I'm pretty sure. If you get the chance to ask my wife, she'll confirm it and you'll be flabbergasted. But, obviously, I hope you never say a word to her about this conversation."

"No. Of course not. I think it's you who—"

"No, no, I have no intention of saying anything."

"You're not going to tell her?"

"I'm aware that it may seem strange to you, and maybe it *is* a little strange. But I don't want to risk any changes. Something like this can make the temperature rise out of control. The consequences of an uncontrolled rise in temperature are not predictable. You should know the perfect temperatures for getting the best chocolate possible from your cocoa butter: 45, 27, 32, right? Well, maybe we could be a little more precise but, basically, that's how things are. Above or below those temperatures, even half a degree Celsius, you only get disasters. Chocolate, like people, has an extremely complex microstructure, so it's better not to interfere with that and do things by the book. Do you understand what I'm saying now? I don't want any change whatsoever in my relationship with Sara. I want her exactly as she is – delightful, perfectionist, arrogant, contradictory, very, very disagreeable at times, always attentive with me, devoted to her family, but with that hint of distance of someone who could have left us long ago but did us the favour of staying. I don't want another Sara. I don't want a shamed, guilty, sadly submissive Sara. A woman like that wouldn't be our Sara, would she? Not *my* Sara."

Oriol's head is spinning when the doorbell rings. Max gets up, looking relaxed and pulling down his shirt-tail. "Great, she's here!

Open the absinthe. We've got a lot to celebrate. And, hey, Oriol, brighten up a bit, will you? You look like someone just died."

Oriol exhales, then takes in a deep breath like a swimmer about to dive into an Olympic pool. He walks a few steps to look at the vigilant, now dark towers of Santa Maria del Mar. Then he notices that the neighbour's hedge has holes in it, and it's possible to glimpse the next-door terrace through the biggest one. He squats and squints, trying to make out what's on the other side. He suddenly feels acutely embarassed by the idea that someone might have been eavesdropping. But, no, he can only see darkness and an empty chair. The metal shutter is up, but it looks as if there's no one there.

"Is it totally smashed? Can it be stuck together?" Hearing Sara's voice coming closer through the dining room, he puts his hands in his pockets and tries to look like a still-attractive man.

"Yes, sure," Max says. "I'll fix it."

When she comes out onto the terrace, in her black dress and with her hair up, Oriol thinks she's more beautiful than ever. He could draw, centimetre by centimetre, the map of the body he still desires. She comes over to him, her eyes shining with emotion, takes his hands and gazes for a second at his Adam's apple, or so it seems to him. Her perfume envelops him with all the intensity of newly resuscitated memories.

"Oriol! You're alive after all! It's so good to see you again," she says moving closer.

They kiss on each cheek. In the next few seconds, when they are swaddled in each other's smell, his heart starts beating wildly.

Sara says, "Did you leave any truffles for me? I need chocolate!"

Max smiles. He's holding the bottle of absinthe and has at least three good reasons for celebrating.

First Interlude

THE LID

"…Yes, of course you can come in, girl. Come on, come on… Can't you see the sign says 'Open'? I know these aren't the usual hours for attending to customers but there are always people who come along, like you now, and they find exactly what they're looking for. Sometimes they find things they don't know they're looking for. So what do you think about that, eh? Things always happen for a reason. Would you say that many people are in the habit of walking into an antiques shop at five in the morning? Maybe there's some object waiting, tucked away in the haven of my shop, and the glow from my window is like a beacon for the wanderer, calling him, drawing him in, even though he doesn't know why. You came here looking for something, girl, and I'm sure you're going to find it.

"Well now, I believe you've found it already. You like this chipped pot? It's an old chocolate pot, made of very fine porcelain. Hold it up against the light and you'll see the quality of the clay. This piece is one in a million, but unfortunately the lid's been lost and the only way you can tell it's a chocolate pot is by the spout. It's very high, you see? This is because, in the olden days, the chocolate had to be served with a lot of foam, and if the spout was too low it didn't pour right. I don't remember the price. Does it say how much on that label tied to the handle? Have you noticed how delicate it is, that handle? Three thousand pesetas, you say? Well, I don't think that's too high, but I can consider a small discount for you. I have the feeling that this piece has been waiting for you. It's been here more than twenty-five years, I'll have you know. More than twenty-five years and nobody's as much as looked at it, nobody's been sufficiently interested, and then one fine day you come along, a mere slip of a girl, at five in the morning, and you find me here by chance, sorting out some papers because I couldn't sleep, and you go straight to Adélaïde's chocolate pot and – bingo! – you like it. You're the one we were waiting for, girl. Things don't happen all by themselves. This chocolate pot has been yours ever since I bought it in a lot which had a bit of everything, and that was in nineteen hundred and… let me think… nineteen hundred and sixty-five! That's right! You weren't even born then, were you? So now you see, you were about to be born and in this world there was a beautiful object that was waiting for you, and you alone. What did you say your name is?

"Sit down, Sara Rovira, and think about it. Have you seen what's written on the base? In that intense, aristocratic blue. It says in French, 'I belong to Madame Adélaïde of France.' I tried to find out more about it at the time. I don't have much else to do in my small part of the world. You don't find such fine porcelain any old where. I think it must come from the Sèvres factory on the outskirts of Paris. It's a little strange that it doesn't bear the typical double-L insignia, with Latinized crossed Ls (which is sometimes called the 'double Louis', as in King Louis), or a third capital letter, which varied because that was the year cipher. But it doesn't matter, because there were exceptions in these places too. I pay more attention to colours. This very intense blue of the letters is highly characteristic and, I'd say, unique. It was used for the first time by the Sèvres factory in 1749. The factory, by the way, was a whim of Madame de Pompadour, the official mistress of Louis XV, an admirable woman who not only shared the king's bed but was a close friend of the queen and hostess of the court's festivities at Versailles. She managed to do all that by the age of twenty-three. Imagine that! How old are you, girl, if you don't mind my asking? There you are... you're almost the same age. Like you, she was another lady who knew very well what she wanted.

"But, as I was saying... we were talking about the Sèvres porcelain factory, weren't we? So, it was founded at the wish of the wonderful Pompadour, with the King's gold, no problem. That's why it became the Royal Porcelain Manufactory, and for a long time it produced only for Versailles. You can't imagine how many people there were in Versailles! And they all needed pots, plates, dainty little cups and bowls, washbowls and figurines – everything in abundance! The porcelain factory produced some really exquisite objects, some of them of incredible opulence and baroque extravagance. Yet, it wouldn't surprise me if they also made small pieces ordered by members of the royal family, tailored to the tastes of each individual. It's well known that the ladies of Versailles were addicted to chocolate, starting with the first one of all, Anne of Austria, such a sad poor thing, the epitome of dullness. The only good thing in her life was drinking hot chocolate with her courtiers. We also know that Adélaïde was the name of the sixth daughter of Louis XV. She was born in the palace, of course, though she died in exile in Italy after the guillotine came down on the necks of a lot of her relatives. She was another remarkable woman who hated her father's courtesans and was as cultured as any prince, a woman who was tired of being a woman, but she had to let people walk all over her precisely because of that. And lovely too! She was really beautiful.

"Sorry, Sara, if I'm getting worked up talking about these ladies of Versailles, but I'm full of admiration and sadness for Madame Adélaïde of France when I think of her fate as a fugitive in an unrecognizable Europe while Napoleon played at being lord of the world, like the brat he was... Poor thing, I wonder when exactly she had to give up the chocolate pot she herself had ordered: 'I want it simple, please, without flowers or naked goddesses, and make it small, because it's just for me and I never take more than three little cups.' It's almost as if I can hear her angelic voice telling her lady-in-waiting to convey her instructions to the messenger waiting outside in the courtyard, hanging around there, watching the clouds float by over those sumptuous façades. I wonder when she saw it for the first time. She would have thought, 'That's exactly what I wanted: simple and elegant.' It couldn't have been before 1749 or after 1785. It's impossible to know the exact moment, but I like to imagine Madame Adélaïde, the one in the portraits in Versailles, with her cheeks as fine as this porcelain and eagle-bright eyes brimming with intelligence and tragedy; a woman who was still young, twenty-five at the most, whose chocolate was served in this very pot every afternoon; who was starting to plot about how to intervene in her father's government and, later, her brother's, because he was heir to the throne and still alive then; and the power that was denied to her, not because she was stupid but because she was a woman.

"I can see that what I'm telling you interests you, Sara. You're one of those people who, like me, think that all these things from the past are still very much alive in us. Well, you've earned yourself a good discount with your enthusiasm. What would you say if I let you have it for two thousand? That makes a difference, doesn't it? Now, while you're thinking about it, I'll tell you the rest of the story, which is about me. About how I found this wonderful piece completely by chance. It was in November 1965, only a week after the death of Senyora Antònia Sampons i Turull, who, apart from being a paragon of rectitude, was very rich and also very ugly. Some people say that this last detail is why she died childless and therefore left everything to foundations, museums and charitable works, but I'm not going to enter into that, because it's not my field.

"Senyora Antònia Sampons i Turull was the only daughter of the chocolate entrepreneur Antoni Sampons, who tends to be remembered today for having given his name to that house in the Passeig de Gràcia, the one which the architect Puig i Cadafalch turned into a marvel of Modernism. Do you know the one I mean? It's right next to Casa Batlló and very near Casa Lleó i Morera. Antoni Sampons pioneered the original, very extravagant renovation, and it's probably his fault that all his neighbours were envious and started that mad race to see who could produce the house with the most colours, the most sculptures, the most windows and the most towers.

"I was lucky enough to get into the Sampons house just a week after the owner died. Very few people can say that. I saw the Roman-style mosaics, the mouldings, the silk-covered walls, the furniture still arranged as she'd had it, the dressing room, the bed, the office where all the windows were stained glass, the music room where she liked to sit and listen to direct broadcasts from the Liceu when she had all but stopped going out. I'd been asked to attend a sort of meeting where the executor of the lady's will was conducting the whole orchestra. There were specialists from the City Council, a historian who was an expert on Catalan industrialization and even a priest, I believe, but I'm not sure since I barely spoke to any of them. What I do recall very clearly is that they'd organized everything into lots containing all sorts of things. The legacy of Senyora Sampons included donations to museums and institutions, and she'd earmarked a certain sum of money to create a foundation with a good part of the works of art from the house. I remember hearing talk of a future chocolate museum. One of the men was there to put together all the pieces that were going to be part of that, including collections of old trading cards (the ones they used to give away with blocks of chocolate), copper utensils, a few pictures and old advertising posters for Sampons Chocolates – 'The best desire of all is desire for Sampons chocolate,' they said – a lot of plans, maybe for industrial machinery (they were very intricate), and the chocolate pots from which Senyora Sampons served her friends hot chocolate every afternoon. Madame Adélaïde's chocolate pot was there too. It had the lid then – with a hole in the middle, as you know, for the wooden swizzle stick – and it would have looked almost new if it hadn't been for the chipped spout. Quite a big bit had broken off and it was very visible. I didn't notice the chocolate pot until considerably later, because I'm not in the habit of snooping around where I'm not wanted.

"'Come through here,' said the very friendly gentleman, the executor of the will, guiding me into a room overlooking the Passeig de Gràcia. 'This is the lot. If you're interested, give me a quote you think is reasonable.'

"I'd been told by a friend that they needed a scrap merchant at the Sampons residence. I was very lucky because it's not every day one can go into a place like that. In my trade, an entrée into such a fine home is guaranteed good business. You always come out with something worthwhile. Even if it's only memories like the ones I'm telling you now. Memories have no money value, yet they're our most priceless treasure, Sara. You know that, don't you? Sometimes it's worth paying something just for a good memory. It's a pity you can't buy memories in an establishment like mine, because I'd get rich, I can assure you. There are some people who'd kill to have memories that are different from the ones they have!

"But let's go back to November 1965. I was telling you that a friend had told me there'd be something there for me, because they were disposing of the assets in the house and there would almost certainly be odds and ends that nobody wanted. I telephoned immediately and they gave me an appointment for the next day. I thought that when a house is being emptied they always need someone to get rid of the rubbish. In this story, I was the rubbish man.

"As I was saying, they took me into a well-lit room overlooking the Passeig de Gràcia, where a heap of stuff was awaiting me: a sewing machine, a dozen and a half unmatched wine glasses and a cat basket. A whole pile of things that only had value for the person who'd wanted them and, even then, they were almost worthless.

"'What is your answer?' asked the executor, appearing out of nowhere with that businesslike air of his.

"'I'll give you four hundred pesetas.'

"'Done,' he said without a second thought. My friend was right. They needed a rubbish man. I should have offered him two hundred pesetas. 'But you have to take it away at once.'

"'Certainly. Right now.'

"The golden rule of my trade is never leave without the merchandise. When you come back something will be missing.

"I started packing up my purchase. I was in no hurry to leave. Out of the corner of my eye I could see how the other gentlemen, all decked out in suits and ties, were busy closing deals. The representative from the future museum was looking at the old advertising posters and making a great song and dance about them.

"'Look! This is one of those incredibly famous drawings by Rafael Penagos. And look at this one. It's by Amadeu Lax! What a magnificent collection!"

"Then I saw him pick up the chocolate pot and start inspecting it.

"'What's this inscription on the base?' he asked. He turned the piece over, taking not the slightest care. The lid fell off and broke into three pieces when it hit the floor.

"'Oh dear!' he exclaimed when he realized what he'd just done. 'I thought the lid was attached. I'll sweep it up. It's the least I can do.'

"The conductor of that orchestra of oafs came along just after that to collect his money for the things I'd almost finished wrapping. He was holding the damaged chocolate pot.

"'If you want to take this too… It's useless in this state. It can't be displayed with the others. It's a pity, because it was one of the finest.'

"He put the chocolate pot on top of the box containing the sewing machine. I had the feeling that the porcelain was muttering, cursing him and that bunch of dolts who had no idea how to handle such beautiful things. I took the money out of my pocket, closed the deal and put Madame Adélaïde's chocolate pot with the other things in my lot.

"So that's the story of how it came into my hands and into my shop.

"At first, when I realized that it could be a very valuable piece, I thought about getting it repaired. Maybe if I spent a bit on it I could sell it for a nice sum. But you know what happens with these plans. You decide, you leave it for another moment, the other moment never comes, and you forget about it in the end, or you can't be bothered, which is the same as if you've forgotten about it. Priorities keep changing over your life, don't they? And we change too. We get lazy. The chocolate pot waited about twenty-five years for me to do something about it. Twenty-five years sitting on a shelf, next to my desk. Then, finally, I looked at it one day and said, 'What on earth is that pot doing there?' I tied a price tag to it and put it in the shop to wait for the person it was destined to go to. All these objects are destined to go to one person or another. Shops like mine are simply a place where the meetings are made possible.

"So what do you think? Now I've told you the whole story with all the details, including things I don't know for sure but can imagine. So, will you give me five hundred pesetas and take it with you? I can't give you a better price than that. This is my tribute to Madame Adélaïde and all the fine ladies of France and to you, because you're very young and it touches me that you like these old things. And because you're very patient, girl. I never imagined that anyone would listen to me for so long, and that needs to be rewarded too.

"Don't worry about the time. Your friends will wait for you. Anyway, the minutes pass slower here in my shop. Can't you see that all these antiques won't let them advance? If time were the same in here as it is in the street, I'd be dead by now. I don't know how many years I've been watching the world going round.

"So, here you are, Sara. It's all yours. I can see you're happy with it. You've bought an object that's full of stories. If you listen carefully, you'll be able to hear them. I'm sure of that. It's as clear as crystal that you're the person we've been waiting for – and almost twenty-seven years. As I always say, things happen when they have to happen and not one second before."

Act II

COCOA, SUGAR AND CINNAMON

Infelice cor tradito,
Per angoscia non scoppiar.*
FRANCESCO MARIA PIAVE
Rigoletto

Tristan und Isolde

You see the scene from the distance of time, but the memories haven't flown with the years. They're as vivid as they were on their first day. 8th November 1899. The Gran Teatre del Liceu dazzles as only it can on opening night. It is a good occasion to be seen, and you are there on the arm of someone who has been very insistent that you should be there with him. Very insistent indeed. Before getting out of the carriage you summon up a prayer you remember, pleading for everything to go well. You do not want the doctor – Horaci, that is – to be ashamed of you.

In the vestibule everyone is chatting happily, without a care in the world, as if the most important event on earth is opening night at the opera. They look at you but are pretending not to, as if nothing strange has happened and that everyone present is in the right place. You know you are a fish out of water and you do not need their reproachful looks to remind you of that. Just a short time ago, when you left the house, you swore to yourself that you would not let it bother you, but there is nothing you can do about it now. You are bothered by it. You smile to hide it. You do not want him to worry and you are trying not to feel so strange and so daunted.

If Doctor Volpi, Horaci, knew how afraid you are, he would try to soothe you, coming out with one of those comments of his like "Do not worry, Aurora, let these upstarts prattle. Can you not see they have nothing better to do?" But you do not want to make him feel bad or spoil his night. When you step out of the carriage and doctor Volpi sends the driver on his way, you are immediately in awe of the dresses of all those bejewelled ladies. They are acting like princesses and want everyone to look at them. The main stairway is a parade of finery. If only you could see all this from outside, you think as you start climbing the stairs. If only you were not part of this event.

Horaci looks very handsome in tails. He's wearing a waist-coat, a gold watch chain and his top hat. His shoes are shiny and hair very neat, with just a touch of brilliantine. He is not dressed in the latest fashion, but you like his slightly antiquated air. He is also one of those naturally elegant men who seem to have been born to wear black tie all the time. You can see at a glance that there is no other man like him. No one can compete with him. The doctor has a special glow about him, perhaps because everything in him radiates harmony, or because he never stops smiling, not even for a second. He seems pleased. There are not many people of his age – and he is nearly eighty – who smile so placidly and naturally as if they have never done other-wise. When he smiles, his blue eyes light up with something that reminds you of a little boy, and you have the impression that he is a boy who does not want to grow up yet. Then you say, "You are like a boy, my big boy, Horaci," and he smiles and says, "Thanks to you, Aurora, thanks to you and you alone."

Then he discreetly whispers in your ear and you can hear in his voice the admiration of someone entering a holy place: "Look, Aurora, this is the Hall of Mirrors."

It is difficult not to make a great to-do when you see it, as you are astonished. You try not to show it and look up discreetly, but you are probably squeezing his arm tighter without realizing it.

Look, Aurora. Who is this impertinent, incredulous woman in that lilac gauze dress, the one who is watching you from this mirror so richly decorated with columns and moulding? With more than four decades behind her, she is not young but, dressed up like this, she looks very different. Her hair is drawn back from her face into a chignon. Her shoulders are bare. They are delicate, like those of a young girl, and nestling in her cleavage there is a white-gold-and-ivory medallion to match her earrings. On her hands she is wearing only a solitaire diamond ring, neither too large nor in any way ostentatious, as she had wished, the priceless testimony of a love she is still unable to believe she deserves. Who is this newcomer? Nobody knows her. Where has she come from? From what netherworld has she been rescued? Who will be the first to notice? How will this person know? What small gesture will betray her origins? Might there be something strange about the way she is dressed, or her manners, or her words? No, there is nothing except, maybe, her extreme caution, like someone walking on eggshells. Even so, anyone can see who she is at a glance. An intruder. Her place is far from all this splendour. She is here but has no right to be here. If the mirror knew, it would refuse to give her back her image. But mirrors are loath to know anything about such complicated matters and play the game of being taken in by appearances.

"Do you like it? Is it not fabulous?" Doctor Volpi murmurs in your ear with that naughty-little-boy look of his.

You nod, because you do not know what to say and your eyes are brimming with tears of emotion. It is much better than you ever imagined when he used to tell you about it, those evenings when you savoured your little cups of hot chocolate together.

"Well, wait until you see the rest," he adds, heading for the cloakroom.

As you are waiting to leave your capes and his top hat, you greet some people. They look at you sideways, with ill-concealed disdain, before offering the de-rigueur greeting.

Horaci introduces you. "This is my wife, Aurora."

Doctor Volpi, Horaci, is admired by everyone. They all respect him, even when he makes one of his reckless decisions. Bringing this common creature to the opera when everyone can see her? Nobody dares to be rude, so they smile and affectedly say, "Pleased to meet you, dear", or very malevolently ask if you like Wagner, to see what you will say, or if you will say anything at all. Horaci comes to the rescue, saying, "Aurora prefers Italian opera, and there is not much we can do about that. As they say, nobody is perfect." And they, the others, the ones who belong here, turn away and start their spiteful mutterings. "His wife? I cannot believe it! No, he could not have married her. It is impossible that he married her!" You are aware of everything, even while pretending the opposite. Every time someone speaks to somebody else, it seems as if they are criticizing you, that they have discovered who you are, that their words are soiling Horaci and making him look bad... and your heart is pounding with all this suffering and apprehensiveness. Horaci, always considerate, can see this, and leans towards you whispering, "Let them burst with envy."

It is a relief to reach the anteroom of the box, although in order to get there you have had to run the gauntlet of many more introductions and looks of surprise, mistrust and condescension. You rest on the settee and sigh. You want to ask him to leave you here, hidden away from all those looks, or, even better, to let you go home and tell everyone you are feeling faint. Nobody would be surprised by that. "It is all too much for her, of course, poor thing. She has never seen anything like this." But Horaci brings you a glass of cold water, squeezes your hand and says, "I am happy that you wanted to come."

This is enough to make you feel strong again. You think you could never say no to this man. You stand up, smooth down your skirt and fill your lungs with this air laden with unfamiliar essences. Then you go to the box. Horaci has told you that Isolde's role is one of the most difficult for opera singers – "Soprano is the right word, but you can call her whatever you like" – and you think about the poor girl who has to appear onstage in a few minutes and wonder who is more afraid, you or her. Horaci pulls out your chair, makes sure you're comfortably settled, sits down at your side, nods at someone and then gives you that enraptured look, that expression of his that transforms you and says, "Everything is as it should be," making you feel worthy of occupying a chair in a box at the Liceu when Wagner's opera is about to start. *You must be insane, Aurora.*

And, good heavens, what a spectacle. You think this even before having time to look at the stage. The ladies' dresses, the dozens of electric lights, the gilding, the velvet, the whiff of grandeur given off by everything. For a moment you forget to breathe. You tug your gloves off very slowly and leave them on the balustrade. Horaci picks them up and puts them on a chair.

"So they will not fall," he says, while glancing at a box on the other side of the auditorium. "Antoni Sampons and his daughter are there, but I do not think they recognize you."

Just then, as if their gazes were drawn to one another, the chocolatier Sampons nods a greeting to Horaci, who courteously responds in kind. You imitate him, doing things the way Horaci has taught you. Antonieta, the daughter, looks up from the programme in her hand, greets you both with distracted aloofness and immediately starts reading again. It is a long time since she was that little girl you remember, and you think you would not have recognized her. She must be – you calculate fast but accurately – yes, that's right, twenty-six. You steal a glance at her, thinking that her face has that whatever it is her mother has, a touch of haughtiness perhaps, or the way her hair frames her face, but the whole effect is that she is not nearly as pretty as Càndida. Those dark unflattering clothes, so unsuitable for such a young woman, do not help, but that is not the problem. Nothing can help the poor girl. She is ugly. Nothing can be done about it, and it is better to tell the truth. She is as ugly as sin, which seems incredible, because her father, sitting beside her, is still a fine figure of a man, and her mother, although she was not one of Murillo's virgins, was pleasing to the eye. It must be because of the terrible thing that happened. People are not left unmarked after such a calamity. You catch yourself at what you are doing and reproach yourself for your unkindness. *What are you doing at the Liceu with such low-minded thoughts about a woman you have known since the day she was born, Aurora? For Heaven's sake, learn to behave like a lady.*

"Is it true that Senyoreta Sampons is still unmarried?" you ask Horaci, who at once confirms that this is so.

Of course she is a spinster. You knew. You only have to look at the poor creature. Now she is picking up some opera glasses and, as she gets ready to watch the performance, makes some comment to her father, who concurs. They make an odd pair and seem to get on very well, apart from being father and daughter and after what happened. It is not surprising she has not married. From here it looks as if she has a moustache. All that dark fuzz on her upper lip. You rebuke yourself again, this time more severely. *Aurora, behave like a lady and do not make the doctor feel ashamed of you. He was so happy to bring you here and he does not deserve that.* You while away the time, chiding yourself inside your head, while, outside, you're wearing an enigmatic smile, which is very appropriate for the occasion.

It is quite a paradox that the only people who really know you have not as much as looked at you, Antonieta because she seems so concerned to study every detail of her programme, and Senyor Antoni because he could not care less about the lives of other people. And, even if he was interested, it is many years since he lost the ability to be surprised by anything at all.

The chocolatier Antoni Sampons, once son-in-law of the deceased, ill-fated inventor of industrial machinery, Don Estanislau Turull – who, moreover, had the adjoining box in the Liceu – never misses a performance at the Liceu, except for *Il trovatore*, the only opera he never wants to see again. Everyone in this small world of busybodies and gossips knows that the rich chocolatier is a true gentleman as well as being a totally devoted music lover, but that he has an intractable problem with the character of Manrico, of whom nobody dares to speak in his presence, or that of his daughter.

And the one next to it must be the Turull box. You do not want to ask about that. You decided some time ago that you must not talk to Horaci about things from the past. In any case, it all seems too long ago, and not worth talking about either. But memory will not lie still, and now that you are here where it all began, looking directly at the box which must have been that of the manufacturer of industrial machinery, Don Estanislau Turull, and his wife, Donya Hortènsia, you do not know how it is that you still have such a clear image of Senyoreta Càndida, all dressed up like a princess, leaving the house on her father's arm. Poor, unlucky Don Estanislau absolutely adored the child. For better or for worse, you never knew anyone like her.

Then you understand why the child used to go to sleep in the anteroom of their box as soon as Act One began, but you also understand why her father was upset because his little girl did not like opera, not even Italian opera. Especially *Rigoletto*. Ah, *Rigoletto*, you will say to Doctor Volpi – you mean Horaci – and you will ask him to take you to see it next time they do it, because you want to know about all those things Senyor Estanislau talked about as if he was under a spell. What you do know is that you can sing a tiny bit of it – the *Bella figlia dell'amore* part – which you heard so many times sitting at Càndida's side.

"Do you know what I heard?" says the doctor, whose thoughts are now in tune with your own. "Càndida Turull has returned to Barcelona."

"She has come back?" you ask. "Alone?"

"I know no more than that. The person who told me did not know much. But it seems she has rented a flat in Bonanova."

"In Bonanova. So far out of town?"

This makes you think how much life has changed. Càndida Turull, alone or in company (who knows?) in Bonanova; Senyor Antoni in the box with his daughter the two of them together, as thick as thieves; and you are here watching them without their recognizing you. Of course they don't recognize you, Aurora because it would be impossible for them to imagine that this lady in the lilac dress at doctor Volpi's side is you. Not even if they knew what you look like now, or if they could see you from such a distance.

"Look, Aurora, my love." The doctor interrupts your train of thought. "The bomb fell there, in Row 13, on the right-hand side. Those empty seats you can see there were occupied by the poor people who died that night. They leave them empty as a sign of respect. It is as if I'm seeing it all over again. They were doing *Guglielmo Tell*," Horaci explains, and you feel a shiver running all the way up your back, because you remember the doctor coming home that night with his waistcoat all stained with blood, and how he told you that the wife of the bookseller Dalmàs had died in his arms and he had not been able to do anything to save her, and that she was not the only one, because the terrible spectacle of death and destruction was truly dreadful. Yet they had to be grateful because there was a second bomb which had not exploded as it had been caught in the skirts of the wife of the lawyer Cardellach, who was already dead. "Oh, God!" Horaci had exclaimed that night, and you had never seen him so upset. "The Liceu will never go back to being what it was, Aurora. We shall never recover from this bloodbath."

But these people were not born to be daunted by misfortune or to waste time brooding over it. You only have to look at Antoni Sampons, sitting there in his box, as distinguished as ever, the memories of his past well protected from further buffeting of the winds of life. He must have heard that Càndida has returned to Barcelona. Of course he would know because news like that circulates very fast. You wonder about the expression on his face when he heard. And the daughter must know, too, that her mother has come back. Does she plan to go to see Càndida or will she shun her too?

Although the lights have not been dimmed the music starts, softly, but the doctor has told you that it will liven up because Wagner always livens up. There is a murmur of protest in the stalls and the boxes. One man in Row 3 is gesticulating and looks very angry. Horaci explains that Wagner has a large group of admirers in Barcelona and they want his operas to be performed properly, in silence, with the lights dimmed so they can give all their attention to the stage, but the director of the Liceu is a fool who does not agree with them, and this is sacrilege against the artist's wishes and art in general. The gentleman in Row 3 is an eminent critic who has now lost his temper. An opera critic in the Liceu who has lost his temper could be a nightmare, as you will find out eventually when you realize that this is a universe with its own laws, and when you start to see where each person fits in. For the moment, you have just arrived, so to speak, and you are trying to understand what is so terrible about leaving these beautiful lights undimmed, but then you get a terrible fright because the violins suddenly start playing very loudly, making a lot of noise because there are so many of them and, when you get the chance, you will try to count them in order to focus your mind on something else. You are also trying to look like a lady who goes to the opera, although you do not know how to do that and, however hard you try, you cannot stop thinking that this is impossible, that you will never do it.

Horaci caresses the back of your hand and says, "The principles of beauty are simplicity and truth."

You look at him wondering why he has said these lovely words, and then his sweet voice adds, "Close your eyes and let yourself be moved by the music, my love."

Docile, happy, you close your eyes. The first thing you understand is that the violins are not frightening when you cannot see them. There are times when the melody is sweet, like a lullaby, and you have the feeling that it is gently rocking all the memories that have surfaced tonight. Suddenly the strings roar and the drums thunder as if the Overture is berating you for something terrible you have done but you do not know what. And the music has your heart racing so fast you do not know what might happen, but it is a pleasurable sensation which you have never felt before, this becoming so emotional without knowing why. Slowly, with your eyes closed, you start wondering whether this is exactly what the lady in the mirror, that impertinent stranger, was supposed to feel, and whether emotions might not be one of the few things in the world that make no distinction between rich and poor. With your eyes closed and Horaci caressing your hand, feeling that, thanks to you, he is the luckiest man in the world, you come to the conclusion that this music and this man are one and the same thing: a miracle that can transform people. That can transform you, Aurora – *Poor little thing, you have been very unlucky in your life and we shall have to make up for that somehow* – into the woman who is sitting at his side. Or maybe into the woman you had inside you but did not know.

I puritani

The day Senyoreta Càndida was born, 12th August 1851, was a joyful one for the Turull house.

How could it be otherwise? The pregnancy had cost the parents seventeen years of Novenas, vows, spas and treatments. Seventeen years of never giving up hope, but with hope dwindling every month. When they finally learned they were going to have a baby, Senyora Hortènsia was thirty-nine and Senyor Estanislau had just turned forty-eight and they did not know whether to give thanks to the Blessed Virgin, the nuns at Sant Vicenç de Jonqueres, the Baden-Baden thermal baths, or more than a dozen doctors of unpronounceable names and a plethora of treatments. When the child was born and turned out to be a girl they were so happy they did not mind a bit.

Like the New Testament prophets or the Blessed Virgin in her various forms Senyoreta Càndida, then, had the aura of a miracle even before she made her appearance in the world. Senyora Hortènsia liked to say that the birth was as pleasant as a summer stroll. Everyone who saw the newborn child fell in love with her pink cheeks and her serene air of happiness. Her father, the always busy, talented Don Estanislau Turull, was so overjoyed that he had a rare attack of generosity and served his best hot chocolate to all the servants in his household. Counting your mother, who was about to give birth, there were nineteen all told.

Four days later, the bells of Santa Maria del Mar rang longer than usual in honour of the baby being baptized, little Càndida, named after a deceased grandmother who was remembered by very few (as tends to be the case). One might say that, in those days, it seemed to be a very appropriate name. Afterwards, the senyors opened the doors of their home in Carrer de la Princesa, and all the *crème de la crème* of Barcelona came to snoop, pay their respects to the happy couple and, while they were there, have a look at the little heiress, who might not be so pretty but she was very rich. In those days, Don Estanislau had made a name among his fellow citizens thanks to sales of machines he invented himself to anyone willing to believe in technological progress. However, since there were very few believers, or they were too young to have any money, his fortune had come from his textile mills and England where he had sold half a dozen patents at a more than satisfactory price.

Your arrival in the world occurred a few days after the re-sounding baptism of the little Turull heiress. The circumstances were different, however. It could not be otherwise. Your poor mother writhed in pain for hours and hours in her cellar room two floors underground until one of the cooks heard her howls. We shall not speak of your father, an elusive fellow who enjoyed flitting from bed to bed. You do not even know his name. They only told you that he was a very good-looking scoundrel and your mother had no idea of what he was like when he beguiled and seduced her. However, none of that mattered in the slightest when the cook went to find Senyora Hortènsia to inform her that one of the maids was dying in childbirth down in the cellars, whereupon she was immediately sent to get the doctor.

When he arrived, it was too late for your mother but, luckily, not for you. The doctor's action, they said, saved you at the last minute but you paid a very high price for your life. One life for another. You always thought that being born fatherless, of a dead mother, was a sentence you had no choice but to serve.

Senyora Hortènsia gave you a name. *Poor little thing, you have been very unlucky in your life and we shall have to make up for that somehow.* She called you Aurora, which means light, sun and beginning so it is a word full of hope. *And beautiful too. A girl must always have a beautiful name because one might also shape her destiny when one gives her a name. You never know.*

You have always been well aware that your great good fortune – life-saving, actually – was coming into the world only a few days after Senyoreta Càndida. The senyors were so happy that their hearts were softened and they could not or would not ignore your situation when they heard the sad story. After all, believing that they were very good people on top of everything else was one of the greatest needs of the richest of the rich in those times. You really gave them a chance to shine. And they certainly shone. They fed you, dressed you (in their daughter's hand-me-downs), educated you (the perfect playmate) and loved you (in their own way, but you cannot ask for more than that) as long as they lived. And when their daughter got married and left home, you also left, because your destiny and that of Senyoreta Càndida were bound together and could never be separated.

At least Senyora Hortènsia had said so.

"You and Càndida are milk sisters. Do you know what that means?"

You shook your head.

"It means you must be united for ever, because that is what God wants. You have to take care of her all your life, whatever happens. I want you to promise me you will do that."

"I promise," you said, somewhat alarmed.

"And that you will never leave her."

"No, Senyora, I shall never leave her."

"And you will be like a sister to her when Senyor Estanislau and I leave this world."

"Yes, Senyora, I shall always take care of Senyoreta Càndida. You do not have to worry."

Senyora Hortènsia smiled and you felt something akin to pride.

"You are a good girl, Aurora. I was not wrong about you."

"Thank you, Senyora Hortènsia."

"You can go now."

You curtsy, carefully taking the skirt of your uniform between your fingers and raising it slightly. You would have liked to ask her some questions, but that would have been unseemly. A maid does not ask questions unless the Senyora invites her to. But the Senyora said something you did not understand, and you would have liked to ask her about it. There was a mystery contained in just two words – "milk" and "sisters" – and, as the years went by, you came to the conclusion that it was impossible to fathom.

You could recall many scenes revealing Senyor Estanislau's great passion for his daughter. The most vivid of them always brings back the song in a foreign language he used to sing to her before bedtime, which is why you believed for so many years it was a lullaby. The caprices of memory want you to see them both now, by the fireplace one cold afternoon at the end of winter. Outside the windows it is dark, and inside the house the gaslights are trembling in fright. Senyor Estanislau is in the rocking chair, with his daughter in his lap, as floppy as if she has swooned, her head resting on his right shoulder. He's rocking in time to the song he is singing, softly, softly, as if to chase away some dark shadow spreading through his heart.

> *Bella figlia dell'amore,*
> *schiavo son de' vezzi tuoi.*
> *Con un detto, un detto solo,*
> *tu puoi le mie pene,*
> *le mie pene consolar.**

Càndida has been feverish for a couple of days. The city has just been scourged by terrible epidemics of yellow fever and cholera, leaving thousands dead. The sight of the carts coming to the houses to collect corpses by the dozen is something nobody can ever forget. The senyors have always taken precautions and thought they had escaped, but Càndida suddenly took a turn for the worse, and her father is desperate when he thinks of the child's beloved body piled on the cart, trundling up the mountain, leaving him, never to return. They have gone to get the doctor, but while they are waiting for him to arrive, Senyor Estanislau has taken the little girl from her bed, all wrapped up in a blanket, and is embracing her, singing very softly that song he always sings. He is so desperate that he believes that, as long as she is in his arms, she will not be taken. He sometimes stops to wipe away an escaping tear, but then he recovers and starts singing again.

Senyor Estanislau remained at the sick child's side twenty-four days, talking to her, singing to her, reading her stories, scrupulously checking every morsel of food she was served and giving her sips of water, until he finally saw she was getting better. Happiness returned, the shadow in Senyor Estanislau's heart shrank and shrank until it totally disappeared, and the little girl opened her eyes wide and said, "Papa, sing me that song."

And her father, in his very best baritone, returned to the quartet from *Rigoletto*.

Bella figlia dell'amo-o-o-o... o-o-o... o-or-e-e!

For some people, Senyoreta Càndida made her real debut in society a few years later, the evening when you saw her leaving the house, dressed like a princess, to go to the Liceu. Don Estanislau was a shareholder in the opera house when nobody in Barcelona believed that the project would flourish, and he therefore considered himself to be a rightful owner, and had decided a long time previously exactly when his little flower would sit in his box and impress everyone. He had chosen the first performance of the 1861–62 season, the year Càndida turned ten, the perfect age for her first acquaintance with opera and the society that applauded it.

Her age and the season were the only two points on which Senyor Estanislau and Senyora Hortènsia agreed. They were at loggerheads over everything else, starting with the most important matter, the repertoire. It happened that Senyora Hortènsia was completely blinded by her passion for Rossini and Donizetti, and she even championed Mozart – to whom Don Estanislau referred as "that idiot" – and, as mother of the child, she would have been very pleased if her little girl could enjoy her first night at the Liceu. She thought, therefore, that something light to make her smile would be ideal, for example *Il barbiere di Siviglia* or *L'elisir d'amore*. Nevertheless, Don Estanislau wanted his daughter to make her debut with a "real" opera, one with a moral and full of epic calamities, because, in his view, "you do not go to the opera to laugh or to see how modern ladies die in bed". He was so determined that the evening should be the way he wanted it to be that he pulled strings to ensure that the opening night of the fourteenth season of the Gran Teatre del Liceu should feature *Rigoletto* – his favourite – or perhaps *Anna Bolena* or *Norma*, but bad luck won the day and he was to be greatly disappointed.

One night, four months before the child's birthday and moments before the curtain rose in the Liceu, a light which had not been properly extinguished set fire to one of the costume storerooms. There was no nearby water supply and the material was highly inflammable. The blaze spread rapidly and, half an hour later, had completely consumed the most European of all the fads Barcelona had ever had. All that remained were smoking ruins and mournful sighs.

The day after the disaster, Senyor Estanislau, as a full member of the board of shareholders, took part in a meeting more doleful than a funeral, but at which important decisions were made. First: ask Queen Isabel II for money to reconstruct the building, because, after all, the first opera house had not been named the "Dramatic Philharmonic Lyceum of H.M. Queen Isabel" for nothing. Second: set up a reconstruction committee and determine the amount that each of the proprietors should pay before work began. Third: send the architect Mestres to Paris, London and Brussels – all three cities with their own experience of charred opera houses – in search of inspiration, after which he was to hurry back home and get to work as soon as possible. Senyor Estanislau's eagerness to take his little girl to the opera cost him fifteen thousand pesetas, which he was all too happy to pay. There were many obstacles. The Queen refused to donate a single peseta towards the rebuilding project, alleging a "depletion of funds allocated to public calamities"; in order to insulate the stalls from the underground installations they had to pay an extremely expensive French architect; despite their asking to be exempted, they had to shell out astronomically high customs fees for the incredibly expensive materials; and a thousand and one other problems had to be dealt with. Twelve months later, the brand-new Liceu was ready for its inaugural season, the shareholders had good reason to be proud of their initiative, and Senyor Estanislau entered the main vestibule and climbed the stairs arm in arm with his little cultured pearl.

Once seated and waiting for the members of the orchestra to finish tuning, the Turulls discussed the latest news with the occupants of the adjoining box, the chocolatier Gabriel Sampons and his delightful wife. "Do you know what that fat Bourbon is doing sitting at the top of the stairs, as if she deserved to be there?" whispered Don Estanislau Turull, referring to a bust of Isabel II, which was even uglier than the Queen herself. And Don Gabriel murmured, "Do not worry, the way things are nowadays, someone will certainly topple her from her pedestal."

Their wives were concerned with other matters. "Do you not think you can see the dresses of the ladies in the dress circle much better now? They must be using brighter gaslights," remarked Donya Hortènsia.

"No, that is not the reason. If you look carefully, you will see they have moved the boxes forward. I think it is a good idea, because they have finally understood what we ladies are here to do! After all, we come to the Liceu to look at the fashions and get ideas!"

The season catered to everyone's tastes. Bellini, Verdi, Rossini and Donizetti, most of them with two operas each. *Rigoletto* was programmed, but second on the list, and Senyor Turull's patience was running out. He had waited too long as it was. He took his little girl to sit in his box on the solemn opening night, 20th April, despite the fact that the work in question was *I puritani*, Vincenzo Bellini's historical drama which Don Estanislau found boring and with far too many Scots for his taste. It did not really matter, though. The main thing was to be there. There would be plenty of time for *barbieres* and *sonnambulas*, and the poor jittery father was dying of impatience. In the end, however, he was not very pleased with his little darling. She found the battles between Cromwell's Puritans and the monarchist Cavaliers, stalwarts of the House of Stuart, intolerably tedious, and not even the heroine's hysterical madness could relieve the boredom. Before the end of Act One, she withdrew to the anteroom, stretched out on the settee and went to sleep. She would have remained there until the next morning if her mother had not woken her up and obliged her to make an appearance, at least to applaud the artistes.

Hence the little girl's debut at the opera was a disaster in her father's eyes. As for her mother, it exactly what one might expect of an evening without Rossini or Donizetti.

Don Giovanni

At the age of sixty-five and still struggling to turn his daughter into an opera lover, Senyor Estanislau was a vigorous man of youthful spirit, only too willing to talk with anyone about the two matters in which he believed even more than his own life: the benefits of technology and the desirability of the Liceu's programming *Rigoletto* every season. It was fortunate for him that the occupant of the neighbouring box was a man as patient as Gabriel Sampons, the second-generation scion of an eminent lineage of chocolatiers and proprietor of an establishment which, in Carrer de Manresa on the corner of Carrer de l'Argenteria, declared in very large letters on its façade, "The best desire of all is desire for Sampons chocolate."

While the ladies did their best to understand the arias, the two men made the most of their nights at the opera to discuss their various interests. Senyor Estanislau, more extrovert by nature, had Senyor Antoni's head pounding like a drum with his descriptions – sparing no detail, right down to the last piston, crank or spring – of the latest devices it had occurred to him to design. Don Gabriel listened, bored stiff, without understanding a word and making no comment. When Turull finished his disquisition and asked him how the business was going, he merely answered, "Getting by, Turull, getting by."

The problem was that there was nothing in the world that did not spark Senyor Estanislau's lively curiosity, including the entire chocolate-making process, which he was only now discovering. He was constantly asking for more details. At first, Don Gabriel tried to spare himself lengthy explanations, begging, "Please, Turull, let me think about something else. Do not be so tiresome."

Soon, however, the chocolatier discovered that if he wished to put an end to the matter, he would have to stop resisting. Going to the opera became a form of martyrdom for the obliging Senyor Sampons, who had to sit near the outside of his box so as to be closer to Turull in his. What with the onslaught of questions there was no way he could hear anything, and he was thus deprived of all the emotions of ill-starred love or direst betrayal. Turull made machines, but the man himself was a question machine.

Mozart was programmed that night. Don Estanislau was sitting sketching in a corner, drawing, gloomy and distracted, until he noticed that they were serving hot chocolate on stage. He looked at the programme notes and then understood: the "extremely libertine young man", Don Giovanni, wanted to pamper his guests. Don Estanislau leant closer to Don Antoni, asking him in a whisper what he thought about this tribute to chocolatiers.

"It is very pleasing, Turull, of course," his good-natured neighbour answered, starting to fear that his interlude of calm had come to an end.

He was not wrong. The scene triggered a barrage of questions.

"Did you not tell me that you have to roast the cocoa first, Sampons?"

"Yes, that is right."

"And then?"

"The beans are husked," Sampons says as succinctly as he can, hoping that brevity will deter this glutton for questions.

"By machine?"

"By hand is better."

"Why is that?"

"Because people prefer it of course!"

"Do you mean they can tell the difference?"

"Indeed they can! Do you think people are stupid?"

"Well, a machine would do it quicker."

"I would not disagree."

"And then?"

"Then it has to be ground. That is the most important phase."

"Using some kind of machine?"

"Not in my establishment, Turull."

"How is it done then?"

"Grindstones, naturally."

"With traction?…"

"Flesh and blood. Three strapping apprentices."

"A machine would do that much better too."

"That may be the case. But machines cannot think or solve problems."

"For the moment, Sampons, for the moment!… Then all the ingredients are mixed together, I suppose."

"Not many ingredients, Turull. Chocolate is not made like it used to be. Tastes are much simpler now. What people want today are simplicity and quality."

"Then what are the—"

"Cocoa, sugar and cinnamon, Turull. Anyone who uses more than that does not know about chocolate. Take good note of that: cocoa, sugar and cinnamon."

"So this is the chocolate that makes desire so good, according to your slogan."

"You are correct, sir."

"Do you have to mix it for long?"

"As long as possible."

"And do your workers not complain?"

"Bitterly!"

"You see? I should make you a machine."

"I have found a solution to the problem."

"Ah yes? What?"

"Any worker who complains too much is sent packing."

"Good God! What antiquated methods!"

"Antiquated? Whatever do you mean? My father, who got onto his knees and ground the beans in front of the client, then took the grindstone home with him, was antiquated?"

Onstage, the manservant Leporello was tallying up the number of women Don Giovanni had seduced.

In Italia seicento e quaranta,
in Lamagna duecento e trent'una;
cento in Francia, in Turchia novant'una;
ma in Ispagna son già mille e tre.

The ladies liked the tenor's voice, but found he gesticulated too much. Turull's daughter was doing the sums to check whether the feat was technically possible, and how many women a man would have to conquer every month before the age of thirty: eleven, according to her calculations, 3.4 per week. She was flabbergasted by her discovery, at a loss for words.

Senyor Estanislau, mulling over what he had just been told, shook his head.

"But Don Gabriel, this cannot be! We are in the middle of the nineteenth century! A man like you! Let me make you a machine and you will soon change your mind…"

Don Gabriel flapped his hands in the air, shooing away the idea. "No, no, please do not talk to me about machines, Turull!"

"If you had machines you would produce twenty times more chocolate!"

"And what do you suggest I should do with so much chocolate? Drown in it? I cannot tell my customers to eat twenty times more!"

"Then go out and find new customers. You only need the means of transport."

"I have that. Two mules. They go up to Gràcia twice a week."

"Mules? What you need is trains! And instead of going to Gràcia you should be going to Paris, Madrid and London."

"Enough, my friend enough! You are not in your right mind."

"It is the future, Sampons, the future riding on a steam engine, or a diesel motor and electric pistons. If you do not climb on board, it will run over you."

Don Gabriel Sampons was flustered at the mere thought of it. Trying to silence this man who was rattling him and depriving him of his operas, he took the path of least resistance. "As for the future, you will have to speak with my son, who is coming back from Switzerland next week. He is young and still believes in this new-fangled nonsense. Now, Turull, please be good enough to let me listen."

But it was too late for Don Gabriel. He did not understand anything, for all his efforts in reading the programme notes and trying to get some idea of what he had missed. When the Commendatore appeared in the last scene, now white from head to foot and turned into a statue, he exclaimed, "But that man, was he not killed? What is he doing onstage?"

The ladies, very vexed by his interruption at such a dramatic moment, just when everything was about to end as they believed it should, shushed him into silence. Onstage, the chorus was making it very clear that such bad men can only come to a terrible end. Don Gabriel peered again and again at the programme notes, trying to work out what was happening and muttering, "This opera makes no sense whatsoever!"

The ladies and young Càndida applauded enthusiastically. Don Gabriel abstained and Don Estanislau agreed with him, "I told you this Mozart has a screw loose."

Senyoreta Càndida preferred Mozart to Bellini, but she liked Verdi most of all, as did a large part of the Liceu audiences. You know this because she told you everything in those days. For example, she said that nothing looked good on Senyora Sampons, because she was like a plump little quail in September, and it was such a shame to see a ruby necklace on that old neck with a dewlap like a cow's! She told you, too, that in a few weeks she was going to meet the Sampons' son, who was coming home after two years studying Heaven knows what in Switzerland, and that Senyora Hortènsia and the plump little quail did nothing but chirp about this, repeating the same thing over and over again: oh, Candideta, you are so lucky because you are going to have someone your own age to talk to at the opera, and you will certainly get on very well, what with all the things you have in common. And when she asked what they had in common, the two clucky mothers said education, coming from a good family, a box at the Liceu, youth, a future... The young lady, understanding the intentions of the two mothers, wrinkled her nose and thought, *That means nothing in common at all.*

When they came home after the opera, Donya Hortènsia kept on and on with her maddening paean to Antoni's virtues. He was such a good-looking young man, so intelligent, hardworking and, naturally, after spending so much time away from home, a very good conversationalist, so he would tell Càndida lots of very amusing and wonderful things – and, who knows, maybe something more than a beautiful friendship would grow between the two young people. "Are you not yearning to meet him, my little one? We are counting the minutes until we can see you together, and we have a feeling that, oh dear, I do not know!... Have you thought about whether you would like to sit in our box or theirs?"

As far as Senyoreta Càndida was concerned, all this boded very ill. She sensed that her mother and the chocolate-monger quail were plotting something, but she was only fifteen and she had birds of quite another feather fluttering in her head. She was not going to be impressed by the first chocolate monger to turn up from Switzerland. She was not remotely interested in Antoni Sampons. She was sure he would be as boring as his parents, always prattling on about chocolate, or presenting her with boxes of the stuff and never missing the chance to spout, "The best desire of all is desire for Sampons chocolate." Senyoreta Càndida did not want a fiancé and if her mother and the plump quail were too insistent, she had already decided her plan of resistance: she would swoon in dismay into the arms of Senyor Estanislau, after which she would shed a few timely tears, sobbing and telling her father that she did not want to leave his side. Never, never! She believed that would be enough to ensure that all the plotting of the two ladies would melt away like a sugar lump in a glass of hot water. No, no, she wanted nothing to do with men who smelt like chocolate, who thought of nothing but their work and making money, and who worked so hard they never had time to spend it. Ugh, no!

What Senyoreta Càndida really would have liked – and you are the only one she told – was to find a Don Giovanni, like the one in the opera by this Mozart, whom nobody at the Liceu had ever heard of. "What a man, Aurora! He is so good at telling beautiful lies! Do you not think that being the lover of a man like that, even if it is only for one night, is much better than marrying a chocolate monger? I think it would be sublime. Imagine being the woman deceived by such a villain, a scoundrel, a real man smelling of wine, sweat and all those other women he has forgotten about when you fall into his arms." You were scandalized on hearing these words, and thought that Senyoreta Càndida was of unsound mind. You heard her out with respect, unprotesting, as you had been taught, but deep inside you did not know what to think, except that the little Turull heiress had become quite unhinged with all those strange ideas of hers.

Sometimes, though rarely, you dared to ask questions. Càndida was different from her mother who had instilled so much respect in you. Although you and Càndida had been raised together, the prudent and indispensable distances were always observed. When you were very small you played together in the courtyard on sunny afternoons. Sometimes you caught a fish for her in the pond where the fountain splashed, the two of you laughing and laughing as you watched it flip-flopping on the tiles before you put it back in the water and saved its life. When you were a little older, you sewed or read the Scriptures together. You recited the rosary in unison and read aloud from the same books. Without you, Senyoreta Càndida would have died of boredom. Without her, you would never have left the kitchen. Sometimes Senyora Hortènsia gave you a hand-me-down, some dress that the little heiress had grown out of but that was invariably too big for you, as she was always chubbier than you, but it did not matter, because her clothes were so pretty. Or she would let you borrow for a night some old doll that her little girl had tired of. As you grew up, your roles were more clearly defined, in keeping with the express wish of Senyora Hortènsia. When you both turned fourteen, she decided that, thenceforth, you would be the young lady's personal maid. You were very pleased by this appointment. It gave you a clearly defined position and allowed you to be useful.

Your new duties meant that you were the first and last person Senyoreta Càndida saw every day, her confidante and perhaps, ever so slightly, her friend. You woke her in the morning, helped her out of bed, got her breakfast, chose the clothes she was to wear, plaited her hair, went promenading with her punctually at noon, listened to her with infinite patience, sat beside her in the church, brought her needlework to her in the afternoon, turned on the lights when she could not see well, fetched her missal and rosary, draped her shoulders with a shawl when she was cold, unplaited and brushed her hair, slid the bed warmer between her sheets, made sure her candlestick was nearby, read aloud to her and, when she was dropping off to sleep, you said goodnight, blew out the small flame and withdrew, happily thanking all the saints in heaven for your good fortune.

One day you plucked up enough courage to ask Senyoreta Càndida the question you had been musing on for so long.

"Senyoreta, do you know who our wet nurse was?"

Càndida had to think about this. "No. Why do you ask?"

"No special reason. I was just wondering."

"You are a strange one, Aurora. You are curious about the oddest things. Why do you not ask my mother?"

"I do not wish to bother her with such trifles."

"I cannot see why she would be bothered."

"It does not matter. It is just a silly idea."

"Oh, Aurora, Auroreta, you are too cautious. Do not worry. I shall ask her."

The answer came some days later. "Mother says she cannot remember the name of our wet nurse. She only knows that she lived in Hortes de Sant Pau and had a little baby. That is the end of the mystery, Auroreta! Are you happy now?"

You were not satisfied with this explanation. "So, while she was feeding us, did she live here in the house?"

Càndida was very surprised by your question. "I did not ask about that."

"I think it is important."

"Ve-e-ry we-e-ell. I shall ask her again. But why do you want to know?"

"There is no reason. I was just wondering. Are you never plagued by questions? When there are things you absolutely have to know, whatever the consequences."

"Oh yes! That certainly happens to me. For example, I want to know how to kiss a man. Do not tell my mother!"

You blushed and did not know what to say. She laughed at you for being such a ninny.

"Have you ever kissed a man, Aurora?"

"Of course not."

"Or has a man ever touched you?"

"What do you mean?"

"My mother says that, below stairs, where you live, things are done differently. Faster or something like that. She says that you people do not feel the same things as us. Do you think she is right?"

Now you were the one who was wide-eyed.

"I think feelings are the same for everyone, Senyoreta."

"Who knows?" the young lady mused. "Anyway, you and I cannot comment because we are still untried."

Once again, the blush rose on your cheeks, but Càndida was unperturbed. She talked very naturally of matters you would not dare to think about.

After a few days, she offered you another answer. "Mother is tired of being questioned about the wet nurse and says she will answer no more questions, Aurora. But she told me that this woman, whose name she cannot recall, never lived here with us. She had her own place and came and went every day in her brother's trap. Then she left when her work was done. Are you satisfied now?"

Your face showed that you were not satisfied. You were still brooding about the matter, and rightly so, because something did not make sense.

"If she came by trap from Hortes de Sant Pau, it must have taken at least an hour," you say, talking mainly to yourself. "It must have taken an hour or more to feed the two of us, maybe an hour and a half. How could she do that and keep going backwards and forwards? Do you not find it strange?"

"It seems she had a family, Aurora. She went off to them and then she came back. What I think is strange is that you are spending so much time fretting about this. That is enough."

But it was not enough for you. Every day you came up with new explanations.

"Senyoreta Càndida. You know what we were saying about the wet nurse… What if she was someone who lived in this house? I think it is the only explanation that—"

Senyoreta Càndida had run out of patience. "I told you very clearly, Aurora, I am tired of your questions! My mother does not want to hear any more of this and neither do I. Leave it! I am not going to say this again."

She was very angry and you did not know why. You told her you would leave it, but it was not true. You asked everyone you could: the cooks, the coachman, the housekeeper. Nobody remembered ever having seen any wet nurse in the house, or any trap drawing up at the door. The coachman was eighty-six years old and his memory was not to be relied on, and only one of the cooks was working in the house in the years about which you were interrogating people, like some kind of police commissioner. She made it very clear that, in those days, she had so much work that she could not talk about anything except whether the saucepans had been put on to boil because she never left the kitchen.

"But the wet nurse had to eat," you said, continuing the interrogation. "And wet nurses are known for eating a lot and having all kinds of whims. If you had seen her you would have to remember her."

"Yes, girl, you're right. Those wet nurses carry on like duchesses! Pity the poor soul who has to serve them!" the cook exclaimed.

"So?"

"So, I do not know what to tell you, Aurora. Locked up down here as I was, I never saw a soul. I never served any food for any wet nurse. And might one know why you are asking so many questions?"

You did not say anything. Neither did you offer any explanation that Thursday afternoon when you went for a walk and, as if by accident, ended up in Hortes de Sant Pau. It was silly of you, but you asked people if they knew a former wet nurse who perhaps used to live there with her family, and who had a brother who took her into the city in a trap, and a child who would be about your age, and all the details you could come up with. In the end, you were none the wiser. Nobody could tell you anything, or offer the slightest clue. That was very rash, Aurora. Whatever came over you? As if there were not hordes of people living in Hortes de Sant Pau.

Norma

We shall let some time go by. The world has kept turning since that opening night of *Don Giovanni*. Don Gabriel has suddenly died after several hours of chest pains, and his son, Antoni, has taken over the business. He is very young – having just turned twenty-one – but thanks to his travels and studies abroad he is quite well equipped and, most important, is very keen to work and highly ambitious. He is thinking that his first step will be to mechanize the workshop of his ancestors and turn it into a proper industry. In keeping with the old tradition of Catalan industrial lineages, Antoni Sampons is of a generation whose turn it is to shine, ensure that the family name becomes even more illustrious and make a fortune. He must puff up like a sponge cake in the oven. His heirs, however, are destined for ruin and suspension of payments, but we shall see soon enough how things turn out in this particular case.

As Don Gabriel Sampons had foreseen, Estanislau Turull, an old man with a young man's soul, and Antoni Sampons, a young man with the ways of an old man, got on very well. Ten minutes after being introduced and having got the formalities out of the way, they were talking about what they had to talk about.

"So you make machines…" the newcomer began.

"And I would make more if they let me."

"You have my congratulations. It is about time someone in this country set about inventing something."

"Just a moment, young man. There is a long tradition in this country of madmen like myself. The other day I heard about a chocolatier who invented a machine to grind the beans and make chocolate for eating. He did that last century. I believe he was the first. A man of progress! And he was from Barcelona as much as you are, as much as I am, and the geese in the cloister of the Cathedral of the Holy Cross and St Eulalia."

"Did the machine work well? Does it still exist?"

"Nobody has any clear idea of what it was like. It vanished without trace."

"Really?"

"Not as much as a sketch remains."

"Is the name of the inventor known?"

"Fernandes."

"Dammit, that is bad luck. With such an ordinary name he will be difficult to track down."

"A needle in a haystack."

The young Antoni was delighted with all this. He was longing to be part of the development of technology in Barcelona. He had brought ideas from the most advanced countries of Europe, for example adding milk to the chocolate to make it sweeter and smoother on the palate. Don Estanislau, very enthusiastic about all these chocolate-flavoured innovations for which he saw a wonderful future, thought about them day and night.

In the early years of this shared project, their conversations were insufferable.

"The problem is the husks, Turull. They never fall where they are supposed to fall. You have to do something about it."

Or: "I need the heat to be turned up or down when I decide, and not when your machine decrees, Turull!"

Don Estanislau was bursting with enthusiasm. He loved refractory machines, because he was even more iron-willed than they were.

These were times of sweeping innovations. Young Sampons decided that he had to travel to Cuba in person in order to supervise the cocoa plantations and decide the best bean for his products, which aspired to excellence for the first time since his grandfather opened the shop in Carrer de Manresa. He then embarked on his endless travels, roaming the world, changing routes over the years and with the upheavals of history: Fernando Pó, Turkey, the north of Morocco, Ghana… He also travelled through Europe, always attentive to what the competition was up to and, while he was at it, garnering new ideas. It was after one of these journeys that he had the inspiration which would change everything. He was so anxious to see it working that, no sooner had he landed than he called his old colleague and – by then – friend to inform him of the marvel.

"The secret is stirring, my friend! Stirring non-stop, with zest and zeal for at least three days. You cannot imagine the difference. The chocolate ends up as sweet as honey and smooth as velvet. Make me a machine that can stir this long and without losing a beat, and I shall fill it with a product that will make us rich!"

Turull pondered his machine, after which he made it and fiddled with it until it worked to perfection. Young Sampons was more than accurate in his prediction. His chocolate inflamed people's desire to eat more.

While he was mechanizing his business, Antoni Sampons was making great progress in another, much more complicated endeavour: convincing his partner's daughter to marry him.

He had to overcome many obstacles, especially in the beginning when he was left to his own devices. Or at least he had to manage without the help of his future father-in-law. It was most inconvenient that they had not yet invented a machine for seducing young ladies.

Senyoreta Càndida was the last piece the young chocolatier needed to slot into the jigsaw puzzle of the perfect future he had planned. But she was enjoying treating him with contempt, denying him even the tiniest spark of hope. It was a kind of game she started playing the first time they met at the Liceu, under the beady-eyed scrutiny of the two mothers. As Càndida had foreseen, Antoni Sampons brought her a box of chocolates. She reeled off the formalities of gratitude, praised the contents of the box, invited the ladies to help themselves and then set it aside as if she had forgotten about it. She spent the whole evening in her seat, pretending to be engrossed by what was happening on the stage – some problem between William Tell and a few Austrian soldiers – without as much as a glance at Antoni.

On two occasions, making the most of the intervals, he tried to engage her in conversation. The first time he offered a not-at-all brief introduction to all the works of Rossini he had seen in the opera houses of several European cities, until he finally got to *Guglielmo Tell* – and, yes, he said it like that, in Italian – which he considered the best of all, although slightly too long. Seeing the scant success of this effort, young Sampons tried again later, this time availing himself of a number of true connoisseur's anecdotes. Did she know, perchance, that Rossini composed most of his best works for his lover, the singer Isabella Colbran, whom he subsequently married? Or perhaps she was unaware that he retired at the age of thirty-seven, at the height of his fame, and no one knew why. Càndida heard him out with a fixed smile, glassy gaze, nodding slightly as if she were fascinated by what he was saying. However, seizing the first possible chance, she slipped away and returned to her seat. The chocolatier was totally unnerved.

The next morning, she was awake and waiting for you, so she could tell you all about something she could only share with you, in fits of giggles. And you wanted to know what had happened.

"A conversation with a candlestick would be much more interesting," she said.

"Then what did you do?"

"I avoided him the whole evening."

"So you do not want him as your suitor?"

"As a what?... Ugh! No, of course not."

"Well, you have acted very properly, Senyoreta. If you do not want someone to be interested in you, it is best to make it clear as soon as you can."

"Auroreta, you do not understand anything. What I want is for him to lose his head over me."

"What?"

"You are such a silly goose, Aurora. Do you not know that the best way to drive a man mad is to show him all the disdain you possibly can?"

You were shaken, as you always were when Senyoreta Càndida talked like this. Yes, you were shaken and did not understand anything.

"But why do you want him to go mad? Do you like him now?"

"Not at all! I cannot bear him! He only talks about dead composers."

"I do not understand, Senyoreta."

"I like the way he looks at me. Do you not like it when men look at you? Does it not make you feel important?"

That was one of the many questions you had never even considered. Men looking at you? No, not at you. You were certain of that. They would never look at you. And if they did, you would not feel important. People like you do not know how to feel important, even if you had the chance.

"And have you thought about what would happen if he asked for your hand in marriage?" Now you are playing your part as devil's advocate. "Your mother is very favourably impressed by Antoni Sampons."

Càndida shrugged. "I shall have to marry somebody, I suppose."

You were not mistaken. Senyora Hortènsia was delighted with her daughter's suitor. He was the living embodiment of every virtue. She was therefore unable to understand her little girl's behaviour and was angry with her all day long.

"Can you not be a little more agreeable with the poor young man? Have you not noticed how dejected he looks whenever he is near you? You hardly glanced at his chocolates the other night and, if it had not been for me, you would have left them in the anteroom. Is it so difficult for you to talk to him, or to be pleasant and attentive?"

"He was talking about Rossini! What do I know about Rossini?"

"You do not have to know everything in order to be able to talk a little. If you do not know what to say, you only have to agree with him. Men are always very happy when we agree with them."

Senyoreta Càndida wrinkled her nose and pouted like a little girl. A sulky little girl. Senyora Hortènsia saw fit to continue with her sermon.

"Do you perchance imagine that there are a lot of suitors like him? That young man is a treasure! He has everything. He is handsome, clever and wealthy, and has ways of keeping busy. That in itself is a great blessing, because men who have no ways of keeping busy get wicked ideas and either beat their wives or run away with a chorus girl. You may not be able to appreciate his virtues, my girl, but this is because you know nothing of the world. I can assure you that if you do not act now, someone else will come along and snatch him away from under your nose, and you will be left in the lurch and as lonely as can be."

"Well, perhaps you are right, but I do not want a suitor!"

"Ah, very well, then I shall go to the Sant Vicenç de Jonqueres convent tomorrow and ask if they have a place for you."

"If that is what you wish, go then!"

"I most certainly shall!"

Their arguments became so heated that Don Estanislau always had to intervene in his capacity as peacemaker.

"Do not take it so much to heart, my dear," he advised his wife in that beguiling voice of his, which would have tamed a lion. "The problem is that our little girl is still too young to be thinking about husbands and marriage. If the Sampons boy is sufficiently intelligent, he will realize this and will wait until she is ready to listen to him. Moreover, an innocent woman is a treasure that a wise man knows how to appreciate."

His reasoning was balsam for Senyora Hortènsia's wounds and soothed her fears. But the wounds were always opened up again when they went to the opera.

Young Antoni Sampons launched into his musical disquisitions because the poor boy believed he would thus dazzle the object of his desire. He had inherited his mother's passion for music. She had begun taking him to the Liceu and the Teatre Principal at a very early age, but in the years he spent abroad he had endeavoured to expand this love for music, shape it and refine it into such sophistication that he became a complete and utter bore. He knew the whole classical repertoire in minute detail, had firm opinions about half a dozen of Mozart's operas which had never even been performed in Barcelona, and was well informed about all the most popular composers of the day, Meyerbeer or Verdi, for example. He could even expound on Wagner, and had friends who had attended the premiere of *Tannhäuser* in Paris. Indeed, he was waiting for the moment when stages all around the world would render Wagner the homage he deserved.

In the box at the Liceu, the only one who really listened to the operatic dissertations of Antoni Sampons was his future mother-in-law, not only because she felt the need to compensate him in some way for Càndida's churlishness, but because she really was interested in everything he said. The moment he opened his mouth, Antoni became a boundless fount of wisdom. He knew singers, conductors and styles, could identify every last thing that tenors and sopranos did with their voices, told them in advance what the best parts of the opera were and, in the intervals, admired the security of the tenor's high notes, or the power and lustre of the soprano's middle range. They no longer went to see anything without seeking Antoni's advice or some anecdote related with the work. And Antoni always exerted himself to please his small audience, which included Càndida, who paid no attention or cast her bored gaze everywhere but at him.

One evening, just before *Norma* was to begin, there was an announcement that the soprano Caterina Mas-Porcell, who was cast as the virgin priestess Adalgisa, had laryngitis, and that her understudy, a soprano with an Italian name nobody had ever heard of – Marietta Lombardi – would be singing in her stead. Senyora Hortènsia asked the young expert what he thought about this understudy and he – a great admirer of Senyora Mas-Porcell – indignantly responded that he had to confess that he had never heard of her.

The performance was one surprise after another for Antoni Sampons. This Marietta had a light soprano voice with incredible treble notes and prodigious phrasing. Everyone was astounded. She was young, very pretty, and performed the role with all the aplomb of a veteran, even though – as they discovered in the interval – this was her debut as Adalgisa and the first time she had sung away from her birthplace, Padua. Antoni Sampons was so impressed that he could not stop singing her praises. The ladies nodded sagely, but they had not really noticed such a great difference.

When the curtain came down, the Liceu audience was in thrall to this beautiful, angel-faced young woman with a wonderful voice. Even the critic Joan Cortada applauded enthusiastically. The impresario breathed a sigh of relief and the soprano, Carolina Briol, who had sung the role of Norma, looked sideways at the newcomer, wishing she could strangle her. Crowned with success, the new star basked in her audience's admiration.

That very night, the inexperienced Marietta Lombardi, who could scarcely believe what was happening, received a spectacular bunch of red roses complete with a card on which was written *"Dal vostro devoto ammiratore, Antoni Sampons"*.

The next day, Antoni Sampons enquired after the health of Senyora Mas-Porcell, and, on learning that she had not yet recovered from her laryngitis, did something he had never done in his life. He went to the Liceu alone. With the expression of an utter neophyte, he sat in his box marvelling once again at the res, mis and even the fas of the lovely Italian. At interval, after very careful planning on his part, Senyoreta Lombardi received a special box of Sampons chocolates, whereupon she asked someone to translate the slogan it proclaimed on the lid. When she opened the box a card fell out. In the most impeccable penmanship it invited her to dinner that night. She sent an affirmative answer to the author of the note, and the show went on.

Antoni Sampons spoke Italian quite well, that is, when he wanted to, because, in Barcelona's social circles, he was known to be quite taciturn. That night he was jubilant and ready to talk the hind legs off a donkey, since he was convinced that inviting a lady he did not know out to dinner was a way of demonstrating that he was a man. He stood in the vestibule smoking, as he waited for Marietta. When he kissed her hand and offered her his arm, he was not at all concerned that somebody might see them. They strolled along La Rambla and then to the Hotel Colón, where he had reserved a table and – just in case – a suite.

There were several familiar faces in the Hotel Colón, as was usually the case, but he did not care. He was a young man, a free man and of a European spirit. He had nothing to fear. Marietta Lombardi, aged twenty-three, was two years older than him and she had round, perfectly located breasts that were even more thrilling than her treble notes. They ate with gusto, not turning up their noses at anything. Offstage, she seemed a simple soul, very different from what he had been told about artistes.

They talked about music all evening, and when, at five in the morning, she said it was very late and that she would have to go, Antoni was so overjoyed with everything that he completely forgot about the suite (for which he had paid a fortune). He had spent the whole time talking about opera and did not regret it for a moment.

When he arrived home with his tails all crumpled and a simpleton's smile on his face, he went straight to bed. He had no idea that his mother had heard the grievous news hours earlier and was locked in her room crying her heart out.

Senyoreta Càndida heard about it from Senyora Sampons, who was telling Senyora Hortènsia what had happened. She was not asking for help, but had to unburden herself because she was "ill with worry". The chocolatier's widow was a cunning woman who knew how to make the best of the few minutes when the men went to get refreshments and to whisper, with the urgency that secrets require, all the details.

"Of course you can see that Antoni is acting strangely. He is not himself! You know that pretty little Italian who was the understudy for our Mas-Porcell in *Norma* last spring – well, my boy is infatuated with her. I thought it would be a fleeting thing, but these artistes are worldly and my Antoni is a very good catch. Need I say more? He started to send her gifts. Flowers, chocolates, some pieces of jewellery and Heaven knows what else. He took her to the most expensive places in Barcelona and did not care if people saw them, which was very reckless of him. The worst of it is not that he is so moonstruck, because, after all, my boy is a man now, and you know what men are like. The worst thing, my dear Hortènsia, is that it is an enduring infatuation and I am starting to think about those long illnesses that end on the deathbed. I fear it might have been going on too long now for anything to be done about it. He got it into his head to go off to Paris, and then we found out that she is going to be there too, singing whatever it is she has to sing. It seems that the little Italian has come a long way since she first sang in Barcelona, and now everyone wants her. The contracts are literally raining down on her, from all the best theatres in Europe. Oh dear, I do hope they ask her to go to Argentina. You know what these people are like, always flitting around from one place to another, with their never-ending performances, rehearsals and recitals, with all the fanfare, musicians, tributes and admirers… and the charms of the young lady are very considerable, and even more so when she is dressed up as that priestess. I am so distressed by this whole situation that I am afraid that one day Antoni is going to come home and tell me he has married her, and then it will be impossible to do anything. Or worse, that she is expecting his child. Oh, horror!"

Senyora Hortènsia covered her mouth with her hand, and tears rolled down her cheeks. This little farce might have been titled *The Lightness of the Light Soprano*, but for the two mothers it was a horrendous tragedy. Just one performance had been sufficient for this girl to shatter the cosy dreams the good ladies had of becoming in-laws. But now that they were fellow conspirators – no, that was an unseemly way of putting it when their aims were so respectable – now that they were associates – ah yes, it is soothing to have the right word for every endeavour – now that they were associates everything would end well, because it could not be otherwise.

Donya Hortènsia wasted no time before she started blaming her daughter.

"I told you, silly girl, that he would be snatched away from you. Are you satisfied now? Are you going to do something about this? Are you happy to see him parading around with that Italian and all that décolletage hanging on his arm?"

The response was so complicated that Senyoreta Càndida judged it best not to say anything. No, Heaven forbid, she was not pleased that Antoni had a lover. Yet she was happy too, because that opened up an array of exciting possibilities. She had a rival! And not just any rival! This was a battle she had to win, joining forces with the two matrons but also making a point of her own audacity in the process. She was certainly not going to permit Antoni Sampons to languish any longer in his love for that singer, Marietta Lombardi.

It was all very thrilling, although she would never confess to anyone that this was how she experienced the situation. Well, she would tell her eternal confidante. This episode had enabled her to see that, slumbering inside the tedious Sampons, there was another man, one that was capable of misbehaving, spending vast amounts of money and – so his mother thought – sowing wild oats wherever he pleased. This, in Càndida's eyes, made him an interesting person. Now she had quite another opinion of Antoni Sampons. She saw him as hers and very much worth fighting for. Thus was born the need to compete with Marietta Lombardi and, most important, to win. Naturally. She was certain she would win.

"I believe you have always been in love with Antoni Sampons," you said when Càndida had told all.

"In love? What do you mean? Have you ever been in love, Aurora?"

You shrugged, not knowing what to answer. If you had been in love, you had not noticed.

"I do not think I have either," she said. "Mother says that one must never lose one's head because of love. But I should like to. Would you like that?"

"What do you mean, lose one's head?"

"But not for just anyone! For a really villainous man, Aurora, one who would make me suffer terribly."

"Like Antoni Sampons?"

"If only it was him, Aurora. If only! Do you think he's depraved enough?" You shrugged again and she sighed, the ingenuous girl who was too young to know what she was saying.

A composed, single-minded Senyoreta Càndida went into battle. First of all, she listened carefully to everything Antoni had to say and – oh, surprise! – she found it interesting. She also started to look at him when he spoke and to respond with more than monosyllables when an answer was required. She wore dresses with lower necklines. "If I must compete with a woman dressed up as a Druid priestess, I shall have to leave a little something bare," she explained to Senyora Hortènsia, who hastened to agree with her. She took to dabbing her cleavage and shoulders with perfume before leaving home and, once at the Liceu, smiled coquettishly and constantly, as long it was at him, a fisherwoman casting her fly right in front of the nose of a splendid trout.

The results were immediately obvious. Antoni, who had recently been so aloof in her presence, started speaking to her again, invited her to walk with him to the hall of mirrors at interval and once again presented her with very large boxes of chocolates.

In one of their little strolls, during an interval of Giovanni Pacini's *Saffo*, he said, "I should like to speak with you about an episode I am ashamed of, Càndida. Some months ago, I was seeing a certain young lady and I did some truly abominable things."

"Abominable? What do you mean?"

"Excessive."

"I really cannot see you as being capable of that, Antoni," she said flashing him a captivating smile and still walking.

"You would be shocked."

"Why do you not tell me, and we shall see if you are right?"

"Never, Càndida, I could not!"

"Ah…"

"I can only say one thing."

"And what might that be?"

"Please forgive me."

"Why? You have not offended me."

"Do you really mean that?"

"And if you had, I should forgive you anyway."

"I do not believe it."

"Test me."

"What did you say?"

"Offend me."

"But, Càndida, whatever are you saying?"

Càndida stopped walking, looked at him with the eyes of a woman who knows perfectly well what she is saying and answered, "I want to have to forgive you for something. Would you do me this favour?"

Poor Sampons must have thought that women are a very odd subspecies, always doing something other than what you expect. "Would you accept me as your suitor?" he blurted out.

"Yes, but on one condition."

"Please tell me."

"I want you to lose your head over me."

"There is no need to ask for that, Càndida. I lost my head over you some time ago. Since you paid me no heed, I had to find a substitute, and she simply could not compare with you."

If Càndida had coached her suitor as to how he should respond, he could not have done better. These were exactly the words she wanted to hear, the ones her pride demanded.

"And now may I ask what you think of me?" he continued.

"You may, but I shall not answer."

"Then I shall ask you again when I am your husband."

"But I shall not answer then either."

Antoni Sampons and the Turull heiress were married in La Mercè Church on 24th May 1872. She was eighteen years old and he was twenty-two. They had just completed the year of mourning for Don Gabriel, and the business in Carrer de Manresa now boasted fifteen machines invented by Antoni's new father-in-law. They were working non-stop.

The young couple had everything: their present of youth, good looks, wealth and excellent social connections, and a future of economic growth and great promise. The output of Sampons Chocolates increased a hundredfold in the first year alone. The innovations began – starting with the milk chocolate invented by the Swiss – exports grew and Antoni kept having such felicitous ideas as giving away sets of trading cards with bars of chocolate, or commissioning well-known artists to provide him with paintings with which to embellish the tin boxes in which his assortments were presented. He also started advertising in the newspapers, which was unheard of at the time. "Sampons

Chocolates adapt to all pockets and all tastes"; "A cup of hot Sampons chocolate is the most agreeable of breakfasts"; "Try Sampons Chocolates when you tire of the rest". The business was thriving, and the young Antoni lived to make it thrive. Ten months after the wedding, a new jewel sparkled in the crown of their good fortune: a baby daughter, Antonieta.

"A year of marriage is blessed when three fill the nest," Senyora Sampons murmured contentedly, gazing at the child, in whom she could only see the features of her late husband.

Senyora Hortènsia and Senyor Estanislau, very satisfied with the way things had turned out, were convinced that, from now on, their life could only be a very beautiful path sloping gently downward through the most marvellous land-scape. They went three times a week to visit their daughter, who had taken up residence in the Sampons house in Carrer Ample as the new daughter-in-law. Here they found a whole universe: Senyora Sampons with hot chocolate and sponge fingers ready to serve, a son-in-law with a host of weird and wonderful ideas he wished to discuss with his father-in-law and you, Aurora, as happy to see them as if you were another daughter. They had their afternoon tea, went into ecstasies over the new little queen of the house, who did not take after anyone but whom they found exquisite all the same – although she was not remotely that, poor little thing – and Senyor Estanislau continued to sing *"Bella figlia dell'amore, schiavo son de' vezzi tuoi"* every time he laid eyes on Càndida, now arrayed in her married woman's dresses and her hair perfectly coiffed.

Naturally, they were also seen at the Liceu, more or less as usual. The young couple, so elegantly turned out, and with that air of having the world at their feet, was envied by everyone. They occupied the usual box, although Senyora Sampons was seen less frequently now, because it was such a bother to get into dresses that looked like curtains and to throttle herself with that ruby necklace cutting into her jowls. During the performances the two men still talked about machines – that had not changed either – while the two ladies, mother and daughter, talked about little Antonieta, or Senyora Sampons, or husbands or a thousand and one titbits that always had to be discussed because, however much they chattered, it was never enough. On the few occasions when Càndida's parents fell silent to check what was happening on the stage, they soon turned back to their child, gazing at her through innocent eyes and thanking Heaven for their good fortune, thanking and thanking because their latecomer daughter was the haven they had found after all the storms of their lives, their greatest pride and joy, the delight and comfort of their old age. Thank you, thank you, thank you.

Then came the premiere of *Il trovatore*.

Il trovatore

The original Sampons family lived in Carrer de Manresa, in the most elegant flat of the building whose ground floor was occupied by the shop which grandfather Sampons opened as soon as he arrived from Molins de Rei. Don Gabriel, however, wishing to satisfy his wife's whim, bought her an old, rather run-down mansion in Carrer Ample, carried out some very necessary although not quite sufficient renovation work and installed her there with all her relatives. The mansion was square and as solid as a rock, with cast-iron balconies overlooking the street, heavily moulded ceilings, a ballroom where nobody would ever dance and even a carriage entrance.

This was where Càndida went to live as the daughter-in-law after she married Antoni Sampons. Her quarters, which had a living room and bedroom, opened onto the street. This was one of the brightest parts of house, since it was on the second floor and the sun slipped easily through the windows as it made its way across the city. Antoni kept his own bedroom, on the same floor, near his wife's, although still separated from hers by several doors, rugs and ornamental mirrors. As was to be expected, you were assigned a small windowless room below stairs, with four grubby walls, a door on broken hinges, a bed, a wardrobe and a chamber pot. A menial's room, not that you expected anything more.

Your life went on unchanged in Carrer Ample. At half-past nine every morning you climbed the stairs, carefully balancing

the tray, which bore a dainty linen napkin, the hot chocolate –
in a white porcelain chocolate pot – the little basket with half
a dozen slices of bread and a small plate of fruit. After resting
the tray for three seconds on the table in the landing you tapped
at Senyoreta – oh sorry, you mean *Senyora* – Càndida's door.
After just two gentle knocks she called out, "Come in, Auroreta,
come in," and you entered the darkened room, the tray in your
hands and the porcelain going ting-ting. You put the tray on
the table, closed the door and opened the curtains of the high
windows, letting sunlight pour in over the furniture, rugs and
decorated wallpaper. The Senyoreta had her breakfast in bed –
because, naturally, a lady cannot get out of bed as soon as she
wakes up – and the day slowly began for her. It had begun for
you hours earlier.

Then you selected her clothes, brushed her shoes, found her
a shawl and went out with her, always punctually at twelve,
sometimes to mass or confession. In the afternoon you brought
her sewing, her afternoon tea and another shawl, the woollen
one this time, because when the sun disappeared it was very
cold indoors. In the evening you helped her to change into
her nightwear, brushed her hair, brought her a glass of water,
kept her company and passed the bed-warmer over the sheets.
Càndida was never quiet – another thing that had not changed
– although there were times when you wished she would hold
her tongue, because she often said things that made you blush.
But you had never known anyone who could make Senyoreta
Càndida stop chattering.

"Oh my goodness, Aurora, the wedding night! Every girl
should be obliged by law to have one even if she does not want
to marry. If you knew all the things I learnt in just a few hours!

So many surprises! For example, did you know that men cannot contain themselves? However well brought up they are, and for all the effort they make, poor things, they cannot help themselves and they explode like a bomb – boom! Well, I do not want to frighten you, so I should say they spurt, yes, yes, that's right, like a fountain, and then they go floppy and seem dazed. They are not themselves for a while. They look at you with owl eyes, embrace you for no reason and mumble things. That makes you feel very lethargic too. You have to make the most of this time to ask them for something you really want, and that would not be easy to get from them, because this is when they can deny you nothing. Do not just ask for the first thing that comes into your head, as that would be a waste. No, you have to plan very carefully what you are going to ask for when the time comes, because his generosity will be as great as the happiness he has just had with you. That is why it is so important to be good to them, docile and obedient, and give them what they ask for. When I went to confession the day before our wedding the priest told me, 'The most important thing, young lady, is to do everything your husband asks of you. You must deny him nothing, even if you do not like it, or do not want to, or are perhaps a little afraid, because sooner or later God will reward you.' And do you know what, Aurora? I believe that this is why women have come into the world: we are here to be rewarded, because we can satisfy this urgent need of our husbands. We let them release all that tension, and when that is done they can go about all the thousand and one details of their business with a clear head. Meanwhile, we can go out for a little fresh air, showing off the proof of our merits with... oh, I do not know, maybe a fur coat, a new brougham or a beautiful ring, for example.

"These men are very amusing creatures. I never imagined such a thing! They have a body that is very different from ours, you know. There is even a part that stands up when you look at it (and even more if you touch it). It looks like one of those red-capped mushrooms. There is no need to pull such a face, Aurora. It does not last for ever, and I do not think it hurts them, except for being a little uncomfortable maybe. Do you know what I mean? I think we women are so lucky to be all of a piece without having to put up with this kind of perturbation. We only have pregnancies, but they are God's gift.

"I have tried to explain all this to you as well as I can, but if you want to understand what I mean you will have to try for yourself. No, no, Aurora, do not look so frightened, as if I am saying something strange. What do you have to lose? You are not married and, as far as I know, you have no suitor, so nobody can call you to account. Who cares whether your maidenhood is intact? Do you not think it is a silly idea to keep it for someone you do not know? It does not matter what the priests have to say, because they do what they like when it suits them – or do you really believe they deny themselves the pleasures of the flesh? Even our Lord Jesus Christ did not do that! Cheer up, Auroreta, be a good girl. Do I startle you? Come on, woman, are you not really dying of curiosity? I should like to see you – yes, you – with a man of your station, through the keyhole. I should like to know what other men do, the ones who are nothing like Antoni, and to see how rough and dirty they are. Oh, it gives me such pleasure just to think about it! Would you let me watch you? No, of course you would not! I do not know why I am asking. Who would we find who would want to take you to bed? But there is one thing I am starting to understand very clearly, Aurora, and that is that if you want to understand men, knowing one man is not enough. I want to be well schooled in this matter, and one man is not even a beginning. Stop looking at me like that. You seem completely thunderstruck! I love shocking you. It is so easy! You get alarmed by the slightest thing, Aurora and at your age! It seems that you have learnt nothing at all. You are lucky to have me to tell you everything, do you not agree?"

The chocolate pot had been there for years, but one day Senyoreta Càndida made you take it out of the glass cabinet and give it a good wash with soap and water.

"It seems that no one has used it for a long time. I asked Antoni if I could have it, and do you know what he said? That everything in this house is mine and I can use whatever I like. Is that not lovely? And do you not think the pot is perfect for my morning hot chocolate? I shall try it tomorrow."

When you washed it, the delicacy of the porcelain, the craftsmanship that had gone into its exquisite lines, the high spout and the generous bow-shaped handle told you that this was no ordinary piece. There was something written on the base in blue letters, in French or Italian but you were not sure which. The swizzle stick had been lost, but you found another one in the kitchen which fitted it perfectly. A chocolate pot without a swizzle stick was an uncomfortable reminder of an open-mouthed child who cannot be gratified. In any case, the chocolate must be stirred or it spoils. What a pity, that ugly chip on the spout. You ran your fingertip along the broken edge. It was rough, disagreeable to the touch. It reminded you of life, but only sometimes. You were in a trance and spoke aloud. "Yes, it is a beautiful chocolate pot. A little bit chipped – such a shame – but it does not really matter."

You asked Senyoreta Càndida about the writing.

"It is French, Aurora," she said. "Look, it says, 'I belong to Madame Adélaïde of France.'"

"And who is that lady?" You are very surprised.

"I have no idea," she said. "You will have to ask my mother-in-law. And Aurora, please stop calling me Senyoreta because I am now *Senyora* Càndida. Or *Senyora* Sampons, if you prefer."

It was hopeless. You could not say *Senyora*, however hard you tried.

Càndida's mother-in-law immediately shed some light on the mystery. "The chocolate pot, you say? That has been here for years. If it could speak it would tell you the whole family history. I do not know exactly where it came from, because my husband never told me. I found it thrown away with the rubbish and rescued it. Imagine that! The shop was very small. It was before we expanded the business. We were very young and newly married. It might have been a gift from somebody, but I never tried to find out. Believe it or not, you are the first person who has ever asked about it."

The chocolate pot only held enough to fill three small cups. Senyoreta Càndida, you mean Senyora Sampons, used to keep saying that, but she rarely had the three cups. Then you helped her to get out of bed, do her hair and choose her clothes, as she prattled on and on.

"Shall I take the tray now, Senyoreta?

"You just said it again, Aurora! How many times must I tell you? *Senyora*! You must call me *Senyora*! What if Senyor Antoni heard you?"

When the Senyoreta – the *Senyora* – gave the order, you removed the tray and took it and her breakfast things down to the kitchen, where you waited for your chance and then hid for a moment in the pantry to scour out the little bit of chocolate left in the pot. It was so good you shivered with pleasure, even though you had to be quick so as not to be caught red-handed by Enriqueta the cook or Quima the housekeeper, the kind of women who could never keep still and who surged out of the darkness like ghosts. Then you very carefully washed the chocolate pot, dried it well and put it in its place on a shelf next to the pantry ready for the next morning. You did this day in, day out. Exactly the same thing every morning for two years, four months and twenty-four days, counting the last one. That was when you drank the whole pot.

The first time Augusto Bulterini sang in the Liceu it was in the role of Don Alvaro in *La forza del destino*, one of those nights when the young Sampons couple, splendid in their family box, were the envy of everyone who saw them. Càndida loved this opera, because it was one of those where the man has no qualms about dying for a lady, and the lady loves him in a very dramatic way, so she trills higher and higher and then the whole thing ends very tragically (especially when it's Verdi), as the trumpets in the orchestra have been portending for some time. She cried floods of tears when Leonora told her lover, "I shall wait for you in heaven, *addio*," and died before she could finish pronouncing his name, because the poor thing had been stabbed by her own brother. Such goings-on! It was a very good thing that a genius like Verdi was there to remind people of these things they used to do.

They spoke very little of the tenor. His style was more than correct, he had a good voice and he looked the part in the leading man's role, although he was not as young as he seemed, which Senyor Antoni pointed out. He had to be at least thirty-five. Senyoreta Càndida thought thirty-five was a splendid age for a tenor, and especially for one as good-looking as this Bulterini, who stalked catlike round the stage and with that glorious mane of black hair. The fickle Liceu audience liked the Italian, and he came back a couple of seasons later, this time as the leading man in *Il trovatore*. The choice could not have been more pleasing to Senyoreta Càndida, who, sitting at her dressing table, told you all about it one morning while you were doing her hair.

"Do you know what, Aurora? Antoni had one of those ideas of his and wanted to give a very fine party to open the new factory premises. He set everyone to work to make the space presentable, with my father's machinery perfectly visible so everyone can see how advanced we are and how we invest our money. There were a great number of guests, of all kinds, including politicians, journalists, architects, businessmen, rival chocolatiers – Amatller, Juncosa, Company and Fargas – writers and personalities from the entertainment world. Of course, there is no lack of people in Barcelona nowadays if you want to have a big party, and it was all as brilliant as one might expect.

"In order to please me and some of our music-loving guests, Antoni invited the company which will be premiering *Il trovatore* in the Liceu tomorrow, so they could entertain us with a little musical offering. The impresario was delighted and it all went wonderfully well. Shortly after refreshments were served they made their appearance with the trio from the end of Act

One, with the Count and the troubadour who are in love with the noble lady, and poor Leonora herself. Everyone was ecstatic when they sang that wonderful part, all shouts and threats, which ends when she says, "*Vibra il ferro in questo core che te amar non vuol, né può.*"* Oh, Aurora, such emotion! Can you imagine what it was like? Then there was an interval, after which they came out again and sang some arias. Signor Bulterini, for example, sang wonderfully about how no power on earth would stop him. What a man! How handsome he is and how all our guests applauded! It was a truly unforgettable evening. The fact is, Aurora, after that, everyone will remember Sampons chocolates, and when they think about us they will remember the music and the good taste with which everything was done. And a great many people will talk about it!

"But there is one other thing I should like to tell you. Before the party began, we were introduced to the artistes. They were exceedingly pleasant with Antoni, who after all was the man in charge, but the one who really stood out was this Signor Augusto Bulterini. Seeing him close up and without his costume and make-up, I was very impressed, Aurora. You could not begin to imagine what lovely black curly hair he has, with a tiny touch of grey at the temples, because Antoni is right when he says he must be nearing forty. What a gaze! It was so intense I could hardly breathe. Signor Bulterini hardly left my side the whole evening and paid no attention to anyone else. His conversation – in Spanish – is most agreeable and natural, with all the poise of a king or a minister. He seemed very impressed by my youth and kept telling me all the things he found irresistible in my face: my eyes, nose, mouth and even my ears. Since he had given me the opening, and I did not know what to say anyway, I asked if he is married. And can you imagine what he answered? He was very bold. 'I am a free man at present, but for a lady like you, Senyora, I should happily let my wings be clipped.' What do you think about that? Are you not amazed? What enchanting audacity, and with my husband standing so near us! If Antoni had heard him, I am sure he would have hit him. How shocking! And if he were not such a civilized man, he might even have felt obliged to challenge the Italian to a duel, to first blood or even to the death. Can you imagine, Aurora, what might have happened if I had not been so discreet? I was very close to being in a desperate denouement, like they have in operas. But, never mind, I knew how to behave. I remained where I was, trapped in conversation with this modern Casanova, without making any fuss at all. After that absurdity about his freedom, Signor Bulterini gave me a roguish smile which made me very agitated. I kept talking about Antoni, in order to remind him of my status as a married woman, but he did not care. He simply did not heed me and kept showering me with compliments, which made me blush. It went on like that until he was called to the stage, but while he sang he kept looking at me, his eyes glinting with a boldness that made me feel quite faint with fear.

"With all these emotions I have not slept a wink, Aurora, just thinking about that brazen look. And now I am all atremble at the mere idea of having to go back to watch him performing in the Liceu, and – to make matters worse – with Antoni, who has no idea that this man is a scoundrel who wants to steal his wife. Yet I am curious to know what this Signor Bulterini is going to come out with today, and am ready for anything, because this man is a devil, Aurora, a devil that will stop at nothing until he gets what he wants. You can be sure of that!"

Il trovatore was a resounding success. Bulterini and the soprano who had been cast as Leonora had to come out for eight encores. Even Antoni Sampons praised the pair, especially Bulterini, whose Manrico was the most brilliant and intense he had ever seen. Everyone knew that Antoni Sampons was not a great admirer of Verdi, but that night the verdict was unanimous. There was only one thing to say: it had been a marvellous evening.

Càndida had been very quiet for a long time. Antoni asked if the opera had not been to her liking. She said she had enjoyed it very much, that it had been marvellous, but she laid her hand on her husband's arm to signal that she wanted to go home. As they descended the marble stairway her heart was galloping. If she closed her eyes, she could see Manrico looking at her from the stage with that air of wanting something from her. Something he could not have. She wanted to slap him for looking at her like that, but also longed to give him what he wanted. The contradictions crowded in her throat, almost strangling her.

"Are you sure you liked it?" Antoni repeated.

"Very much. It is just that I dozed a little in Act Four. Such a pity. It is a shame we cannot see it again."

Antoni Sampons pulled a face. "I am going to Madrid on the stagecoach that leaves at nine in the morning."

"Yes, of course," she said and let the ensuing silence fill the conversation with ideas.

"Maybe you could ask your father to go with you," suggested Antoni, always quick to pander to his wife's every whim, however trifling it might be.

"I could also go alone. I would be perfectly all right."

"Alone?" Antoni looked at her with a mixture of fascination and pride. "You liked it that much?"

Càndida smiled.

"Very well. There's no need to discuss the matter any further. After all, you are a married woman and everyone knows that."

"Oh Aurora, I am consumed with anxiety and I cannot tell anyone. I have not slept for three nights, I cannot eat and I am unable to think about anything else. Come here, Auroreta. You must listen to me in this, my most difficult hour. You have always been at my side, you know me better than anyone else and will be able to tell me what I must do. Do you remember Signor Bulterini, the Italian singer? I told you about the shameless things he said to me at Antoni's party in the new factory. Well, two days later he did it again and was even more brazen. I had to hear him out, poor me, what else could I do? I was alone in the box and he came in and locked it from inside with the key. A woman cannot face a situation like that all alone, without her husband at her side to defend her. You cannot imagine all the preposterous things I had to listen to, my dear Auroreta. He says he cannot keep on living if not at my side. Imagine! He says that ever since he first saw me he can only think of me and when he will be able to enjoy my company again! He used all kinds of adjectives and my poor head was spinning. And he speaks so beautifully, and with that accent… it was as if he was hypnotizing me. Perhaps he did hypnotize me. I cannot be sure. But wait, there is more. He wants me to go with him to Naples and be his lover. To Naples! Can you imagine? And me, his lover! This man thinks we are in an opera. He says he cannot bear the idea of me being in the arms of another man, that he has a storm in his heart that only a look from my eyes can calm. It must be true, yes, because he looks at me in a way that is not at all normal! The worst part is not what he says with his words, but what he makes me understand with his eyes. They bewitch me, undress me, possess me. It is like looking at a wild beast. Are you shocked, Aurora? Now do you understand why I am in such a state? What I am telling you, is this not hell on earth?"

You understood much more than you dared to say to Senyoreta Càndida. Much more than you could digest, and much more than she would be willing to hear. You always had a very clear idea of your place, even when she proclaimed so emphatically that you were friends and that was why she was seeking your advice. No. You were not friends and never would be. Too many things came between you. What Senyoreta Càndida was looking for – and this was one of the things you understood but could not say – was your complicity in her mischief. She wanted you to encourage her, to push her into it and thus free her conscience of guilt. You, however, could only tell the truth, even if it was a fearful, incomplete truth.

"This fire you are fuelling is very dangerous, *Senyora*," you said.

"Dangerous, Aurora? I would say it is lethal. Do you know what Augusto did to me the other night in the anteroom of my box? No, it would be better if I did not tell you, because I do not want to make you suffer. I already told you that I was alone and he took advantage of me. He is very experienced and you can see that at a league's distance. When he looks at you in that way it is as if he has poison in his eyes, a paralysing poison that quells any resistance from his victim. I was a puppet in his arms, a doll with no will of its own, under the spell of his hands and his words. Yes, Aurora, now do not cry, I let myself be seduced by another man, but I am not the only guilty party. Where was my husband while I was struggling for my honour? Did he do anything to prevent this outrage? Did he perchance forbid me from going to the opera alone? Was he concerned about what might happen to me? Do you not think he was careless? And that libertine, did he remember that I belong to another man and desist from assaulting me? Of course he did not! He carried it through to the end and has made me mad with anxiety. And now I do not know what to do if I must pass my days without him."

"You must forget him," you told her, even more upset than she was. "Heed the advice of friendship."

"Forget him, you counsel? You do not know what you are saying, you poor thing. Do you think he would let me? Do you think I could? Do you think my husband will do something to get me out of this? When he only thinks about his journeys and his machines? You do not know anything. One day you are going to come in here looking for me and I shall be gone. I shall be gone for ever, Aurora. What I feel cannot be put into words. It is as if I am intoxicated and only I can understand how. As if destiny has shown me a path and my future can only be at the side of... I do not want to say his name again because it burns inside me. I must live for what I have, Aurora. Or die."

How horrified you were. The Senyora was mad, stark raving mad. You could not think what to say or what to do. You wondered if you should go and tell Senyor Antoni, or go to the Turull house and tell Don Estanislau and Donya Hortènsia. But you decided against that. What if it was all just fantasy? Or one of those strange notions that Càndida sometimes had, like wanting to find a Don Giovanni who would make her suffer? Maybe there was no need to worry.

Then you saw that the Senyora was sitting in her chair, sipping the hot chocolate you had served her, staring out on to the street and sighing. "Bring me my sewing, Aurora. I should like to do some embroidery."

While you went to fetch her embroidery hoop and the little box of needles, you tried to breathe normally again and told yourself that it had only been her excitable imagination, that she had not done anything with the tenor, and it was all just the folly of a pampered girl. Deep inside, you had always known that Càndida, Senyora or Senyoreta, had never changed. She had always been an insufferable spoilt brat.

You put the embroidery hoop on her lap. She asked, "Will you sit awhile and embroider with me?"

You came out with the first excuse that came into your head. There was a lot of work in the kitchen and you had to help Enriqueta to pick through the legumes and then make the desserts. She nodded but, before giving her attention to her embroidery, she gave you one last, slightly lost, sad look, and murmured very quietly, "May she who loved so much one day never live to regret it."

You left her there by the window with her strange attack of melancholy and went down to the kitchen to cry with fright.

La traviata

It was no fantasy. You discovered this all of a sudden with horror in your heart.

You remember it as a nightmare. It was 16th October 1874. Senyoreta Càndida did not answer when you knocked twice at her door. You knocked again. Silence. You thought she must have slept badly and was having trouble waking up. She had often had problems sleeping recently, or she would wake up in the night with one of those nightmares she confided only to you. You decided to go in anyway, even without permission.

The room was in darkness. You did what you always did: tray, door, curtains. The sun was shining down on Carrer Ample, as it did every day. Everything strove to keep up the appearance of routine, pretending that nothing had happened.

But the room was empty. The bed had not been slept in.

This cannot be. All the words that Càndida had been pouring out for hours and hours over the last few days battered your head like blows. *No, this cannot be.* With hope that was really despair you searched the whole house. You looked in all the logical places, like the garden, and also the most unlikely ones, those she never entered, like the kitchen and your room. You asked the coachman if the Senyora had required his services that morning. No, the Senyora had not asked for anything. "And yesterday," you asked with a shrinking heart.

"No, she said nothing yesterday either," he said, and then added, "But yesterday afternoon a brougham stopped at the entrance."

"A brougham? Whose was it?"

The coachman only grimaced, as if to say, "How should I know?"

A brougham. Your heart was racing. You were not innocent. You knew things and had your suspicions. No, not suspicions, Aurora – and now you cannot deny the evidence – because you knew you were faced with certainties. Certainties as big as cathedrals! How could you have been so blind? It never occurred to you that the Senyoreta meant what she said… You always believed she was talking for talking's sake and that she was not really capable of… You have been stupid, blind and deaf, Aurora! Yes, that is what you have been! And now you felt guilty, as if you had dreamt up this perfidy yourself.

Then you remembered the child. Little Antonieta. You found her happily occupied in her playroom, combing a doll's hair with her fingers, watched over by a bored-looking young maid. You asked if the Senyora had looked in that morning. You do not know why, but you still cherished some hope. You *needed* some hope. Your spirit was shrouded in black.

The little girl, poor child, chortled over her small diversions. The maid said, "I have not seen her."

No one had seen her.

You were the only one in the house who knew, Aurora. You and you alone. That was the woeful privilege reserved for the bastard servant, a dead woman's daughter, miraculously saved. That October morning you wished you had never been born. You could not bear the idea of facing Senyor Antoni, coming back from his journey, asking about his beloved wife, surprised that she had not come out to welcome him home and, in the end, incredulous and all but mortally wounded on hearing the whole truth from your lips. This truth had been tearing at your entrails, but now it was bearing down on you like a mountain.

In a flash you foresaw what was going to happen, as if you were a witch gazing into a crystal ball. As you stood there next to the Senyora's impeccable, undisturbed bed you understood that this was the end (and rarely in one's life does one recognize such a thing so clearly), and there was nothing you could do about it. People like you do not hold the reins of history. People like you can only suffer the consequences.

You turned the key in the lock, from inside, and sat down at the table where Càndida would never again have breakfast. You unfolded the linen napkin and spread it on your lap, as you had seen her do so many, many times. Then you poured some hot chocolate into the little cup. Three whole cups, every last drop held in the chocolate pot of the mysterious Adélaïde of France. You sipped it, looking down onto the street, with the calm of a woman already condemned. It was not sweet but it was very velvety. Once you finished that, you devoured the bread and the fruit, leaving the plates as clean as if they had just been washed.

For just one second, you thought you deserved it.

The nightmare had three acts, like Senyora Hortènsia's favourite operas. In the second act, Senyor Antoni returned from his travels. If anyone had composed a homecoming prelude, it would have begun with a very quiet *adagio*, moving slowly into the *allegro* and then a *presto* clanging with cymbals, of the kind that prepares the audience for the bad turn things are about to take. Oh yes, and the trumpets! We must not forget the trumpets, the harbingers of fate. Then there would be a duet – you and the Senyor – in the traditional style. First, you tell him what has happened, then he has his say, and only at the end do your voices mingle. This is be followed by a highly dramatic aria, sung by Senyor Antoni with his little daughter in his arms, cursing the woman who has abandoned them, the day he married her and the Neapolitan tenor who stole her from him. The denouement is a furious *cabaletta* in which he swears to God that he will devote himself body and soul to his daughter Antonieta, and raise her far away from the painful, damaging memory of her mother. Curtain. Applause.

But life does not happen like an opera on the stage. You were dying of fright, waiting for something to happen and not daring to confess the truth. The hours went by after her flight. Càndida had been gone for three days and a sad, silent torpor fell over the house. Visitors came. You heard them climbing the stairs behind the housekeeper and you heard them leaving. Senyor Antoni had his lunch served in his office. You had little to do and, for the first time in your life, you were bored. Sometimes you looked in on Antonieta. You were as sorry for her as you felt for yourself. You went back to your room, your lair, and let time pass by, listening to the noises coming from upstairs and wondering whether you should have said something to Senyor Antoni. And you wept in fear and rage.

"Aurora, you are wanted in the parlour," said Madrona, poking her nose round the door, hanging askew on its broken hinges.

You went upstairs immediately, your hands trembling with fright, tension and sorrow.

Senyor Antoni was standing by the fireplace. His mother sat in the chair next to the curtains. With a very serious expression, Senyor Estanislau was holding Senyora Hortèn-sia's hand. She looked as if she had been crying a lot. They asked you to stand in the centre of the room so they could all see you clearly. Senyor Antoni asked if you knew where Senyora Càndida was.

"I do not know with any certainty, Senyor, but I can imagine."

"And what do you imagine, Aurora?" he asked.

"Please do not make me say it, Senyor." Your voice broke. You were terribly afraid, and had been for days.

"Tell us why then. Why do you suspect her of something? Did she tell you?"

"Yes, Senyor."

"Did she speak to you about Signor Bulterini?"

You were shocked to hear Senyor Antoni's voice pronouncing the Italian singer's name, to watch him say it without the slight-est quaver or doubt, as if it were just any name.

"She spoke to me about him on some occasions."

Senyora Hortènsia, very agitated, suddenly interrupted. "And did you say nothing to her, you nincompoop? Did you not tell her to forget those foolish ideas and remind her that she is a married woman and mother of a little daughter?"

"Yes, Senyora, I did, but I did not believe that Senyoreta – I mean, Senyora – Càndida meant what she was saying. I thought it was one of her fantasies."

"The housekeeper has informed me," Senyor Antoni contin-ued, "that three nights ago she saw you leaving the house after ten, in a great hurry, on an errand for the Senyora, and that you came back after half-past eleven."

You could feel your heart swelling, filling your whole breast, and for a moment you thought you were going to die then and there, in front of all of them. Darkness misted your eyes and you thought, *I am lost.*

"Is that true, Aurora?"

"Yes, sir."

"Would you tell us where you went?"

"To deliver a letter."

"Where?"

"The stage door at the Liceu, Senyor."

"To whom did you have to deliver it?"

"Signor Bulterini's manservant, Senyor."

"Did you do that?"

"Yes, Senyor."

"Did the Senyora tell you what was in the letter?"

"Yes, Senyor."

"So you were fully aware of what you were doing, for Heavens' sake!" shouted Senyora Hortènsia, her voice breaking.

You could bear it no longer. You started crying like a little girl. You could not breathe. You thought you were going to faint. That was the last thing you wanted to do. You did not want to do anything to upset them further.

"Senyora Càndida…" you whimpered almost inaudibly, "Senyora Càndida deceived me."

"What do you mean she deceived you, Aurora? Explain what you mean!" Senyora Hortènsia was yelling. You had never heard her screech like this before, but the one who really made an impression on you was Senyor Estanislau. He had not moved. His eyes were glazed, staring at the tassels on the curtains. The only way you could tell he was alive was the fact that he occasionally blinked.

"The note…" you sobbed, devastated by this situation, "I believed it was to bid him farewell for ever. That is what she told me. I recommended that she should write it."

"Are you telling the truth?" Senyor Antoni asked.

"Yes, Senyor, I swear it."

"Do not swear, you impertinent girl!" screeched Senyora Hortènsia. "And stop crying!"

Your legs started to buckle beneath you and Senyor Antoni gave you his arm. If he had not, you would have fallen to the floor.

"I feel unwell," you whimpered. "I have done nothing wrong. Senyora Càndida is headstrong when she wishes. She would not listen to me. I believed she would come back. It cannot be that she will not come home. She will come back when she understands what she has done. I am sure of it."

You were bawling like a small child. You were such a sorry sight that Senyor Antoni asked Donya Hortènsia if you were a good girl and if you were to be believed. Then Senyora Hortènsia replied, "Aurora is a good girl. I know her as if she were my own daughter. I can vouch for her."

Your tears stopped falling. You were still standing there, paralysed in the middle of this gathering, once again waiting for something to happen. A clock struck six.

"You may go now, Aurora," said Senyor Antoni, in the mild tone he had used all this time. "You are not responsible for what has happened."

You left, barely able to walk in a straight line. Everything was so strange that it felt as if these things were not happening. Life seemed unreal. As you went down the stairs, you could hear

Senyora Hortènsia's quavering voice: "Why has this happened to us? Why?"

You had not got halfway down when you stopped. Senyor Antoni's mother was talking about you. "Well, she cannot stay in this house. I hope you understand that. It would be better if she goes with you. We could not recommend her to anyone either, after what she has done."

Senyora Hortènsia did not defend you, or defend herself. "Very well."

Very well. It took so little to change the course of a person's existence.

Your belongings were soon bundled together, still fitting into the same piece of cloth you used to wrap them in when you arrived.

Once everything was packed up, you sat on the kitchen bench, fearful and waiting. Then a bad idea lit up in your head like a glow-worm: the chocolate pot. You could not leave it there all by itself on the shelf next to the pantry. Nobody would miss it when you left. In that house they had plenty of other problems to deal with before anyone might wonder what had happened to the chipped old chocolate pot. As tends to happen in such cases, one bad idea led to another and you were soon telling yourself that, even if they did look for it, they would all imagine that Senyora Càndida had taken it with her, and it was evident that no one would be able to prove anything. You had had a dreadful day, your heart was beating very fast, and this was your chance, because you were alone in the kitchen and you could not even hear Madrona marching around like a French soldier, always everywhere at once. Such a disagreeable woman. You acted fast, without a second thought, the way these things are done. You were impelled by a strange desire to possess an object that, for you, was much more than that. It was part of a still very much alive but already buried past. You wrapped it in an old rag and put it in the bundle with the rest of your belongings. Then you went to the bench in the entrance of the house and sat there waiting for your heart to stop pounding.

The family remained in the parlour for a long time. They had to deal with many problems and make some difficult but necessary decisions. Disinheriting Senyoreta Càndida in favour of Antonieta, to begin with. Talking about the specific clauses of the separation document, which Senyor Antoni's lawyer had already drafted. Two very important conditions were clearly stated. Càndida would not see her daughter again until Antonieta was of legal age, and she was barred from setting foot in her husband's house, ever again, no matter how many years had gone by.

You were later told that, when this last clause was read out, Senyor Estanislau murmured, without looking at anyone, "It would be better if she never comes back."

After all that, you could see that the third act would be terrible. It would finish more or less like what is portended in *La traviata* by the prelude of Act Three. Nothing can stave off the disaster, however much the public wants a happy ending.

You had never seen any mother more desperate to erase the memory of her daughter than Senyora Hortènsia, or a more shame-faced father than Senyor Estanislau, who was devastated by everything. You never knew which of the two decided to remove the furniture and all the things that still remained in Càndida's bedroom, bring them out into the courtyard, pile them up and burn them. Senyora Hortènsia locked herself in her room so she would not have to witness it. Senyor Estanislau, however, sat in a rocking chair and did not move until the blaze died down to embers, and the embers to ashes, and the ashes to such bleak and bitter thoughts that his heart turned to stone.

Meanwhile, he sat there, rocking gently and singing "*Bella figlia dell'amore, schiavo son de' vezzi tuoi*", letting his memory hurt him so badly that he would never recover. That was the last time anyone ever saw him singing that part from the famous quartet in *Rigoletto*. The next day when, as a logical result of everything that had happened, he had the music room closed, he muttered, "Everything I wanted in life has turned against me."

From time to time he asked, "Are there any letters?" They would hand him the mail, which he distractedly glanced at before getting on with his work, although it was clear that he was increasingly oblivious to everything. He no longer went out. Unable to keep up appearances, he could not bear to see the faces of his old friends, or put up with polite silences. He gradually lost interest in inventing new machines. "There is an abundance of machines in the world! Why should I bother?" He retreated into impenetrable silence, moving further and further away from everything.

Then he had the attack of apoplexy, which took him almost totally away. His affliction pervaded every room of the house, which like him, were now mere shadows of their former glory. White sheets shrouded the dining-room and smoking-room furniture. The desk in Senyor Estanislau's office, once strewn with plans, sketches, formulas and order sheets for his materials, was cleared and locked. The curtains, rugs, tapestries and bedspreads, which were changed twice a year, remained frozen in perpetual winter.

Senyora Hortènsia dismissed all the servants. You were the only one left. "You and I shall take care of everything from now on, Aurora," she said, and then added, "Senyor Estanislau would not want anyone to see him like this. Except you. You have always been like a daughter to us and, as it turns out, you will be much more so than we ever imagined."

Poor Senyor Estanislau. You felt so sorry for him! This man – so strapping, as strong as an oak, happy as a lark, agile in his mind and on his feet, accustomed to doing as he pleased without having to give explanations to anyone – was suddenly condemned to having to spend all day being moved from bed to window and back again, sipping broth which you or the Senyora had to feed him with a small dessert spoon because he was no longer able to open his mouth by himself. If you looked into his eyes you could see the boding of death. The same could be said of Senyora Hortènsia, who ever since that day when you came back to the house in Carrer de la Princesa had been shrivelling away, like fruit drying in the sun. She never went out, hardly ate, and always dressed in mourning, although nobody in the family had died. One day she asked for the lawyer and, in a trembling voice, gave the order, "I want you to sell our box in the Liceu."

Long gone were the days when Senyor Estanislau, pointing at the heavens and in the thunderous voice of the god Odin at the end of *Die Walküre*, proudly proclaimed, "I would sell the house before selling our box at the Liceu!"

It was difficult to know which of the two was more afflicted. At least Senyor Estanislau was no longer really present, although he sometimes had a madman's smile on his face as he sat there by the window, eking out his placid – absent, but placid – existence. The Senyora, however, could only weep in secret, when she thought no one could hear her, repeating over and over again, "Why did this have to happen to us? Why has this happened to us?"

It was very sad to witness that premature decline, especially for someone like you who still had such clear memories of the splendour of the days when there were always parties, surprises and flurries of dressmakers, watchmakers, lawyers, friends coming for afternoon tea, washerwomen and ironing women. And the nights at the opera. In those days, when they used to talk such a lot about every new season at the Liceu, the biggest problem was that *Rigoletto* was not on the programme.

Senyor Estanislau died, sitting in his chair by the tall windows overlooking Carrer de la Princesa, with that smile of remote happiness still on his lips. You believe that he did not suffer and that he left this world peacefully. A huge crowd came to his funeral at the cathedral. Senyora Hortènsia reminded you of a little bird fallen from a very high nest. Antoni Sampons sat in the front row, with his five-year-old Antonieta. People were whispering a lot, ugly words swirling in their murmurings: "shameful", "betrayal", "loose woman", while many crocodile tears were compassionately and sorrowfully shed.

Antoni Sampons took his leave of his mother-in-law in the square and walked home with weary step, holding his little daughter's hand. Senyora Hortènsia could hardly look him in the eye.

The next season at the Liceu, the first without Senyor Estanislau, a magnificent *Rigoletto* was one of the highlights.

Even before leaving the Sampons house, you regretted what you had done. That is not like you, Aurora, an inner voice scolded.

How dare you! How could you take something that does not belong to you? That is stealing. Yes, that was the word: stealing. An ugly word. You dislike that word, Aurora.

All the excuses you invented for yourself, pushing you to take the chocolate pot off the shelf and hide it with your things, had evaporated. You tried to conjure them up again, inside yourself, but to no avail. The glow-worm of the original idea had also flown. You were left with remorse, guilt and self-disgust.

You always were a little excessive, Aurora. You might at least recognize that.

Before leaving the Sampons residence, under the tutelage of Senyor Estanislau and Senyora Hortènsia once again, all three of you with sorrow etched on your faces, you had already decided what you had to do, although it would by no means be easy. Nobody told you this, not even your whispering inner voice, which was now treacherously silent, but you knew: you had to return the chocolate pot to the place you had taken it from, without permission. That was what you had to do.

How? You had no idea, although you imagined it would not be easy.

The first morning in the Turull household you got up very early, before dawn, and wrapped the chocolate pot in many layers of white tissue paper. You tied up the packet, now as roly-poly as a well-swaddled infant, with a white ribbon. As a sign of respect, you put on clean clothes. You left the house before daybreak, and only half an hour later you were standing at the entrance of the house in Carrer Ample. Your heart was thumping when you took hold of the heavy door knocker. That blockhead Enriqueta opened the door and the moment she saw you her whole bearing changed.

"What are you doing here? Why have you come back?"

"I have come to deliver something."

"We are not interested." She cut you off before you could explain.

"Listen to me. This is not mine."

"We want nothing from Senyora Càndida."

"Enriqueta, keep quiet and let me speak."

"I cannot, I really cannot." With that, she started to close the door, grumbling, "For Heaven's sake, Aurora, do not come back. Senyor Antoni has suffered enough. I shall tell no one I have seen you."

It would have been worse with Madrona, you thought. You turned on your heel. You had no choice. *Very well, Enriqueta, I shall tell no one I have seen you either.*

The fine porcelain was burning in your hands as you and the chocolate pot went back home.

After the funeral came days of silence and windows that were never opened. You were afraid the Senyora would die of grief, because she picked at her food like a little bird and gradually lost the habit of speaking. Then, one day she said, "Please sit down, Aurora." You clasped your hands on your lap and she looked at you in a special kind of way, as if she loved you, and then made an announcement that you did not expect.

"Very soon I shall be going to live with a niece of mine with whom I have come to a certain arrangement with a view to my future in the years that are left to me. It is nothing sophisticated, I can assure you. I have bought some small flats in Bonanova, and have put them in her name, in order to recompense her for the bother of looking after me until I die. As you know, I do not lack money. Senyor Estanislau's patents are still very lucrative. I have more money than I need, and more than I can spend. When I am no more, it will all go to Antonieta, who is my only heiress after what happened with Càndida. However, I do not wish to make these changes without making sure that you will be well looked after, Aurora. I should never forgive myself if anything bad befell you." Senyora Hortènsia paused and asked you to move a little closer. It was difficult for her to speak and hard to hear what she was saying. "I want you to know that your mother was a good girl. You must bear her no grudge for what happened to her. She was deceived by a bad person, who only cared about himself. I believe that you have never felt rancour towards your mother."

"No, Senyora. I have never felt rancour towards anyone."

"Listen carefully now. Before your mother died, I promised her I would take care of you. I think I have done that quite well. I have never gone back on my word, never in my whole life. Neither do I wish to do that now by leaving you in the hands of fate. I hope that you will never reproach me for that."

"Senyora Hortènsia, I do not reproach you for anything. On the con—"

"Let me finish." She smiled, just a little. "I have spoken with my friend, Doctor Horaci Volpi. Do you remember him? You would have seen him in this house on some occasions. He was a very good friend of Senyor Estanislau's. They loved to sit at the coffee table talking until very late. The way these men amuse themselves! The most important thing is that he is a gentleman through and through, a man in the old style. He has been living alone for some years now and very urgently needs a housekeeper to put him in order."

"Put him in order?"

"Take charge of him, look after him and keep his house clean and tidy. A young woman, if possible." She paused. "I told him about you, Aurora. I told him you are a good person and very willing to work. I also told him about the promise I made to your mother and how I have taken care of you all these years. He has accepted my recommendation and I believe he is happy about it. I can assure you that you will feel at home there, just as you do here. As I said, Horaci is the kind of gentleman who is a rarity these days."

"Maybe I shall not know how to do all these things…" you ventured.

"Do not be silly! Of course you will know. Do not let me down."

"No, Senyora."

"You must be there tomorrow morning at nine. Here is the address." She held out a piece of paper on which it was written.

"Tomorrow?"

"At nine. Be punctual."

You did not imagine things could move so fast.

"Yes, Senyora."

"Dress yourself properly. Wear the linen uniform."

"Yes, Senyora."

"And do not be late, but do not arrive too early either."

"No, Senyora."

"Are you happy?"

"I am very happy, Senyora. But, what will you—"

"Ah, do not worry about me. I can look after myself. Besides, that is now the job of my niece and why I made my arrangement with her. Think about yourself, Aurora. You are still a young woman. You need a place to live now that our lives have been ruined."

You spent that afternoon crying. You would have given anything to be able to stay there. That was your home, the place where you were born, and where you had played as a child. The house you left and then returned to. You could not get it into your head that there was another world, different from that one. The idea of being the servant of another person, a doctor, a man who lived alone in a house you had never seen, was very frightening.

Now things could not get any worse. This finale had been looming on the horizon for a long time. Life has no preludes, or intermezzos, or an orchestra which suddenly starts getting clamorous to warn everyone of what is to come.

In life, things start by themselves and end when they please. If you are not prepared for that, then that is your bad luck.

Don Pasquale

You did everything Senyora Hortènsia had asked: linen uniform, hair neatly parted, shoes shining and face well-scrubbed. You arrived early and waited until the bells of Santa Maria del Pi struck nine. The last chime was still echoing when Doctor Volpi opened the door. He looked at you through narrowed eyes, frowning, with his glasses perched on the tip of his nose. He was wearing a stained-silk dressing grown and his tousled hair stood up in a grey halo round his head.

"Good morning, doctor," you greeted him, with a nice little curtsy. "My name is Aurora. I have been sent by Senyora Hortènsia, the widow of—"

"Come in, come in young lady. I was expecting you, but my friend Hortènsia told me you would be here on Wednesday at nine. Good Heavens, is it nine o'clock on Wednesday already? The days fly away like swallows in autumn. Sit here, or there, or wherever you can. I shall be with you in a moment. Let me tidy myself up a little. Since I was not expecting visitors... Come in, do come in, young lady."

From the entrance, you glanced into the parlour. Well, it was not a parlour, to begin with. It was full of shelves crammed with books, right up to the ceiling. In the central space there was a rug, some chairs, an armchair, a reading lamp... all higgledy-piggledy, in any old place, as if they had just been unloaded from a cart and left there. The disarray was daunting. You did not want to go inside. Heaps of books and papers lay on the chairs, there was a pile of newspapers in the middle of the – very grubby! – rug, curtains trailing on the floor because the hems had come unstitched, cushions with their stuffing spilling out, and you counted as many as seven hats, all dusty, occupying the round table. *What a mess! Cleaning all that up is going to take weeks.* Fortunately, the flat did not seem to be very big. *If the parlour is in such a state, what must the kitchen be like?* You remained where you were, in the entrance, your feet close together, without taking a single step and your overcoat still buttoned.

"Come in, come in, young lady." The doctor had changed into another dressing gown, this time without stains, and had combed his hair off his face. "Ah, you must forgive me! As you can see, I do not have many visitors. I do not even have anywhere for you to sit. What a disgrace! Let me, let me find somewhere. We only have to put all this somewhere else…" He picked up a whole pile of papers from an armchair, walked around the room a couple of times and, not seeing anywhere to put them, threw them into the fireplace, where a fire was burning. A cloud of ashes billowed through the room. "There you are, now! They will not cause us any more problems."

You sat down facing the doctor, making an enormous effort to conceal your discomfiture.

"I am sure that Senyora Hortènsia has spoken very highly of me," he said, now also seated. You examined him carefully, believing that he did not notice. First you stared at his hands, white hands with delicate skin, clean, neatly trimmed nails and criss-crossed with blue veins. A gentleman's hands, as you would say later. "Well now, Senyoreta Aurora, you are gravely misinformed. I am a hopeless case. Three months ago, when my last housekeeper left, I thought I could manage alone. I know this is somewhat unusual, but I am a hermit, you see, a man living alone who needs very little and spends the whole day reading. I usually go out for lunch, the nuns in the Montsió convent do my washing and I do not need to bother anyone to pass the bed-warmer over my sheets. That is all you need to know. It seems that I am less competent than I believed. In fact, Senyora Hortènsia warned me, but I was obstinate and wanted to prove her wrong. Stubbornness is another of my serious defects. I am hopelessly stubborn and presumptuous and, it would seem, too inept to live alone. Now, my poor girl, if you accept this job, you are going to have a terrifying amount of work. And it is all my fault…"

Doctor Volpi was tall and thin, with a distinguished air about him that not even the grubbiest dressing gown in the world could disguise. He was fifty-six years old, his skin was starting to look transparent and his hair was greying, but his long lean body was the same as it had always been. It was a body that, now that he was on the threshold of the winter of life, made him look more attractive than he had ever been in its spring and summer.

"You have no questions?" he asked.

You had several, which you ranked in order of importance, from greatest to least.

"I should like to know why the former housekeeper left," you said.

"Of course, Aurora, I should have explained. Poor Joana was working here for forty-seven years. She was eighty-eight and could hardly stand on her feet. Sometimes I had to help her do up her shoes. Imagine that. Towards the end, her health was very delicate. One day I said, 'Senyora Joana, what do you think about going to live with some relative who can look after you?' I had to repeat it several times, as she was getting deaf. Finally, she understood me. She asked, 'But, doctor, do you mean that? How will you manage without someone to look after you?' The poor woman did not realize that, for some time, she was more like the lady of the house and I her manservant. This house was rather like an operetta by Donizetti. Do you know Donizetti, Senyoreta Aurora?"

"No, Senyor."

"It does not matter. These things can always be remedied. You look very young and as if you can do up your own shoes."

You let out a muffled laugh. You did not want to, but you could not help it. *Behave yourself, Aurora!*

"Yes, Senyor, I can do that by myself. I am twenty-four years old."

"That is excellent news, Senyoreta. I cannot tell you how relieved I am to hear that. And, woman, laugh as much as you like. Laughing is good for your digestion and prolongs life. Did you know that? We have come into this world to laugh! As they say, *cessa alfin di sospirar*,* which is such a great truth it is used to end operas. Imagine! Now come, come with me and I shall show you your room. We must talk about all these things before you make any commitment. Come here, follow me, and you will see that my flat is nothing out of this world. I moved here after my wife died. A man living alone does not need a big house, you know. Big houses were invented so ladies would not squabble. With their husbands or with other ladies. Have you not noticed that ladies confined in small spaces are much more quarrelsome? So the more rooms you have the better, because then they never cross paths. Do not let that worry you, for this problem is as general as it is inconsequential. As they say, *così fan tutte*." He paused and looked at you. "Do you understand what I just said, Senyoreta?"

"No, I understood nothing, doctor."

"'Thus do they all' – Mozart. You do not know it? It is an opera buffa, like *Le nozze di Figaro*. *Buffa* means it is a comic opera, to make you laugh, but with no loss of elegance, eh! With this fellow Mozart, one always laughs elegantly. Look, your room is here. What do you think?"

This whole conversation took place in a dark, narrow passageway, which made a couple of sudden, right-angled turns, as if the architect wanted the flat's inhabitants to engage in a perpetual game of hide-and-seek. Your room was next to the kitchen, but it looked onto the light well, so some daylight came in. It was much bigger than any of the rooms you had ever had, with a wardrobe, a bedside table, a chair, and there was still enough space to walk across it and open the window. The only problem was the light. You had never slept in a room that was not completely dark, and were not sure whether you would be able to sleep with light coming in. Yet you were quick to respond, "It is a very nice room."

"You will need to buy sheets. Tell me what they cost and I shall give you the money," Doctor Volpi said.

"If you agree, I can make them myself and then they will be cheaper," you offered.

"Oh really! That is a very good idea. Yes, yes, an excellent idea! Then… have we come to an agreement, Senyoreta?"

"What is over there?" You gestured towards another right angle in the passageway.

"Oh yes, of course. Come with me. There is a dining room I do not use. The front part of the flat is enough for me, and it is warmer too." The doctor showed you a small dining room, which also opened onto the light well. There were more piles of paper, a few chairs and two paintings, so dark it was impossible to see what they represented.

"I suppose your room is over there," you said.

"Yes, yes, that is my room. Would you like to see it?"

"No, thank you. There is no need. We should speak of my weekly wages, perhaps."

"Oh yes! Of course we must speak of your wages! A very important matter, Senyoreta! I agree. Tell me what you would like to be paid."

"Senyora Hortènsia paid me six pieces of eight every week."

"Then there is no more to be said. Senyora Hortènsia is a good example."

"However, I should prefer to be paid seven or eight. Things are more expensive nowadays, and sometimes I do not have enough to buy as much as a handkerchief."

"I like you, young lady. I like you! You have not yet started to work and you asking for a higher wage. Very well. Seven or eight? Which do you prefer?"

"If eight were possible…"

"Yes, this is the more sensible answer. Then that is the end of the matter. I shall pay you eight. Is there anything else?"

"I also used to have a free afternoon. On Thursday."

"Whatever you say."

"And would you give me your permission to go to Mass on Sunday mornings?"

"Go to Mass? Of course you can go to Mass, woman!"

"There is one more matter."

"Tell me what it is."

You remained in fearful silence for a moment, for you were not sure of what the effect of your next words might be. Nevertheless, you continued.

"I am... all alone in the world, doctor. Alone and defenceless, I mean. I have come here because Senyora Hortènsia told me to, and because she says that you are an old-style gentleman."

"She said that? Good Lord! What kind of recommendation is that?"

"If it were not for that I should not have come. I do not wish to offend you, but you are a man who lives alone and I am a poor girl who has never—"

"You do not offend me in the least! If you believe that all men are blackguards, I would say you are totally right to do so! You do well to be wary! I do not know what I can say to put you at your ease, because all wolves know how to dress up in sheep's clothing. Perhaps you would feel safer if we put a bolt on your door. Do you believe that would be sufficient?"

"I think so."

"Well, that is decided. Is there anything else?"

"Only when you wish me to start."

"Could it be at once?"

"I shall go and fetch my belongings and return at lunchtime tomorrow, if you agree."

"Senyoreta, I find this fascinating! I can only say yes to everything!"

You were never easily daunted. If things turned out to be a little more difficult than they appeared to be, you were simply more patient. Cleaning up his flat, for example, did not have to be done in a single day. Nobody obliged you to do that. First of all, you went about the more urgent chores, like the hems on the curtains, which made a very bad impression. As for the papers, you thought you would ask the doctor to help you with them, but, finally, since you did not want to bother him you tidied them into neat piles and stowed them in a wooden box. Then you were able to attend to the rug, which was very dirty, and could not be left even one day more. You found a home for all the hats on a shelf in the entrance and, in order to make sure they would not get soiled by direct contact with the wood, you made a linen runner finished with a lace edging which looked very nice when placed on the shelf. When the doctor saw it, he smiled happily and said, "It is easy to see that this house is blessed with a woman's touch again!"

The doctor was not at all miserly with the household expenses, and neither did he interfere with the shopping. He let you decide things for yourself so when you told him you needed three pesetas to buy material to cover the chairs in the parlour and make yourself some sheets, he gave them to you without asking any questions. Neither was he interested in seeing receipts. He was too trusting. Anyone could have cheated him, and it would not have surprised you to learn that his old housekeeper had filled her pockets before leaving. You would not do such a thing, because you were another kind of person.

The doctor was pleased with everything from the very first day, but you were not sure what to think. This disaster of a man was a doctor? A doctor of what? Of clouds of dust and pleasantness? You never understood why he seemed so happy, or why he addressed you using the respectful form, *vosté*, or why he called you *senyoreta*. You had never met anyone like him. He was full of surprises, he was disconcerting and he often left you speechless. When you thought he was going to say one thing, he said the exact opposite. His behaviour was extravagant. He would come into the kitchen every few minutes to ask what the lovely smell was, or call you with great urgency in his voice, as if the house were burning down, only to ask you what day it was. Sometimes he would spend twelve hours reading in the parlour without coming out for anything. On other occasions, he would ask for a carriage at nine in the morning and would not come home until midnight. You saw no sign of his having any amorous relationship, not even the disreputable kind. No friends came to call, but from time to time he asked you to help carry a patient into the library and to lay him down on the rug. He never raised his voice and never rebuked you for anything. You had not seen him get angry. Nothing ruffled him, not even the convolutions of politics, or the cold of winter or the heat of summer. He was a serene, peaceful, different kind of man, and life in his house was all smooth sailing. Naturally, you realized that this was a very good situation. In fact, maybe it was *too* good, as if such perfection was not possible and there had to be some dark mystery lurking beneath the beautiful surface.

"We only have one life, Aurora! Do you think it would be right to waste it on such disagreeable matters as politics? I could not care less about all these Bourbons, Carlists, republicans, federalists and that ridiculous Italian king who came here to make such a spectacle of himself. They are of no interest, and I certainly do not wish to waste my breath talking about them!"

The doctor had just arrived, taken off his hat and left it on the table, which was now clean and uncluttered. With leisurely curiosity he glanced at his mail – which you had placed in a little silver basket – as he drew off his gloves. You had made him a small treat, which you brought in on a tray, concealed under a napkin.

"Mmmm… what is that lovely smell?" he asked distracted by the fragrance drifting from the tray.

"So, doctor," you asked, "if you do not wish to speak of politics, what do you talk about at your weekly gatherings?"

"Ah, at these gatherings we talk only about things that are worth talking about! The ones that make the world a pleasant place to live in."

You looked at him wide-eyed, as if trying to understand something.

He explained. "Opera. Theatre. Poetry. Painting. Architecture…" he lowered his voice slightly and added, "And ladies!"

"And is there such a lot to say about these things?"

The more he told you the more complicated it all seemed. How could they spend a whole afternoon talking about such matters? Whatever would they say?

You glided round the flat, light-footed and silent. You picked up his hat and put it on the shelf in the entrance, neatly aligned with the rest on the linen runner. You helped him to take off his cape, which you carefully folded and left on the settee. Then you knelt to take off his boots.

"You would be very surprised, Aurora, by the heated discussions I get into with my friends. I am sure that the supporters of Queen Isabel and those of Archduke Charles of Austria are more restrained, even if both parties are rivals for the throne of Spain. In our group we have also declared war! It is one of the most ferocious kinds, Aurora: between the champions of the tenor Gayarre and the staunch defenders of Masini."

The expression on your face said *I thought that opera could not offer a great deal of conversation*, but then you felt nervous because you knew nothing of wars, except that you did not like them at all because they were horrible.

"I shall tell you all about it," he said. "But such a momentous subject as this cannot be so easily addressed when one's stomach is empty and one's throat is dry. Would you mind if I flavour our conversation with whatever this is you have just brought me? It smells so heavenly an angel must have made it." Staring at your shoelaces, you did not respond except for smiling timidly as he went on. "Whatever can this be? Juice squeezed from a cloud in paradise? Essence of a one-eyed cherub's wing?"

You giggled when he said these silly things. He seemed happy with you.

Once his boots had been put away, you slipped out to fetch his dressing gown – now clean, with the buttonholes mended and hems stitched again – and his slippers. You held out the belt for him so he would not have to fumble to find it, but he was already groping for it and your hands touched for a moment. You could feel how soft his were. Yours were like two cold fish. You were startled and thrust them into your pocket, your fingers nervously twining and untwining. You blushed, which only added to your confusion. *What is this, Aurora? Is there a name for it? Would you dare to say it aloud, even if only to yourself? No, of course not! Some emotions are difficult to name. These feelings are not for someone like you.*

The doctor sat in the armchair and looked at you in the way he always did. You never knew why, but it reminded you of the tenderness with which Senyor Estanislau had gazed at Càndida when she was a little girl.

"You guessed once again that I would come home late today?"

You smiled in response.

"Do you not think you treat me too well?"

"No, Senyor. I believe you deserve it." You lowered your eyes.

You liked to offer him some small treat every time he came home, and waiting up late for him to arrive was no bother at all. You felt better knowing that he would not be going to bed with an empty grumbling stomach because he had not eaten since Heaven knows when. In the afternoons you cooked up something in the kitchen because you had nothing better to do, or in case the doctor came home tired after so much talking and needed something restorative. Since he had a sweet tooth and was quite demanding as well; one of his favourites was Sampons hot chocolate. You made it with a touch of cinnamon, a heaped spoon of sugar and not much water so it was nice and thick. You served it using his special little cup and saucer, with some sugared bread fingers and a glass of cold water, because hot chocolate excites a thirst that must be quenched immediately.

"Now that is Barcelona chocolate as it should be served," the doctor said, sweeping away the napkin like a magician revealing some kind of wonder.

"Yes, but it is different today," you proudly announced.

"In what way is it different?"

"Taste it and tell me what you think.

The doctor let it cool, as he usually did. Meanwhile, he tried to help you understand the Opera War. It seems that there were two singers – he called them tenors, but the word meant nothing to you then – and each one wanted to sing louder, higher, longer, more often and more highly paid than the other. One was called Julián Gayarre, and he was Spanish, and the other, an Italian, was called Angelo Masini. They never sang together, because each one believed that his voice was too marvellous to mix with the other's. Most important, they would have ruined any impresario who might have been tempted to contract both of them at once. In Barcelona, where people liked to be different, they preferred Gayarre, but the opposition, the Masini enthusiasts – the doctor among them – were gradually gaining ground. Not long afterwards they brought him to sing in the Liceu, where his audiences were completely dazzled. The doctor said that being a Masini man was not unlike being a Catalan nationalist. Both nationalists and Masini supporters were right, and this correct view in itself would eventually win the day because, sooner or later, some sensible person would recognize the truth of the matter. The main thing was not to despair. His voice was still vibrant with his bellicose zeal for Masini's cause when he added, "Aurora, if we are to taste this, we shall need another spoon!"

"What did you say, doctor?"

"Another spoon, Aurora. I shall not taste this unless you have some too."

"Oh, no, Senyor. The chocolate is for you. Heaven forbid! Whatever next!"

"Did you not say this is a new recipe? Then let us invent a new way of enjoying it. Like two old friends after a spirited conversation. Come on, bring yourself a cup too."

"No, Senyor. That would not be right. I shall keep you company though."

"No, no and no, Aurora! You will never win any stubbornness contest against me." He crossed his arms like a fractious little boy. "I shall not yield. And I am not going to taste it alone. I am going to get the cup myself…" He stood up.

"Oh, what a cross I have to bear with you! Stay there, doctor." You sounded so high-handed that you were surprised at yourself. "Can you not see that you do not need to fetch anything for me? If you continue like this, you might even end up tying my shoelaces, as you did with your other housekeeper. Please, please, stay there. I always have to do things your way."

"*Davvero?*"* He frowned. You stood up and went into the kitchen.

He would have gone himself. You were sure of that. The doctor sometimes got overexcited and had very strange ideas. It was certainly not beneath his dignity to sneak into the kitchen like a wayward little boy, and start lifting all the lids to see and sniff what was cooking. If he was looking for something he could never find it and always left chaos on his wake. You had to keep an eye on him.

You came back from the kitchen with the cup and spoon, the smallest of each you could find. The doctor was sitting in his armchair, one leg elegantly crossed over the other, jiggling his foot in the air, keeping time to a little song he was singing softly to himself.

> *Com'è gentil*
> *la notte a mezzo april!*
> *È azzurro il ciel,*
> *la luna è senza vel:*
> *tutt'è languor,*
> *pace, mistero, amor!**

"Have our crockery and cutlery shrunk, Aurora?" he asked when he saw you coming in with the diminutive items. You could not help laughing. "And why do you not sit down, woman? Is this how you eat with a friend? This is most discouraging!"

You did not know how to sit. Sideways, with one leg out in front of you, perched on the edge of the seat or sitting further back?… You felt very uncomfortable with the doctor watching you eating. You had never eaten in front of anyone like him and, in fact, had never eaten outside the kitchen. You felt so strange, so different, so clumsy, so out of place… But the last thing you wanted to do was to offend him, so you made an effort. You put so little chocolate on the spoon that you could hardly taste it, opening your mouth to about the size of a pine nut, which must have looked very comical. But the doctor did not make fun of you. He made everything seem natural and easy. Even his way of gazing at you started to seem normal, although sometimes it made you blush.

"Are you going to tell me what your invention is?"

"I made it with water and milk, in equal quantities."

He raised his eyebrows, very surprised. "Ah…" he said.

"It is the latest fashion in Vienna and Paris."

"And how do you know about these things, Aurora? Have you ever been to Vienna or Paris?"

"Me? No, of course I have not, a poor girl like me! I read about it in some foreign magazines," you said, your cheeks reddening as if you had caught red-handed, up to some kind of mischief.

"Of course! I keep forgetting that you can read, Aurora! You are somewhat strange too. So, do you buy foreign fashion magazines?"

"With my wages, Senyor. But only sometimes, when I have saved a little, because they are expensive. They are written in foreign languages, but if you read them again and again you forget about the words and end up understanding what they are saying."

"Really?" His eyebrows remained raised. The doctor peered at you as if you belonged to some strange species. "Well, Aurora, let me tell you that I wholly approve of the fashions of Vienna and Paris! Would you like to go to these places?"

"Of course not! What would a simple soul like me do there?"

"Drink hot chocolate with milk?"

"I am already drinking it here, and that is astonishing enough." You laughed, and this made the doctor laugh. His laugh was deep, bass-baritone, although you did not know that expression then, and laughing together really did give you the feeling that you were like two friends.

"Now listen to me, Aurora. From now on I want to include some foreign magazines in the household expenses."

"Oh no, doctor! There is no need for that. That is an extravagance we can very well do wi—"

"No, it is an essential item! How, otherwise, are we to know that they are changing the way of drinking chocolate in Paris and Vienna? Please do as I tell you, Aurora. Buy the fashion magazines or, better still, send off a request for subscription."

You shook your head, as if the doctor had completely lost his mind or had asked you to do something bizarre.

"To Paris?" Shock pushed your voice an octave higher than usual.

"Wherever you like, girl! Send it off and that is the end of the matter. Do it in your name, naturally. Please do not make me a subscriber to any French fashion magazine!"

You kept shaking your head, but let him persuade you. It was too tempting, too generous to refuse. You frowned, as a girl in your position should, but you could not stop wondering how all this had come about. How could you have been so fortunate? That man was like first prize in a raffle, which you had won without knowing how. You, who had never had anything!

You went back to Senyor Antoni's house with the chocolate pot in your hands a couple more times. The door remained closed, but behind the spyhole you could glimpse Enriqueta's sour face.

"You here again?" she grumbled the moment she saw you.

You could see her staring at you. You had put on a little weight and looked healthier now. You were also better dressed, because the doctor let you make your own clothes and you did not have to wear a drab uniform of the same colour all the time, although you were well aware that you had to dress in keeping with your station.

"Listen to me, Enriqueta." Your voice had changed too. It was more self-assured than before. "This is the last time I am going to come here and I wish to speak very clearly. When I left this house, after what happened with Senyora Càndida, I took something that was not mine. I do not know why I did it, but I was young, upset and I suppose I was not thinking straight. I have greatly regretted this, almost from the moment I walked out this door. Ever since then, I have wanted to return what I stole, but you always answer the door with that nasty expression on your face and bar my way. I believe it is time to stop this silliness and put the matter behind us. Do you not agree? I beg you, take the chocolate pot and then we can forget about it." You held out the packet, but she was not very interested.

"A chocolate pot?" she said, pulling a face as if you were talking about some monster from the depths of the sea.

"A white porcelain chocolate pot."

"And who will remember that, Aurora?" She sneered, showing her disdain. "This does not make sense. It is eight years since Senyora Càndida ran off with that man."

"That is not the point. The chocolate pot is not mine. It belongs here. It meant something to Senyor Antoni's mother, or so she told me a long time ago."

"Aurora, the Senyora is dying. I swear that this is not a good time to go stirring up problems from the past. This thing does not belong to anyone now. Why can you not just keep it? It is more yours than anyone else's, if you think about it. Please do not come back. We have a lot of work here."

Who are the owners of lost things? To whom do they belong, these objects that someone once loved when that person is gone for ever? Do they want another person to keep them, cherish them and become their owner? Is there a place where lost objects hope to be found? Do things need an owner or are they happier when they are free? Would not the security of belonging to someone be better?

"Very well, Enriqueta, I shall not come back." You were already turning away from her.

The spyhole snapped shut and, once again, you were in the street holding the chocolate pot.

You walked slowly, meandering through the labyrinth of streets. Carrer Agullers seemed longer than usual. In Carrer Espaseria you heard the bells of Santa Maria del Mar, and it seemed that the echoes paused to caress your cheeks as they flew like arrows to the sea. You were drawn to the old basilica, like an insect attracted to light. You stayed inside for a while, in this beautiful place which had always enraptured you. Then you left by the door on the Banys Vells side and continued your leisurely wanderings, now turning left into Carrer de Brosolí. You made the most of your walk to put your thoughts in order because, from time to time, one should do some spring cleaning inside one's head, get rid of all the useless odds and ends and dust down the good pieces. Otherwise, time covers everything with the same veil.

Carrer de Brosolí opened into Argenteria, the street of the silversmiths, just opposite the corner of Carrer de Manresa, where the Sampons chocolate shop was. You stopped to look at the display, as bright and shining as a guardian angel, all those dainties so beautifully laid out on plates and nestling in bowls. There were glossy strands of spun sugar which made you think of a fantasy in ice, coffee-flavoured sweets wrapped in silvery paper, cones of cocoa powder for making hot chocolate, all kinds of chocolates with fillings made of the most sophisticated blends of ingredients and, as a backdrop to the whole exhibit, a lovely painting of a very elegant lady sitting in her library and sipping from a little cup of hot chocolate. At the bottom it said, "The best desire of all is desire for Sampons chocolate." Your eyes strayed behind the boxes of different colours and sizes, full of delicacies you had never tasted. It seemed that the great attraction was a kind of chocolate called *gianduia*, piled into gleaming pyramids in a prominent position in the shop window, as if they were the keystone of the whole array. Then, lined up like soldiers, were blocks of chocolate: big, small and medium-sized, *a la pedra** (according to the wrapping) and milk chocolate, another strange new invention. The prices were not shown, but you had some money with you and thought it would be sufficient to buy a little surprise for the doctor.

You pushed open the shop door, making a bell tinkle inside. The smell was heavenly and you would have remained where you were, in a trance, just inhaling it, if a friendly woman's voice had not asked, "How may I help you, Senyora?"

Senyora.

You looked at the speaker, a young woman with big twinkling eyes. She could not have been more than twenty. Apparently, thanks to the uniform you had made for yourself, she had not noticed that you were not a senyora but a servant. From a good house, yes. Luckily that much was true. This girl could have addressed you informally if she had paid attention to your appearance. That was her right, but she preferred to say, "How may I help you, Senyora?" You asked for some chocolate powder for making hot chocolate nice and thick, the way the doctor liked it and, since you were there, a small block of milk chocolate. The girl wrapped your purchases in tissue paper, smiling all the while.

Meanwhile, you looked at some photographs hanging on the walls. Some were of dark-skinned men picking cocoa beans from crooked-looking trees. Beneath it, a sign proclaimed: "Sampons Chocolates: Cuban plantations." There was also a portrait of Senyor Antoni standing next to a pile of cocoa beans drying in the sun. The sign said, "Antoni Sampons in Santiago, Cuba, supervising the drying of the cocoa crop, 1878." Then there was another sign, in very conspicuous black letters:

SAMPONS CHOCOLATES

FOUNDED IN 1877

Prize-winning products in every competition

owing to their excellent quality

Approved and recommended by

THE ROYAL ACADEMY OF MEDICINE AND SURGERY

OF THE CITY OF BARCELONA

Sold in reputable patisseries and apothecaries' establishments

"One peseta and three reals please," the girl said. You took the coins from your pocket and put them in her hand.

While you were waiting for your change, you saw a way of doing what you had tried so hard but failed to do. It seemed logical and right. You stealthily put the package containing the chocolate pot on a nearby chair, on your side of the counter. The shop assistant's back was turned and, in any case, could not see the chair from where she was. There were two other customers in the shop, but they were distracted by other matters. A man was agonizing over which would be the best chocolates for a gift, as if he were buying precious stones, and a fat woman was scolding a small child who wanted some rock sugar. They presented no problem. The chocolate pot lay sideways on the chair, so discreet that no one would notice or say anything. They would find it when they were tidying up at closing time.

"Here is your change, Senyora. I am sure you will enjoy your chocolate," the girl said.

So now it seemed that you looked like a person who ate chocolate regularly. Is that what the shop assistant thought? That you had bought it for yourself?

You pushed open the door and, once in the street clutching your delicious purchases, you breathed a sigh of relief. *You have done it. You have returned it. You can stop worrying about it now.*

You strode off with your head held high.

Like some small animal that gets lost in the street and then immediately finds its way home, the chocolate pot wasted no time in returning to your hands, your life and your honest woman's conscience. The smiling shop assistant restored it to you. You had gone back to get some chocolate powder for the doctor, as you planned to make him the hot chocolate you now prepared with milk, following the dictates of fashion in Vienna and Paris, and while you were waiting you were gazing at the wrappings of the sweets and chocolates, the cards given away with blocks of chocolate for the children to collect and trade. When the girl handed you your change, she said, "Wait a moment, please." With that, she disappeared into the back room and returned with her ever-radiant smile and held out the chocolate pot, still wrapped in tissue paper. "You left this on the chair the other day and I put it away because I was certain you would return."

You took the packet, trying to look pleased. "Thank you. I believed I had lost it."

"I am happy to help, Senyora," the girl said.

Senyora.

When you got home, you hid the packet in the back of the wardrobe. Now you were not sure when you would have another chance to free yourself of this burden. Or if you ever would.

As the old man with whom you lived so happily, without really understanding why, had once said, the years fly away like swallows in autumn. But the doctor said so many things you did not understand.

Sometimes a comment he had made a long time previously suddenly made sense. It might take years for this to happen. It was like the day when you looked in the mirror and saw a woman with a full face, a lock of hair falling on her forehead and clear, untroubled eyes. *How can this be?*

How was it possible that you were thirty-nine and had been living for fifteen years in that flat in Carrer del Pi, where every inch spoke of your presence, where Doctor Volpi's hair had turned white, and where you still listened to him with the same admiration and astonishment you felt on the very first day? How could it be that, after so much time, he still made you laugh and blush?

Within those four walls, the years did not fly away or, if they did, they were always singing the same song. The doctor locked himself away to read or went out very early and did not come back until his discussion group had finished for the day. You always had the hot chocolate ready, with bread, or sponge fingers, or little cakes, or brioche, he told you what he had talked about with his friends, or complained that a lot of people were getting sick because it was so cold, and you helped him into his silk dressing gown and slippers. Then he would say something like, "Goodnight, Aurora. I am happy today, because next week they have programmed *Guglielmo Tell*, and I love operas in French!" And he would go off to bed, humming, and you would say, "Good night, Doctor Volpi. Sleep well. I shall see you in the morning, God willing."

In the afternoons you read the fashion magazines, which now came every month. You could hardly keep up with them. Sometimes you went out for a walk along La Rambla, because you enjoyed seeing all the hustle and bustle of the cafés and theatres. Then you came home, lit the lamps and wondered, *How is it possible that nothing ever happens, but the years slip away like water trickling through a wicker basket?*

Of course there were some upsets, for example the first night of the accursed opera *Guglielmo Tell*: that damned first night – and may Heaven forgive you for your thoughts – when the doctor came home early in a terrible state with his white waistcoat covered in blood. You almost died of fright when you saw him and thought he was injured. Still in a state of shock, he sat in his armchair and, while you helped him to take off his dress boots, he told you how the wife of the bookseller Dalmàs had died in his arms, and he had been unable to do anything to save her, but she was not the only one. The sight of all that death and destruction had been horrendous. And only one of the two bombs thrown had gone off. The second, by some miracle, had been stopped by the skirts of the wife of the lawyer Cardellach, who had also died. God bless the poor soul.

"Oh Lord!" exclaimed Doctor Volpi, and this was the first time you had ever seen him so distraught. "The Liceu will never go back to being what it was, Aurora. We shall never recover from this bloodbath."

You suddenly dropped the second patent-leather boot on the rug. Kneeling there beside the doctor, you burst into tears. He was shocked into silence and was staring at you. You were sobbing like a small child, with tears pouring down your cheeks, more and more uncontainable tears. *Where has all this dread come from? What is happening to me*. The doctor wondered the same and feared his conclusions.

"But Aurora," he said, "come on, get up. What is wrong, woman? Do not cry like that. Speak to me, please."

He took one of your arms and pulled, trying to help you stand, but you, what with all your crying, instead of standing up, fell down with your skirts all puffed up, so you looked like a great big onion lying there on the rug. He was increasingly astonished and increasingly desperate.

"Aurora, please, listen to me. What is wrong? Tell me why you are crying. Are you crying, perhaps, for the people who were killed by the bomb?"

When you calmed down a little, you burbled a few incoherent words, trying to give some kind of explanation.

"All that blood… It gave me a terrible fright… I thought… You seemed to be injured… The blood… Thanks be to God… You are unharmed… I was so terribly afraid…"

He helped you to stand, gazing at you. "Aurora, little one!… But, then… all this crying was only on my account?" Doctor Volpi's eyes filled with tears, and his hands were probably trembling too, but you did not notice, because you were so overwhelmed by your own distress.

"Sit down, Aurora, please sit down. I am going to get you a handkerchief."

He hurried out of the room, leaving you alone, staring at the boots, which were also bloodstained, and the more you looked at the blood the more you sobbed, imagining what might have happened to him, and the more you sobbed the more sobs came out, and the more you looked at the boots… and it was like one of those annoying little ditties that never comes to an end.

The doctor brought you a handkerchief and a cup of hot chocolate and tried to soothe you with words, sweet artless words, like he might have said to a small child, words unlike any that had ever been said to you before. Then he told you to go to your room and sleep off the fright. He remained alone, wide awake, sitting in his armchair in the parlour, staring at the books which had witnessed so many things in his life, as if he was seeking words of wisdom from them, or trying to share his surprise with them. Doctor Volpi thought a lot that night, perhaps as he had never thought before, or at least he had never been aware of thinking like this. At daybreak he decided he should get some sleep and went to bed.

He slept soundly, because he had come to something that slightly resembled a decision.

"I should like to speak with you about something, Aurora. Would you please sit down for a moment? Here, in front of me."

Poor Doctor Volpi had no idea of the task he had ahead of him. Even if he had suspected, he would have continued anyway, because he was one of those headstrong men who will not let trifles stand in the way of a decision.

You sat on the chair, your legs close together, hands in your lap and the wrinkle of a frown crossing your forehead. You smoothed your skirts. You seemed calm except for your flushed cheeks.

"Yes, doctor, what is it?"

"The matter is… well, for some days I have been thinking about a question that concerns you and, naturally, me too somewhat, and I believe the time has come to tell you what I am thinking, supposing I find the way to do it, because, as you may have noticed, I am not very sure of myself. In any case, the matter is… and if I must be sincere and, well, it seems easier in theory, or when I was rehearsing what I want to say before asking you to come and listen to me, but the truth of the matter is I do not even know where to start. How silly, and at my age too!"

"Is there any way I can help, doctor?" you offered.

"The problem is that it is one of those things one does not say very often. Do you know what I mean? I am an old man now and I have only done this once in my life and that was a very different matter. I believe I was not so aware of what I was doing then. Ah, youth! What a malady of awareness! But, please bear with me, I shall do it. This matter… Aurora, do you recall how long you have been my housekeeper?"

"Since November 1877," you answered, the wrinkle in your forehead deepening.

"Then…" the doctor counted, "that makes nineteen years. Good Heavens, time has simply flown by!"

Your alarm came out in the form of a question. "But, is something wrong, doctor? Should I be worried? Have I done something to vex you?"

"No, no, no, no, Aurora. Please hear me out. Nineteen years is a long time…"

"Nineteen years and twenty-one days."

"Well… what I wish to say might sound somewhat strange to you, coming out all of a sudden like this, but the truth is that, for these nineteen years and twenty-one days, no man on earth has been as well cared for as I have."

You were flattered and smiled. Yet fear made your body shrink inside your bodice. His words had a recognizable ring of farewell, of conclusion, of something that was about to end.

Whatever was happening, it was important. You were starting to understand that clearly enough.

"Are you unwell, doctor? Are you feeling ill?"

"Ill? No, not as far as I know. At my age, the worst thing that is happening to me is being my age. Do not worry, Aurora, and please let me speak."

Do not worry. That is easy to say. You said nothing, gritted your teeth and let him speak, but he was soon rambling again.

"I should like to think that you, too, have been happy here in my home these last nineteen years," he said.

"But is there some problem? Have you got involved in politics?"

"Please, Aurora, just be quiet for a moment... I am asking you so boorishly, because if you do not stop talking, the little bit of courage I have will desert me and you will be left with the mystery *ad æternum*, which is a very long time."

"No, no, please, for Heaven's sake. I shall not speak."

You went quiet, clenching your teeth even harder. This situation was increasingly difficult. Almost impossible. Pure torture.

"I should like to think that, for you, there have been moments in which you forgot you were working for me, that I was the master of the house and all these stupid conventionalities, and that we have been two friends, who enjoyed sitting down for a nice chat and to drink chocolate together."

Your eyes were as wide as saucers. You still had no idea where this was leading. Was this a farewell? Did he want to die? Was he going to live abroad? If martyrdom is worse than torture, this was turning into martyrdom.

Now he was staring at you, waiting for something, and you were unsure what you had to do.

"Could you please confirm that what I have just said is true, Aurora? It is important for what I wish to say next."

"Of course, doctor. What was it?"

"Are we friends?"

"Of course we are not, doctor! You are the master here and I am your housekeeper."

"But could we be friends?"

"No! It would be a very serious breach of respect if I were to think of myself as your friend. I am not your equal and I am very well aware of that."

"But, would you like us to be friends?"

"Please, doctor, I have never had a friend." You could see him wilting, as if this was all too much for him. Nevertheless, you continued. "I think that having friends is not something that people like me can aspire to. Friends do not let you work, and I came into this world to work. There is no more to be said."

You crossed your hands in your lap, feeling proud of your words. The doctor frowned, stared into space for a moment and then rubbed his hands over his face.

"This is hopeless, Aurora. I do not know how to do this. It is more difficult than I imagined."

You started. You were alarmed and disconcerted. You had no idea what was happening. This man was not the Doctor Horaci Volpi you knew. The worst thing was that you did not know why.

"Please do not alarm me any more, doctor," you begged. "Tell me what is wrong. I can see you want to tell me something. Let me help you. Is it something terrible? Is it bad news?"

"Oh, little one, I pray you will not think so."

"I shall not. Well, then… then is it… well, different news?"

"Yes."

"Is it strange?"

"Very strange!"

"Disagreeable?"

"Not necessarily."

"Could you be leaving Barcelona?"

"No, woman! Where would I go, at my age?"

"Are you ill? Are you going to die?"

"Of course I am going to die! But I should not like it to happen right now."

You could think of no more possibilities.

Think, Aurora, think. What is making him so agitated? It is something he dares not tell you, something that makes his voice go hoarse and makes him behave like a little boy who has been caught in the middle of some mischief... Ah, now I know! Of course. It could be nothing else.

"Then it must be a matter related with a lady."

"You are as bright as a button, Aurora." The doctor smiled delicately at your insight.

"Do you wish to marry? Is that what you are trying to tell me?"

"*Bravissimo!*"

This answer to your questions was a blow. He wanted to bring a lady into the house! After all this time, having to answer to a lady would be an upheaval, and a terrible upheaval at that. Now you would have to do everything her way and she would make your head spin, giving you orders every two minutes, wanting to supervise housekeeping purchases, to change things – and you could say goodbye to your fashion magazines – wanting to keep a close eye on expenses and fill her own pockets of course. If she did not want to fill her pockets, what woman would want to marry Doctor Volpi, an old man of seventy-five with such a dull existence, going from his books to the men's discussion group and from the discussion group to his box in the Liceu? She would no doubt be a crafty young woman… But, oh dear, how young? If you had to put up with a young lady of twenty-five, with a supple, girlish body and face like fine porcelain, rummaging in your cupboards all day long, it would make your blood boil! Or worse, if you had to watch this good man Doctor Volpi doing his utmost to keep up with a young fortune hunter! And he would certainly consent to her every whim, as he was incapable of saying no to anyone. Then he would lose his true personality, because everyone knows that women like that have more influence over men than anything that has ever been invented, and you did not know how you could bear it.

You were immediately ashamed of these thoughts. Who were you to be thinking such things about the doctor's decisions? *Have these years of privilege gone to your head, Aurora?* Did you think that, just because some ingenuous shop assistant called you "Senyora", you had some rights over him? You felt ashamed of yourself, while your inner voice admonished, *Aurora, how could you have imagined that this would go on for ever? You should be grateful, because you have spent nineteen years in a bed of roses. You came into the world alone, with nobody to care for you. You, a woman who does not deserve anything.*

Meanwhile, the silence grew and became very uncomfortable. Doctor Volpi's breathing sounded ragged, because he was very anxious and he had been waiting so long for your answer, but you did not know what to say or how to continue the conversation.

"Listen to me, Aurora. That is enough! I cannot bear this any longer. I shall say it simply and without further ado, and it will be better for us both, do you not think?" You nodded. "Well, Aurora… I should be very happy if you would marry me."

You are bad, Aurora. You are a woman who is as bad as the Devil himself. You have had uncharitable thoughts about the doctor and, with your wicked ideas, you have soiled the only truly good person you have ever known. The only thing that has happened to this poor man is that he has lost his head. He has gone completely mad. Look what he has come out with now! He wants to marry, and marry you! You could burst out laughing. But be careful, because he is taking this seriously. Be kind.

"No, doctor, that is not possible," you heard yourself saying, very firmly and with utter conviction.

"And why ever not? Are we not free, you and I?"

"Well, it cannot be, because it is not right. You and I are not the same. We are not free in the same way."

"Ah, no?"

"No, doctor. I would not know how to be your wife. I could not go out anywhere with you."

"And why not?"

"Because people would talk. Do you not know that?"

"They already talk. I would prefer them to talk about my getting married than to spread all kinds of ridiculous rumours about why I am not married. I did not know you were influenced by such tittle-tattle, Aurora."

"It affects me when they gossip about you, of course."

"Well, listen to me. I should like to give them a reason for talking about us."

"Heaven forbid! No, no, no, no," and you shook your head to emphasize every negative with another negative. "You have not thought about this properly. This is a kind of strange attack you have had. Surely you know that they would see you as an irresponsible person."

"I do not care how they see me. As long as you know that I—"

"No, no, no, no. This cannot be. No, no, no…" and you were still shaking your head. "You are not well, doctor. They will know I am your housekeeper!"

"I could not care less."

"They will laugh at you."

"Yes, but dying of envy."

"What ever are you saying, doctor? I have never heard such nonsense. And might one know why you have got this idea into your head now?"

Doctor Volpi let out a sigh. A long sigh, laden with mysteries. A sigh that concealed more than a thousand reasons why he wanted you, Aurora, to be his wife.

"Moreover," you continued, "I do not know anything about men. I know nothing at all. I have never… I have not… I am still a virgin, and that is the truth."

"And I have been a widower for almost thirty years, little one. I have never been a libertine. I believe I have forgotten everything I ever learnt. But I think we shall manage. Do you not agree?"

"No, no, no…"

"Now, listen to me, Aurora, it is not as if I have not thought about these things. For me you have the grace and beauty of the goddess Charis. More than her, because you are real and you are here, in my home. The fact is, when I think about you and myself and a future together, I do not think about lustful things. Do you understand me?" You kept shaking your head at every expression like "together", "our" and "future", like a stern mother chiding her little boy for saying something silly. "It must be something to do with age, and I have never been very forward about these things, but the first image that comes into my head is of you lying in bed at my side and holding my hand under the sheet. Or you laughing about something I have told you, the way you do, like a little songbird warbling, or the two of us at the Liceu, enjoying something lovely like *La sonnambula* or *Aida*, and strolling together along La Rambla, and going to have hot chocolate in Carrer de Petrixol. That is what I think about, and when I do, I am almost faint with happiness."

"The Liceu? Please, please, do not say another word! You poor man, Doctor Volpi. Tomorrow you will greatly regret that you have said these things to me. But you need not worry, because I shall act as if you have not said anything. I think you have worked too hard today. Now, this is what I suggest... you should go to bed. I shall bring you a little cup of chocolate, just the way you like it, and then you will close your eyes and have a nice sleep. Are you listening to me?"

"Of course I am listening to you."

"Well, that is what you must do. Tomorrow you will see things very differently."

"And if tomorrow I do not?..."

"No, please, say no more now. It is not good for you to keep talking now, doctor. Tomorrow will be another day, a completely new day. Come with me now. The bed-warmer must be cold by now."

It was a long night. You did not want to think about it, but Doctor Volpi's words kept coming back relentlessly, again and again, swirling in your head – *beauty, goddess, songbird* – words you never imagined could be addressed to you, just to you, and even though you did not match up to them, they sounded lovely. You liked them as much as you liked the way the doctor looked at you, the tone of his voice when he was talking about the future and even the blue veins on his hands. In the still of the night, which always makes things more confusing, you even stopped thinking for a second that it was a ludicrous idea and started wondering what if...

What if?... All the changes in the world, all the revolutions, all the conquests, anything that was worth the effort, always began when someone asked, "What if?..."

And you kept asking yourself the question so insistently that you had to leave your bed and go and get a glass of water, because your throat had suddenly gone dry. And while you were in the kitchen, staring, as if in a trance, at the wrapping on a block of chocolate, reading over and over again those words, "The best desire of all is desire for Sampons chocolate", you asked yourself, for the first time, what you wanted. What was your wish? What would you have liked if you had been born to another life? The answers made you very afraid.

When you went back to your room, you could hear that the doctor seemed to be singing to himself, as usual. He was always singing. You listened carefully and recognized one of those Italian songs you had sometimes heard before. You did not understand why he was singing so happily. You shook your head, yet again that night, which was so loaded with every no-no-no you had said, and went back to bed escorted by the cheerful tune:

> *La moral di tutto questo*
> *è assai facil di trovar.*
> *Ve la dico presto presto*
> *se vi piace d'ascoltar.*
> *Ben è scemo di cervello*
>
> *chi s'ammoglia in vecchia età;*
> *va a cercar col campanello*
> *noie e doglie in quantità.**

Rigoletto

"Do you know what I heard? Càndida Turull has returned to Barcelona." That is what the doctor – you mean Horaci – said when you were sitting in the box waiting for *Tristan und Isolde* to begin. When you left the opera house he was so elated, telling you why Wagnerian sopranos had to be as strong as Valkyries, and he was so full of praise for the beautiful way Isolde had died for love that he talked of nothing else all the way home, and you did not dare to interrupt him with your questions.

You decided to wait until the next morning, for the idle hour after breakfast.

"Doctor, do you know if Càndida Turull has really come back to Barcelona? I should like to see her again."

Horaci put on his stern expression. "Aurora, how long are you going to keep calling me 'doctor'? We have been married for nearly a year!"

Of all the changes that had taken place in your life, those of the last year were the hardest to adapt to. How to address him? It was so complicated! How can you change your ways when you have been doing the same thing all your life? How can you rise in status if you have never had any self-esteem?

"If I do not call you that, I have the feeling that I am not talking to you, doctor," you tried to explain, or perhaps to defend yourself. "I mean, talking to you, Horaci! Please be patient with me and I promise I shall try harder. At least it does not happen any more in public, does it? But do not worry, because even if I call you 'doctor', I love you just the same."

His smile was so dazzling that you were totally disarmed. He always ended up agreeing with you. Moreover, you were a good pupil, much better than he had imagined you would be. In one year you had learnt more than you had in your whole life, from the purely mechanical abilities – like eating a lobster using little silver pliers – through to more artistic skills – dancing a waltz, spinning one way and then the other – and the whole series of rules and regulations that you have to know if you are to mingle with people who notice every single slip as if examining you through a magnifying glass.

That is not important, you thought, because deep inside you everything was much easier, even though there had been some very significant changes, of course. Now the doctor – Horaci – no longer ate alone at the small round table. And you no longer had dinner by yourself in the kitchen at half-past seven. You ate together in the parlour, after the clock had struck nine – the dinner time of elegant people – at an English-style table, which you had chosen in the furniture section of El Siglo department store, nicely set with a tablecloth and napkins stitched by your own hand. You no longer sewed in the kitchen or in your bedroom as you used to do, but sitting in a rocking chair in the glassed-in balcony, watching the people walking up and down Carrer del Pi, or waiting to glimpse your husband coming home so you could leave everything to be with him. And very often, although you had to overcome your fear of being watched by everyone, you ate out in some restaurant, like Can Culleretes or the Colón, after which you strolled around looking in shop windows, laughing softly or covering your mouth with your gloved hand, because you had learnt that a lady does do not stop in the middle of the street laughing heartily, doubled over with her hands on her hips, as you might have done a year beforehand.

The nights – oh the nights! – you went to bed together, still a little awkward, each of you with a candlestick and a solemn expression. The doctor – Horaci – told you all about opera. Rossini, Donizetti, Verdi, Mozart, Wagner, Bellini... and at first the names were strange and the titles very complicated, so it was difficult for you. He sang you his favourite passages and you laughed or were horrified by the whole incomprehensible assortment of stories where anything could happen – forgiveness, revenge, a bloodbath, three weddings all at once... but always at the very end of the final scene. Your husband's passion when he talked about these things made him seem younger. His eyes shone with enthusiasm like a little boy's, and he laughed when his voice broke because he could not sing the high notes, while you kept asking very elementary questions like "What is a *cabaletta*?" or "When the arias are not sad, are they no longer arias?" and he explained everything in detail, because he was so happy to have awakened in you an interest in one of the most beautiful things in the world. On cold nights he held your hand under the bedclothes and then he had an urgent need to blow out the candles. And in the dark – oh, the dark – it was all much easier than you had imagined. He acted as if he was in bed with a queen and it was not at all difficult to do what he wanted, to follow his lead without denying him anything, to love him without words or fuss, but with all your heart and soul. When you woke up in the morning, in a hurry to make the doctor's breakfast and with senseless fright in your heart, you had to remind yourself that things were different now.

Aurora, you silly goose, things are very different now. Can you get that into your head for once and for all? Now the servant is Clara, and she is in the kitchen getting breakfast. You are the lady of the house and it is your obligation to laze in bed and get up very slowly so you do not feel faint, and then put on your silk dressing gown and slippers before spending ten minutes at your dressing table. That is what you have to do, Aurora, whether or not you believe that it makes no difference if it is ten minutes or half a minute, or whether your heart keeps telling you to hurry off to the kitchen to get the tray and set it with cups, coffee pot and plates. But you have to do all this for him, the doctor – Horaci – so he will think that you have turned into a lady who does not have to worry about anything.

While you were thinking all this as you brushed your black hair, your husband watched you contentedly from the bed and clinking plates and cups in the kitchen announced that, yes, things really had changed, however difficult it was for you to call the doctor "Horaci", and even though you had just told him that you would like to see Càndida again.

"I know what we can do," your husband said. "The lady who told me about Càndida Turull has invited us to come and see her at her new home in Passatge de Domingo, where she and her family have just moved. We shall accept her invitation and, while we are there, we shall bring up the subject and see what she has to say. Her name is Maria del Roser Golorons, the wife of the builder Rodolf Lax. I am sure you will like her very much. You do not have to worry about anything; she is certainly not one of those insufferable strait-laced ladies."

Going visiting and social gatherings still intimidated you. Horaci sent your card to the house in Passatge de Domingo and, a couple of hours later, a brougham was waiting at your door, ready to take you up Passeig de Gràcia and even higher up, to the zone where the city's well-to-do people had decided they wanted to be seen.

"Does it not bother them, living so far away?" you muttered as you got into the brougham.

"I believe that when you are so rich nothing bothers you," the doctor said.

The brougham went along Carrer del Pi to Portaferrissa, where it turned right to go to Plaça de Catalunya through Portal de l'Àngel.

"We are already outside the walls and we did not have to pay anything," the doctor said, happily looking up at towers of old city walls that only endured in his memory. "This is one result of getting old: they suddenly change the sets, the plot and the conductor of the orchestra, but you want to keep playing the same role."

You were very impressed by Senyora Maria del Roser Golorons. She, like you, seemed to be an impostor, but in reverse. She was a lady who could have disguised herself as a maid without anybody noticing, because she was so pleasant, simple and open. She welcomed you from the foot of a sweeping marble stairway. "Be careful with the vine leaves," she said, gesturing at the moulding on the balustrade, which was far too ornate for your liking. You picked up your skirts, not too much and not too little, trying not to show your ankle or to stumble, and followed your hostess upstairs.

The mandatory but pleasant tour of the house began with the courtyard, where the plants were still very small, and then proceeded through the large drawing room with its fireplace, the library, the sewing room and the playroom, where the three formally dressed children of the family were introduced to you as the two sons, Amadeu and Joan, and a tiny toddler daughter, just over a year old, whose name was Violeta. The nursemaid, Conxa, was also welcoming. On returning to the main floor, you glanced into Senyor Lax's office and, leaving that, you were shown a locked space under the stairs, home of the prodigious invention which all visitors to the house admired. "This is where we keep the telephone!" Senyora Lax triumphantly announced. The doctor was immediately fascinated by the strange object and our hostess assured us that it was extremely useful for speaking with the people in charge of the factories in Mataró, because Senyor Lax no longer had to make the journey every time he needed to tell them something. Horaci kept nodding and repeating, "Of course, of course, Mataró…"

"Can the people in Mataró really hear you speaking into this machine?" you asked.

"I promise you, Senyora, it is as if you were standing beside them!" your hostess said. "I also found it hard to believe the first time I set eyes on this contraption, which looks more like a lightning conductor."

Chocolate was served in the drawing room with the fireplace, a sculptured work which was too ostentatious for everyone's taste, except for Rodolf Lax, who tended to excess in everything. Even so, the doctor – Horaci – found something to praise.

"Do you like it?" asked Maria del Roser, sipping from the little cup the maid had just served her. "I think it is a horror, but there's nothing to be done about it. After all, my husband is the one who gives the orders! The other day we were visited by Antoni Sampons, the chocolatier, and he also liked it very much.

In fact, he was so impressed with it that he is getting the sculptor to make him a similar one in the house he has just bought in Passeig de Gràcia. It seems that one of these architects that are so in demand nowadays – Domènech i Cadafalch or Puig i Montaner? – has already begun the renovation. Well, it does not matter which one it is. But, Heavens above, one hopes that it is not one of those men who cannot make a single straight wall! If that is the case, poor Antonieta will not be able to hang a painting anywhere for the rest of her life. These people are quite terrifying! Do you know what they say about the Marchioness of Vinardell? Well, the architect made the walls so crooked that there was not enough space for her grand piano in the music room and, when she protested, this shameless man said, 'Senyora, I suggest you learn to play the violin.' That is how things work today!"

It was perfect that Senyora Lax should have raised the subject, and Horaci immediately took it up.

"Ah yes, that reminds me… Maria del Roser, did you not tell me the other day that Càndida Turull has returned to Barcelona?"

"Indeed I did, doctor. It seems that she is living in a flat in Passeig de Bonanova, a gift from her saint of a mother, who was always so concerned about everyone. In this family we dearly loved Senyora Hortènsia, may she rest in peace. I believe her granddaughter is very like her, at least insofar as she is a very good person."

Senyora Hortènsia was the theme of our conversation for the next few minutes, and rightly so. All three of you spoke of her with heartfelt affection, remembering her mildness, her simple nature and her way of always being concerned about other people.

"I owe everything I have to Senyora Hortènsia," you said, trying very hard to stop the tears from brimming over. "I was greatly affected by her death."

"I imagine" – and now Horaci said what you had not dared to utter – "you know that my dear wife was born in the Turull house."

Maria del Roser Golorons put her cup down on the table. Her movements were gentle, without the slightest trace of malice, like her words.

"I am aware of that, doctor. I might add that when you were married a year ago, people talked of nothing else. Everywhere one went it was the scandal of the day." She smiled and looked at you both, slightly tilting her head. "People cannot bear it if someone else is happier than they are."

"Then you will understand Aurora's interest in Càndida is a very personal matter. They were raised together, so to speak. Aurora loves her like a sister."

You added, "I promised Senyora Hortènsia that I would always look after her daughter and to make sure nothing happened to her, but now I am not sure if I wish to see her for Senyora Hortènsia or for myself."

Maria del Roser Golorons was a veteran of many wars. Hearing these words, she fell silent and pursed her lips. "Senyora Càndida has not made it at all easy for you to keep your promise, but it is very noble of you continue being true to your word, my dear. Tell me what I can do to help."

"I only need her address, if you would tell me what it is."

"Of course I can do that. I shall also give you some advice, if you will permit me." You made a very convincing gesture with your hand. "You must be prepared for the likelihood that your nobility of spirit will not be returned."

How ingenuous you were! It still hurt you to hear anyone speaking badly of Senyoreta Càndida. Senyora Càndida. Càndida.

"I believe she is not receiving visitors," Senyora Lax continued. "I am informed that she lives alone with hardly any servants. However, it would appear that she sometimes sees Antonieta. This does not surprise me, because Antonieta is an angel, with a heart as big as a cathedral. I have heard that mother and daughter met again some months ago. Imagine, they are almost strangers! If she were not blessed with this daughter…"

"You mean that…" Horaci was very upset by the story.

"I mean that if Senyoreta Sampons did not make sure that her mother lacks for nothing, she would not even be able to eat. It seems that the singer abandoned her after subjecting her to all kinds of horrors. Even while the idyll lasted, he did not exactly treat her like a princess. A terrible disaster… If poor Senyor Estanislau had known…"

The doctor – Horaci – pulled a face to show his disgust. "What a dreadful thing, this story of Càndida Turull."

"Indeed it is, doctor… Indeed it is," your hostess concluded. "Oh, listen, I believe I can hear Rodolf. He will be very happy to find you here. Let me pour you a little more hot chocolate. And we shall change the subject, because these dramas upset him greatly."

Despite Maria del Roser Golorons's comments and your own misgivings, you decided to go to see her. You called for a carriage and asked to go to Passeig de la Bonanova. The doctor

– Horaci – came with you. At the entrance, he asked you, for what must have been the hundredth time, "Are you sure you want to go in alone?"

"Yes, I am sure."

"Very well. I shall come back for you in an hour. But will that not be too long? What if it goes badly?"

"It will go well. Please do not worry."

You carried a packet in your hands. Yellowing tissue paper tied up with white ribbon. It reminded you a little of those mummified animals that are sometimes found in ancient tombs.

You rang the bell twice before a scrawny major-domo came to open it.

"What did you say your name was?" He made you repeat it while ushering you into a gloomy entrance hall, where he indicated you should wait.

"Aurora. Doctor Volpi's wife. If you say Auroreta, Senyora Càndida will know who I am."

Your heart was racing, as it did when you were a little girl and Senyora Hortènsia called you to reprimand you, saying that "with all your chit-chat" you were keeping her daughter from her studies. Or when you were in the Sampons house, sneaking away to drink the chocolate in the bottom of the pot, terrified that someone would come into the kitchen and catch you. Or the morning when you went into Candideta's bedroom and found that her bed had not been slept in.

You heard voices at the end of the corridor. Càndida was probably making her major-domo repeat your name. Perhaps he had said a "senyora" had come to visit. A senyora. Poor Càndida probably did not understand anything. The wait was starting to drag on a little too long when he came back and announced in a languid voice that the Senyora was ready to receive you.

You thought your heart was going to explode before you reached the end of the corridor. You looked to your left and saw a huge, tiger-like cat, which hissed ferociously. You almost jumped out of your skin, and then you heard a coarse chuckle. In the living room a stout woman sat on a sagging sofa, still snickering, flapping an oriental-style fan and peering at you through rings of wrinkles.

"Aurora?" She drawled your name as if pronouncing it slowly would help her to believe what was happening. "Can this be you?"

She did not get up, of course. Neither did she greet you in any of the ways in which she should have welcomed the wife of a doctor. She examined you a little longer with her owl's eyes as you remained standing before her, letting her peruse you. Finally she said, "What a pretty dress. Let me see. Turn around."

Oh, if Horaci could have seen you turning round to show Càndida your dress, he would have been very angry! Luckily you had come in alone. It was only then that you realized that Càndida was the only person in the world for whom you were the Aurora you had always been.

"Goodness gracious! What a change!" she said.

"May I sit down?" you asked, but did not wait for her answer, just in case. You sat in the chair facing her, which gave you the best view of the whole living room, with her sitting opposite you, in the middle, something like a classical Venus.

You started to wonder why you had come. And the conversation had not even begun.

"I very much wanted to see you," you confessed, not at all surprised to hear yourself still using the *vostè* form. It would never have occurred to you to use the informal *tu*. "I have thought so much about you all these years! I was so happy to hear that you were here!"

"As they say, Auroreta, around the world and homewards hurled."

"How are you?"

"You can see for yourself. Fat and old."

"Please do not say that. We are the same age!"

"Then you are as old as I am."

The major-domo suddenly appeared, like a ghost. It was de-rigueur formality to ask if the ladies would like anything. Càndida answered for us both.

"No, there is no need for you to bring anything. Go and feed the cats. They have been waiting for a while."

The obsequious major-domo bowed slightly, said, "Yes, Senyora," and disappeared again. You were a little thirsty, but did not dare to say so. You looked around. There were a few books – very few – a pile of magazines, a sewing machine and a phonograph. It was the first time you had ever seen one, and it seemed to present a way of lightening the conversation.

"It is wonderful to be able to listen to music," you remarked, looking at the newfangled device.

"So you like music now, Aurora?"

"I am becoming interested, little by little."

"That is good. Things should be done little by little. I hardly ever listen to anything now. Music makes me agitated."

On the table, next to the phonograph, there were half a dozen cylinders, each in its own box. You could read familiar names: Wagner, Rossini, Puccini, Verdi. The only box that was open and empty read: "*Rigoletto*: *Quartet*". The cylinder must have been in the machine. Perhaps she had been listening to it shortly before you came. All at once you felt sad to imagine Càndida, sitting on that sagging sofa, alone or with a cat in her lap, as a voice sang from the phonograph:

Bella figlia dell'amore,
schiavo son de' vezzi tuoi.
Con un detto, un detto solo,
tu puoi le mie pene,
le mie pene consolar.

The silence, while you were thinking these sad things, was total and more eloquent than any word could possibly be. All those years and neither of you had anything to say.

"Are you not going to explain?" Càndida asked, looking meaningfully at your clothes.

You were angry because your words came out with a hint of apology, as if you had done something wrong. There are some people who turn everything into something bad. Until that day, it had never occurred to you that Càndida was one of them.

"When Senyora Hortènsia went to live with her niece, she sent me to Doctor Volpi to be his housekeeper. After I had been working there for nineteen years he asked me to marry him. As you would agree, the idea was madness, and at first, of course, I said no, but then I reconsidered and, in the end—"

"It was not madness," she interrupted in a flat, indifferent tone. "That is called being clever. I never imagined you were so wily, Aurora. How do you like men?"

"I am true to just one man," you said.

"Oh, you are a simpleton. You should never say such a thing," she said, waving a plump hand. "Men are slippery by nature and easily distracted. Always distracted. You can never totally trust them. So if you want a man you must put him on a short leash and never let him off it. He has to understand that the paths to your heart are difficult to find, like the right way through a maze of mirrors. The man who wants to understand will have you for ever. And the one who does not... Well, that one, so much the worse for him."

You did not agree with her but kept silent. You changed the subject slightly and it worked. Talking about men with Càndida was the last thing you wished to do.

"In fact, I owe everything to your mother," you continued. "If it had not been for her—"

"Neither you nor I would be in this world if it had not been for my mother."

"Yes, that is true." Another silence, this time shredded by loud meows. The cats were probably happy to smell their food. "I think of Senyora Hortènsia every day. The more the years go by the more I marvel at what she did for me and the more grateful I am."

"What are you talking about, Aurora?" When Càndida frowned she looked ten years older.

"I am talking about the wet nurse. Your mother got her to feed both of us, remember? It was natural that she did it for you, because you were her daughter. But me? Getting a wet nurse to feed me? I was an insignificant creature who meant nothing to anyone."

"What wet nurse, Aurora? What are you saying?"

"Do you not remember?" You were breathing easier at last. This was a subject you could both talk about naturally, without acting like a pair of statues. "When we were little girls we talked a lot about the wet nurse. You asked Senyora Hortènsia and she said we had one who lived in Hortes de Sant Pau. I actually went there to see if I could find her."

Càndida's expression suddenly turned vicious. It was like an attack.

"Aurora, are you really still so naive, and at your age? I invented that story about Hortes de Sant Pau so you would stop badgering me. Have you not worked it out yet? Good Heavens, woman, there was never any wet nurse! My mother suckled both of us."

You felt as if she had punched you. Blackness spread, a dark veil swiftly covering your eyes. Càndida's gleeful words came from far away.

"I cannot believe you never suspected anything! My lies were not at all convincing and you always identified the weaknesses in my story. Do you not remember? There was not enough time for the wet nurse to keep coming back and forth to feed us. The cook had never seen her… and you, always acting like the chief of police with all your questions… Yet you believed every word. That was the most amusing part!"

"Senyora Hortènsia?" you mumbled, still not quite understanding what you had just heard. "Your mother put me to the breast? But why?"

"Ah, you should have asked her."

"That is completely topsy-turvy," you pronounced. "Ladies do not put servants' babies to the breast. That is turning the world on its head!"

"Well, it is not unlike the way things are now!" Càndida said. "You look more like the Turulls' daughter than I do."

"Why did your mother never tell me?" you asked.

"You know what my mother was like. Nothing pleased her more than that old biblical precept about the right hand not knowing what the left hand was doing. She was being a Good Samaritan... As you can imagine, she bought me this flat, but she did it with money she had taken from my father without his knowing. So what do you think of that?"

You did not think anything. You just wanted to cry.

"I have brought you this..." you said, trying to fill the anguished silence. You placed the package on the table.

"What is that? I do not want anything that reminds me of the old days, Aurora. You know me well enough. The past and I have not been on speaking terms for a long time."

"Do you not wish to open it?"

"Tell me what it is." Her voice, harsh and peevish, cut like a knife.

"It is the white porcelain chocolate pot. The one with the inscription in blue letters."

The cats had stopped yowling and the silence was so absolute it seemed that the world had forgotten to turn on its axis. Càndida's brittle voice broke the spell.

"Take it away. I do not even want to see it." A pause, perhaps reflective. "Please," she added.

Your visit ended before you had imagined it would, and you spent twenty minutes waiting for the doctor – Horaci – at the entrance. When he came you were in a state of great distress, trying not to cry and cradling the chocolate pot in your hands. On the way home, he held you to his breast and let you cry your heart out. Then he listened to everything you had to tell him.

Before going to bed, you returned the chocolate pot to its place at the very back of your wardrobe. *Let it rot there*, you thought, because you had no intention of taking it out ever again.

"Why is it that all your old demons sometimes get stirred up, Aurora, my dear?" Horaci asked. How right he was to ask! There were times when you felt overwhelmed by something you could not explain, especially when you realized that the years were going by and you could do nothing about it, or when you had a bad day, or when you were sad, like the day in August 1910 when you learnt that Antoni Sampons had died at the age of fifty-nine.

You went to the wardrobe to get the chocolate pot. The tissue paper had turned yellow and the ribbon was frayed. You tied it up with a new one and then wrote a note saying, "I pray that you will accept this object, which has always belonged to you. With my admiration and sincere condolences. Your Aurora." You called Clara and said, "Please take this to the Sampons house in Passeig de Gràcia. Make sure it is given to Senyoreta Antònia Sampons and that she knows we have sent it."

You waited until Clara returned, pretending to be sewing next to the window. The doctor – Horaci – was reading and coughing in the parlour, and every cough almost made your heart stop. Now you only thought about the past, because the future was full of dark mists.

Clara was young and fleet-footed. She returned quickly. You expected to see her carrying the chocolate pot, but this time was different.

"And the packet?" you asked as soon as she came in.

"You asked me to leave it…"

"Yes, yes, I know what I asked you, but did they accept it?"

"Yes, they did."

"Who opened the door?"

"A housekeeper."

"Young or old?"

"More or less like me" – *Thank Heavens, new blood!* – "and they have sent you this," she said holding out a small envelope.

Inside was a card, on one side of which was the name "Antonia Sampons i Turull". On the other were a few brief, healing words:

> *I greatly appreciate your kind gesture at such a time. When I have recovered a little, I should like to invite you to come and have afternoon tea with me. Please give the doctor my kindest regards. Antònia.*

She had used the formal second-person form. You flopped into your rocking chair and looked out at the street. The hot chocolate made by Antònia Sampons's cook was reputed to be the best in Barcelona.

"May I leave now, Senyora?" Clara's tone was querulous.

"Yes, of course. I am sorry."

Clara left the room. You read the note six more times, imagining the promised afternoon tea.

Rarely do they appear so clearly. They tend to be evasive, mistaken, fleeting or nocturnal in their ways. But not this time. Now, this time, it was evident. This was an ending.

Second Interlude

THE CHIP

It is a sweltering morning in the summer of 1834. The city is ailing and semi-deserted. Anyone who can do so has fled. To the country, to the seaside, to the foot of a mountain, as far away as possible from the foul stench of death. Not even the birds have dared to stay in the trees on La Rambla. The hush of the cemetery hangs over the world's liveliest promenade. Every day at first light the dead cart comes to take the bodies from the houses. In some places they find a corpse, all by itself, with only the cheapest coffin for company, waiting in the doorway. The relatives have taken flight, leaving the body behind, alone and delivered to an inevitable destiny. When cholera strikes there is nothing to be done. Four days, a week at the most, and then you are a corpse. Unfortunately, in this case, death is not dealt out equally. Some people have somewhere else to go, an escape.

In a dark corner of Carrer de Trentaclaus, in a room with a wall covered in red silk and lying on a similarly upholstered bed, yet another victim is breathing her last. The priest has just come to administer the last rites, staring at everything as if he has never seen such a house (and perhaps we shall have to believe him, poor man). He asks the dying woman what her name is, and her age. She can barely muster the whispered words: "Caterina Molins. Seventy-four."

Agnès, who has been living in this house for fifteen years and has spent the last four sleepless nights sitting in a chair at the bedside, starts in surprise when she hears this name. She has never heard of Caterina Molins, but believes that the last frontier must be crossed telling the truth and without disguises. It is a poor skimpy thing the truth that we all bear within us. Caterina Molins could be the name of any woman: a fishwife, a weaver's spouse or a chambermaid in a good house. Once upon a time, a long time ago, all these things were possible. But that was a long time ago. She has only known *Madame* Francesca – *madame* pronounced French-style, and her first name the Italian way – who, for her and the other girls, has been a kindly, caring mother. She has taught them to cherish their dignity as they carry out the duties of this soiling, degrading profession, has come to their rescue when things became difficult, has protected them from men who do not wish to understand anything; has paid them well and has even watched over them when they were ill.

On nights when there was not a lot of work she used to regale them with stories of the days when Francesca was the most famous whore in the city, but only for men with well-lined pockets. The rest could not even get close enough for a whiff of her.

"You must have seen many things, Caterina," the priest says with his benevolent good man's smile just before administering the Last Sacrament.

Caterina frowns and nods almost imperceptibly in agreement with this servant of God who, by the sound of his voice, must be a young man. She cannot see him well because, for some years now, her sight has been blurry, like memory and like the future.

If her words were still as nimble as her thoughts she would say, "You would swoon, my good young fellow, to hear the things I have seen and especially those I have done."

On his way out, the priest blesses the entrance of the establishment. He likes to do this whenever he takes the Last Sacraments to a brothel, because he believes somebody might benefit from it. It is quite shocking to see this house now, all empty rooms and silence. The customers have fled, as have many of the girls. Almost all those who have remained are sick. Agnès is the only one not stricken by the disease. The priest blesses her too, at the threshold of the main entrance. "God will reward you for what you are doing," he tells her. He walks away with his mournfully tinkling little bell, leaving a line of God-fearing women kneeling in his wake.

When Agnès returns to the dying woman's bedside, she finds her lying very still with her eyes closed. Her heart stops. *She is gone! After all my long vigil, she has died the only minute I leave her alone.* But she is mistaken. Madame Francesca has not died, but is peacefully resting as she feels her future trickling away. What a pity this sensation is so short-lived. It is so agreeable not having to think about anything. Tomorrow she will be no more. It is a delightful thought.

When she opens her eyes again, Caterina points vaguely at something. Everything is very laborious now, even telling Agnès to give her a cardboard box which she will find under the bed. Fortunately, her young attendant is a resourceful girl who understands even without words. She kneels down, gets the box and sits in the chair again.

With trembling hands and clumsy movements, Caterina removes the lid.

"Look for…" she orders, summoning the little breath she has left.

Agnès looks. Inside the box she finds a rosary, a wooden swizzle stick, the kind used to stir hot chocolate, a silk handkerchief, an ivory comb and a crumpled piece of paper. Caterina gestures at the paper. She wants Agnès to look at it and read.

It is a receipt from a nearby Mount of Piety, the Church's pawnbroker, with a date – six months ago – a figure and a name: Caterina Molins.

"Go..." Madame Francesca goes back to sleep.

She does not wake up.

Agnès waits in the queue at the Mount of Piety. Madame Francesca died four weeks ago, but the establishment has only opened today. It seems that the cholera epidemic has almost run its course, and the city's streets look more normal now as businesses and cafés reopen.

When she reaches the window, Agnès hands over the receipt. "That will be sixty-four copper reals," the man said.

Agnès leaves the coins on the rough wooden counter. The man disappears with the receipt, rummages around somewhere and, a few seconds later, returns with an object in his hands. He puts it on the counter.

"A coffee pot?" Agnès asks.

"A chocolate pot," the man tells her as he takes her money. "I clearly remember the lady who brought it here. She said it was a valuable piece, a gift from somebody who had gone away for ever. I asked her who this person was and she said, 'A friend. The only one I ever had.' 'And did she go far away,' I asked. She said, 'She never told me. That was the last I knew of her. She must have died by now. I too shall soon be dead.'"

This story means nothing to Agnès. She has not come all the way here to listen to fairy tales, but to collect an item which she imagined was a kind of treasure. And this is what she gets.

What a blow! She would like to forget the whole thing and ask for her money back, but is too embarrassed.

"Is it worth anything?" she asks.

"The porcelain is very fine. And it is old, at least fifty years. But I am no authority in these matters."

Agnès resignedly picks up the chocolate pot and lets the next person in the queue take her place at the window. What a waste of time! Truth to tell, she was hoping for a ring, a medallion, a pair of silver buttons or a silk dress perhaps. Anything but this porcelain thing. What is she supposed to do with a chocolate pot? If she had known she would not have bothered to come, let alone pay for it with good money. It is a crying shame!

She has not even emerged from under the porch of the Mount of Piety before she is wondering how she can get her money back. Then she remembers the chocolatier who set up shop in Carrer de Manresa before the epidemic, Gabriel... whatever his name is. She has only walked past once, but the fragrance from the shop filled Carrer de l'Argenteria, making her long for a nice cup of hot chocolate. Agnès loves chocolate! Moreover, it is good for her work, because it keeps your organs young and strong and makes you want to... makes you want to do what Agnès does half a dozen times every day.

On the way, walking fast so as not to waste any more time, she thinks about lost-and-found objects. To whom do they belong, these objects that someone once loved when that person is gone for ever? Do they want another person to keep them, cherish them and become their owner? No, of course not. What would they care? She curses Madame Francesca. It's all her fault. What is this rubbish she has inherited? Could she not have just left it where it was instead of causing all this bother?

If she does not get something out of this, she is going to be even angrier. Now she can see the chocolatier's shop. GABRIEL SAMPONS, it says in gold letters on the door. She has made up her mind. She pushes the door open and is at once enveloped by the wonderful smell. The chocolatier immediately comes out from the back room to attend his customer. But he stops short when he sees Agnès. He does not know her, which is not exactly the case with some of his customers. He is a young man, very busy, recently married, and the last thing he wants is trouble. No whore is going to get rich from his savings. Neither does he want her in the shop in case she upsets one of his distinguished customers.

"What do you want?" he asks.

"A matter of business," she says. When it comes to plain speaking, no one can compete with Agnès.

Don Gabriel trembles to see people admiring his shop window, fearing that they might come in and find him talking with this young woman of easy virtue.

"I am listening."

Agnès puts the chocolate pot down on top of the display case.

"A swap. I shall give you this chocolate pot. It is very fine porcelain and is more than fifty years old."

Don Gabriel frowns.

"And what do you want in return?"

"What can you offer?" she asks craftily.

Don Gabriel scowls as he studies the piece. As its owner claims, the porcelain is of very high quality. On the bottom there is some kind of trademark, in French, which clearly suggests that it once belonged to a high-born lady. Adélaïde? He has never heard of anyone with this name. Of course, he is no expert in history and with these complicated matters one must always seek competent advice.

"Is there no swizzle stick?" he enquires.

Agnès does not know what he is talking about. She shrugs.

"The swizzle stick! The long-handled wooden cylinder for stirring the chocolate."

Oh lawks! Agnès remembers that there was a swizzle stick in the box Madame Francesca kept under her bed. She now realizes that the two pieces, chocolate pot and swizzle stick go together.

"Never mind, I can find another one," Don Gabriel says, his mind made up. "I shall take it. Four blocks of chocolate."

Agnès is used to doing business with men. She has done nothing else since she grew breasts.

"Could it not be six?"

A lady has just come out of Carrer del Brosolí and is strolling towards the shop. Don Gabriel recognizes her. A good customer.

"Yes, yes, very well." Now he is in a hurry. "Here, take them and be on your way."

Agnès looks at the shop window, understands and plays her part. When a proper lady appears, all men suddenly turn into something else. She has known that for a long time. She takes her blocks of chocolate, flashes him a lovely smile by way of farewell and leaves the shop before the good lady sees her.

Don Gabriel hastens to hide the chocolate pot behind the counter. He is somehow fearful, as if he is concealing something that might offend the eyes of a proper lady. He clumsily knocks the spout against the iron frame of the display case. The dry crunch only augurs one thing. A few porcelain splinters fall on the bench. The chip has appeared and is there for ever.

The proper lady is gazing in the shop window as if she is having trouble deciding. Don Gabriel clicks his tongue in annoyance and runs a fingertip over the newly inflicted wound. It is jagged, like his feelings. The object has only just come into his hands and now he cannot sell it. What a pity. He had thought he might put it in the shop window, where it would have looked very nice. He is to blame, and all because of his clumsiness and haste. He throws the chocolate pot into the rubbish bucket just as the proper lady pushes the door and enters his shop.

Madame Adélaïde's poor chocolate pot languishes with the rubbish all day long, until the evening, just as they are about to close, when the chocolatier's wife spies something like a very fine porcelain handle poking out of the rubbish and carefully extracts it.

"What is this doing with the rubbish? It is such a beautiful chocolate pot. A little chipped, but that does not matter. Oh dear, these men, they never know what is of value and what is not," she mutters to herself, as she locks the door from inside and goes upstairs, carrying the chocolate pot.

Act III

PEPPER, CLOVES
AND ACHIOTE

If you are not feeling well, if you
have not slept, chocolate will re-
vive you.

MARIE DE RABUTIN-CHANTAL,
MARQUISE DE SÉVIGNÉ
Letter sent from Versailles, 11th February 1671

One

Madame,

It is my pleasure to inform you that our legation arrived in
Barcelona yesterday at about six o'clock in the afternoon after
a fourteen-day journey in which there has been more dust than
rain, more cold weather than fine and more sour faces than
pleasant words. We are very well accommodated in the Fonda
de Santa Maria, an establishment that is not far from the port
and very near a church known by everyone as Santa Maria del
Mar, one of the magnificent buildings which have given Barcelona renown as "the city of three cathedrals". The innkeeper is a
likeable enough Italian by the name of Zanotti, who, no sooner
than he set eyes on us, informed us that he had received discreet
orders to ensure we were well treated. "Orders from whom?"
asked Monsieur de Beaumarchais in quite acceptable Italian. "If
I told you they would no longer be discreet," the man said. "But
it is sufficient for you to know that there are people in this city
who wish to please such high-ranking ambassadors, *signore*."

The three master chocolatiers in our company were not surprised by these words for the simple reason that they understood
nothing, for, as I said, they were speaking Italian. However, I
could see that Monsieur de Beaumarchais was vexed to learn
that our presence is not as inconspicuous as we should have

liked. We had certainly not announced our coming and neither were we met by anyone. He was fretful all night, even as we dined and settled into conversation after the meal. After brooding at such length on the matter, he went to sleep with a deep frown scoring his forehead. Naturally, I did not close my eyes until I was certain that he was fast asleep, which is not difficult to ascertain, for a snoring Monsieur de Beaumarchais snorts like an angry boar. The window of our room looks onto the street, and since it is next to the main entrance, a couple of lanterns which burn well into the early hours of the morning provide some light in the darkness. I therefore believe I shall take a little time every night, once the good Beaumarchais has gone to sleep, to write you my secret chronicle of our adventures in this land, as you requested. This is the safest time. Snoring time (if you will forgive me for mentioning it).

Let me begin, Madame, by informing you that five gentlemen make up the French legation, three of whom you know very well: myself, your devoted servant; Monsieur de Beaumarchais, serving the interests of your nephew, His Majesty; and our Labbé, head pastry chef at the palace, who has turned out to be not at all bothersome as a travelling companion. As soon as he gets into the carriage and is rocked by the rhythm of the roads, he is overcome by a passion for sleep which he is helpless to resist. He slumbers curled up in any corner (as you know, he is not much taller than a mushroom) and does not stir until we have arrived. The other two, chosen – as you are well aware – for the excellence of their work, are Monsieur Delon, in the name of the Corporation des Chocolatiers of the illustrious – and sweet! – city of Bayonne, and Monsieur Maleshèrbes, of the chocolatiers guild of Paris.

This Maleshèrbes is a second cousin – or so he claims – of the minister of the same name who has been serving your nephew for the last couple of years, but unfortunately for us, apart from lineage, I fear the two gentlemen have nothing in common.

As for Delon, this thin-faced gentleman of about fifty years old seems to be something of a weakling, but appearances are deceptive. In fact, he is a pleasant, even-tempered fellow, of serene intelligent conversation, an excellent mediator in disputes and scrimmages, however heated they may become, always able to find fitting words and with sufficient mettle to support both sides impartially without offending anyone. We are fortunate to have him with us, because this Maleshèrbes, representative of the Parisian chocolatiers, is like one of those storms with a great deal of thunder and lightning but never letting fall a drop of rain. He is tall and thickset, a mountain of a man, as red as the devil and with the evil temper of a ferret. His bad character, expressed in the most uncouth, asinine language, explodes when one least expects it. If I had made a note of all the occasions during our journey in which he got his way by bellowing, they would run into four figures. In the town of Millau, he bawled so loudly next to the carriage that one of the horses fell unconscious to the ground. He seems to delight in striking terror into innkeepers' wives. At least half a dozen ran away weeping, poor simple creatures. Our Labbé, who has the misfortune to share a room with him, swears that, even when asleep, he roars and is very frightening. I shall only tell you one more thing about him, an episode which occurred before we left Paris, to give you an approximate idea of the nature of the man.

Monsieur Maleshèrbes kept us waiting for more than an hour on the day of our departure and, when he finally appeared, he had three trunks that were so enormous they were more like coffins. Beaumarchais informed him that he could not travel with so much luggage, to which Maleshèrbes replied, "Ah no? And why not? Who says I may not?"

"I say so, sir." Beaumarchais puffed out his chest.

"And, might one know, who are you?"

"Pierre-Augustin Caron de Beaumarchais, sir, secretary to the King and leader of this expedition."

The chocolatier raised his eyebrows, showing his contempt. "Beaumarchais? The author of those comedies?"

"The very same, sir," our man replied.

"And why should I heed a man who writes comedies?" Maleshèrbes was getting redder and roaring loud enough to put the fear of God into everyone around us.

"Because if you do not heed this man, the comedy might very soon become a tragedy," Beaumarchais responded, slightly opening his dress coat to reveal the sword which was well concealed beneath his travelling clothes.

Maleshèrbes rudely pushed his way into the carriage, grunted at the three of us who were tired of waiting for him and sprawled on the seat, taking up two places. I did not hear him say a single word in the next nine hours, and I can assure you that that it was better when he refrained from speaking, for this man is of the kind that only opens his mouth to provoke. After just two days he had quarrelled with everyone.

He picked a fight with me when we stopped after the second day. With the disdainful air of someone accustomed to giving orders, and without even looking at me, he said, "You, whippersnapper, take my trunk to my room and be quick about it!"

"I am sorry, sir, but I am not your servant. I am Monsieur de Beaumarchais's assistant. However, I should glad to help to find somebody to carry the trunk to your room."

He was astounded. "Assistant to the King's secretary on a foreign mission? How old are you?"

"Eighteen, sir," I told him.

"And you have sufficient experience to accompany the King's secretary on such a mission?"

"I believe I do, sir." Naturally, I did not inform him that this was not the first time.

"What is your name?"

"Victor Philibert Guillot, sir."

"I have never heard of you. Are you at the Palace?"

Yes, I am, sir. I am the personal secretary of Madame Adélaïde and her sister, Madame Victoire.

"Well, well, well…" he grumbled, his humours roiling inside him like a volcano about to erupt. "I believe it would be good for you, since you are such a puny fellow, to heft a trunk or two. You would be a much better servant for all these people if you were somewhat sturdier."

"I serve my mistresses not with brawn but with the power of my intellect, sir," I interrupted.

"Ah, intellect!" mocked Malesherbes, in an affected voice, raising his eyes heavenwards. "Our country would have advanced much further if we had fewer people who think and more people who haul. Out of my way, boy. I shall do it myself. I have no time for intellect!"

I could describe further disagreeable encounters, but do not wish to tire you with trifling anecdotes. Now, if you will permit, I shall try to sleep a little, because Monsieur de Beaumarchais has decided that, with the first light of day and having breakfasted, we shall go out to accomplish our mission.

I now take my leave with the utmost respect, Madame.

Your faithful servant,

Victor Philibert Guillot

Two

Madame,

Yesterday began inauspiciously. We were dressing and about to go downstairs for breakfast when word came that three gentlemen were waiting for us at the entrance to the inn. We found this very strange, as we had arranged to meet no one. Monsieur de Beaumarchais and I went out to learn who these gentlemen were, and the innkeeper, Zanotti, introduced us.

"This gentleman is the Captain General of the Fourth Military Region, Senyor Francisco González i de Bassecourt, and his two companions are his trusted men, both with positions in the municipal government. They have come to welcome you to the city."

My first thought was, the politicians of this country are certainly well attired! You should have seen them, Madame. They were wearing long, freshly powdered wigs, shoes with gleaming buckles and dress coats abundantly embroidered in gold, as if they were about to attend some very dignified ceremony or receive a prince.

I must add that the Captain General is a strapping, muscular man – especially his arms – but he has a shrill voice with nothing remotely military about it, and a potato nose which makes one want to burst out laughing. I say "potato", Madame, although I have observed that people here are very averse to potatoes. Can you believe that? Indeed, they hold them in contempt and use them for animal fodder. At some point I shall have to explain to them how mistaken they are, and tell them about our fervour for consuming this tubercle in Versailles, and how right Monsieur Parmentier was when he sang its praises. I cannot understand why they do not follow our example here!

However, to return to this Captain General Potato Nose, I wondered, how is it possible for this man, with such attributes, to give orders to his troops? Later on, Beaumarchais confessed to me that he had imagined the gentleman quite differently, for he had been informed he was an enlightened man, a lover of literature and patron of the performing arts. As you see, people can be very different when you see them at close quarters.

It is also odd that they should have spoken to us in English, or at least they tried, since the skills displayed by our hosts in this barbarous tongue were not exactly impressive. Only one of the three, the smallest among them, opened his mouth and, with considerable difficulty, translated what was said to his two companions who, looking like a pair of oafs, nodded constantly, saying "Yes, yes, yes" all the while. No doubt you will be wondering why we did not change the language when Monsieur de Beaumarchais has such a good command of Spanish. I would venture that, from the very beginning, it did not seem good policy or polite to flout the wishes of these most unexpected hosts. Since both Beaumarchais and myself are fluent in the language they speak in London, thanks to our journeys to that evil-smelling city, we had no objections to using it for a while.

The captain and the two city councillors had come, we understood, after considerable effort, to invite us to join them on a tour of their city which, for some reason, could not wait. Monsieur de Beaumarchais did his best to explain that we had work to do before permitting ourselves the distraction of such an outing, but the three gentlemen were of another opinion: first the jaunt and then work, which they said in so many words, in their ill-bred way and with such insistence that Monsieur de Beaumarchais had no choice but to capitulate.

"We shall humour them while also making sure that they do not delay us very long and then proceed with our own plans," he whispered, sending me off to fetch the three chocolatiers.

Our tour, on foot and in the freezing cold, which we did not expect in this southern land, began with a walk along a crooked promenade running from one end of the city to the other. In the morning they sell foodstuffs there while, in the afternoons, the people stroll up and down, watching the troops parading. They are constantly constructing new palaces and you can hear Mass being said in the churches. They call it La Rambla and it is the liveliest street in the city. Monsieur de Beaumarchais was keen to learn more about it, but our hosts only smiled, nodded and said, "Yes, yes, yes."

After that they wished to show us the waterfront landscape from the ramparts walk, where we were buffeted by a damp and terrible gale which left us frozen to the bone. On top of the wall we began a concert of sneezing which reminded me of the chorus of those infernal deities of that lyrical tragedy you like so much… What was its name? It was one of the works by our maestro Lully, but I do not recall the title. Never mind, I always mix them up. You will know the work to which I refer. There was a hero and a chorus, as in our long walk. Maleshèrbes took the lead and with every detonation issuing from his nose one feared the apocalypse was nigh. Labbé, Delon and I echoed him with a melodious chorus of sneezes. For the time being, Beaumarchais resisted.

Our hosts declared that we had to do something to drive out the cold, and shepherded us to a tavern where we were served glasses of brown liquor made from flowers, herbs and walnuts, they informed us, but its name is difficult to remember. We soon finished a whole bottle, but the café owner brought us another and yet a third. The drink was most palatable, and our guides poured us one glass after another, urging us to down them all with an insistence we began to find suspicious after the fourth glass. Beaumarchais, a man experienced in such matters, as you know, ordered our party to drink no more, but for some that was too late. Our puny Labbé could not stay upright. Delon, with a frown on his face, stared at the dust in the street. My head was spinning without respite. The worst problem was Maleshèrbes who, after the order to stop, wanted to keep drinking and belligerently challenged Beaumarchais.

"And who are you to tell me not to drink? I shall drink if I judge it right and proper."

"Not here, my good sir. We are leaving now."

"Another glass, waiter!"

"I said no! Stow your bottle, waiter!"

"Bring it here. I want two glasses!"

"Maleshèrbes, get outside immediately!"

"Carry me out if you can, you and that stripling you call your assistant!"

"Do not rouse me to anger, Maleshèrbes."

"Do not make my blood boil, Beaumarchais."

This time Beaumarchais was in no mood for argument, and neither was he disposed to assert his authority. I believe he was too dizzy to start shouting at the man and only wanted to return to our lodgings and lie on his bed. Meanwhile, the wise and prudent Delon emptied his stomach on Captain General Potato Nose's dress coat. More foresighted, Labbé spewed all over a poplar trunk while the municipal authorities, sitting in a couple of the chairs they hire out on La Rambla, looked on, making no secret of their disgust.

As you will understand, Madame, this setback has thrown all our plans into disarray. We left Maleshèrbes in the tavern, calling for more drink and, with some difficulty found our way back to the inn where we went straight to bed without any wish or opportunity to think about what had happened to us. Delon seemed more composed after his vomiting attack. He even wished us goodnight. Monsieur de Beaumarchais was unable to answer, for his head was lowered over the washbasin ejecting prodigious quantities of acrid liquid. I knew nothing about Labbé or his whereabouts. As for myself, the last thing I recall seeing was the smirking face of Captain General Potato Nose as he tucked me into bed, perfidiously urging me to rest (in Catalan, the local language they use for everything): "*Descanseu, jove, descanseu.*"

As you will see, we ended our first day in this city in a most ignoble fashion: sleeping off our debauchery in an inn. In our defence, I can only say that our hosts were as treacherous as the liquor they served us.

I cannot end my missive, Madame, without warning you that I must confess to having some horrible news for you. However, since I have the most appalling headache today and can barely sit up straight, I shall postpone writing about that until tomorrow. Meanwhile, I beg you not to be angry.

I now take my leave with the utmost respect, Madame.

Three

I must now tell you the dreadful news I was in no condition to convey yesterday: Captain General Potato Nose and his two officials have robbed us! Now we know why they were so solicitous when accompanying us back to the inn and putting us to bed. When we went to sleep they went through all our belongings and stole anything that took their fancy, by which I mean money, gold and jewellery, leaving our whole group destitute. On discovering this, Beaumarchais was so desperate I feared he would leap out the window. They have taken everything, and I have the impression that "everything" in this case is even more than we believe.

I was the only one whom the thieves distinguished by another kind of treatment. Besides gold and money, they took an object from my luggage. Can you guess what it was? It was, of course and to my great sorrow, the gift you sent for Maestro Fernandes, which I was to deliver to him with your letter. Please do not worry about the letter. I still have it, but the gift has vanished. Monsieur de Beaumarchais said, however, that we shall very quickly recover what has been stolen from us, and to this end he had decided to visit the Captain General in his office in the Viceroy's Palace (which I shall tell you about forthwith). Meanwhile, he sent me to wake up all the members of our legation and tell them that we were waiting for them before having breakfast.

As you can imagine, Madame, upon discovering the disaster our mood was very glum. Delon immediately came down to the dining room and confirmed everything I have just told you about the theft. More trouble began when I came to the room shared by Maleshèrbes and Labbé. Knock as I might, and however loudly I called out their names (to the point of indiscretion), there was no response. The silence in the room was so sepulchral that I believed for a moment – simpleton that I am – that they had gone to early Mass. I then recalled that Maleshèrbes is no friend of the clergy, whereupon, in the name of the King of France, I asked the innkeeper for the key and entered the room, determined to discover what was happening.

What was happening was disgraceful. There was an appalling stench of ill-digested alcohol in the room. Both men lay in the shadows of drawn curtains, belly up on their beds. Maleshèrbes – what a sight! – was half undressed. Monsieur Labbé was still in his street clothes. Scattered around the floor I counted as many as six bottles of that home brew which had been our ruin the previous night. One of them had tipped over and had spread its contents all over the tiles. Ashamed by the conduct of these two subjects of His Majesty, I tried to wake Labbé, in whom I have more confidence, and only managed to do so after shaking him with all my might, as if he were a tree laden with ripe fruit ready to be picked. Only after great perseverance did I get him to open one eye and to look at me, but he could not have been truly awake, because he said, "Holy Mother of God, I see before me a shrivelled cod," at which point he lapsed back into semi-consciousness to continue sleeping.

I was unsure as to whether the cod referred to myself, as a nickname the members of our party might have given me. I looked at Labbé's belongings and Maleshèrbes' trunk. They too had been ransacked. The thieves had come with a clear purpose and had plotted the perfect strategy for achieving their aim, while we had behaved like perfect dolts in making it so easy for them.

This is what I was pondering as I went downstairs to inform Monsieur de Beaumarchais of the situation. Naturally he was angry and, after a meagre breakfast, went off to the Viceroy's Palace to demand explanations.

"Wait here for me, Guillot," he asked, "in case the slumberers wake. Do not, under any circumstances, permit anyone to leave the inn; I shall have returned by lunchtime."

I ran to ask Maestro Delon to do what Beaumarchais had just required of me. He promised he would do his utmost, but could not assure me that he would be able to stand in the way of Maleshèrbes if that human mountain decided to leave the inn. As you requested, I immediately left to follow Beaumarchais, fearing that I might have lost him in that maze of streets. I was fortunate, because I soon sighted him, after which I stuck to him like a shadow, although very discreetly so he would suspect nothing.

First, he went to the Viceroy's Palace where he had been told Senyor González, the finely arrayed gentleman of the previous day, had his office. He asked for him, presenting himself as "Ambassador of His Majesty, King of France". As you might imagine he was immediately received. What transpired inside the office, I was unable to witness with my own eyes (I waited in the square, admiring the grandeur and majestic proportions of the place, but trembling with cold, for the cloak I was wearing was insufficient to keep it at bay). When Beaumarchais emerged from the palace he was more serene, smiling as he strolled at a leisurely pace, as if well pleased by what he had been told. He continued his walk, turning to the right, into a street as long and narrow as the blade of his sword and aptly named Espaseria, no doubt after the swordsmiths whose establishments were clustered there. I kept following without letting him out of my sight for an instant. He was walking with such assurance that anyone might have imagined he was returning to the inn.

I was surprised to see him following the lateral wall of the church of Santa Maria del Mar, after which he turned again, this time to the left into a street full of palatial mansions, known as Carrer de Montcada. I drew closer, with the sharp instinct of the spy who is no novice, helped in my endeavours by the liveliness of the street, which was full of people coming and going and merchants proclaiming the virtues of their wares in their own language, which is not Spanish, and neither do they wish it to be.

Monsieur de Beaumarchais did not slacken his pace until he was approximately halfway along the street, where he stopped, looked up and, it seemed to me, hesitated a moment, before deciding which door he had to knock at. He eventually decided. He rapped the knocker at the entrance. The door immediately opened and he was ushered inside. I had the impression that he was no stranger there. I waited a long time for him to come out, hearing the bells of Santa Maria del Mar striking ten and then eleven. Just when I began to fear that I would still be there at midday, the door opened and Monsieur de Beaumarchais emerged, his expression as serious as it was on entering, but now with a hint of mystery showing on his face. By this I mean that, if one might divine such a thing, he seemed to have satisfactorily negotiated some profitable business.

This time, I correctly surmised that he was returning to the inn, and hastened to move ahead so as to be there before him (I am long-legged, nimble and twenty-seven years younger than he is, and might therefore inform you that it was not difficult for me). On arriving I asked Delon if he had any news, and was informed that the slumberers had not left their room. I sat at a table in the dining room, pretending to read a publication called *Gazeta de Barcelona*, and feigned great surprise when I saw Beaumarchais coming through the door.

Monsieur de Beaumarchais was breathing fire when he recounted what he had discovered in the Viceroy's Palace.

"Do you know, Guillot, that those thieves who left us with just the clothes we were wearing have no connection with the Captain General or with the City Council? Just as I suspected. The real Senyor González i de Bassecourt is a cultured man, as we had been told, a patron of the performing arts in this city and an avid admirer of my comedies, all of which he has seen. We spoke in French without the slightest difficulty. He is distressed by my account of the events and has promised to everything within his power to detain the malefactors."

"Then," I asked, "who were the three impostors?"

"That is what I am asking myself, Guillot. The very same question."

Just as Beaumarchais had said, an investigation was carried out. The Captain General's men interrogated Zanotti, who claimed, "I merely conveyed what they told me. What would a poor man like me know about these charlatans, when I had never seen them in my life?" They made an inventory of what had been stolen from us and, when they spoke to me, were surprised.

"A chocolate pot?"

"In white porcelain, from the Royal Factory of Sèvres, although it does not bear the typical double-L insignia. It was wrapped in turquoise velvet."

"Is this chocolate pot very valuable?"

"Its value is incalculable, sir. It is a unique piece."

"May I satisfy my curiosity?" one of them asked. "Why are you travelling with a chocolate pot?"

I no longer trusted anyone. I had no wish to mention you or Senyor Fernandes to those men, and therefore answered, "I never travel without it, sir."

The high point was when the policemen woke the two liquor bibbers, although I must say the interrogation yielded little. When they left, Beaumarchais in person threw the entire contents of the washbowl over the heads of Maleshèrbes and Labbé. This had a galvanizing effect.

"Now let us see if this revives you. And, for Heaven's sake, cover yourself my good man!" Beaumarchais pointed at Maleshèrbes's thighs, which looked for all the world like a pair of hams, the streaky-bacon belly and the limp little sausage which, amid all that abundance seemed unsure where to reside. "And I would ask you to behave like gentlemen, or must I remind you that you are High Commissioners of His Majesty, King of France, the greatest nation known to—"

"Very well, very well," Zanotti interrupted. "May I be of help in any way, and will you permit me to return the washbowl to its stand?"

In the end, the remedy was a large pot of lukewarm coffee which had been brought to the boil five or six times. As you know, this disagreeable-tasting medicinal beverage is now recommended by all the doctors in Europe.

Four

Nevertheless, my chronicle of misadventure is far from ending here, Madame. Once we were all ready to go out, with clearer heads and lighter feet, we saw that it had started to snow. Since we had had a surfeit of the cold the previous day and were in no mood for any more sneezing concerts or for catching terrible colds, Monsieur de Beaumarchais became apprehensive as he stared at the sky.

"Is this weather normal, Zanotti? I believed you had a milder climate here in Barcelona."

The innkeeper shrugged. "The world is becoming very strange, sir."

We remained there for quite a long time, all five as silent as the grave, looking at the sky and waiting for the snow to stop foiling our plans. The exact opposite happened. It reminded me of a snowfall I once saw at the Palace, which had left the guards at the gate almost buried beneath it. It was getting dark, and Beaumarchais was increasingly desperate, because yet another day had slipped by without our achieving anything of note. He then came over to me and said, "Guillot, since you are elusive by nature and of nimble feet, could you go ahead of the delegation to the establishment in Carrer de les Tres Voltes? You only need to inform Senyor Fernandes that we shall all do him the honour of visiting him tomorrow."

I assented, of course, and was happy to be able to move around a little. I ran upstairs to fetch the letter you gave me and, bearing it well protected inside my leather pouch, sallied out into the relentlessly falling snow. It was so cold that my cape was useless, however hard I tried to wrap myself in it. With great strides I covered the distance to the Plaça de l'Oli, which I reached with even the hairs on my head shivering with cold.

I found the square by asking people in the street. In Passeig del Born they said, "Oh, it is quite a long way!" In the middle of Carrer del Rec they replied, "You are close." Finally, as I walked downhill towards the prison, they told me, "You are almost there. Go down Carrer de la Bòria until it opens into a square." This is what I did. It would have been much easier without the freezing cold, obviously, but I came upon a locked and barred wooden door on which a faded sign said:

FERNANDES

MASTER CHOCOLATIER

PURVEYOR TO THE PRINCESSES OF FRANCE

There was not a soul to be seen, the windows looked like tightly closed eyelids and snow was piling up in the streets. I could no longer feel nose, hands or toes inside my shoes. I knocked at the door but nobody opened. I feared I would freeze to death if I stood there much longer, so I began to knock with an insistence which would seem to typify my approach to closed doors since arriving in Barcelona. Do not imagine for a moment that it was opened immediately. I had time to say several prayers as I sought refuge inside my cape and the porchless doorway with snow sliding down my nose and freezing my wig. I beat at the door as many times as despair counselled. Finally, with the shred of voice that was left to me, I called out, "Senyor Fernandes, for the love of God, open the door or I shall die here like a dog. My name is Guillot and I have come from Versailles, sent by Madame Adélaïde and bringing you a…"

You must know, Madame, that your name worked like a password. Just when the snowstorm had worked itself into such a fury that it was impossible to see six inches in front of my nose, a ray of hope opened up in the chocolatier's doorway and a pair of jet black eyes perused me at length. I begged, "Senyor Fernandes, I am freezing. Please let me in."

The door charitably opened, and I finally found refuge in a room, complete with a long counter, a marvellous aroma of chocolate and a brightly burning fire.

I felt a blanket being draped around my shoulders and heard the dulcet tones of a female voice.

"Sit down by the fire and you will soon recover."

Perhaps you are wondering what language was used to pronounce these words. I must admit I cannot be sure. The woman who opened the door was not wholly ignorant of some of the secrets of our beautiful tongue, but to claim she spoke it would be to exaggerate. In a manner of speaking, I would say I know a few words in Catalan and fewer in Spanish, but I could make myself understood. As you know, I have always had a good ear for foreign languages. In a mixture of the three languages, then – although I could not guarantee that some passing phrase in Italian did not form part of the blend –this ministering angel who had saved me and I were able to communicate, and, as you will see, not too ineptly.

I call her a ministering angel not only for the warm blanket I mentioned, or the delicious cup of hot chocolate she regaled me with immediately afterwards, thereby bringing me back from the dead. It is more because of the exquisite expression on her face that I give her this name. My saviour is a woman of some twenty-five years at most, with dark eyes shining like stars in the light of the flames in her fireplace, gracefully shaped cheeks, hair the colour of old copper and lips like velvet. I was so astounded by this extraordinary beauty that I was struck by the thought that had I died on her doorstep I should not have liked the angels of heaven nearly so much.

"You speak my language, Senyora…" I said admiringly.

"No, really I do not…" she replied, "but I understand it. I have a considerable number of customers who speak like you. There are many French people in Barcelona."

I recalled that Beaumarchais had warned me as we were leaving Paris, "You will discover, my dear Guillot, how Barcelona is the most French of all the foreign cities."

I finished my cup of chocolate and the woman asked, "Did you say that Madame sent you?"

"*Oui.*"

"Do you have proof of this?"

"*Naturellement.*"

"May I see it?"

"I shall show it to Senyor Fernandes. Is he at home?"

"No, not at present."

"I shall wait for him then."

"I would not advise it. He may take some time."

"I am in no hurry."

"But I am. Please give me your credentials and I shall show them to Senyor Fernandes."

"Are you his servant?"

"No, sir, I am not."

"Is Senyor Fernandes a relation of yours? Your father, perhaps?"

"No, he is not."

"Will you tell me or shall I be obliged to guess?"

"He is my husband. And now, will you show me what you have brought for him?"

I confess she made me waver. I was on the point of showing her, but remembered in time how we had been cozened so soon after our arrival, and therefore reconsidered.

"I am not certain that I can trust you, Senyora."

"I share your uncertainty, sir."

"Where is Senyor Fernandes?"

"Give me your credentials from Madame and I shall tell you."

"You tell me first and then you shall have them."

"I cannot accept these conditions."

"Neither can I."

"Do you mistrust me?"

"Unfortunately I do."

"Do you have reason to mistrust me?"

"More than enough!"

"And I have, perchance, harmed you in some way?"

"You have not, but others have."

"And I must pay for sins I have not committed?"

"As everyone must, sooner or later."

"If you give me your credentials we shall have no further problems."

"Or we may have more. One cannot be sure."

"Good sir, do not be so harsh."

"I am diligent and proud to be so."

"Please let me see them."

"As I told you, I shall not!"

"You must leave, then."

"I most certainly shall not!"

"For such a young man you are as stubborn as a mule."

"And you, for a woman, are the same."

It was then that someone began beating at the door in a way that could, under no circumstances, be interpreted as friendly. Bam! Bam! Bam!

"I am lost! It is the people from the guild! They have heard us. They know I am here!" my angel cried, her face contorted in a grimace of utter terror.

The beating persisted. Bam! Bam! Bam! The wood shuddered with the blows. A voice thundered in English, "Open up, in the name of King George!"

"So, our man does business with the English?"

I may have murmured it, but I was very angry.

"No, sir. To my knowledge he does not."

"Then what do these people want?"

My angel shrugged.

"Open up, in the name of His Majesty King George III!"

"What shall we do?"

"Open the door, of course," I declared with all the power and conviction of a Titan setting out to avenge, single-handedly, our lost honour in the Seven Years' War.

And that is what she did. She flung the door open, upon which I was confronted with the red nose and several rolls of wart-infested chins of a round-bellied figure, more toad than man. He was more warmly clad than I and three times fatter, which is no doubt why he shivered less. He was in the company of two soldiers, decked out in uniform with lances and all, who addressed him as "sir".

"I greet you, Senyor and Senyora, in the name of His Majesty King George III, King of England, Ireland, Menorca, India, Dominica, Granada, St Vincent, Tobago, Florida—"

I interrupted, "Yes, yes, yes, we know all that." These English, always with their victories rolling off their tongues, are insufferable. "How may I be of service?" I enquired.

"First of all, let us in, if you please."

I stood aside and signalled to the woman to do the same. The three men entered the room with all their paraphernalia and closed the door. For a second we all shared the relief of having shut out the darkness and the snow. The Englishman glanced around and I sensed from a barely perceptible twitching of his lip that he approved of what he saw.

"In the name of His Majesty King George III, I order you to show me this device of your invention which produces chocolate," declared Sir English Toad, who would seem ill disposed to waste time on introductions or niceties. As he spoke, his rolling chins wobbled with such efficiency.

A glance from my angel revealed that she was very afraid of these men. Her eyes besieged me, waiting for me to act.

"They believe you are my husband," she murmured.

"So I see," I replied.

"And what do they want?"

"To see the machine."

"I will not allow it! I do not want them in my home!"

I must recognize that I was greatly pleased by her response and the antipathy she showed towards the Englishmen.

"Do you really want them to leave?" I asked.

"I certainly do."

"Well, show them the machine."

As we were having our muttered conversation, the toad became impatient and started stamping his feet and grunting. Although I feared she would refuse and that Sir English Toad would declare war on us then and there, the wife of the chocolatier Fernandes decided to heed my advice, and ushered us through to a back room.

"After you, my good sirs," I said bowing at our visitors, knowing that nothing beguiles an Englishman as much as deference.

There, in the back room, was the mechanical prodigy, the wonder of all of civilized Europe. It is a six-legged apparatus made of wood and metal with four large handles and very elegant wheels, both ratcheted and smooth. From what I could understand of my angel's account, the cocoa beans are fed in, mixed with sugar and spices inside the device, after which it emerges in the form of an exquisite paste which one might dub, without the slightest exaggeration, the best chocolate in the world. The Englishmen were full of praise, pronouncing that such an invention could only come from the imagination of a genius. They immediately concerned themselves with the machine's functioning, which she explained in great detail and I translated, omitting, perhaps, some of the more astounding details. With every word I was cursing our ineptness in letting that delegation of savages gain an advantage over us.

The subjects of King George III also wished to know what spices were mixed with the chocolate paste. My angel explained that a great variety could be used, but it should always contain fourteen grains of black pepper, half an ounce of cloves and a large seed of the reddest achiote. Some apothecaries recommend the addition of cardamom, cinnamon, vanilla bean, almonds and even orange flower water but she – or so she says – much prefers simple recipes.

"People today do not like elaborate food as much as they used to." She was truly bewitching. "The important thing is that the chocolate should be of the best quality and with very few additives."

Forgive the digression. We were admiring the machine, which so pleased the Englishmen that they were speechless (as I was also, although I was obliged to conceal my wonder). The two soldiers brazenly took measurements in hand spans and even weighed it by taking up position either side and lifting it, as if to calculate how many men would be needed to bear it away. Meanwhile, their leader stood back, doing and saying nothing.

"Might I ask the reason for all this zeal, sir?" I asked.

"King George has heard about your invention, Senyor Fernandes, and has done you the honour of showing you his interest. He is a lover of chocolate, which he takes three times every day. It helps him to think and gives him the strength of six bulls."

I simpered as if flattered, but all this was auguring very ill indeed. The men were finishing their measurements, or so it seemed, when the toad spoke again.

"I have a question, Senyor Fernandes, and only you can satisfy my curiosity."

I thought, *now I am the one who is lost. If he asks me about some small detail of the construction or functioning of the machine, he will discover my subterfuge and, in his rage, will squash me like a mosquito.*

"I shall answer as best I can."

"How is it that you speak English with such a strong French accent?" the King's emissary wished to know.

"Ah, this question…" I smiled as I thought up a sufficiently credible response. "I had a French nursemaid."

"I am informed that you were an apprentice of Maestro Lloseres, whose premises were nearby."

"That is correct, sir."

"How old are you? Are you not very young to have done so many things?"

"My looks are very deceptive, sir. It is because I am slightly built. However, I have just turned thirty-one."

"Really?"

"I swear it is true."

The English toad stroked his chins. "It could be the chocolate. The King's advisors say that chocolate is most effective in conserving the vigour of youth."

"I would not contradict you, sir!"

It seemed he believed everything.

"I have one more question."

Heaven spare me such suffering!

"Once again I shall try to answer."

"Do you know my country?"

"No, I do not, sir," I lied.

"We English are hospitable people of good taste, and we greatly admire people like yourself who are able to bring progress to the world with new, useful and practical ideas and mechanical marvels. This is also true of His Majesty, naturally. Not long ago I acquired, on behalf of the King, a diving machine, which is most useful for recovering objects lost in shipwrecks. And a device which can produce bas-relief portraits of three people (and you only have to turn a key). His Majesty, King George, is a great believer in all these things and convinced that progress in the world will be wrought by these wheels, cogs, handles and pistons with which you are so familiar. His Majesty would like to know if you and your lovely wife would accept his invitation to reside in Buckingham Palace for all the time you would need to construct another machine like this one."

I was petrified by his words. Fortunately, I gathered my wits enough to respond, "I shall need to discuss this with my wife, sir."

"Naturally. I understand."

"You understand?"

"Indeed I do. If I had such a lovely wife, I should not move as much as a finger without consulting her. Please, go ahead." The toad waved his hand in the direction of my beautiful angel, a spark of admiration lighting in his eyes – or it may have been covetousness.

"Would you be so good as to allow us to speak in private?" I requested.

"Do what you must." He sounded resigned.

Sir English Toad and his stalwarts withdrew from the back room leaving the machine (and us still more) in peace. I translated all the words we had exchanged without missing a single one. As soon as she began to understand what was happening, she started shaking her head, saying, "No, no, no, no. This cannot be. My husband will not be making any more machines."

"Think about it, woman. This is an excellent opportunity to make a lot of money."

"I said no. This cannot happen!"

"Do not be so rash. These matters require due consideration."

"There is nothing to consider. Tell him I decline his offer."

Since it seemed foolhardy to risk the wrath of the Englishman with such a forthright rejection, I deemed it more prudent to proceed with caution. I came out of the room with the chastened look of a henpecked husband – which always makes a great impression among men – saying, "My wife needs to think about it. If you would be so good as to tell me where I might bring you her answer, you will have it in a few hours."

The Englishman wrote the address on a piece of paper, which he handed to me. They were staying in the Manresa Inn, in the street of the same name.

"I shall give you two days. Do not try my patience, Senyor Fernandes."

"No, I shall not, sir."

"Ah, Fernandes…" He suddenly turned towards me, "One more thing."

"Yes, sir."

"Might you have seen a legation of Frenchmen snooping around the city?"

"Frenchmen, sir? There are so many in this ci—"

"These are emissaries of King Louis and arrived two or three days ago. They are lodged in the Santa Maria Inn."

I was surprised, I must confess, that he was so well informed of our movements. For a moment I was certain that these were the people who had robbed us, but then I remembered the way those scoundrels spoke and dismissed the idea. However bumbling the English may be, they are still able to speak English. And those other bumpkins spoke not a word.

"No, sir. I have seen no such Frenchmen."

"Well, if by any chance you should see them, we do not wish you to have any kind of dealings with them. Do you understand me, Fernandes? I mean…" and he corrected himself, looking at my angel with his dead-fish eyes, "that His Majesty, King

George III would be sure to recompense you if you refrain from dealing with those uncivilized people and confine your trade to our great nation."

"I understand, sir. We shall trade only with you," I assented, very much against my will but acting the part with great finesse.

If I had not always believed that Englishmen know no feelings other than hunger, fatigue and bestial lust, I might have sworn that this bloated-toad manikin was gazing at the chocolatier's wife with lovelorn eyes.

"Then there is no more to be said." He seemed content. "Long live the King! Until we meet again."

They all proffered something akin to a military salute and left the establishment, slamming the door. It was evident that drawn-out farewells were not to the taste of this madman.

Now, with your permission, Madame, I shall rest my hand a little before continuing my account of the latter part of the profitable afternoon I spent in the home of Senyor Fernandes and his beautiful, captivating wife.

Five

Having partaken of two dry figs and a sip of water, your most devoted servant, who is loyal to you above all living beings, is now ready to resume the chronicle of events which were interrupted at the end of my last missive. I shall begin where I left off. We are in the establishment of the chocolatier Fernandes, and the English toad has just left in the company of his small retinue, slamming the door as he went.

With all the hurly-burly, my poor angel was greatly frightened. She was standing by the machine, weeping copious tears, but do not ask me why.

"They want to steal it from me. They all want to steal my machine," she sobbed.

I begged her to calm down a little, made her sit by the fireside and tried to make her understand the more positive aspect of the whole affair. If her husband were sufficiently quick-witted and able to leave aside political affiliations – which never lead to anything good – he should be able to make a tidy profit from these perfidious Englishmen and their king, who, from what I am told, is of very unsound mind.

"Senyor Fernandes is a truly fortunate man," I added – and, I must admit, I was only partially referring to the business at hand. However, she kept shaking her head and weeping disconsolately.

"I tell you, this cannot be."

"But why not? What is the reason for all this obstinacy?"

She kept shedding tears upon tears and gave no answer. I understood nothing, neither the reason for her tears nor her husband's unwillingness to fleece the Englishmen. I should have been delighted at such a chance to penetrate the palace of our arch enemy and should certainly have taken the uttermost advantage of it.

"I still do not know your name, sir," my lachrymose angel blurted out.

"Victor Philibert, your humble servant, Senyora."

"My name is Marianna."

Forgive me if I divulge an intimate impression, Madame, but on hearing this name I thought that heaven and earth had rarely come to such harmonious concurrence. The name did perfect justice to the lovely creature.

"Marianna is a most beautiful name," I said.

"It was given to me by Monsignor Fideu. Do you know him? This man is a saint. I owe him my life, my good fortune and everything I am."

"Is he really called Monsignor Fideu?" This surprised me, because this word in her language means "noodle".

"It is amusing, is it not? Many people think it is a nickname because he is so fond of noodle soup. Yet it is his true family name! Such strange things happen in the world." She smiled, still lovelier now she was happy. "Monsignor Fideu is the priest at Santa Maria del Mar, which is my parish. How fortunate I was! However, instead of listening to the story of my life, which is not very cheerful, would you please show me the proof that it was Madame who sent you?"

"Very well."

I fumbled in my leather pouch, looking for your letter. Unfortunately I was unable to deliver the gift it promised, and which I should have liked to give her first of all.

"Do you know Madame?" I asked as I was groping for it.

"No, of course I do not. But I have heard so much about her that I feel we are old friends. Her orders come to us with such frequency! Did you know that the chocolate we make for her is exclusive? It is for her and her alone."

"Here it is." I handed her the letter.

"Would you read it to me?"

"Do you not know how to read?"

I should have imagined this, for she was only the wife of a chocolatier. The lovely, delightful wife of another man.

"They tried to teach me, but I was a dunce," she smiled.

"I shall be very pleased to oblige. You will, of course, convey to your husband every word it says?"

"You may rest assured of that."

I began to read:

"Dear Senyor Fernandes, to whom we are indebted for so many sweet moments, I am sending you these words with my secretary, Seny—"

"How is it possible that she writes such good Catalan?" Senyora Marianna was beginning to cede ground.

"Madame is attentive to every detail." I smiled, proud to be able to make such a declaration.

"Can it be that she speaks our language?"

"I do not believe so, Senyora, although Madame Adélaïde's learning is extensive and includes subjects that would surprise us both, yet I am of the opinion that she found someone to translate her words. You must know that at Versailles we have so many people that one can always find someone who is well qualified to carry out whatever task is needed, however unusual it is."

"Oh, of course, of course."

"...I am sending you these words with my secretary, Monsieur Guillot, who at my orders will deliver this missive to you in person. Senyor Guillot may appear to be very young for such a task, but do not be deceived by appearances. He is an honest man and enjoys my absolute trust and that of my sister Victoire."

"Do you see how well she speaks of you?" Marianna was moved, but I responded with a gesture, modestly trying to convey that Madame is too generous. I did not wish my listener, who was already somewhat absent, to be further distracted and thus continued.

"I should like you to know that, in our palace, your chocolate is what ambrosia was to the gods of old, and equally sought, to such an extreme that we must hide it so only we know where it is. My sister and I count the minutes until the next time we can savour it. We have hot chocolate for breakfast and afternoon tea, and enjoy it so greatly that we had some special chocolate pots made to the measure of three small cups in the belief that this would make it last longer. We thought that you might like to possess one of these porcelain treasures produced in the factory that the late King, our father, so wisely had built in the

nearby town of Sèvres. We are sending you one, bearing my name and from my own personal effects, as a sign of admiration and fraternity, and in the hope that it will be to your liking."

"You read Catalan very badly!" Marianna giggled.

"Have you understood what the letter says?"

"Yes, she is offering me a chocolate pot."

"No, not you, your husband."

"Yes. And where is this chocolate pot?"

"It was stolen. But when we recover it, I shall bring it to you."

"Ah, it was stolen?"

"Yes, Marianna, to our great misfortune. But listen, for you are about to hear the most important part.

"Let us see what it says."

"I would also venture to ask you a small favour. My emissary, who will deliver these words to you, is a member of a commission of gentlemen sent by the King himself, my nephew, Louis XVI. As you will know, our beloved monarch is an enlightened man who is interested in any evidence of modernity which may appear in the world. Accordingly, your device for manufacturing chocolate has awakened his liveliest curiosity, and he has therefore wished to send our palace chocolatier, Monsieur Labbé, so that you can instruct him in its secrets. I beg you to receive him with all the honours due to a man who sweetens the existence of the King of France and to repeat the favour with the other members of the legation, consisting of two gentlemen, from whom you will shortly be hearing, and the royal secretary. If I am telling

you all this, it is to beseech you, knowing you to be a just and upright man, to receive these gentlemen with the same grace as you would welcome myself or His Majesty, and to assist them to carry out—"

"All these people have come here with you? Oh, dear God, I am truly lost now!" Marianna interrupted once again.

"Wait a moment, please, before you speak, Senyora. I am almost finished now. Listen carefully to what comes next," I begged her.

"...assist them to carry out their mission. Similarly, it is my sorry duty to inform you that we are apprised that the King of England, the abominable George III, hearing of our plans, has decided to send a delegation to the city of Barcelona with, we believe, the intention of visiting your establishment. These are not people to be trusted by noble spirits, Senyor, and, deeming myself a friend of yours, I feel obliged to warn you of their designs. I beg you, on behalf of my nephew, not to speak with them under any circumstances, unless you wish to be robbed, murdered, or to suffer a still worse fate."

At this point, Marianna frowned.

"Senyor, do you know what they could do that would be worse than murdering me?"

"Shhh! Only the closing words are yet to be read!"

"Since I am aware that this situation will occasion you some difficulties and the last thing in the world I wish is to be

responsible for such an unhappy eventuality, I have asked my
secretary, monsieur Guillot, to—"

"Oh, she speaks of you again!"

"Yes, indeed, but listen to me, woman. You talk too much!"

"…I have asked my secretary, Monsieur Guillot, to place
a large order with you, sufficient to assure us warmth and
comfort in the chill gloom of our palace winters in the coming
years. Once our ambassadors are satisfied and have left your
premises, Monsieur Guillot will give you further details and
will pay you a proper price for your work and availability.
I assure you that this is a generous sum in recompense for
any trouble we may cause you, while countervailing this is
the fact that you will have the satisfaction of having offered
a most useful service to the French Crown. To conclude,
Senyor Fernandes, I should like to repeat that you have my
gratitude for the wonderful afternoons your beverage has af-
forded us. If only you knew how beautifully your chocolate
combines with our violin exercises and reading in the modest
chamber occupied by my sister Victoire and myself as grey
afternoon skies glower over the parade ground… these are
the components of the evenings we spend in our apartments
of the palace.

> *I am your most affectionate friend,*
> > *Madame Adélaïde of France"*

There was a slightly distressing silence.

"Is that all?" Marianna asked. When I nodded, she sighed and
added, "Then I am lost!"

"Remember that I have come as part of a delegation that wishes to see the machine—"

"I have understood everything except the part about the business and the payment."

I smiled to see that she was interested in the part that would benefit her most.

"It is simple, Marianna. Madame wishes to compensate you for any problems you and your husband may have."

"And does she wish to compensate us with a large or small amount?"

"A very large amount."

"In cash?"

"In gold."

"Soon?"

"Madame wishes you to be rich before I depart from the city."

I remained as silent as the tomb with respect to the circumstance that we had not a single real after being robbed the previous night, praying that Monsieur Beaumarchais had spoken truly when he assured me that we would recover everything that had been taken from us.

"Would you say that your compensation is greater or smaller than the offer made by the Englishmen?"

"Senyora, do not offend me! Although it were the same sum, you would always be better served if you dealt with the great country of France!"

Marianna's eyes glowed with emotion. I would venture that your offer interested her much more than she dared to say in words, but do not ask me why I believe this. She cringed as if to conceal valuable information from me or, perhaps, despite the words I had just read out to her, she did not yet trust me or our intentions.

"And tell me," she said, "would the legation that you represent continue to deal with me without seeing my husband?"

"Naturally we could not, Senyora. Your husband was the object of our visit."

"I believed that the machine was the object."

"It is, of course, but your husband must show us how it works and give us a demonstration…"

"I can give you the demonstration. I know all the secrets of this machine. I helped to devise and assemble it. I have been using it for months without help from anyone."

"I am not sure. We had not foreseen this circumstance." I hesitated a moment before asking her, "And why must you do it? Are you so sure that Senyor Fernandes will not return? Is this not unwarranted obduracy?"

There was an eloquent silence followed by the mournful words, "Alas, Senyor, people do not return from the place where my husband has gone."

Since I did not fully apprehend her meaning, she lowered her voice and moved a little closer to me. "He is dead, Senyor. The greatest obduracy of all."

"Dead?" The surprise must have made me raise my voice inordinately, upon which she looked very afraid.

"Shhh! Do not shout! No one knows."

"When did this happen?"

"Almost six months ago."

"Six months! And why does no one know?"

"Because I have kept it secret."

"Why have you done this?"

All at once, someone began pounding on the door with brute force and in a manner that led us to believe the English plenipotentiaries had returned. A strident, penetrating voice soon disabused us.

"Eh, you, woman! Open up or I shall kick your door down!"

She went pale and I had the impression she was trembling.

"It is Mimó!" she said.

I shrugged as if to ask who this uncivil Mimó might be. She explained, "A despicable wretch who is adamantly obsessed with the idea that he will have me. You must hide."

The blows and shouting at the door became so violent that the pots of chocolate on the shelves were shuddering, as were our hearts.

"Marianna! Open up!" shrilled the voice.

Marianna pointed at a man-sized hole under the counter. I crawled into it, contorting my body as much as I could, just in time to foil the threats of the brute.

"Marianna! If you do not open up I—"

Marianna opened the door before he could act. An icy, damp gust swept inside, almost enough to make one cry. I overheard the entire conversation, which I understood without difficulty, as if my ear were becoming accustomed to this language which is not my own but bears some resemblance to it. What follows is a transcription of the words they spoke, from memory but no less precise for that.

"What do you want, Mimó?"

"Will you not let me in?"

"I shall not. What do you want?"

"I have come to see your husband."

"My husband is away."

"Still? And when will he return?"

"I shall let you know when he does."

That voice, Madame... I recognized it at once. There cannot be many as disagreeable as that in all the world. I listened attentively in order to be sure.

"Do you know how long your husband has been away, Marianna?"

"That is no concern of yours."

"By my reckoning it is at least five months. Perchance he has left you and you are in need of another man?"

In sooth, I was in no doubt. That was the voice of Captain General Potato Nose! Or, rather, that of the lying scoundrel who had visited us at the inn the previous day, pretending to be the commander of the military region.

"If I needed another man, it would not be you, Mimó,' my doughty angel replied, not mincing her words.

This man Mimó was none too happy to hear this. His voice became even more obnoxious when he threatened, "Do not be haughty with me. We can close your business."

"You and who else?"

"I and the other chocolatiers. In our guild and elsewhere we are all in agreement on the matter."

"The apothecaries also?"

"And the millers."

"Aha! You have been busy, Mimó."

"I shall be even busier if you allow me, Marianna." Now he was softening, he was slimy as a slug. I was longing to emerge from my hideaway and have words with that man.

"Go now and leave me in peace. We have had this conversation too many times."

"Why are you so stubborn, Marianna? Do you not understand that your husband has abandoned you? Do you not know what I can offer you?"

"You? Do not make me laugh."

"I and none other. I have money and shall have even more. We shall be the richest traders in the city. With my talent for business and your smile behind the counter no one will compete with us."

Marianna gave a weary sigh. "Go now, Mimó. I have heard this story too many times."

With some effort, I extracted a leg from my lair and knelt behind the counter. My heart was galloping, for I knew my life was at risk, but I had to be certain. I raised my head very slowly, like a puppet in its theatre, until I glimpsed the man in the doorway who was speaking so insolently to my poor angel who was in danger of catching her death of cold. Indeed, Madame, my instinct had not erred. It was that blackguard! The potato nose confirmed it at once, even though he had changed his disguise for a trader's apparel. He had the brawny, muscular arms of a chocolatier and the same hideous brigand's face. He was staring at Marianna like a cat at a plate of cream and was moving so indecently close to her that I wanted to vomit. Forgive the crudeness of my words, Madame, but it would have given me great pleasure to give that imbecile a sound thrashing then and there, for Marianna, for the money and for the chocolate pot! I was restrained only by my desire not to sully my angel's reputation (and also because he would have made mincemeat of me). Much against my will and biting my fists, I curled up like a worm and crept into the hole beneath the counter once more, trying to make sense of this predicament as I peered out through a crack in the counter.

The conversation continued, as sharp as the cold gusting in from the street. Now, in his spite, Potato Nose revealed his knavery.

"I see that, like your husband, your clients have forsaken you."

"Yes, thanks to you and your minions. Do you believe I am unaware of what you have been saying about me?"

"It is untrue, perhaps?"

"You are vermin, Mimó and can only covet what you cannot have."

Potato Nose puffed up like a singer to adopt a peremptory and still louder tone. He loomed over Marianna, but she did not retreat. What a valiant woman! I believe that seeing her defiance of this bully made me love her even more.

"Do not provoke me, woman, for I shall not be responsible for the consequences."

"If you do not like hearing words truly spoken, then desist from coming to this house."

"I come here because I know that, sooner or later, you will have sweet words for me. I must only wait."

"As you wish."

"You women yelp loudly at first but then you come whimpering back to seek a protector."

"Have you finished? I would like to close the door."

"I have not yet informed you of what I have come here to tell you. I have been sent by the guild."

"Which guild?"

"Ours."

"To tell me what?"

"The dignitaries of our guild require your husband to pay his dues."

"We owe nothing."

"Five months' membership fees. And interest. It is a large amount. We want your husband at our next meeting, on Wednesday this week, bringing what he owes and an explanation."

"Leave my husband in peace. I am the person you must speak with."

"This is a matter for men, Marianna. It is the law."

"When the law is no longer valid it must be changed."

"Why are you so inflexible? Come with me, Marianna. We shall present a united front, you, me and the machine. That will see an end to all your problems. Ours will be a prosperous business."

"I already have a prosperous business, although you obstruct me in every way!"

"Yes, but only until we take your machine…"

"You are a vile wretch, Mimó!" Marianna tried to close the door, but he stopped it with his foot. I felt the coldest chill in the world enter through the open crack. I do not refer to the snow falling from the sky but to the words I heard.

"Do you not understand? You are a woman! Women cannot be master craftsmen in this trade. You cannot keep this machine. You need a man."

"What would you know about what I need? Go away, Mimó. There is nothing more to say and it is very cold."

"You are determined to bring misfortune upon yourself, Marianna, when you could have everything."

"So you say."

"You will regret this."

"Let me close the door."

"Do you not hear what I am telling you?"

"Of course I hear, you worm!" Now it was Marianna who took command, with the voice and will – Heaven knows where it came from – to defend herself. I had the impression that this was not the first time she had done so. "I hear you all too well. I shall regret it, you say? And what will you do to me this time? Tell more lies, like the vile story you have been spreading lately? Who invented this perverted story that I adulterate the chocolate with menstrual blood, like a witch? That could only come from the brain of a rancorous oaf like you. The only impurity in my chocolate is you and your bile. That is the only thing you have: bile aplenty! And envy that corrodes your very soul. You want everything my husband has, do you not? Me, the machine and a prosperous business. Do you think I did not see the way you looked at me, even when my husband was beside me? You shall have nothing that is his. You shall never have anything of his, however long you wait, and however often you come with your caterwauling to my house. Do you understand me? Never! Never, never, never!"

Mimó, shocked by the power and truth of Marianna's words, took a step backwards. He lamely added, "We shall see about that!"

The door slammed in the perplexed face and tuberous nose of the chocolatier. Bam! Poor Marianna, now shrunk to a shadow of the woman who had defied Mimó, collapsed on the ground like an empty sack and wept, her face hidden in her hands. I wanted to speak with her, ask about all the distressing things I had overheard and console her with soothing words, but she was unable to speak or stop weeping. She waved her hand vaguely as if to say we would meet again, and perhaps indicating that I should leave.

I must confess, Madame, that I was overwhelmed, incapable of uttering any word or making any gesture that might assuage such despair. I could not help thinking that, when women lament their own misfortune, a man can only be a clodpole.

I left, still thinking about this knave Mimó and how I might find him, but the darkness was all but complete in these streets with no torches or lighting of any kind. Then I stopped to listen to some footsteps crunching in the snow. There were very few people abroad in this weather and at this hour. I only needed to follow my ear and my instinct, like a wild animal.

All at once, on rounding a corner, I saw a moving patch of light and recognized that whoreson Mimó, who was entering a building with his lantern in his hand. I took careful note of our whereabouts with a view to returning later, perhaps in company. We were in Carrer de les Caputxes.

On my way back to the inn, in the dark and shivering with cold, I was assailed by an unwelcome murmuring in my head. *If everything is worrisome today, tomorrow will be worse.*

Six

Madame,

In my zeal to make your reading more pleasurable by finishing yesterday's chronicle at the most apposite moment, I omitted a detail of some significance. On my arrival at the inn, after that evening of frights and freezing, Beaumarchais was not there to receive me. I was most surprised by this. I asked Zanotti and was told, "When he left through that doorway he said he was going to the theatre, but that was not true, Signore."

"What emboldens you to assert such a thing?"

"Because the doors of the Comedy Theatre are locked and barred, Signore. It is two years since it has opened its doors to the citizens of Barcelona for any performance, sung or spoken. It is said that opera is too costly for the city to afford in these times of crisis. It is enough to make a man weep that we should meet in such circumstances. How can a man live without music or theatre?"

I was still more taken aback when Beaumarchais did not appear during the night, and I had to sleep alone after having written for a considerable time in the bright glow of the streetlamps. At breakfast time no one had seen him, and his absence left the entire legation leaderless and ignorant as to what to do.

"We cannot go to visit Senyor Fernandes without him. That would be most discourteous!" the always polite Delon ventured.

345

"Well, I have no intention of waiting for him for ever!" pronounced Maleshèrbes, who was busy gobbling up three slices of bread with cheese.

"Perhaps we should inform the Captain General? He may have been kidnapped." Labbé was alarmed.

Delon replied, "Say no more about that, sir. We would know if he had been kidnapped."

"We would? How?" asked Labbé.

I intervened. "Gentlemen, we should not precipitate matters. He has only been missing for a few hours. Let him return by his own devices without involving the Captain General."

"So much the better. This Captain General is a good-for-nothing," Maleshèrbes submitted, his mouth still full. "Our stolen money is proof of that. Would you say he has lifted a finger to recover it?"

After some moments of troubled reflection, Delon spoke. "Tell us, Guillot, what are the plans for today? Thus apprised we shall know what we must do."

"I?"

"Naturally, in the absence of Beaumarchais, you must take command."

Heaven have mercy on me! If there is one thing I cannot do it is taking decisions. Not even for myself, Madame. When I must decide something I am all of a tremble. Once I have decided, it is still worse, for I always believe I should have chosen what I discarded. The torments of hell could not be worse.

Faced with this situation which, although not desperate, was grave enough, I granted the members of the legation a day of rest.

"And what do you wish us to do with all this time and not a single real among us?" Labbé quite sensibly enquired.

"I shall go back to bed," declared Maleshèrbes, with the contented air of a well-gorged piglet. "Inform me when lunch is served."

"The man lives only to exercise his jaws." Delon was horrified.

"Would you care to join me, sir, for a walk along the top of the city wall?" Labbé asked his colleague from Bayonne.

Thus, leaving them more or less composed, I used my time as best I could, and I believe I used it most profitably, as you shall soon see.

I began by visiting my chocolatier angel. It was delightful walking in the city that morning. The City Council had dragooned its prisoners into sweeping the streets. Snow was neatly piled on the corners. A bright but far from warm sun shone down and everything smelt new.

In the establishment in Carrer de les Tres Voltes, I found Marianna behind the counter, still lovelier than the previous day and smiling at a customer who had just bought a pound of chocolate.

"The chocolate from this house has no equal," the woman affirmed. "My husband and I will have no other."

Marianna nodded, well pleased.

As the customer was leaving she added, "Give my respects to your husband."

"I shall do that, thank you," Marianna replied, a dark cloud crossing her face.

When her eyes met mine, her smile broadened, suggesting that she was pleased to see me.

"Are you recovered?" I asked.

"Greatly, thank you."

Another customer came in, a maidservant from a wealthy household it seemed. Marianna left me for a moment in order to attend to her.

"My master and mistress wish to know if the chocolatier can come this afternoon to make the chocolate."

"My husband is travelling," Marianna informed her with the dazzling smile that turned all lies into truth. "I shall come myself."

"You? You can make chocolate?"

"I most certainly can, and it will be as delectable as my husband's."

"And the grindstone?"

"I shall bring it myself, as is usually done."

"Do you kneel on the ground, like a man?"

"Of course I do. Do I not have knees?"

"You have knees. But strength? Do you have that?"

"You will be astounded."

The maidservant from the rich man's house shook her head.

"Goodness gracious! I think not. My master and mistress will not suffer seeing you kneeling." With a speculative glance through narrowed eyes, she added, "And the authorities permit you to make chocolate in people's houses, working like a man?"

Marianna sighed in resignation. She did not like lying and was beginning to believe that hers was a lost cause. She did not deign to reply. The maidservant continued, "It would be preferable to seek a man to make the chocolate. Do you know where I might find one?"

Marianna allowed herself the luxury of an impish smile. "I am sorry, but I know of none that is man enough."

The customer looked at her as if she were certain that she was entirely in the right in this very straightforward matter and indignantly swept out of the shop.

"Are you really able to use a grindstone?" I asked.

"Of course I am. It is the simplest thing in the world."

"I believe it requires exceedingly strong arms."

"I have unimaginable strength, sir, particularly when I am angry."

"I may be able to help you. Would you show me how to do it?"

"To make chocolate in rich people's houses? But have you looked at yourself?" She giggled. "You are as thin as a reed! You would not even be able to lift the small grinding stone we call the *mano*. And you will soil your clothes. No, no, it is more than evident that you were born to shuffle papers and books. And to think. This is no task for you!"

"Truth to tell, I should do anything to make you happy." She huffed in resignation once again. "In order to remain by your side I would soil myself through to my very soul. I am your most fervent admirer, Marianna!"

"Lately they have been coming to me in all guises!" She was mocking me slightly, but soon spoke seriously. "I am most grateful that you wish to help me."

"Yesterday I wanted to break that Mimó's nose!"

"You would achieve nothing by that. To my great misfortune, he is not mistaken. Whatever I do, I shall have to close and they will take the machine, which is what they want."

"What is this? You yield? You?"

She shrugged. "I am weary of struggling against everything and everyone."

"And how will you survive?"

"I shall have to return to the House of Charity. They still remember me and I know people there, old and young. I have discussed it with Monsignor Fideu. He will help me."

"House of Charity?"

"I left there to marry, once again due to the good offices of this saintly man. One day I shall tell you about it. Mine is a most improbable story. I was very fortunate to be able to marry, and I loved my husband dearly. But my luck suddenly changed and then every opportunity was thwarted." She lapsed into silence, but soon recovered the smile that always lights up her face. "But at least I shall not surrender myself to Mimó. Does that console you?"

She laughed again, giving me no time to respond. I left her there, because another customer had entered and I did not want to keep the woman waiting or to disturb Marianna. I assured her I would return, probably in the company of the legation I represent, and went outside into the square, where I spied a man who, leaning against a wall, was engrossed in watching her establishment. I wished to ask him what he was doing there and who had sent him, but I judged it wiser not to call attention to myself, at least for the moment, and to go about my business.

Since everyone had a rest day, and there are many hours to fill in a day, I resolved to pry a little into my angel's life by visiting the saintly priest of whom she so often spoke. I set off for Santa Maria del Mar, that great stone vessel moored to the life of a whole neighbourhood, which was starting to become my own. You may think I have lost my wits, Madame, but that very moment it seemed to me that, whatever came to pass and however much I roamed the world, that place would always be mine. There will always be a part of me that belongs to these streets and tiny squares, that nostalgically recalls the constant hubbub of different accents and busy voices, and that will cherish in my heart the simple names of these streets, which denote the trades of humble citizens: Vidrieria, Esparteria, Formatgeria...

glassmakers, wicker workers, cheese makers. Strange are the designs of the heart, Madame, but it is the heart and only the heart that decides where it wishes to belong.

My heart has recently declared that it belongs to Barcelona, to the neighbourhood of La Ribera, and I realize I can do nothing about it.

As I walked, I had time to ponder my quandary and how to remedy it. Does it not happen to you, Madame, that your thoughts move with your feet? As I discovered long ago, I think much better when I am moving. Hence, if I wish to cogitate I go out for a long walk in the palace gardens. Heavens above! Did I really need all that immensity? I would almost say they were expressly designed so that a vacillating soul like myself can clarify his thinking and come to conclusions.

To return to my thoughts as I was walking round Barcelona, it occurred to me that, like myself, you perhaps are in need of explanation. Hence, in the time it takes to walk from Carrer de les Tres Voltes to the priest's door, I shall inform you that the Barcelona chocolatiers' guild is newly founded. Seven years ago, after forty-eight years of squabbles and legal wrangling, the old chocolate makers' association, which is dedicated to St Anthony of Padua, managed to get the court to recognize it as an independent guild. You should also know that, before then, only the apothecaries had permits to sell chocolate, and that the College of Apothecaries and Sugar Confectioners did everything within their power – legally and illegally – to protect this monopoly. And, to boot, the cocoa millers began claiming the right to sell the product they ground, this being denied to them by the apothecaries, who for many years spared no effort when deeming it necessary to dictate their demands to the judges.

Since its inception, the guild has had its own rules and regulations, and its membership is exclusive to master chocolatiers. Only members of the guild may sell this sweetmeat, whether retail or wholesale. In order to become a master chocolatier, one must undergo an apprenticeship of at least six years, and must religiously pay all the dues the guild demands. An apprentice may only change his master twice and must also pass an examination. This test, notorious for its difficulty, is divided into two parts, theoretical and practical. The latter part includes grinding the chocolate before the examination committee using a mealing stone they call a *metate*. Each candidate must show that he knows how to light the fire and, if he is skilled at that, his examiners are well pleased. He must also analyse different types of cocoa beans and classify them according to species, origin and quality. Once he has passed the examination, he must only pay the fees in order to call himself a chocolatier. Any man who neglects to pay his dues four times is expelled from the guild, although he may keep the status of master chocolatier. Women may not apply to take the examination and, accordingly, by virtue of their sex, cannot be master chocolatiers or become members of the guild. As the local refrain goes, chocolate is men's business.

Having offered my explanation of the situation, in the hope that it will clarify matters, I have now reached the door of the parish priest of Santa Maria del Mar, Monsignor Fideu by (true) name. I hope it will not bore you when I inform you of the interesting things I learnt from him about our Marianna, which I shall describe in detail in my next epistle. My poor hand is now in need of a rest (and my belly is growling for some dry figs).

There is just one more small detail.

You may very well believe that such concern over the problems of this woman is irrelevant to my commitment to further the interests of our legation. Being so perspicacious, you may be of the opinion that if I am moving so much through the frozen streets of Barcelona, if I am questioning strangers and if I am exerting myself so much, there must be some other inducement.

Madame, I wish to confess the truth before you discover it. I am sure you would have discerned this infatuation of mine some time ago. I may perhaps be disappointing you, and Monsieur de Beaumarchais might punish me on learning of it, but I shall willingly accept any punishment and then turn the other cheek, for I can do nothing about it and, moreover, am disposed to suffer it for her sake.

I acknowledge that Marianna fills my thoughts, day and night (and I pray His Majesty and you yourself will forgive me).

I am madly in love, Madame.

(And now, although you may rebuke me for neglecting my responsibilities, you will never be able to accuse me of not knowing how to end a chapter.)

Seven

I beg you to forgive the unexpected twist in my story, of which I am about to offer you one more chapter, this time concerning the conversation I had in the Santa Maria del Mar parish office with the holy priest, Monsignor Fideu. After the introductions (brief) and the formalities (essential), I directly addressed my chief concern, Marianna. I was unambiguous in acknowledging that I was captivated by her beauty, and still more by her courage, which I had witnessed, curled up in my hideaway beneath the counter. The priest heard me out as if he had nothing to do all day, a small smile playing on his lips and his hands folded on the table before him. The sight reminded me of the images of those God-inspired hermits in the Lives of the Saints.

I made no bones about my interests, telling him that if I lived in the city or planned to settle here I would not waste another moment but would immediately propose marriage to a woman like Marianna and found with her a large family, the more numerous the better, but since, regrettably, I have many weighty obligations binding me to my nation and the palace at Versailles in your service, Madame, I was obliged to find another solution, which may also be satisfactory. Under no circumstances can I accept Marianna's having to return to live in that charitable institution, and, still less, to be at the mercy of that beast Mimó and others of his ilk, who only wish to harm her and who ogle her... I am sure there is no need, Madame, to tell you what they ogle.

Monsignor Fideu nodded in agreement with everything he heard. "You do very well to be concerned for her, Monsieur. I am an old man and shall soon be called to render accounts before my Maker. When the Lord God asks me about Marianna, I should like to tell Him that she is in good hands."

"That is why I am here, Monsignor Fideu, but to achieve certain ends I have in mind I shall need your help and support. Marianna holds you in high esteem and heeds your advice. She says you have known her all her life. Nobody better than you can tell me, then, certain things I must know before taking my first step. If you are willing, of course..."

"Do you wish to know if Marianna is honest and trustworthy?"

"You have guessed correctly."

"This means you have come in search of a story..." Well content, he slowly drummed the tabletop with his fingertips. "The story of Marianna the chocolatier, you mean?"

There was no hint of demurral in his voice. Rather, he seemed pleased.

"If you would be so kind."

"It will be my pleasure. Make yourself comfortable in your chair, because it is worth taking pains over this story. I shall tell you everything you wish to hear. It all began when, as a very small child, Marianna was orphaned of both her parents. Someone took her to the House of Charity, where they receive destitute children. She grew up there, as healthy and well fed as the tertiary nuns could manage. I met her, together with the other poor children, in my work as their confessor. Marianna stood out for her goodness and unworldly charm, and also for her incomparably exquisite face. She was beautiful even as a very small girl. Everyone praised her to the skies. The nuns said she was an intelligent, hard-working child and, most important of all, they had never known such a good-hearted one.

"You may be unaware of the customs of Spanish monarchs in these realms when they have some money to spare and are of good cheer. Our esteemed King Charles III was so overjoyed with his newborn grandson (although the poor child lasted less than three years) that he organized a competition in this city for poor girls of marriageable age. He promised dowries of six thousand reals for three poor, orphaned and honest damsels, aged between fifteen and thirty-five years. They had to make a submission in writing with one of God's ministers as their character witness.

"As soon as I had news of this contest promising to choose three fortunate winners from all the entries, I thought of Marianna. She was unrivalled in her virtues, yet without dowry or parents she would never leave the confines of the House of Charity. Have you ever known such an unjust fate for such a perfect creature? Praised be King Charles III and his whimsies! He would not appear to be his father's son were it not for his zeal in trying to make everyone speak Spanish – such folly! – as if we would not continue speaking as we wished, whatever he pronounced. In brief, this was a blessing from heaven for the child. I hastened to obtain all the documents she needed: the death certificates of her parents, a certificate of good health, another stating that she abided by the precepts of the Church, and yet another attesting to her condition of 'disgraceful' poverty (the things they think of!), and then penned a letter confirming that she was a chaste, righteous maiden, well raised, natural daughter of her late parents, duly honest and with no deformity of face that might detract from her other merits. I signed it myself, 'since she is unable to write', and presented her submission.

"Marianna's eyes were was as big as saucers, poor child, when I told her what I had done, while also assuring her that no one deserved the King's largesse as much as she. She was only sixteen years old, highly intelligent and resigned to life as a member of the Third Order, the only respectable option she had if she were not to die in abject poverty. After I had given my account of the papers I had presented, she suddenly asked, 'And who should a poor girl like me marry, when I only know old people, orphans and nuns?'

"I then understood that obtaining a dowry for her was not sufficient. I also had to find a man worthy of her, and that would take more time. I set about the task immediately. I am known to be a serene, affable fellow but, I can assure you, I am constantly vigilant and nothing escapes me. From that moment on I began to scrutinize all the unmarried men in the city, but none seemed worthy of my Marianna. Some were crude of speech, others too dull or too sharp, or too hairy or too lazy, and I even disapproved of a young man whose only defect was that he came from l'Espluga de Francolí. I feared that I was becoming deranged with my obsession, but then I met Fernandes, the chocolatier.

"What a fine, clever man! He was a good Christian, far-sighted and hard-working – and to think I met him by chance! I went into his shop in Carrer de les Tres Voltes one afternoon in order to satisfy my whim of indulging in a little cup of well-spiced hot chocolate. It would seem that those uncivilized Indians on the other side of the world say their chocolate is food for the gods!

After tasting their heavenly beverage, I am not surprised that it is so difficult to convert them to the true religion. Fernandes served me, poured a cup for himself and closed the door of the shop, wishing to convey to me his most intimate woes. As you will know, we priests are well accustomed to listening to private torments.

"Thus I learnt about the woes of this poor man. He suffered greatly and worked still more. He had ever greater numbers of customers beating at his door but, being alone, was not able to serve them all. Moreover, of course, he went to the houses of the rich to prepare their chocolate himself, as is the custom. He could have looked for an apprentice, but was wary of the authorities of the guild, the apothecaries and, still more, the millers. He preferred not to tell his secrets to any stranger and had decided to keep them to himself until the day when he could share them with a person he could trust. I noted that his voice was breaking with despair when I asked him what troubled him, and he answered me.

The chocolatier Fernandes longed to wed. He was thirty-three years old, still single and had no relatives in the city. Since his arrival, having walked from Mataró carrying his *metate* and *mano*, he had worked from sunrise to sunset. Sometimes, on raising his eyes from the cocoa beans, he dreamt of a wife who would comfort him in the sorrows of his solitude, which were numerous (some of which assailed him by day and others by night). He had no experience of courting or time to do anything except make chocolate and more chocolate, and now that he had reached the age of thirty-three, when gods die and which, as the ancients taught, is midway through life, he was in despair to think that the chocolate that was sweetening the lives of the rich was so embittering his own.

As he described his tribulations, I was looking at him, this man Fernandes, just as I am looking at you now, and within me I was brimming with joy. I let him finish, because words such as those I had to say are more effective when one's listener has unburdened himself. Then I said, 'You may be surprised to learn, Fernandes, that I am very pleased to hear of your sorrows and travails.'

"Naturally, he was taken aback by this. He asked why I was so content when he had spoken only of adversity. 'Because I have the remedy for your suffering, Fernandes. Permit me to do what I must do and you will see.'

"I should not like you to think that I influenced the competition, but I did speak with two or three people of influence who always heed what I have to say (and especially when I prescribe their penance). I had no need to exaggerate anything and thus confined myself to offering an accurate account of the true qualities of my candidate, and they all agreed that I was not mistaken. I subsequently learnt that one thousand eight hundred and eighty damsels had presented solicitations, of which three hundred and nine had been eliminated since they did not comply with all the requirements, which left one thousand five hundred and seventy-one. The fact that Marianna was chosen was an act of almost divine justice, I can assure you, and her union with Fernandes the best idea I have ever had.

"Theirs was a marvellous marriage. She found a haven and he found happiness. With Marianna's help the poor man was at last able to think about other things. Then I learnt that they had invented a chocolate-making machine. At night, when they closed the shop, so they told me, they talked of devices and planned their future. I chided them, saying, 'Bringing children into the world is what you must think about when you close your doors at night!' I felt as if they were duty-bound to make me a grandfather, but to no avail, for they were consumed with constructing this machine they had contrived. And they did it! There was nothing those two could not do together. Do you understand what I am saying? They were like one of those September tempests, stopped by nothing and sweeping away everything in their path."

Monsignor Fideu's eyes filled with tears as he spoke of his protégée and the chocolatier.

"This machine you have seen, then, is like the son or daughter they never had, because they were too distracted with other matters. They made a fine pair, and I believe they deserved another destiny, a less truculent fate. Sometimes Our Lord's writing is far from intelligible."

I waited until he regained control of his emotions and tear-filled eyes, after which I asked whether he was completely sure that Fernandes had died.

"Of course I am sure he is dead! I buried him myself, right here, in the rectory vegetable patch."

"You buried him yourself?"

"Marianna asked me to help her to ensure that the poor man had a Christian burial, and to keep his death a secret, so that the members of the guild would not close the shop. Since I can deny her nothing, I did as she asked. May God have mercy on me! Sometimes she comes to visit the grave. Only we two know where it is. It is strange to see such a beautiful young woman praying and weeping amid the broccoli and cauliflowers. If the sacristan asks what she is doing there I say that suffering has unhinged the poor child."

"What was the cause of the chocolatier's death?"

"Measles. What a catastrophe! One day he was feverish, and two weeks later we had buried him."

I was very moved to hear the story of my angel and her chocolatier, while also pleased that I had visited Monsignor Fideu, because I could see that he was the perfect man to help me achieve my aims.

"Monsignor," I said, "I am under the impression that you are not well pleased by the idea that Marianna should become a nun and enter the House of Charity, never to leave it again."

"Of course I am not pleased by the idea!" His tone was sharp. Then, more dejectedly, he added, "What more can I do? As I have said, I am no longer young and do not have that—"

"Please let me speak, Monsignor. I have come here in search of a story. That is true. You, however, are still unaware that I wish to pay a good price for it."

"Really?" He opened his eyes wide and then frowned. "What might that price be?"

"An ending."

As I had foreseen, he was most interested to hear this. Before I gave him the details, I asked, "Would you be free to see me the day after tomorrow at five in the afternoon?"

Eight

When I arrived at the Santa Maria Inn that evening, Zanotti was waiting for me.

"I may be interfering where it is not warranted, sir, but I have news that Monsieur de Beaumarchais has been sighted at the port, in the company of a uniformed soldier."

"What uniform? From here or elsewhere?" I was intrigued.

"French, Signore. The Royal and Military Order of St Louis."

Zounds! That greatly shocked me. What was Beaumarchais's purpose in cultivating such friendships? Since my besotted state still permitted me to think a little and had not annulled the deep sense of duty which has always been my forte, I asked the way to the port and set out at once, accompanied only by an oil lamp which the innkeeper lent me.

On the way, I thought of nothing but your words.

It is as if I can see you, Madame, seated in your small drawing room, with a violin lying in your lap and, before you, the tray on which the chocolate, now cold, had been served. You sighed and, with a most serious expression, told me, "This may sound strange, Monsieur Guillot, but my sister and I have powerful reasons for believing that Monsieur de Beaumarchais is hatching something, which has led him to journey to Barcelona under the pretext of protecting the chocolatiers' legation. Both Madame Victoire and myself are almost certain that he will use his stay in this beautiful city to meet a person he cannot see in

Paris, or perhaps engage in some kind of business. We do not know whether he is under orders from the King in making this move, or whether he is impelled by personal interests, but we feel obliged to ask you to watch him closely and inform us of everything he does."

I must admit that, at the time, I believed that your suspicions were somewhat excessive. Yesterday, however, while I crossed the Pla de Palau in the stygian darkness of the night, looking for the city's seafront entrance, I realized that this notion of mine had been most ingenuous. How right you were, Madame! And how painful it would be, if your misgivings were confirmed, to be obliged to speak ill to you of the secretary of the King, for whom I have such great respect and admiration.

I had located the seafront entrance through which I had to pass before they closed the city gates when I heard a clamour of male voices behind me. Instinct made me turn, but only to ensure that I was in no danger. You would not believe the sight that greeted my eyes!

Some twenty-five paces away from me was a party of friends, or so it would seem, in high spirits, as if returning from some kind of revels. One of them, a squat, toad-like fellow, was so inebriated that two men were holding him up. His bearers, it must be said, were most finely arrayed, with new wigs, gold-buttoned military dress coats and shiny buckles on their shoes. One of them was translating what they said in such bizarre English that I almost laughed aloud. One man stood out from the others in the party. Also dressed most luxuriously, laden with embroidery, great quantities of gold and lavishness in everything, he boasted in the centre of his face a large nasal protuberance so resembling a potato that once again I had to wonder why the people of this land are so adverse to eating potatoes, as if seeing this man and thinking such thoughts were all of a piece. There were two more individuals, one of them vomiting over the spindly trunk of a newly planted tree and the other one watching as if to say, "Be quick about it; it is my turn now."

Are you too exclaiming over the fact that I should have stumbled on such select company? It is true, Madame. The same thing was happening again! The chocolatier Mimó, disguised once more as the Captain General, had decided to sally out again to indulge in his beloved pastime of robbing foreigners. This time the victims were to be Sir English Toad and his two stalwarts who, on this carousing expedition, had left their lances behind them. When I came across them they must have been carrying at least five bottles as they walked to their inn in Carrer de Manresa, where I knew they would be robbed of everything the moment they closed their eyes to sleep off the effects of their wassailing.

I confess that this conviction confronted me with a most uncomfortable dilemma. Should I spare from suffering these men whom I deemed to be enemies of my nation and my king? Would I not serve my country better if I took the side of the malefactors? Yet, if I took their side, would I not be betraying myself, for I too had been their innocent victim? Is it not the duty of true gentlemen to come to the aid of a person in need? And is it not human – and common sense? – to join forces in the face of adversity? Should I serve France before my own common sense? And since I had not come to any decision and the men were moving past me, I hastily made my choice (and, as you know, I do not excel at this).

I hurried towards the group and stood before the toad. He was trying to see me but unable to open his eyes properly. Nonetheless, he mumbled thickly, "You, Fernandes?"

"Yes, sir. I have come to give you my answer about the machine," I said in very fine English and with great resolve.

I could see Mimó-Potato Nose staring at me without knowing where I had come from or what I wanted – and, to my great good fortune, without understanding a word I uttered.

"Must it be here and now? Do you believe this is an appropriate occasion?" my enemy asked.

"I can wait no longer," I lied.

"Very well." He was making an effort to speak. "So, what have you decided?" He lowered his voice to add, "Speak softly, for I wish no one to know of our business."

"I understand. We accept your offer."

"You will come with us?"

"Yes, sir."

"And the device?"

"It will be yours."

"And your wife?"

"No. Do not as much as entertain the idea."

"I mean, will she be coming with us?"

"She will."

The toad's mouth twisted into the toothy smirk of a jocund hake. He attempted to pronounce the words "Magnificent tidings", but burbled instead "Mafnisent tind..."

At this point his stomach went into spasms, and what it manifested bore no resemblance to words. It left Captain General Potato Nose's dress coat in a horrible state.

Once recovered and having set aright his wig, he resumed our conversation, pale and sweating but with all the exaggerated display that Englishmen confuse with good manners.

"I shall come to your establishment tomorrow to conclude our agreement."

"I prefer the day after tomorrow."

"I have no objection to that. What time?"

"Would five in the afternoon be a suitable hour?"

"Agreed. We shall come then, bringing the duly stamped documents."

The walnut-and-herb liquor gushing from the Englishmen's stomachs made them look for all the world like human fountains. Undeterred, the toad was still cock-a-hoop, which he expressed by making a little speech, slurred to be sure, but also exalted, in the way that liquor exalts one.

"What a marvellous city this is, sir! How many wonders it offers! What congenial people! A man could believe he is in paradise here. Splendid drinking, fine food, excellent friends" – with which he heartily slapped his escort's shoulder – "and lovely women! Do you know what?" He now whispered in a confidential tone. "This afternoon I bedded a most distinguished lady, only a few hours after meeting her. She is lodged in the inn where I am staying. She is a fervent admirer of the English Navy and tells me she finds me handsome. You cannot imagine such bounties! I was a little puppy in her arms. I even went to sleep! That has never happened to me before, not even with strumpets I have known for many a year! Here I have discovered how sweet it is to sleep with my head in a lady's lap as she runs her fingers through my hair. How enchanting it is! And what a fine chunk of womanhood! Excuse me for a moment, please."

As the Englishman turned away to vomit more at his ease, that dolt Mimó watched me most attentively. He was most certainly pondering how my presence would jeopardize his interests. Before leaving I approached the Englishman with the excuse of removing a lump of partially digested beef from his dress coat and whispered in his ear, mumbling but making sure I was understood, "Have a very pleasant evening, sir."

Mimó was full of suspicion, which is exactly what I wanted.

Yes, I know, I could have said something. I had the occasion to warn the man of the danger he was in, but did not take advantage of it. Please do not reproach me. Before writing another word, I accept you are right. I intended to warn him of the thieves' intentions, but changed my mind at the last moment. Damnation! I have no talent for making decisions and can never determine what I must do and what I must not.

The toad was a model of impassiveness, although he surely expected more portentous words to go with my gesture. As grim-faced as if he were about to die for the sake of honour, he replied, "I wish you the same, Fernandes!"

I then turned towards that fool Mimó, swept off my hat in most ceremonious style, as I addressed him in my still-incipient Catalan.

"Senyor Captain General, what a pleasure to see you again."

I then hurried off across the Pla de Palau, because time was not in my favour.

Nine

I reached the seafront entrance to the city just as the great doors were stridently creaking closed. However I pleaded with the watchmen to let me out, invoking the names of the French King, the Spanish King, their honour and my word, I was unable to convince them. It would seem that my arguments were less than adequate. They looked at me as if I were a mangy cur and went about their business as if I were not there.

I had no choice but to climb up to the ramparts walk by way of the sloping bank near the Convent of St Sebastian in the hope of glimpsing something. The port area began at the foot of the wall but extended a great distance, and everything was plunged in darkness. In order to remain unseen, I extinguished my lamp so that my shadow melted into all the other shadows of the night. Everything was whimpering with cold. You cannot imagine, Madame, what a freezing gale was blowing in that place and at that hour. With the first blast I could have snapped the nose off my face. I had to keep clutching my hat and wig which were struggling to forsake my head and fly away. To add to my woes, it was a pitch-black, moonless night.

I told myself to be patient. "Patience is a tree with bitter roots that bears sweet fruits." I reminded myself of what the classic poet said. Who was it? I could not recall. Ovid perhaps? Horace? Or the great Petrarch? All at once I had a vision of your father's library and those delightful afternoons – so warm and comfortable by the fireside! – of ordering the books, separating those which had to be sent to the binder, and silent readings of the Italian poets, whom I have always appreciated. How happy I should be if I could reside for ever in the palace library, Madame. If this mission ends with the results you desire, I may perhaps dare to request that you recommend me for the post of librarian. I believe I would be well equipped for it, since one is not required to make decisions more difficult than having to decide whether to shelve the *Divine Comedy* under D for Dante or A for Alighieri, and because the serene stillness of objects suits my nature very well.

Books are the best company, would you not agree? The wise and beautiful words they contain make us better people. There is a difference between someone who has read and someone who has never touched a book. It might be said of the former that he has probed many different spirits, while the latter, poor wretch, has never gone beyond the bounds of himself. If I were called upon to acknowledge my masters, I should certainly cite the Italian poets first of all. Is it not miraculous that a perfect stranger born three hundred years ago is able to tell you things about yourself you did not know? That night, as I shivered and shook with cold on top of the wall, their verses came to my rescue. The first was by the great Petrarch, and of course his words were most fitting.

> Alone, and lost in thought, the desert glade
> Measuring I roam with ling'ring steps and slow;
> And still a watchful glance around me throw,
> Anxious to shun the print of human tread.

But after that, love poems which I had never fully understood flooded into my head, filling it with new, intense, overwhelming feeling. Marianna, her face, her voice were everywhere. *The moment I saw you was the very first day, and I resolved to love you true. With my eyes and mind, lady, between us to shorten the way... Oh my first love, you!* As if enticed by the lure of her memory, more verses appeared, mixed together in great tumult, but as true as the feelings burgeoning in my breast. *An instant of the heart one a lover makes. Every thought of love partakes... and my heart is all atremble...* Now I understood the anguish and fears of those old poets.

Does it happen to you that the more you sing the more you want to sing? This is what happened to me that evening. Once I had begun to sing the praises of my love in other men's words I was unable to cease. I whispered through chattering teeth ... *I wish to speak and am in bewilderment bound... But if will is the wish of fate, must I with this sorrowful soul stay my ground?... Love is my guide... And I know the pain will ease only when I have died.*

To my misfortune, life proceeds in prose and the fevers of love bring no warmth. All at once, as I stood there shivering and shaking, I thought I saw a tiny spot of light moving along the wharf, and was obliged against my will to forgo the poetry recital I was performing for myself. I squinted, doing my best to keep the light in sight.

It was like watching a slow-moving glow-worm. Someone was taking his time as he strolled along the wharf. It was someone, or maybe two people, and perhaps they were coming... Little by little I elucidated the mystery. The light was moving closer, but was still far away. It shone on a conversation. There were two people. Two friends, perchance? Or two lovers? Shadows are always deceptive. It was only when they drew a little nearer that the wind – now blowing in my favour – bore their voices to my ears. One was high and nasal. I could not tell if it was a man's or a woman's, but it was rather jarring. As for the other, it would be much easier for me to describe its consistency and tone, but there is no need for that: I shall only say that it was the very distinctive voice of our dear Monsieur de Beaumarchais.

Here we have the secretary of the King in the company of his friend, the Commander of the Royal and Military Order of St Louis, I thought, before seeing Beaumarchais delicately taking the hand of his companion. I knew he was eccentric, but not so eccentric as to kiss the hand of an army officer. Then I realized that the shadow of the discordant voice was wearing a skirt and had a halo of very nicely coiffed ringlets. I could not see the face, although it seemed to have a jutting jaw and a very square chin, which was not exactly delicate. It let out a giggle, as brassy as every other sound issuing from that throat, and then disappeared in the direction of a motionless shadow that was waiting not far away. It was one of those two-wheeled carriages with a single seat they call a tilbury, for the use of one, or at most two people. She climbed into the seat, gracefully sweeping up her skirts with one hand and waving goodbye to Beaumarchais with the other. He waited there a few minutes longer and then did likewise. He got into another carriage – hired, it seemed – and I lost sight of him as well.

So, it was nothing more than that, I surmised: an assignation with a lady.

I sniggered to myself to think that Cupid's arrows had also pierced the heart of our cold, imperturbable, strategist

Beaumarchais. The two of us afflicted by the same malady! I wanted to give him a fraternal embrace and say, "Sir, I am willing to share my Italian poets with you and your paramour." But we were separated by a great wall.

I thought it would be wise to return to the inn and try to sleep a little. As I walked through the deserted streets there was only one question in my head: what is it about Barcelona that makes even the most sublime spirits find there what they did not know they were seeking?

Ten

Beaumarchais returned to the inn at daybreak, took off his shoes, stockings and breeches and then stretched out on the bed.

"Monsieur," I said, "I believe that tomorrow afternoon at five would be a good time for our party to visit the establishment of the chocolatier Fernandes, so that we may see this invention which is the reason for your journey. By then you should have been able to rest and the…"

However, it was clear that Beaumarchais was exhausted – and perhaps well satisfied – because the only answer he gave me was a snore.

I left my bed feeling uneasy, filled the basin and washed my face. The mirror gave me back my usual simpleton's expression, although it was further marred by the blue bags under my eyes. I had not slept a wink. Nonetheless, I had to see my Marianna at once. My heart would brook no more hours of separation.

My clothes, unlike those of the King's secretary, were carefully folded on a chair. I dressed, spurred on by my impatience, yet when I was about to put on my shoes I was most nonplussed by what I saw.

A package wrapped in turquoise velvet, which was very familiar to my eyes, had appeared on the table as if by magic. I silently confirmed my surmise: it was the wrapping of your chocolate pot, the one you gave me together with your letter. I removed the velvet cloth and found the delicacy of the white porcelain, the elegant handle, the lid, the spout and the inscription on its base: *Je suis à madame Adélaïde de France*. I was in no doubt. It was your chocolate pot! The very same that had been stolen from me on our first night by that blackguard Mimó disguised as a captain general! How had it come to be here, now mixed up with Beaumarchais's belongings?

I had no qualms about shaking the gentleman awake. An explanation was required.

"How is it that you have Madame's chocolate pot in your possession? Where did you find it?"

The slumbers of the King's secretary withstood all my efforts, and I only drew from him a few mumblings.

"Chocolate pot... Ah... yes... Take it. I brought it..."

He turned onto his other side and emitted a thunderous rumble.

It was evident that this was no time for explanations. That was of little matter, however, because the chocolate pot gave me the perfect excuse for going to visit my Marianna and – at last! – to satisfy your wishes.

I placed the chocolate pot in my leather pouch and ran downstairs like a man possessed, as fast as my youthful spindleshanks would carry me. The last thing I wished was to encounter any of the three French chocolatiers. However, as tends to happen with all base thoughts, Providence punished me by immediately effecting the contrary. To my great dismay, I ran into a very choleric Malesherbes.

"You are avoiding us, Monsieur Guillot? You are playing at cat and mouse?"

"No, sir, I most certainly am not!"

"Well then, where would you be going at such an hour and without having breakfasted?"

"I have personal matters to attend to."

"That is what Beaumarchais told me when I saw him scurrying off yesterday. And what personal matters might need your attention in a city that is not yours and with empty pockets? My colleagues and I are tired of all these mysteries."

"There is no mystery. The appointment has been made."

"Ah, indeed? And when is that to be?"

"Tomorrow afternoon, sir, at five o'clock sharp. We shall all meet in Senyor Fernandes's shop."

The man was a mountain blocking my way! Although I had told him what he wished to hear, he would not let me leave.

"And now, what is the problem?" I asked.

"Why should I believe a hobbledehoy like you?"

I was tired of this. The only thing that occurred to me was to drop to my knees and crawl out between his legs, shouting as I went, "Tell the others, Maleshèrbes! Beaumarchais as well!"

I strode through the streets, which were easier to navigate now that the snow was melting. The weather was far from the sunny clime one would expect from a coastal city, but at least I could feel the benefits of my cape now.

I reached Carrer de les Tres Voltes in no time at all and was surprised to find two armed sentinels at the door. My Marianna was attending to the real Captain General, that gentleman González de Bassecourt who had not yet resolved our problems. I immediately understood that he was not there to buy chocolate.

Sweet Marianna was sitting on a chair in front of the counter while he was lumbering around the room, his shoes making a great racket. He was firing one question after another at her, all in an inquisitorial tone.

"Pray, do not make me waste my time, Senyora. I have some highly important and most vexing matters to attend to. Arms trafficking, no less! Yet I must come here to speak of chocolate! There have been many complaints about you of late, and this is not acceptable. The King is a customer of yours! If you are poisoning him and I do nothing to prevent this, I shall be summarily hung. Pray, answer me! And tell me the truth!"

"I have told you the truth, Senyor. These complaints are baseless. You may confirm that for yourself."

"Why are there so many? And all at once?"

"Because there are many people who wish to harm me, Senyor."

"So you would swear that you have never adulterated your chocolate in order to reduce costs?"

"I have never done that, Senyor."

"And you have never added any repellent ingredient in order to take revenge on somebody, or to cast a spell?"

"Of course I have not, Senyor. I am a chocolatier and neither alchemist nor witch as they would have you believe."

"Are you aware of the vile additives you are accused of putting in your chocolate?"

"Indeed I am, Senyor, alas."

"And you would swear before a judge, should this be necessary, that these are false accusations?"

"I would swear it before God. Moreover, I could demonstrate that they are false."

"You claim people wish to harm you. Could you be more specific?"

"The whole of the chocolatiers' guild. And the apothecaries' guild and those of the sugar confectioners and the millers."

"Begad! You accuse a great number of people. And have you done anything to all these men?"

Seen so close, the Captain General gave the impression of being quite a poor-spirited fellow. He was gazing at Marianna as if into a crystal ball and expecting some magic result. In fact, he was caught in a great dilemma: should he be influenced by the complaints against Marianna (and he was rather too swayed by them) because the King was such an enthusiastic consumer of hot chocolate, or was he perhaps committing an injustice and should therefore heed his own heart and set this beautiful creature free? Senyor González was floundering in doubt.

"Senyor, if I may be so bold" – I intervened for I was in danger of exploding had I not done so – "I shall answer your questions in the lady's name, for she is too modest to tell you the whole truth. The reason why all these ruthless gentlemen wish to close this shop is only one: Marianna is the best chocolatier in Barcelona. Oh but why should I say Barcelona? In all Catalonia! In all Europe! In the whole civilized world!" I made a lengthy pause. "Do you like chocolate, sir?"

"Greatly." Now his expression was almost mischievous.

"And have you ever tasted the chocolate of this house?"

"No. To my great misfortune—"

"Stand up, please, Marianna, and let the Captain General sit down. He has a difficult day ahead and needs to gather strength. Arms trafficking, you said! What a responsibility! Make yourself comfortable, Senyor." I led him, gently guiding him by the shoulders to the chair, watching the two soldiers at the door from the corner of my eye. "Let us offer you a small taste of this delicacy which is so appreciated by His Majesty King Charles, whose tastes do not entirely coincide with those of his distant cousin, King Louis XVI of France. As we know, they are not on the friendliest of terms. Once you have tasted it, you may decide which side you wish to take."

"I do not know… Senyor… I do not know if… and who might you be, Senyor?"

"Victor Philibert Guillot, Senyor, your humble servant and most fervent devotee of the chocolate made by Senyor Fernandes and his wife. I have come directly from Versailles to admire it in person." I think he was impressed by my presentation, but still more so by what I said next. "I believe that you very recently had the opportunity to meet the leader of our mission, the famous comedy writer Caron de Beaumarchais, who visited you in relation with a most disagreeable affair in which we were the unfortunate victims. Do you recall the meeting?"

The Captain General rolled his eyes heavenwards at the mere thought of Beaumarchais.

"Oh, that man, how I admire him!" he exclaimed. "If only you knew how I laughed when I saw *Les Noces de Figaro*! I believe it is the best thing ever written!" He was silent for a moment, as if to allow the memory of *Figaro* pervade and then fade away in the atmosphere, and, somewhat crestfallen, continued, "I am therefore so desolate at having been unable to set to rights this matter of the robbery! We have been most unfortunate that so many calamities have beset us at once."

"Do not concern yourself about us! With a city full of arms traffickers, I am not surprised that you have better things to do!" I absolved him (because that was what suited my purposes, of course).

He gave a sigh of relief and I imagine he felt understood.

"It is not only a matter of arms traffickers, Senyor, but still more serious matters!"

"What matters might they be?"

"Unfortunately, I am not at liberty to tell you."

"Oh, that is indeed a pity. I must admit you have aroused my curiosity. However, do not think of such baneful matters now, but sip a little of this beverage, the most comforting in the world, made by snow-white hands and served in a cup and saucer expressly made for it, as is presently the custom in the Americas. They are made of Ligurian majolica, the finest there is, expressly brought to Barcelona to satisfy the most exquisite palates. Do you see the foam? Do you note a hint of peppercorns? This is the way King Charles drinks it every afternoon. The Pontiff in Rome is also fond of it prepared like this. You will know that chocolate began as a delight for aristocrats, monarchs and the Vatican, despite the fact that it has now fallen into the grimy, hairy hands of commoners. Now, do not forget to wipe your moustache. It would not do for people to see where you have been!"

Somewhat averse and mistrustful, the Captain General sniffed the contents of the cup before taking the first sip. Then he could not stop. Marianna went into the back room to fetch something.

"Do you see?" I continued, observing the pleasure on his face. "This chocolate, taken with bread fingers or freshly picked fruit, is what the Baron of Maldà, one of the most illustrious customers of this house, enjoys twice a day. Do you know him? Of course you must! What an obtuse question! Naturally, friendships abound among people of such quality. Now, do savour this delicacy which the lady of the house has just brought for you and you will see how you wish to repeat the pleasure."

"What is this exactly?"

"It is solid chocolate and you have surely tasted nothing to equal it."

"Solid? I did not know this existed."

"Now you see that it does. It exists because her husband is a genius. I can assure you that if Senyor Fernandes were here with us, he would be delighted to regale you with the host of philosophical, economic, gastronomic and even astrological theories he took into account when he devised this marvel. It is a great pity that he is travelling and shall not return for some time. I am sure that those gentlemen who are hoping that Senyora Marianna will fail have come to you with their malicious rumours…"

"In fact, they have told me that he will not return."

"Falsehood upon falsehood! He is in Versailles. Do you believe that Versailles is a place from which people do not return? Look at me. I come and go as I wish. Senyor Fernandes will do the same once he has completed the secret task with which he has been entrusted by His Majesty King Louis."

"Secret task?"

"Swear to God you will not tell a soul." I lowered my voice. "Senyor Fernandes has been summoned by the King's daughters. They wish to have for their own use a chocolate machine like the one he has made in Barcelona. The men of the chocolatiers' guild are sick with envy. Here the talent of others is felt as a scourge."

"How right you are, Senyor! This problem bedevils me every day," the Captain General confided with his mouth full.

"I can well believe it, Senyor. Yes, I can very well believe it! And the chocolate, do you find it to your taste?"

"Delicious!"

"Are you slightly less bothered now?"

All the confessions had softened the Captain General, who now reciprocated with one of his own secrets.

"I can have no relief from being bothered, Senyor. I am surrounded by inept and unlettered ignoramuses who do not even know where America is!"

"Can this be true?" I made a great show of my surprise.

"These arms traffickers I mentioned… do you remember?" I nodded. "Well, they want independence in the American colonies."

"Independence? And why would those barbarians want to be independent?"

"I am unable to answer that, Senyor. They are benighted beings and will not be better treated anywhere than under the guidance of civilization. Govern themselves? What an absurd idea. They do not even have a king! And when they have failed, they will come creeping back, tails between their legs, begging for a true government to protect them. Then we shall see who rules the world, and the price of all this petulance."

"I most wholeheartedly agree! You have just summoned the future!"

"Well, these mischief-makers I am pursuing want to send money and arms to the rebels so that they can fight the British Empire. And they want to send their cargo from the docks of Barcelona. It is a most disturbing affair, as you can see!"

"I certainly do see. Have you searched the ships?"

"All of them, one by one, but I have found nothing."

"Are the mischief-makers very numerous?"

"I have not been able to ascertain this. At times it seems there are many, and on other occasions one man alone."

"What a harrowing situation! Eat, do eat, Senyor, and gather strength. Marianna, please serve the gentleman another plate."

"I am in despair, Senyor Guillot!"

"I share your distress, my friend. Perhaps you need a little help."

"I have help, believe me, and from no less than a *commandeur* of the Royal and Military Order of St Louis. He has been visiting Barcelona these last few days and has made it his business to search the ships one by one. He is a most rigorous gentleman."

"The Order of St Louis?" I was very startled.

"Charles by name. Perhaps you know him?"

"Charles?" I pondered this for a moment. "No, I do not know the gentleman."

This conversation was affording me more information than I had anticipated. In order to cultivate a soothing atmosphere, I changed the subject to chocolate again.

"Do taste this, Senyor. This is made from the very same cocoa that Hernán Cortés brought on his first return from Mexico. No one knew what to do with it, so they sent it to a convent, and the nuns had the idea of mixing it with sugar. And then they claim that religious orders serve no useful purpose!"

"Indeed."

"Do not hold back! This food will help you to bring this whole sorry affair to a successful conclusion, I am sure. It is a great source of energy. All the doctors say so. And its effects are nothing less than miraculous. Perhaps you know of the case of Senyora Rosa Catalina Font?"

"Rosa Catalina… No. Who is this lady?"

"Senyora Rosa Catalina Font lives in Carrer dels Mirallers and, although you may not believe me, I can tell you that she is about to turn one hundred and two and she is as healthy and strong as an ox."

"Ah, really? And how is that?"

"At the age of eighty-five, she began as a servant in a house which she managed alone until the age of ninety-three. How did she do this? Every day she ate some vegetables from the garden and drank two little cups of Fernandes chocolate. I can vouch that she has never fainted or even had the slightest spell of dizziness. At the age of a hundred she was afflicted by erysipelas on her head, but they bled her two or three times and she was very quickly cured. To this very day she spins and sews, dresses herself and does her own housework. Do you not find this marvellous? That is what is what they sell over this counter."

"It is all most interesting. You cannot imagine how grateful I am for your sustenance. I must leave now. Those traffickers—"

"Naturally, Senyor González de Bassecourt. The traffickers are your first concern! But, please, take this small portion of chocolate remaining on the plate to enjoy along the way. And do return when your spirits are low, for there is nothing like chocolate for treating this malady."

The Captain General left the shop with renewed energy, while I sat on the chair trying to make sense of this puzzle which was becoming more and more convoluted.

I asked Marianna if I might also have a small cup of chocolate, and then I remembered that I was still carrying your...

However, I beg you to bear with me, wait, Madame, for I shall pause here in case anyone has anything important or urgent to do before savouring my coming words. Indeed, I have plenty more to say.

Eleven

"This is for you, Marianna. It is the gift from Madame Adélaïde which I was not able to deliver before," I said, taking the bundle wrapped in turquoise velvet from my leather pouch.

"You have recovered it?"

"Fortunately."

Marianna gave me an enchanting smile.

"And what might it be?" she asked, unwrapping it.

She giggled nervously, probably because she is unaccustomed to receiving gifts. She carefully folded back the cloth – two layers of velvet – to reveal the porcelain chocolate pot. It looked new, as if just out of the kiln.

"A chocolate pot. How beautiful it is!" She turned it around in her hands, looking at it from every angle. Seeing the blue letters on the base, she questioned me with her eyes.

"It says, 'I belong to Madame Adélaïde of France,'" I translated. "This is the only piece of its kind in existence. May I tell her that you like it?"

Her eyes were shining.

"Of course, you must! Would you like to try it? I can serve you the chocolate in it."

"I should like it more if you were the one to try it."

"We shall try it together then."

What a mystery words are! What Marianna had just said – "together" – made my heart leap.

Perhaps you will be ashamed of me, Madame, but then I lost contact, not with the conversation but with existence itself. Gazing at Marianna, I was utterly entranced. Those eyes, those lips, those breasts worthy of a Greek statue. As if my body had arrogated command of itself, I realized that I was gradually bending forward, closer and closer to her, staring at her lips, longing to fuse them with my own. I do not know what I might have done if her gentle voice had not brought me back to the world again.

"Are you well, Senyor? Can you breathe?"

I started, took her hand and kissed it lightly, an inadequate kiss that in no way reflected everything she inspired in me when she was near (and even far from) me. Then, as if the world were calling me by name, I heard the unmistakable sounds of a vehicle approaching along the street: creaking parts, a trotting horse… I glanced outside and saw Beaumarchais on the driver's seat of a tilbury (perhaps the same one as the previous night), accompanied by the ringletted lady.

I assure you, Madame, I have never been so full of merit when obeying your orders as I was at that moment. Very much against my will – for you and for France – I left Marianna and hurried out of the shop after a hasty farewell, looked in every direction and followed the squeaking of the tilbury's wheels, although I saw no sign of it. It is not easy to follow a carriage on foot but, as you know, I am swift and my senses are alert.

I was just in time to see Beaumarchais entering the inn in Carrer de Manresa behind his lady.

Twelve

I do not know how, but I followed the pair of them up the stairs without being seen, crouching on the landings and peering through the banisters. Once they reached the second floor, the lady drew a key from her cleavage, turned it in the lock and entered the room. Beaumarchais looked all around him before following. The door closed on their secrets.

I cautiously crept over to the door and looked through the keyhole, but saw nothing. Beaumarchais is an old fox, and had, no doubt, taken the precaution of hanging some item of clothing over it. Striving to keep all my senses alert, I did the only thing I could do in such circumstances: trust my hearing. I imagined that I would discern the kind of noises that tend to issue from a secret assignation between a man and a woman in a hostel, but soon realized that nothing sounded as it should. There was no creaking bed, no muffled moans, no banging of furniture (not the style of Beaumarchais, I admit), or any grunts like rutting beasts. None of that. The only thing I heard was a conversation which I shall now transcribe from memory and with the utmost fidelity.

"You have everything ready?" This was the voice of Beaumarchais.

"I have not overlooked a single detail."

"What is the name of the ship?"

"*Libertas*. It is a Latin name. Will you not write it down?"

"I prefer to remember it. That is safer."

"You do well. A man of experience."

"The ship is a brigantine?"

"Sailing under a Spanish flag. It is engaged in the cocoa bean trade with Venezuela."

"The perfect hiding place."

"I hope that will prove to be so, sir."

"Then… shall we meet there tomorrow at quarter to five?"

"I shall be waiting for you on the wharf."

"I shall bring everything with me, as agreed."

"I am so agitated that I believe I shall not be able to sleep tonight."

"I doubt I shall either."

"Do not be late. The *Libertas* sails punctually at seven."

"There is no need to worry. I am a man of his word and my word is law."

"So you have demonstrated."

"Farewell then. Until tomorrow."

"Until tomorrow."

When the door opened again I had hidden behind a corner in the passageway and poked my nose out just enough to discover what was happening. I saw Monsieur de Beaumarchais sauntering out and making his leisurely way down the stairs as if he had not a care in the world. His movements made me think of a man who has just made a decision of great import. Then everything was silent.

I took advantage of the hush to calm myself a little. With so many shocks my heart had been pounding and missing beats for quite some time. I thought I should let it rest while I gave some thought to what I had just learnt. Beaumarchais was leaving us in the lurch and was about to flee to the Indies with the mysterious lady. So these were his intentions when he joined our mission! You were right to be mistrustful of the man from the very beginning. Who could have imagined this of such a high-ranking gentleman?

I then began to wonder who would miss Beaumarchais at court; who would lament his absence. I recalled that lady, Marie-Thérèse de Willer, I believe she is called, who is so dazzled by him. Apart from her and a handful of flatterers who want to steal his ideas and copy his comedies, I could think of no one else. Monsieur de Beaumarchais has not cultivated many friendships in Versailles, perhaps because someone as talented as he is does not readily make friends. It sometimes seems to me that not even your nephew esteems him greatly, but sends him off on all those missions abroad in order to be rid of him. Perhaps there is some truth to all the rumours accusing him of dreadful things like falsifying documents or embezzlement. As for me, Madame, to think I shall never see him again fills my heart with sadness. Even if everything they say about him is true.

Then again, there is the lady. I wonder who she is. In her manners she shows her position and her apparel bespeaks wealth. She is not young but rather the contrary. Among her virtues, beauty is not one of the most prominent, yet she has an agreeable way of speaking, like a well-instructed, enlightened woman, although there is a disagreeable, discordant tone of I know not what in her voice, which I also noted last night from the top of the wall. It is a perplexing voice, even when heard near at hand. It is impossible to tell whether it has come from the throat of a man or a woman. Moreover, it is clear to me that she and Beaumarchais have known each other for some considerable time. No man plans to flee with another person to a faraway continent unless he has sufficient faith in the other, would you not agree? And how long must it be since... On what occasion have they...

I swear, Madame, that my head was in turmoil with all this brooding and pursuing answers to such indiscreet questions. Now that I had calmed my heart my head was frightening me.

I had not yet come to any conclusion when the door of the room opened once more and someone came out. Fortunately, I had not moved from my hiding place and I was able to peep out around the corner. I expected to see the mysterious lady turning the key in the lock. Great was my surprise to see that the person locking the door was a *commandeur* of the Royal and Military Order of St Louis, in full regalia, including a long, straight-bladed sword, which seemed very light and ideal for city skirmishes. I could catch but a glimpse of him, but my impression is of a well-built man, neither old nor young, with blue eyes, a square jaw, rosy cheeks and thin lips. He had a fine black moustache which he kept caressing with a fingertip as if afraid it might fall off. There was something familiar about him, which made me wonder whether I had seen him before, or in some other place. I also wondered, naturally, why I had not heard his voice in the conversation between Beaumarchais and his lady, when he was in the same room. Had he too been hiding perchance? Had he been lying in wait for them? What if he was a criminal, a thief, a killer, a spy? Mysteries and more mysteries...

Once he had locked the door, the *commandeur* tucked the key inside his dress coat, straightened his tricorne hat, checked that his sword was properly sheathed and rushed downstairs in very great haste.

Thirteen

You may, perhaps, believe that this was the end of the episode of the stairway of the inn. No, Madame, it is my unhappy task to relate now a very important part of what followed. With my hand on the banister rail I prepared to go downstairs, still greatly bewildered by the tangle of thoughts I could not unravel when I heard what seemed to be a whole army ascending the wooden stairs. I rushed to hide again behind my corner in the passageway and from there I heard the voice of Sir English Toad commanding, "Make haste! This is our chance! Enter the room!"

Vandals that they are, the two soldiers who always escorted that squat little man hurled themselves at the door of Beaumarchais's lady's room, staving it in with the second attempt. The method was that of a group of conquerors securing strategic territory. I was appalled at the thought of the lady, still inside the room, alone and unable to defend herself against those brutes.

Is it not the duty of any man worthy of the name to defend a lady who is assailed in such a way? This time I was in no doubt. I sallied forth from my redoubt and hastened to the room, determined to prevent them from committing any outrage against Beaumarchais's lady. I was not bearing arms of any kind, but my sense of righteousness spurred me on enough to shout, "Stop this at once, gentlemen. I shall not permit what you are about to do!"

The three men stood stock still and then turned towards me, enraged until they recognized me. Like the hunter relaxing when he sees that the prey is inoffensive, the toad laughed and said, "Ah, so it is you, Fernandes. Might one know what you are doing here?"

I glanced around the room. It was empty. The bed was impeccably made and there was no trace of the lady. The window was closed and her trunks open and ransacked. On the floor I recognized dress coats in different colours – beige and deep red – a truly eye-catching yellow silk skirt, white stockings which I believe were for a man and two wigs, one a man's and the other a lady's. I believe that, even with time to ponder, I would not have made sense of what lay before my eyes, but with two soldiers pointing their lances at my nose I was not thinking at all clearly.

"For whom are you working?" the toad demanded to know, in a tone that was rather less amicable than that of our previous meeting.

"Me? I work for no one, sir. I work only for myself."

"What are you doing here, then? Would you be looking for something?"

"I am a friend of the lady who occupies this room," I lied.

"Are you now?" Sir English Toad's expression was malicious, almost certainly because he had attributed his own particular meaning to my use of the word "friend". "In that case, I believe you have considerable competition, young man."

He jerked his head so that his nose pointed at the uniforms lying on the floor. There was no doubt that they journeyed in the same trunk as the silk skirt. It was also evident that they did not belong to Beaumarchais. I understood nothing.

"And tell me…" the toad continued, "your friendship with the lady who occupies this room, is it a very close friendship?"

"A gentleman would never answer such a question, sir," I said, raising my chin and acting very offended.

Then I felt the coldness of a lance tip between my chin and Adam's apple.

"Do you believe you could make an exception?" the toad wished to know, holding up his hand to stay, for the moment, the soldier who was about to puncture my neck.

"It is quite a close friendship," I lied again, believing that mendacity would save me.

It was soon obvious that I chose the wrong option.

"Well, well, well… this is most useful for us, most interesting indeed." The Englishman rubbed his hands as if it helped him to think. Then he added, "So you must be apprised of the fact that you and I have something in common…"

I broke out in a cold sweat with these words. The English toad was the lover of Beaumarchais's lover? But how many lovers can one woman acquire in a city? I know I am young and somewhat raw, Madame, but this was beyond my comprehension. Yet I sought to soothe the offended sentiments of the cuckold and embroidered my lie.

"I must confess I have not touched her. She would not allow it. She is very taken with you, extremely taken with you."

It was too late, or perhaps I was disproportionate in my flattery (lack of experience, as we know). The toad looked at me with an air of resignation that boded very ill, saying, "Enough of your claptrap, Fernandes. That trollop robbed me down to my last gold coin. She slipped into my bed, lulled me to sleep and then made a wax copy of the keys to my trunks, after which, seizing her chance when we were making merry that night we met you in the Pla de Palau, she fleeced me. When I returned to the inn my trunks were empty... Not a jewel, not a scrap of silk, not an inkpot, not a single real was left! I believed there was nothing to be done about such a regrettable situation, but now fortune has placed you in my way and I have every intention of seizing this opportunity. You will be the remedy to what ails me. You could not have appeared at more propitious moment." He paused, cleared his throat and said to his men. "Truss him up well. He must not escape. Senyor Fernandes will be our hostage. Let us see, Fernandes, if the lady loves you enough to pay the ransom I believe I shall ask."

"Hostage? Whose hostage? Why? No, no, you must not ask for a ransom! She will not..." I had many things to say and a host of questions occurred to me, but I saw that these men were not at all disposed to respond. On the contrary, they went about their work, taking not the slightest notice of me. With a great smirk on his lips, the toad was writing a letter wherein he informed the lady in very few words that he was holding Senyor Fernandes captive and, in return for his release, he wanted everything she had stolen from him two nights earlier.

Meanwhile, the two soldiers were expertly binding me with very thick rope. Hands, feet, my whole body, until I was verily a human sausage... I tried to convince them that I had lied about everything in order to save my skin, that I had never made the acquaintance of the lady in the room and that, indeed, I was not Fernandes. They turned a deaf ear. They went about their work. Then one of them approached me with a greasy handkerchief in his hands, his eyes focused on my mouth.

The toad held up his hand and the handkerchief bearer stopped.

"Before we gag you, Fernandes, I should like you to shed some light on a question I have... With that glorious piece of womanhood you have for a wife, how could you bed that old cow?"

I shrugged as the soldier tied the gag so tight that my jaw was almost dislocated. I sighed resignedly as the two boors swaddled me from head to foot in a sheet and carried me thus bundled down the stairs. As they walked past the innkeeper I heard them nonchalantly greeting him. He, pleased to oblige them, returned their salutation.

I believe this city would be even more agreeable if it were not possible to buy everything and everyone with money.

Fourteen

If you asked me the colour of the hours that followed my transformation into a human sausage, I should say black, very black indeed. The English toad's men carried me for a considerable time on foot, after which they threw me on a cart and we rattled along our way. I could not guess where they were taking me, but knew we had gone outside the city wall when I heard the voice of a guard who let them through without inspecting the merchandise and because, once we were on the wooden drawbridge, the wheels stopped clattering. I then had to endure some twists and turns in all directions and I heard gruff voices, near and far, giving orders in different languages and dialects.

Thanks to this sorry situation, aggravated by all the bumping along the way, I was well and truly battered when we reached our destination. I was beginning to think they would untie all the ropes which were cutting into my whole body, but soon discovered that they had no intention of removing as much as the sheet. One of the men flung me over his shoulder and carried me down some narrow wooden steps to a place with a strong reek of damp, where his footsteps echoed. Was it a secret hiding place? A cellar? The men spoke vulgar English, which I found difficult to understand. Nonetheless, I divined that they were leaving me there with a guard who was not one of the two soldiers, and they had no intention of giving me as much as a drop of water. I tried to move a little, dragging myself across the floor like a worm. I also asked for water but, since I was gagged, I was not understood. Instead of water I received a kick in the ribs, which took away any desire I might have had to speak. Then I heard them leave. This was the beginning of the darkest hours of boredom.

To begin with, I was curious about the sounds. I needed to know where they had left me. Alas, it was all too easy to discover. It only took two minutes of being left alone before I ascertained the truth. There was a slow movement, as if something was rocking the room in which I was held, and a glub-glubbing, which sounded like something bubbling or a fish tank. They had brought me to the hold of one of the ships in the port. It was logical: the distance we had covered, the narrow steps leading down, the coarse voices of the dock workers... And if I were not sufficiently convinced, I suddenly heard a small shrill squeal and felt some animal running over my feet. I swept it aside, convinced it was a rat, and I can assure you it was not my last encounter that night with this loathsome creature.

I do not know how I managed to fill the hours of my captivity. I exhausted my repertoire of Italian poems, tried to sleep a little – helped neither by my posture nor the company I was in – thought at length about Marianna, revised Latin declensions, fretted over the questions of Beaumarchais, his lover and the *commandeur* of the Royal and Military Order of St Louis, trying to deduce something, dwelt on my travelling companions and felt sad to think that they might be missing me. Then there was total silence, broken only by snoring nearby. I remembered Beaumarchais and could not help shedding a tear.

If you are ever gagged, Madame (Heaven forbid!), do not cry. It is not sensible. Mucous accumulates between one's nose and nape of neck in a ball which cannot be dislodged. I had great difficulty breathing, a problem which has dogged me from a tender age. Meanwhile, my guard slumbered on and the rats were wide awake. It was the most horrendous night of my life. I hope I shall be able to say the same thing when I die of old age, for I pray I shall never again suffer anything remotely like this.

The morning which followed upon the night was more of the same. Nothing had changed: no one paid the slightest attention to me, I could hear distant voices on the dock and wondered how long I should have to remain there, numb, dying of thirst and full of apprehension. What would become of me if the ransom were not paid? Would they throw me overboard without even removing the sheet that swaddled me? Would mine be a baffling death in the fetid waters of the port? Was it not a pitiful thing to die in such a way when I was only eighteen years old? I even thought about my mother, poor woman. If she had known I was going to come to such an end, she would not have taken so much trouble to feed me when I was a puny, impudent child.

Yet the black hours ran their course, Madame. It must have been mid-afternoon, more or less, when I heard the most raucous shouts, and then the whole boat shook with a great thwack. There were more blows, groans and running feet and, all of a sudden, the rasping voice of Beaumarchais's lady saying, "Take me to the prisoner immediately or I shall behead you here and now!"

This did not impress me as very feminine behaviour, but my surprise was much less than my joy on hearing a familiar voice, even that one. There were other people present. I heard them purposefully crossing the deck, although they spoke not a word. Perhaps the lady had come with an escort of armed soldiers, like the heroine in one of those comedies where everything is based on lies but all ends well.

When I felt hands turning me over to loosen the knots in the sheet, I thanked Heaven (although I am not exactly a believer). At first I was unable to see the face of my benefactress, because the hours in darkness had rendered me temporarily blind. I slowly began to adapt to my new situation and, as those hands kept releasing me from my bonds, I turned to see who my rescuer was.

Zounds! I was thunderstruck!

There she was, as I had imagined before I was able to see her: Beaumarchais's lady. Her ringlets were impeccable, as was the yellow silk skirt I had seen lying on the floor of her room, and she was wearing matching velvet gloves. However, over her elegant skirt, and securely attached to her slender waist, a sword nestled in its sheath. Now that I could see her at close range, I could admire her almost transparent blue eyes, her fine lips and rosy cheeks. Her movements were extremely graceful, but her hands were fleshy and arms well muscled.

"Are you well enough to walk?" she asked in her jarring voice.

"I believe so."

"Very well. Try to stand. You may lean on me."

Before we left that lair, I noted with some satisfaction that I had not been mistaken. We were, as I had imagined, in the dank, filthy hold of a ship. Coming out by way of the narrow hatchway – I had also been correct in thus identifying the narrow steps – I saw that it was a frigate sailing under an English flag. I also noticed the toad's soldiers sprawled on the deck, both of them gagged and bound hand and foot. I cannot deny that I was deeply gratified to see them in the same sorry state in which they had left me for so long. There was a third man, a strapping, brutish fellow, dressed only in sailor's breeches and a shirt. He too was bound and gagged. I suspected that this was the guard who had snored through the night instead of doing his job. Half a dozen soldiers – and I do not know whether they were French or Catalan – guarded the prisoners. Two more were stationed on the dock.

"I should like to know the name of the lady who has delivered me," I ventured, feeling braver with my feet on the ground.

"For you, I am Mademoiselle d'Éon," she responded with an enigmatic but delightful smile. One could not say that she was a beautiful woman but, seen at close quarters, she had a siren-song allure.

There was still some light, and I guessed that it must have been about four, or half-past four in the afternoon. With a little luck, I should be able to accompany the master chocolatiers to Marianna's shop as planned. I only had to hurry.

The soldiers carried the prisoners down to the dock and stopped in front of Mademoiselle d'Éon, who gave the order, "Take them to the hold of the *Libertas* and ask Monsieur de Beaumarchais where he would like you to leave them."

I started. Beaumarchais was also there? I recalled the secret conversation in the inn before all my misfortunes befell me. They had arranged to meet at quarter to five in the afternoon. Fate had chosen me to witness, I thought, the most intimate secret of the man I admire most in the world.

I could see him in the distance. Beaumarchais was on the dock standing near a brigantine flying a Spanish flag. He had the contented look of a man who, finally having achieved everything he wants, has dispensed with all formalities. He glanced at the prisoners and said, "Take them astern. Their officer is in the hold in the bows and I do not wish them to have any visual or spoken contact until the ship docks in Boston. In any case, once they know where they are going, they will have scant wish to speak."

Thus I learnt that the English toad had been captured and that Beaumarchais had some plan for him, which escaped me. Maybe he was going to sell him as a slave? Ask for ransom? Torture him to obtain secret information?

As I was thinking about this, an unbelievable spectacle was unfolding before my very eyes. Mademoiselle d'Éon had raised her skirts and was donning some beige chamois breeches. She removed her dainty silk shoes and replaced them with black leather boots. Then she rid herself of bodice and stays to array herself in a deep-red dress coat trimmed with silver thread. She was taking these items from a bundle hidden in a tilbury she had waiting in the shelter of the wall. She also took out a man's wig which she exchanged for the ringlets that adorned her head. The velvet gloves gave way to others in dark leather. Instead of jewels, her breast was adorned by a sash from which hung a military decoration in the form of a cross. The false eyelashes were stowed in favour of an equally artificial moustache, which she very skilfully attached to her upper lip. The final touch was the tricorne hat, complete with silver braid and white cockade. When she had completed her transformation, the only detail that had not changed was the sword.

"Why are you gaping at me like that, Guillot? Are you shocked to see how a lady undresses, or an officer dresses?" Mademoiselle asked as she checked with a fingertip to make sure her moustache was in place.

In a trice, with the deftness of one who has done it a thousand times, she had become the *commandeur* of the Royal and Military Order of St Louis whom others had seen in Beaumarchais's company. The very gentleman I too had seen, leaving the room at the inn in Carrer de Manresa. Now it happened that he and the mysterious lady were one and the same person. I should have liked to have the wit to clarify certain matters, but my admiration was so complete that I was bereft of speech. I was beginning to divine a glimmer of sense in this complicated affair, although I was far from any real understanding of what was happening.

"You really looked like a woman," I said.

"Naturally, because that is what I am."

"But now you are a man."

"That too, that too! Let me present myself once more. My name is Charles de Beaumont, better known as Chevalier d'Éon, loyal servant of our king and also your friend, if you so please." He accompanied his words with a very military clicking of heels.

"I believed it was not possible to be a man and a woman at the same time…"

"Well, now you know! I was born like this. When they saw me, my parents were so disconcerted that they gave me three male names and three female names so they should not have to decide what I was. I do not know which to settle for either, so I am one thing for a while and then the other."

"What do you feel you really are, Mademoiselle or Chevalier?"

"It depends on the day and my needs," he replied.

"Of course," I persisted, "but who are you?"

"Someone who unsettles those who believe that the world is simple."

"Begad! I am utterly bewildered," I confessed.

"Believe me, Monsieur, bewilderment is the least of the effects I have on people. You will recover."

"Is it true that you seduced the English toad?"

"Toad? Ha! Now that is very good!" He smiled, showing perfectly white, feminine teeth. "You are sharp-witted, Guillot, and this is pleasing! Yes, I seduced him. Sometimes one has to make sacrifices for France!"

"And did you rob him?"

"Naturally I did. Such a nauseating deed is not done without a price. It was so easy…"

"And, of course, you are also helping Captain General González to catch the arms traffickers."

"Helping him? That is not a word I should use. Let us say I distract him… get him to look elsewhere."

"Because…" and now I voiced my most risky conclusion, "you are also the arms trafficker."

He gave me a sly grin.

"You ask too many questions, Guillot. You will go far. Unless they slit your throat first, of course." With a very crude, masculine gesture he adjusted the sword at his waist, turned around and marched away, leaving me with an unanswered question and feeling ridiculous.

The brigantine was still being loaded. After the prisoners had been stowed, the dock workers were bringing large, dark wooden boxes, which seemed very heavy. Each one required four men to carry it, and they moved them very carefully into the ship's hold. It was a slow, delicate operation overseen by Beaumarchais's eagle eye. From time to time he urged them to hurry, while giving instructions to an overseer who was bustling up and down the gangway. When the work was done, the men boisterously bade each other farewell and moved away from the ship. Two sailors, armed to the teeth and already in position, were sufficient to guard the cargo. Only then did Beaumarchais relax slightly. He came over to me and, with a penetrating gaze, asked, "What do you suspect is stowed in the hold of this brigantine?"

"The English hostages," I replied.

"Anything else?"

"I have seen nothing else, Monsieur."

"Do you know the destination of this ship?"

"I heard it was bound for Venezuela, but just now it seemed you were speaking of another port. I did not recognize the name and immediately forgot it."

"And what will you tell Madame Adélaïde in these missives you write her?"

"I shall only tell her what I have seen and heard, Monsieur. That is what I always do."

"You will also add that if any person requires further details about this ship, its cargo or where it is bound, he should ask the King, whose interests all of those present are serving."

"I shall do that if you so wish, Monsieur."

I stood there, confounded by my own insignificance in this affair while the two men finalized their business from their respective heights of greatness.

"I would say that is all then, Beaumarchais."

"So I believe, Beaumont. Will you remain on the dock until she weighs anchor?"

"I shall not move from here until this brigantine disappears over the horizon."

"And after that?"

"After that… this is something one can never know."

"Shall we meet again?"

"That is difficult to foresee. Do you have plans for the future?"

"I wish to write two or three comedies that are buzzing in my head. The King will have them performed at his birthday celebrations. And your own plans?"

"I may come to visit the court. It is so long since the last occasion… I yearn for the perfect rows of trees in the gardens. Outside Versailles, everything seems so disorderly… Nonetheless, I may stay in London for a time, incognito, to savour the delights of English high society, which is the best in the world."

"I do not know how you can bear the stench of London, my dear friend."

"Familiar stenches do not offend as much as foreign stenches. Paris does not exactly smell like roses."

"If the winds carry me to England, I shall come to visit you."

"May they blow strong."

"It is always a pleasure to work with you, Beaumont."

"I was about to say the same, Beaumarchais."

I was captivated by their conversation and could not but think of how many adventures these two veterans had shared. What they must have seen. My imagination was soaring with the gulls when Beaumarchais's voice brought me back to earth. "Wake up, Guillot. Wipe that idiotic expression from your face and get up on the tilbury. We have an appointment with some chocolatiers and I do not wish to arrive late."

Fifteen

(*The shop of the chocolatier Fernandes. Marianna is straighten-
ing the crocks on the shelves next to the counter, singing softly.
She seems happy. A nearby bell rings five. With the final peal, the
shop door opens. Enter Guillot, Labbé, Delon and Maleshèrbes.*)

GUILLOT: Here at last, Monsieurs! Please, come in, come in.
(*To Marianna*) Senyora, I wish to present France's finest
chocolatiers who have come here to learn about the device
invented by your husband.

MARIANNA (*slightly bowing her head*): You are most welcome,
gentlemen.

DELON, LABBÉ, MALESHÈRBES: Senyora…

MARIANNA (*indicating the white porcelain chocolate pot she
has on the counter*): Would you like a cup of chocolate? It
is freshly made.

LABBÉ (*the most relaxed in the party*): I would not decline.

DELON: I would not either. It would be most welcome, in this
cold.

MALESHÈRBES (*to Guillot*): Why did you not tell us that we were
to be welcomed by this nymph? Such a lovely creature! How
fortunate it is that her husband is not here!

MARIANNA: I regret to say I have only one chair. You will have
to remain standing.

MALESHÈRBES: I would even stand on my head here.

405

MARIANNA (*places three small cups on the counter and pours the chocolate, filling each cup to the brim*): Exactly three cups. How should I serve your chocolate, Monsieur Guillot?

GUILLOT: I have of late endured some difficult hours and am half-starved. I shall be well pleased, however you serve it.

MARIANNA (*to the three chocolatiers*): The chocolate pot is a gift from Madame Adélaïde. Is it not beautiful?

LABBÉ: I knew it looked familiar...

MARIANNA (*with a radiant smile*): Do taste the chocolate, Senyors. I should very much like to know if you find it to your liking.

LABBÉ (*sips*): The flavour is interesting.

DELON (*sips*): It is quite good.

MALESHÈRBES (*drains his cup*): Delicious! Sublime! Very sweet! The best I have ever tasted!

MARIANNA: And now you have pampered your stomachs a little, I imagine you would like to see the machine.

LABBÉ: This is the purpose of our long journey, Senyora.

MALESHÈRBES: Laying eyes on you is reward enough.

DELON: If you will permit, I should like to address a few words to our hostess. Senyora, you are most kind in your willingness to show us the machine when your husband is absent.

MARIANNA: Senyor Guillot has informed you that?...

DELON: That he is travelling.

MARIANNA (*aside*): Ah, all the better. (*Going into the back room*) Follow me, Senyors.

MALESHÈRBES: I shall always follow you, Senyora.

GUILLOT: I shall come too.

(*Marianna and the four men disappear into the back room. Just then the street door flies open and a wrathful Mimó charges into the room, more like a beast than a man.*)

MIMÓ (*shouting*): Marianna! Is anyone here? Marianna! Come out at once!

MARIANNA: What is this? (*The frightened expression on her face changes when she sees who it is.*) Ah, you Mimó. If I had known, I should not have come out.

MIMÓ: Out of my way! I have come for the machine.

MARIANNA: What did you say?

MIMÓ: I am taking it.

MARIANNA: No.

MIMÓ: It is confiscated.

MARIANNA: You will not take it.

MIMÓ: You would be wise not to resist. The machine belongs to us now.

MARIANNA: And who might "us" be?

MIMÓ (*pompous*): The Illustrious Chocolatiers' Guild of the City of Barcelona.

MARIANNA: Not even in your dreams!

MIMÓ: I shall not leave without it. The law is on my side.

MARIANNA: We have discussed this matter on many occasions. The law is not concerned about me and neither am I concerned about the law.

MIMÓ (*with a sneering grin*): I knew you would not see reason. I have therefore not come alone.

(*Enter Captain General González de Bassecourt.*)

MARIANNA: Senyor González? You?

CAPTAIN GENERAL: I greatly regret this, but have no choice in the matter.

MARIANNA: Only two days ago you were here enjoying free chocolate, all fawning and flattery!

CAPTAIN GENERAL: Yes, yes. Please forgive me. I am a great admirer of your chocolate and your person.

MARIANNA: You have a very strange way of showing it.

CAPTAIN GENERAL: I cannot break the law. Mimó is right: the regulations stipulate that a woman may not manage a business alone.

MARIANNA: How many times must I tell you that I am not alone? I am a married woman and my husband is travelling.

MIMÓ (*sarcastic*): He must have gone to the ends of the earth.

CAPTAIN GENERAL: I am very sorry, Marianna, but I must close your shop until your husband returns.

MARIANNA: I understand. And you will steal my machine as well.

MIMÓ: It is con-fis-cat-ed! The machine is *confiscated*, as surety. When you pay your debt to the guild, we may see fit to return it.

MARIANNA (*lowers voice, addressing Mimó*): You are a bad man, Mimó. My husband always knew it. But you are even worse as a chocolatier than as a person. The only thing you can is steal other people's work.

MIMÓ: Do I imagine it or did you just speak of your husband in the past tense? You see? You too know he will not be returning.

MARIANNA (*to the Captain General*): Have you nothing to say? These people burst into my premises, ill-treat me and you consent to this? Have they muzzled you with a bribe? Do you not understand that without a shop and without my machine I shall have nothing? How am I to live? Does this not concern you? Are you without a heart or conscience?

MIMÓ: Ask for charity. With such a comely body you should have no difficulty finding someone to keep you.

MARIANNA (*clenching her fists*): Get out of my house!

MIMÓ: No, not this time, woman. This time you will not make me leave. I have come to get something that is mine. Out of my way!

MARIANNA: No!

MIMÓ: As you wish. You force me to do things I would prefer not to do.

(*Mimó roughly pushes Marianna aside and enters the back room.*)

VOICE OF MALÈSHERBES (*enraged*): You? My God! Exactly the man I was looking for! Take this! And this!

(*Blows are heard and something cracking. Mimó staggers out, his hand to his nose, which is spurting blood.*)

MIMÓ (*henceforth sounding very nasal*): What is this man doing here? Where is the machine?

MALESHÈRBES (*emerging from the back room and pointing at Mimó*): This is the man! The scoundrel who robbed us of everything we possessed! Whoreson dog!

CAPTAIN GENERAL (*in a state of confusion*): What is this you are saying? The most eminent man in the guild?

MALESHÈRBES (*to the Captain General, his fist ready to punch Mimó again*): Detain him or I shall carve him up.

LABBÉ (*emerging from the back room and addressing Maleshèrbes in alarm*): Be reasonable, my friend. He is smaller than you.

MALESHÈRBES: So what? If I heeded that argument, I should never be able to hit anyone!

DELON (*also appearing*): Begad! Such a disagreeable spectacle.

CAPTAIN GENERAL (*raising his voice*): Pray, calm down, Senyor.

MALESHÈRBES (*once again punching Mimó on the nose*): Where is our money? Confess, blockhead, or I shall squash you flatter than a cocoa bean!

MIMÓ: Please! I am an innocent man!

MALESHÈRBES (*punching Mimó on the nose yet again*): A liar as well! I shall beat you to a pulp!

CAPTAIN GENERAL: Senyor, I order you to stop!

MIMÓ: Help! Senyor González, get this animal off me. He is going to kill me!

CAPTAIN GENERAL (*unsheathing his sword*): Silence!

(*They all obey. Mimó, his nose broken, groans on the floor. Marianna watches the scene sheltering in Guillot's arms. Labbé and Delon look on expectantly. Maleshèrbes is bright red and itching to pummel Mimó some more.*)

MALESHÈRBES: Tell us what you have done with the property you stole from us! Where have you hidden our money?

MIMÓ: I have nothing of yours, Senyor. I swear it.

MALESHÈRBES: Do not swear a lie, you thieving wretch! (*Hurls himself on Mimó*). I shall make mincemeat of you! You will end up as lard!

MIMÓ (*terrified*): For the love of God, listen to me! I wish to say something but cannot speak if you keep beating me.

MALESHÈRBES: I do not wish to hear anything from you.

CAPTAIN GENERAL (*to Maleshèrbes*): Senyor, pray restrain your-self and let the thie... er, Senyor Mimó, speak.

MALESHÈRBES: I have no interest in anything he might say.

CAPTAIN GENERAL: Senyor, if you do not desist, I shall be obliged to arrest you.

LABBÉ (*trying to placate his wrathful companion*): Maleshèrbes, my friend, please calm down a little.

MALESHÈRBES: That is asking the impossible!

DELON: It will be very difficult to resolve the matter like this.

MARIANNA (*her voice tremulous*): Please, Senyor, will you do it for me?

MALESHÈRBES (*reluctant*): Very well, but only because you have asked.

CAPTAIN GENERAL (*to Mimó*): You have your opportunity to explain yourself, Mimó. We are disposed to listen.

MIMÓ: It is true that two colleagues from the guild and I myself stole all your belongings. (*Exclamations of fury.*) We did it because we made a mistake. An anonymous informer told us that a group of Englishmen had come to the city with the in-tention of taking Fernandes's machine. He even told us where they were staying, namely the Santa Maria Inn. The English mission turned out to be French, but when we discovered this, it was too late. We believe that somebody deliberately gulled us, but we do not know who. We were only trying to stop those people from taking away the machine. Foreigners always get besotted with everything we have, and come here with their pockets stuffed with money. We could not allow that! We must have the machine, at least until Fernandes pays all his debts.

MARIANNA (*furious, addressing Mimó*): Wicked man! Why do you not tell them that you also want me and that you are taking my machine because I will not be yours?

MALESHÈRBES (*thrashing Mimó again after hearing Marianna's words*): I shall pound you to a pulp! I shall pulverize you! I shall pestle you to pieces!

(*Three men restrain Maleshèrbes so Mimó can finish.*)

MIMÓ: Yes, we robbed you. I have admitted that. After we got you drunk on ratafia.* But only one day later someone robbed us of our booty. It must have been that anonymous informer of whom we saw neither hide nor hair again. He used us for his own plans. That is why we do not have anything of what we took from you, Senyors. Believe it or not, that is the truth.

MALESHÈRBES (*struggling to free himself from the men holding him back*): I do not believe even half a word of it! Filthy swine!

CAPTAIN GENERAL: One moment please, Monsieur Maleshèrbes. I believe him. (*Addressing Mimó*) Then you confess that you are a thief?

MIMÓ: If a man steals only once and to save his guild, is he then a thief?

CAPTAIN GENERAL: He is, Senyor, just like all the others.

MIMÓ: Of course he is not! Those Englishmen wanted to take the machine! The machine is for the chocolatiers of Barcelona and we cannot permit them to take it. I did it in the name of our interests!

CAPTAIN GENERAL: I believe you are excessively diligent in the name of your interests, Mimó. You are under arrest.

MIMÓ: What? You cannot...

CAPTAIN GENERAL: Indeed I can. I am the authority here and that is why you asked me to come. (*To his men*) Seize him.

MIMÓ: What are you doing? This makes no sense. Are you behind this, Marianna? Is this all your work? Moreover, the machine is not there. It has disappeared.

MARIANNA: What are you saying? When I went to sleep last night it was here. Did you perchance steal it in the early hours of the morning, as you have threatened so many times?

MIMÓ: Of course I did not.

MARIANNA: I do not believe you and no judge will believe you either.

MIMÓ: Hogwash!

MARIANNA: You have just confessed that you are a thief, Mimó! Who would believe you now?

CAPTAIN GENERAL (*nodding*): The lady speaks truly. When the judge learns that you have confessed to a crime before all these witnesses, he will not see you as being very innocent. Crimes are never committed alone and criminals tend to acquire a taste for them. Every judge knows that.

MIMÓ: I have never heard such balderdash. I do not have the damned machine!

MARIANNA: So those Englishmen have stolen it perhaps? They also wanted it, and Englishmen have no taste for bargaining.

MALESHÈRBES: Or it might have been us because we also wanted it. Did you think of that?

CAPTAIN GENERAL: This is a most complicated case with a host of suspects. As if I were not already overburdened!

MIMÓ: Marianna, you will not forget this as long as you live!

MARIANNA: For once we are in agreement, Mimó.

CAPTAIN GENERAL: Pray, take this unruly fellow away, directly to the prison in Plaça de l'Àngel.

(*The two men drag Mimó out into the street and disappear with him.*)

GUILLOT (*euphoric*): One potato nose less! (*Pensive*) This is most vexing: I shall have to leave here without knowing why the people in this land are so adverse to eating potatoes. I know, of course, that you are Spanish and not Catalan, but can you explain this, Senyor González?

CAPTAIN GENERAL: I have never given the matter any thought. Yet, knowing the Catalans as I do, I should not be surprised if it were because you French are so insistent they should eat them.

GUILLOT: Ah, I had not considered that. That is most interesting.

CAPTAIN GENERAL (*to Marianna*): My dear lady, you cannot imagine how much this pains me.

MARIANNA: Do you still intend to close my shop?

CAPTAIN GENERAL (*dejected*): I do not wish to do so, but lament that I must. There are a great number of complaints about you, and serious accusations. The most eminent gentlemen of the three guilds – the chocolatiers, the millers and the apothecaries – have declared war. They are all against you. I fear that if your husband is unable to silence them, I have no choice. I must board up your door to make sure that no one enters.

MARIANNA (*thoughtful*): I suppose I saw this coming. Must you do it now?

CAPTAIN GENERAL: The sooner the better.

MARIANNA: Very well. Take this (*she hands him a key*). Please go now and lock the door from without. Do what you must do.

CAPTAIN GENERAL: Believe me, I am most grieved—

MARIANNA: Do not prolong this, Senyor González. Lock the door.

CAPTAIN GENERAL: And you? And your visitors?

MARIANNA: We shall leave by the back door.

CAPTAIN GENERAL: Very well. It is with great sorrow that I must do my duty. It has gone seven and I must still go to the port to check for suspicious movements. Marianna, I wish you luck.

MARIANNA: I wish you the same.

CAPTAIN GENERAL (*waves*): Farewell, all of you.

(*The Captain General goes into the street and closes the shutters of the shop. The key is heard turning in the lock and then the sounds of his men nailing boards across the door using large hammers. Henceforth the action takes place with this background of hammering noises. Inside, it grows slowly darker.*)

LABBÉ: I was not aware of a back door.

MARIANNA: There is no back door.

LABBÉ: Then… How do you?… Are we trapped? Might one know how we shall leave if this man is sealing the only door?

MARIANNA: We shall leave. Do not worry, for everything is planned. Is that not so, Monsieur Guillot?

GUILLOT: To the smallest detail.

MALESHÈRBES (*looking rather foolish*): I have total confidence in you, Marianna. I find this situation most original and highly amusing.

MARIANNA: Thank you, Monsieur Maleshèrbes. You are most gracious.

MALESHÈRBES: Call me Auguste, please.

(*A gleam of light appears, shining from the back room. Monsignor Fideu suddenly appears holding a box of already lit lanterns in his hands.*)

MONSIGNOR FIDEU: Good evening and God bless you all. (*To Guillot*) Did the comedy end as you wished?

GUILLOT: Even better! There have been some surprises. González has arrested Mimó.

MONSIGNOR FIDEU: Wait, for we are yet to have a denouement. Are you all ready?

GUILLOT: We are all ready. What must we do?

MONSIGNOR FIDEU (*handing the lanterns to the chocolatiers*): Senyors, please take a lantern to light the way. Monsieur Guillot, who knows where to go and has tested the route, will lead you. I shall take up the rear, but first of all I must ensure that the entrance to the secret passage to the tunnel is well hidden. You did not imagine that you would end up in the sewer, I am sure. As you will discover, the Romans left us a city full of holes. I do not know why they wanted all these secret passageways, although we find them most useful. Take a lantern, please. Collect your belongings. Do not stumble. You would be wise to hold up your capes. These underground passages are not always as clean as they might be and you could be soiled. You have nothing to fear. Beaumarchais is waiting at the other end with a carriage at the ready. Please, go ahead. I shall follow.

(*They leave the scene in the following order: Guillot, Labbé, Delon and Maleshèrbes. Marianna picks up the chocolate pot and wraps it in the turquoise velvet cloth. She cradles it very gently, like a newborn child. Marianna and Monsignor Fideu are left alone.*)

MARIANNA (*close to tears*): Monsignor... How is this possible? Are you saving my life once again?

MONSIGNOR FIDEU: My dear little Marianna, what silliness is this? Only God can do that. I am only helping a little.

MARIANNA: How can I repay you?

MONSIGNOR FIDEU: I shall tell you how. When you are living far from here, when so many people are enamoured of you, the King sings your praises and everyone wishes to make the acquaintance of the beautiful young chocolatier who has left Barcelona to come to Versailles, and when you are the most admired, desired and exalted of all the women in the palace, remember where you have come from and that this part of the world also has its good things. Remember that your first admirer was here and he was this poor priest with a name that makes people laugh.

MARIANNA: Oh, Monsignor Fideu, the things that occur to you. What could be better than this? And who could be better than you? I shall remember you every day I am away. And when I am able to return, I swear by all—

MONSIGNOR FIDEU: Sssh! Do not swear. That is unseemly. Now, go. They are waiting for us.

(*Marianna smiles, wipes away a tear and leaves. Monsignor Fideu is left alone, lit by his lantern. His face is somewhat ghostly in the surrounding darkness. The Captain General's men must have finished their work, for it is silent outside.*)

MONSIGNOR FIDEU: It has gone seven and a boat has sailed from the port. The Captain General is unaware that there is no back door to the shop. At the end of the tunnel a carriage awaits the legation. The chocolate-making machine, dismantled into twenty-two pieces, will be stowed inside the carriage. This time tomorrow, those men and the machine will be on their way to Versailles. Marianna will be with them, still convinced that she will return one day. Guillot, her young swain, will be a happy man. Beaumarchais... ah, about Beaumarchais, I dare not breathe a word. The man has too many secrets, all of them very important. I should only like to ask him, "Senyor playwright, does the comedy end when the lights dim or, in the darkness, must we still expect that something will happen?"

(*Monsignor Fideu exits. The tenuous light from the opening of the underground passageway is no longer visible.*)

(*DARKNESS*)

Sixteen

Madame,

It is my pleasure to inform you that our legation will be leaving Barcelona tomorrow morning before eight, as soon as they open the gates in the wall. If we all remain in good health and are not delayed by rocky roads, chasms, storms or thieves, we should be in Hostalric by dinnertime. At this rate, bearing in mind that when one travels such great distances there are always unforeseen circumstances that thwart one's plans, we should be at the palace in no more than fourteen days.

On its return journey, the French legation consists of five gentlemen and one lady. I believe that if you have read my chronicle carefully you will be able to say that you are perfectly aware of who they are. Nevertheless, I shall list them: I myself, your faithful servant; Monsieur de Beaumarchais, serving your nephew's interests; our own Labbé, chief pastry chef at the palace; Monsieur Maleshèrbes, head of the chocolatiers' guild of Paris; and Monsieur Delon, representative of the chocolatiers of Bayonne. The lady's name is Marianna, and she, the best chocolatier in the city of Barcelona, is travelling to Versailles longing to meet you and to reveal her skills to its cultivated court. All members of the delegation believe that, in her company, our homeward journey will be shorter and much more agreeable than the outward one. I concur with them.

Our final hours in this city have been full of surprises, all of them magnificent. The first was to find in the tunnel, where we were led by Monsignor Fideu, some small carts (with large wheels) bearing Senyor Fernandes's chocolate-making machine, now in pieces to facilitate its transport. With the exception of Marianna and very little difficulty each of us wheeled part of the invention through the tunnels, and thus we left the shop, the neighbourhood and even the walled city.

What a surprise it was, after travelling underground like moles, to find Beaumarchais waiting for us in the driver's seat of a carriage. He was in the company of two burly fellows, probably dock workers, who helped our gentlemen with the machine, which they loaded onto a sturdy cart. That done, they took it away to hide it until the morrow, and to prepare it for the long journey, or so they informed us. Monsignor Fideu was with us, saying that one of God's ministers is always useful in difficult situations. We said our farewells, almost tearfully. Before we parted, he gazed into my eyes and murmured, "Something tells me you will be back, Guillot. We shall soon meet again in these damp streets."

We had emerged from the tunnel outside the city walls. Hence, once we were in the carriage, acting as if we had spent a day in the country, we entered the city once more through Portal Nou without raising any suspicion. Everyone was full of admiration for the way in which the manoeuvre had been planned, and still more so when they learnt that it was the work of Monsignor Fideu and your humble servant, although it would not have been possible without Beaumarchais.

"Such are the mysterious designs of our leader," said the always conciliatory Delon.

Since it behoved him to speak, the King's secretary turned slightly towards us from his position on the driver's seat and said yes and no, that his secret designs had not always been concerned with saving Marianna and her machine but rather with certain endeavours which he was unable to divulge, for they were highly secret. He did, however, make the most of the occasion to give us some splendid news.

There was an air of great expectation in the carriage, so much so that the mules – two of them and very ancient – flicked their four ears the better to hear what Beaumarchais had to say.

"I have recovered everything that was stolen from us our first night in this city. You will find it when we arrive at the hostel."

There was an explosion of joy which startled the mules.

"Everything? Including the money?" asked Maleshèrbes, who was in such high spirits he did not seem to be himself.

"Everything!"

We had one night left in Barcelona and the chocolatiers, now with their pockets replenished, made plans to give the city a fitting farewell. I heard them saying that they wished to return to the tavern where they had tasted ratafia for the first, and who knows whether for the last time. Even the temperate Delon was wagering how many bottles he would down before losing his senses.

Beaumarchais made no attempt to chide them. After all, we are on foreign soil and everyone knows that people do not behave when away as they do at home. And there is nothing amiss if a few honest men wish to enjoy themselves.

I spent the afternoon recovering from my ordeals and packing my few belongings. I had almost finished when there was a knock at the door. Beaumarchais entered, closed the door behind him and said, "I must repeat my earlier request, my dear Guillot. Will you give me your word that you will not say a word about what you have seen me doing here?"

"You have it. Except for the chronicle I have written for Madame, I shall not—"

"That is precisely what I am referring to. Your chronicle. You must give it to me."

"I beg your pardon."

"It is too dangerous. I imagine you have mentioned Mademoiselle d'Éon."

"Naturally."

"And our business at the port."

"That too."

Beaumarchais shook his head. "Give it to me."

"I cannot. I gave my word to Madame before speaking with you."

"Guillot, if you resist, I shall have to take it by force."

"Are you capable of that?"

"I am obeying orders."

"Whose orders? The King's?"

"That is no concern of yours."

"And your concerns are so important?"

"They are, at least until we receive news."

"News from Boston. I hear that the people there long for freedom. Do you believe that France will grant their wish?"

He peered at me through narrowed eyes. "You said…"

"That I did not remember the name of the city for which the ship was bound. I know I said that."

"But you do remember it."

"As you can see."

"What else do you remember?"

"Ah, little more. I know that Monsieur Beaumont is a spy in the service of France, and probably the best we have. I also know that, in the palace, they wager fortunes on his true sex, which no one has yet been able to ascertain."

"You surprise me."

"I suspect, what is more, that you are aiding the Americans not only in the name of the King. I believe you have invested your own fortune, which is no bagatelle."

"There are many gentlemen in France who, in the name of freedom, support the Americans' struggle to break free of English shackles."

"Naturally. I understand. The newly freed men will be in your debt."

"That is enough, Guillot." Beaumarchais seemed tired of this chatter. "I should like to use my free afternoon to revise a scene of the comedy I am finishing. Would you be so good as to tell me what you have to offer?"

"I shall give you the notebook in which I have written my chronicle for Madame Adélaïde."

"I am pleased to see that you still have your good judgement."

"Upon our arrival at the palace I shall tell her, and you will attest to this, that it was stolen by thieves at a wayside inn."

"An excellent idea."

"I shall recite my chronicle from memory if Madame so wishes, but shall remain silent about the episodes you wish to remain secret."

"You are an intelligent young man."

"Then there is no more to say. I shall give it to you tomorrow. You have my word."

"Tomorrow? And why not now?"

"Because I wish to complete it. An author should never leave a work unfinished, however minor it may be, as you would know. One can never be sure which eyes will peruse those pages. Tonight, when I have completed my chronicle, the notebook will be yours."

"Very well."

"I should like to ask for something in return."

"I was wondering when you would. Careful, young man, because I can always unsheathe my sword and put an end to the negotiations."

"It is not difficult. I beg you to recommend me to the King for a certain position."

"A position? Do you propose to tell me that you wish to be a minister?"

"Better. Librarian."

His eyes glittered, with emotion perhaps, but also with the pleasure of seeing that it was ending well, without further problems.

"The palace librarian?"

"That is correct."

"You are aware that the royal library contains a host of books?"

"The more the better."

"And that they are all in utter disarray?"

"I shall then have years of work."

"And that the dust of ages is piled upon those books?"

"I shall learn to use a duster."

"Librarian?" He squinted at me. "It may very well suit you. You have my word, Guillot!"

That is how two gentlemen concluded their pact. At no point did I dare to tell him that my admiration for him is so great that I wrote one of my chronicles in the style of a final scene in one of his comedies. I thought he would discover it when he read it.

I used the waning hours of this last day to keep a promise I had made to my beautiful Marianna, who had asked, "Would you accompany me to the House of Charity? I should like to take my leave of someone there and am afraid to venture out alone in these dark streets." We set out at twilight.

The House of Charity is a large, derelict building in Carrer del Carme. The name of the person Marianna wished to see was Caterina Molins, a girl of little more than fifteen whose face I could barely see in the darkness. She appeared to be tall, shapely and fair of face. I then discovered that the reason for the visit was that Marianna wished to make her a gift of the chocolate pot you sent her, still wrapped in the turquoise velvet. Perhaps Marianna feared it would be broken on the journey. Or maybe this Caterina is so important to her that she did not want to leave without giving her some special memento.

The two young women wept, embraced and whispered to one another. I know that it is not becoming to a gentleman, but I eavesdropped a little and hence am informed of what they said.

"When will you come back? What shall I do without you?"

"Please do not make this more difficult for me, my little Caterina. I tell you, I shall return but do not know when. When I do, I wish to find you in better circumstances than at present. Heed what the nuns say. Find a good house where you may enter into service. Go and speak with Monsignor Fideu. Do you understand what I am telling you?"

The girl nodded and Marianna stroked her hair.

"You are my only friend, the only person I have in all the world. You must promise me that you will stay well and that you will not succumb to dissipation or seek your own damnation. If you do not pledge me this, I shall leave with such pain in my heart that I shall die before reaching Paris."

Shocked by this pronouncement, Caterina opened her eyes wide. "I promise."

"I have brought you some money. Do not spend it all at once. I should also like you to have this chocolate pot. It is valuable. If you ever need money, you can pawn it for at least fifty reals. If you do not pawn it, I should like you to keep it close, in memory of me. Will you do that?"

"Of course I shall." The girl was inconsolable and wept copiously, clinging to the chocolate pot.

'I shall be back, Caterina. I promise. I want to find you a happy honourable woman, at peace with God and humankind. Will you promise me this?'

Caterina did not speak. She could only wipe away the tears falling from her eyes.

The conversation lasted only a little longer, until Caterina offered a wan smile and Marianna felt able to leave. When we went out into Carrer del Carme, we could hear the bell tolling to announce that the city gates were being closed.

* * *

This is the end of my chronicle, which you will not read, Madame, unless it is placed in your hands by one of those states of confusion occasionally wrought by time's passing.

It is written by your faithful servant with the sole aim of being true to you, Madame, and true to the events herein described, which took place in the city of Barcelona in the icy winter of 1777.

I kiss your hand, Madame, in enduring affection. I am eternally yours.

Victor Philibert Guillot

Finale

MADAME ADÉLAÏDE

My dear Victoire,

Yesterday, having overcome my reluctance, I went at last to visit the porcelain factory which our father has of late re-established nearby in Sèvres. I was received with all due honours by its director, a garrulous man who was determined to show me every last corner of the premises, from the iron fence surrounding it to the workshops under the roof on the third floor. I must confess it made quite an impression on me. All the craftsmen working there – sculptors, turners, engravers, painters, gilders, kiln operators – produce the most splendid work, which I may not have praised sufficiently during my visit, for reasons that you and I very well know. After all, those workers are our father's subjects and have done nothing to earn my disdain. I should not wish them to think that I object to their presence so close to the palace. Indeed, I approve of it. I am pleased to have such a sophisticated industry so close to home. I am happy that France has this. Like you, I admire the subtle art of porcelain and celebrate the fact that we Europeans have at last understood its mysteries and that we no longer have to buy everything from China, as we did in the past. I consider it a great advance that there are porcelain plates, jars, jugs and ceiling lamps made by French hands. No one can accuse me of not wanting the best for my nation. Yet I could cry tears of rage only to think that, if all this exists, it is because of her.

While the long inspection of the factory lasted – tiring for the feet of my ladies-in-waiting but not for mine – I forced myself to smile a little, although she frequently came to mind. Such aversion! I did not wish to remember her and, before entering the factory, promised myself I would not, but even so... I am loath to write her name on this paper. To write something is to make it present and tangible, and to bring it back to life. Her name must not endure anywhere, although I know it will, and perhaps even more than ours, my dear sister. If anyone had asked me yesterday morning what this woman's merits are, I should have answered, "She has none." Or perhaps, worse, I might have said something spiteful, dripping with the poison of irony: "Oh, does she have demonstrable merits out of our father's bed and dressed to go out?"

Yesterday, after my visit to the porcelain factory I wished to be left alone in the carriage for a while. I needed to think. There, left to my own thoughts, I had to recognize that a person who wished to create such a place must have some merit. At least the merit of exquisite taste. Did you know that an alchemist at the factory has invented a colour for her and her alone? It is a pale pink and not at all unsightly. The painters apply it as she requires. And it would seem that she requires it for many objects. I had the impression that the artisans were pleased to work for her, which suggests that she is a generous mistress. I never imagined I should be capable of saying such a thing but I believe that Madame de Pompadour has done something that benefits our nation. There, you see, I have written her name. As is well known, one only needs *not* to want to think about something in order to be unable to stop thinking about it for a single second. As I said, she was in my thoughts all the time I was walking around the factory. Although I am no longer doing that, she is still with me. Do not think for a moment that I suddenly commend her past and present lasciviousness with the King. I shall never do that. I am of the view that if one wishes to favour the arts it is not necessary to bed anyone, although I also accept that there are women who lie with all and sundry and then do no good afterwards. I shall say no more, for I might yet end up forgiving her.

My visit ended on the first floor, where the clay and other raw materials are stored. Trying to flatter me, the director of the factory brought me a basin and, holding it out to me, said, "Perhaps, Madame, you would like to choose some clay for some personal object you might like us to make. If you could tell us what that is, we shall make it according to your wishes."

I did not waver for a single second. "I should like a chocolate pot," I said.

"Ah, of course," the director said. "Everyone in France knows that the Mesdames are great connoisseurs of the art of drinking chocolate."

"It is true that we are great devotees. It is a family trait."

"Oh yes, indeed! Your ancestors made it fashionable in the court, did they not?"

"You are well informed. Anne of Austria, the mother of my great-great-grandfather, brought it here for the first time, before anyone had tasted it. She was the daughter of Philip III of Spain, the only country which knew its virtues at the time. After that, my great-great-grandmother, Maria Theresa, made it popular in the palace. Despite being the wife of the Sun King, she was not a brilliant woman. Rather, she was the saddest queen ever to set foot in Versailles. She was the first queen to live in the palace, but she never liked it. Before her husband came to the throne, it was just a gloomy wooden hunting lodge. I believe that the only moments of happiness my great-great-grandmother had were when she was sipping hot chocolate in her small apartments, hidden away from all the splendour which only cast gloom on her spirit. They say that the first time she looked out over the garden from a balcony of the Hall of Mirrors she had the mad temptation to jump off it, hoping thus to die. Alas, she did die not long afterwards, consumed by a mysterious malaise. I say it was sadness. The sadness of Versailles can be lethal, in case you are not aware of it."

"I am surprised, Madame. You are a fount of wisdom," the director said.

"I like to be well informed."

"It will be a pleasure to make a chocolate pot that would honour this lineage of women you have just told me about, as well as pleasing you, if it were within my power. What colour would you like?"

"White. White soothes me."

"Would you like it decorated?"

"I prefer it unornamented."

"I see that you know very well what you want. Is there any other detail? What size should it be?"

"Neither big nor small. Enough for three small cups, which is what I have every afternoon."

"That is easily done. It will be a privilege to serve you."

"Oh, and one more thing."

"Do tell me, please."

"I do not want it marked. I know it is the custom to stamp the crossed Ls on everything you produce."

"Yes, Madame, that is correct. It was the wish of Madame de Pompa—"

"I should prefer not to see them. Would that be possible?"

"It is more than possible, if that is your wish. We shall add an inscription that will recognize you as its owner, if you agree."

"I agree."

"Am I correct in believing that you would prefer the letters to be in blue, rather than pink?"

(The man had begun to understand the situation, by which I mean his surmising that I did not want my chocolate pot to have as much as a single colour in common with her.)

"You are correct," I said. "Blue."

"An excellent choice. Our blue is most elegant."

"Then it is decided."

"That is most pleasing, Madame. Now it is only a matter of selecting the raw materials. Would you do me the honour?"

The director showed me some boxes full of different kinds of clay and powder in colours ranging from pink to marble white, and showed me the exact amount that was required of each type. I removed my glove and was pleased to play at being a potteress, following the instructions I was given.

Accordingly, I placed in the basin four handfuls of some white clay called kaolin, followed by a handful and a half of quartz powder and, finally, half a handful of some ground stone known by its Latin name of *albus*. That done, the director drew my attention to the small mound of clay I had made in the bowl.

435

"Here you have your chocolate pot, Madame. I hope it keeps you good company for many a year. In a few hours you will be able to fill it with chocolate."

I shall leave you here. The chocolate pot has just been delivered and I am eager to try it. You know what our ancestors, the sad princesses, pronounced: the desire for chocolate cannot be kept waiting.

I send you a kiss in true sisterly love.

Your,

Adélaïde

Notes

p. 5, *che dirsi... dalla parola*: "That can hardly be put into words" (Italian). From Leonora's aria, *Il trovatore*, Act I.

p. 20, *torrons*: Torró (plural: *torrons*): a confection made of honey, sugar, egg white, almonds or other nuts and, more recently, chocolate. It is usually shaped into a rectangular tablet and consumed as a traditional Christmas dessert.

p. 26, *ensaïmada*: Ensaïmada (plural *ensaïmades*): from the Catalan *saïm*, meaning animal fat. A traditional pastry product from Mallorca, it is basically sweet bread in the form of a coil and made with pork lard.

p. 32, *botifarra*: This famous Catalan sausage made from raw pork and spices is based on ancient recipes going back to Roman times. It comes in several shapes, flavours, forms and colours.

p. 43, *catànies*: A typical sweet from Vilafranca del Penedés (Catalonia) consisting of an almond covered in a paste made of almonds, hazelnuts and cocoa and then coated with a fine layer of chocolate.

p. 45, *sobrassada*: Raw, cured sausage made with ground pork, paprika, salt and other spices, from the Balearic Islands.

p. 67, *Sares... tortell de reis*: Sara (plural *sares*): Small cake with cream topping and filling, covered with toasted flaked almonds. *Crema de Sant Josep* (literally: St Joseph's cream): a lemon-and-cinnamon-flavoured version of *crème brulée*.

437

Coca de Sant Joan (plural: *coques*): a sweet, soft, light-textured confection made from eggs, butter, flour, milk and yeast and formed into a cake with a topping of candied fruit and a filling of cream, sweet pumpkin, marzipan, cream or chocolate. The classic *coca*, served on the feast of St John, or midsummer's eve, is anise-flavoured with candied fruit and pine nuts. *Tortell de reis* (literally: kings' cake): a special Epiphany treat, this round confection topped with a crown is made of brioche, filled with marzipan or custard and studded with candied fruit, pine nuts and sugar. Hidden inside are a dried broad bean and a tiny king. The person who finds the former has to pay for the cake and whoever finds the king is declared monarch for the day and wears the gold paper crown that comes with the cake.

p. 70, *escalivada*: The name of this appetizer is taken from the Catalan verb *escalivar* (cook in hot ashes, *caliu*). The two main ingredients are aubergines and red peppers, which are served in strips with a touch of garlic and olive oil.

p. 73, *neules*: *Neula* (plural *neules*): a rolled sweet wafer traditionally eaten with Christmas lunch.

p. 85, *coca de pa*: Flat bread, usually oblong, with different savoury toppings.

p. 93, *Bunyols... torrons de Xixona*: *Bunyols de Quaresma*: Anisette fritters made of egg batter and dusted with sugar, typical of Lent. *Panellets*: the traditional dessert of the All Saints' holiday, small cakes in different shapes and flavours mainly made of marzipan. *Torró de Xixona*: this is a soft-textured *torró* made of almonds, honey, egg white and almond oil.

p. 147, *Infelice cor tradito... non scoppiar*: "O wretched heart betrayed, / do not break for sorrow" (Italian).

p. 164, *Bella figlia dell'amore... pene consolar*: "Fairest daughter of love, / I am a slave to your charms; / with but a single word you could /relieve my every pain" (Italian). From Giuseppe Verdi, *Rigoletto*, Act III.

p. 208, *vibra il ferro... né può*: "Plunge your sword into this heart / that cannot, will not love you" (Italian).

p. 235, *cessa alfin di sospirar*: "Cease sighing at last" (Italian). From the finale of Rossini's *La cenerentola*.

p. 245, *Davvero*: "Really?" (Italian).

p. 245, *Com'è gentil... pace, misterio, amor*: "How soft the air / in April night so fair! / The blue sky so serene / the moon in cloudless sheen: / all, all the senses move above / to mystery, peace and love!" (Italian). From Ernesto's aria in Gaetano Donizetti's *Don Pasquale*, Act III.

p. 250, *a la pedra*: Chocolate a *la pedra* (stone-ground) takes its name from the way it is made. Pure cocoa beans are toasted over a fire and, while still hot, are ground to a fine powder on a large grinding stone (*pedra*) using a heavy stone roller.

p. 267, *La moral di tutto questo... doglie in quantità*: "The moral of the story / is very easy to see. / I shall tell you quickly / if you would listen to me. / It is a very foolish head / that leads an old man to wed / for to seek at will a wife / brings pain and problems rife" (Italian). From Gaetano Donizetti's *Don Pasquale*, Act III.

p. 412, *ratafia*: A liqueur typical of the Mediterranean areas of Spain, Italy, and north-east of France. More than a thousand years old, the Catalan version is made of macerated green walnuts and can be flavoured with lemon peel and spices such as nutmeg, cinnamon, clove, rosemary, anise, etc.

List of Characters

ADÉLAÏDE, MADAME (1732–1800): Real character. Sixth child (fourth daughter) of King Louis XV of France and Marie Leszczyńska; great-great-granddaughter of Maria Teresa of Spain; and aunt and godmother of Louis XVI. Learned, restless and actively engaged in the politics of her day, she never married and remained in the Palace of Versailles, where she and her sisters were known as the Mesdames. She bitterly opposed her father's relationship with Madame de Pompadour, who was one of his favourites. After the Revolution, in which her godson, many members of her family and the court were guillotined, she was obliged to flee, thus beginning some years of wandering in Europe. She finally settled in Trieste, where she died at the age of sixty-seven (*III*).

AURORA: Servant in the house of the Turull family (*II*).

BEAUMARCHAIS, PIERRE-AUGUSTIN CARON DE (1732–1799): Real character. Courtier, politician, spy and author of such well known plays as *Le Mariage de Figaro* and *Le Barbier de Séville*. In his own name and in that of the King of France, he played an active role in the American Revolution and helped to finance the rebels (*III*).

BEAUMONT, CHARLES-GENEVIÈVE-LOUIS-AUGUSTE-ANDRÉ-THI-
MOTÉE D'ÉON (CHEVALIER / MADEMOISELLE D'ÉON) (1728–
1810): Real character. A French spy in the service of Louis XV.
His sexual identity was an enigma throughout his life, since
he alternated male and female personalities for many years.
The adventurer Giacomo Casanova claimed that d'Éon was
a woman after seducing her in 1771, and a group of French
doctors came to the same conclusion. She lived as a woman
for thirty-three years in London's aristocratic circles. When
he died, it was found that he had male sexual attributes,
although he was beardless. Others believe he may have been
a hermaphrodite (*III*).

BULTERINI, AUGUSTO (1835–1923): Italian *tenore di grazia* (light
tenor), a Verdi specialist (*II*).

CHARLES III, KING OF SPAIN (1716–88): Real character. Fifth son
of Philip V, and eldest by his second wife, Elisabeth Farnese.
He was King of Naples and Sicily, as well as Spain from 1759
until his death. Notable among his typically enlightened
policies were his economic reforms and emphasis on urban
planning and culture. The birth he celebrated in 1771 (with
a public competition for poor and honest maidens in the
city of Barcelona) was that of his grandson Carlos Clemente
(1771–74), first son of the future Charles IV. If the child had
lived he would have been the older brother of Fernando VII
and, accordingly, heir to the throne.

DELON (1741–1805): A chocolatier established in Bayonne. Part
of the legation that visited Barcelona in 1777 (*III*).

ENRIQUETA: Servant in the Sampons household (*II*).

FERNANDES (?–?): Real character. A Barcelona chocolatier, member of the chocolatiers' guild and supplier to the Versailles court. His invention of a chocolate-processing machine aroused the interest of the chocolatiers' guild in Paris, which sent a mission to Barcelona in 1777 to seek information about the device. According to the chronicler Ramon Nonat Comas (1852–1918), it was exhibited for some time in the guild's headquarters, an anecdote later repeated by the historian and folklorist Joan Amades (1890–1959) (*III*).

FIDEU, MONSIGNOR (1715–91): Santa Maria del Mar parish priest and Marianna's protector (*III*).

FONT, ROSA CATALINA (1674–1777): Real character. She resided in the town of Vic and was famous for living until the age of 103 in very good health. According to the obituary published in *La Gazeta de Barcelona*, she drank chocolate every day (*III*).

FREY, MAX (1971–): Chemist and husband of Sara Rovira (*I*).

FREY ROVIRA, AINA (1998–): Daughter of Max Frey and Sara Rovira (*I*).

FREY ROVIRA, POL (2001–): Son of Max Frey and Sara Rovira (*I*).

GOLORONS, MARIA DEL ROSER (1866–1932): Wife of the industrialist Rodolf Lax, she eventually went to live in the Passeig de Gràcia. She is a friend of Dr Volpi (*II*).

GONZÁLEZ DE BASSECOURT, FRANCISCO, MARQUIS DE GRIGNY, AND FIRST COUNT OF ASALTO (1726–93): Real character. He was born in Pamplona, but his family was Flemish. He fought against the English in Havana. Captain General of Barcelona from 1777 to 1789, he was known for his urban-planning initiatives (the most important of which was opening up the street – now named Nou de la Rambla – running between La Rambla and the city wall and for many years called Carrer del Conde del Asalto in his honour) and his support for the arts, theatre in particular. He was removed from his post and recalled to Madrid after refusing to use force against Barcelona's population in the 1789 Bread Riots.

GUILLOT, VICTOR PHILIBERT (1759–1832): Secretary – and something of a spy – in the service of Madame Adélaïde of France, he lives in Versailles and aspires to the post of palace librarian. (*III*).

HORTÈNSIA, SENYORA: Wife of the inventor Estanislau Turull and mother of Càndida (*II*).

LABBÉ: Royal chocolatier, first to Louis XV and then his grandson Louis XVI. He lives in the palace at Versailles and is part of the legation that travels to Barcelona (*III*).

LOUIS XV, KING OF FRANCE (1710–74): Real character. Originally so appreciated by his people that he was called "*le Bien Aimé*" (the Beloved), he was later notorious for his fleshly indulgence and scandals. Two of his favourite mistresses, Madame du Barry and Madame de Pompadour, figure among the best known and most influential personalities in the history of France. Married to Marie Leszczyńska of Poland, he had ten children including Louis, Dauphin of France, father of Louis XVI, who died before coming to the throne. Notable among his daughters, most of whom never married, were Madame Adélaïde and Madame Victoire.

LOUIS XVI, KING OF FRANCE (1754–93): Real character. He spent his entire life in Versailles and reigned from 1774 to 1789. On 21st January 1793, he was executed by guillotine, as were his wife Marie Antoinette and other members of the royal family.

LOMBARDI, MARIETTA: Opera singer born in Padua (*II*).

MADRONA: Housekeeper for the Sampons family (*II*).

MALESHÈRBES: French chocolatier, head of the chocolatiers' guild in Paris (*III*).

MARIANNA (1754–1824): Chocolate trader, wife of the chocolatier Fernandes, she single-handedly runs a chocolate shop in Carrer de les Tres Voltes. Her character is based on the life of the Barcelona chocolatier Eulàlia Gallisans, who had a shop in Plaça de la Llana, which she had to run clandestinely after the chocolatiers' guild tried to close the business down (*III*).

MAS-PORCELL, CATERINA: Real character. A Catalan soprano who was one of the star performers in of Barcelona's Liceu Opera House for four decades (1838–78) (*II*).

Mimó: Barcelona chocolatier and leader of the chocolatiers' guild (*III*).

Ortega: Chocolatier and mentor of chocolatiers, including Oriol Pairot (*I*).

Pairot, Oriol (1970–): Self-taught chocolatier. Friend of Max Frey and his wife (*I*).

Pompadour, Madame de (Jeanne-Antoinette Poisson) (1721–64): Real character. The most famous of the lovers of Louis XV and a great promoter of culture and the arts in the period in which she was most influential. She was married to Charles-Guillaume Lenormant d'Étioles and had two children who died at an early age. At twenty-three she became the King's lover and went to live in Versailles, where she was given the title of Marquise. In the next twenty years she was a patroness of Diderot's *Encyclopédie* and the work of other writers and painters, as well as founding the porcelain factory in Sèvres, which employed many craftsmen and artists. Her favourite colour was produced there and named Pompadour Pink. She died in Versailles at the age of forty-three, perhaps of tuberculosis, although some speculated that she was poisoned by the King's favourite, Madame du Barry, who was twenty-two years younger.

Rovira, Sara (1969–): Daughter of chocolatiers and wife of Max Frey, she has a chocolate shop in Carrer de l'Argenteria (*I*).

SAMPONS, ANTONI (1851–1910): Son of Don Gabriel Sampons, chocolatier in the Born neighbourhood of Barcelona and founder of a chocolate empire (*II*).

SAMPONS, ANTONIETA (OR ANTÒNIA) (1873–1965): Only daughter of Antoni Sampons and Càndida Turull (*II*).

SAMPONS, GABRIEL (1806–1870): A chocolate artisan, he has a shop in Carrer de Manresa. Father of Antoni Sampons (*II*).

TURULL, CÀNDIDA (1854–1951): Only daughter of Estanislau Turull and Senyora Hortènsia and wife of Antoni Sampons (*II*).

TURULL, ESTANISLAU (1799–1873): Barcelona inventor and designer of machinery during the nineteenth-century years of industrialization (*II*).

VICTOIRE, MADAME (1733–99): Real character. Daughter of Louis XV of France and Marie Leszczyńska, and aunt of King Louis XVI. She lived almost all her life in the palace at Versailles with her sister Adélaïde. She never married. The Revolution obliged her to flee to several French and then Italian cities. She died in Trieste.

VOLPI, HORACI (OR DOCTOR): (1820–1911): Doctor, friend of Senyora Hortènsia, opera lover and habitué of the Liceu Opera House (*II*).

Author's Note and Acknowledgements

The poems recited by Guillot in Part III, Chapter Nine, were written by Dante Alighieri, Petrarch, Angelo Poliziano, Pietro Metastasio and Benedetto Gareth. The conversation between Aurora and Càndida in the chapter '*Il trovatore*' takes some of the repartee from Salvatore Cammarano's libretto for Verdi's opera of the same name.

I should like to express my gratitude to the following people and institutions to which I am indebted: Xaxier Coll, Núria Escala, Enric Rovira, Txell Forrellad, Claudi Uñó, Manel Carque, Francisco Gil, Santiago Alcolea, Nicole Wildisen, Raquel Quesada, Francesc Gràcia Alonso, Ángeles Prieto, Montserrat Blanch, Trinitat Gilbert, Claudia Marseguerra, Clàudia Torres, Deni Olmedo, Ángeles Escudero, Xocolates Simon Coll, Arxiu Històric de la Ciutat de Barcelona (Historical Archive of the City of Barcelona), Arxiu Històric de la Diputació de Barcelona (Historical Archive of the Province of Barcelona), Museu de Xocolata de Barcelona (Barcelona Chocolate Museum), the Musée Gourmand du Chocolat – Choco-Story (Gourmet Chocolate Museum – Choco-Story) in Paris and the Institut Amatller. These pages also owe a great deal to a certain bibliography consisting of works by Roger Alier, Laura Bayès, Chantal Coady, Albert Garcia Espuche,

Nèstor Luján, Ramon Morató and Montserrat Carbonell i Esteller.

Finally, I wish to thank Sandra Bruna for this time we have spent. And Berta Bruna for her faith in me. Without them, this story would not have been told.

THIS NOVEL WAS WRITTEN
IN MATARÓ IN THE SPRING
AND SUMMER OF 2013